Totally
Brilliant

Cathy Hopkins is the author of the incredibly successful *Mates, Dates* and *Truth, Dare* books, and has just started a fabulous new series called *Cinnamon Girl*. She lives in North London with her husband and three cats, Molly, Emmylou and Otis.

Cathy spends most of her time locked in a shed at the bottom of the garden pretending to write books but is actually in there listening to music, hippie dancing and talking to her friends on e-mail.

Occasionally she is joined by Molly, the cat who thinks she is a copy-editor and likes to walk all over the keyboard rewriting and deleting any words she doesn't like.

Emmylou and Otis are new to the household. So far they are as insane as the older one. Their favourite game is to run from one side of the house to the other as fast as possible, then see if they can fly if they leap high enough off the furniture. This usually happens at three o'clock in the morning and they land on anyone who happens to be asleep at the time.

Apart from that, Cathy has joined the gym and spends more time than is good for her making up excuses as to why she hasn't got time to go.

Truth Dare
Kiss
Promise

Totally Brilliant

Cathy Hopkins

PICCADILLY PRESS • LONDON

This edition first published in Great Britain in 2007
by Piccadilly Press Ltd.,
5 Castle Road, London NW1 8PR
www.piccadillypress.co.uk

Text copyright © Cathy Hopkins, 2007

Previously published seperately as:
White Lies and Barefaced Truths © Cathy Hopkins, 2002
Pop Princess © Cathy Hopkins, 2002
Teen Queens and Has-Beens © Cathy Hopkins, 2003

The right of Cathy Hopkins to be identified as Author of this work
has been asserted by her in accordance with the Copyright, Designs
and Patents Act 1988

A catalogue record for this book is available from the British Library

ISBN-13: 978 1 85340 946 2 (trade paperback)

1 3 5 7 9 10 8 6 4 2

Printed in the UK by CPI Bookmarque, Croydon, CR0 4TD
Text design by Textype Typesetters
Cover design by Simon Davis

White Lies
and
Barefaced
Truths

Truth Dare
Kiss
Promise

White Lies
and
Barefaced
Truths

Cathy Hopkins

PICCADILLY PRESS • LONDON

Big thanks to the team at Piccadilly, Rosemary Bromley as always, and Alice Elwes, Lauren Bennie, Scott Brenman, Becca Crewe, Jenni Herzberg, Rachel Hopkins, Annie McGrath and Olivia McDonnell, for answering all my e-mail questions.

Truth, Dare, Kiss or Promise

'TRUTH, DARE, kiss or promise?' asked Mac as he attempted to light the fire for the third time.

Becca leaned back against a rock and nuzzled her feet into the sand. 'Truth,' she said.

'OK, you have to tell us who you fancy.'

'Easy,' said Becca. 'Brad Pitt.'

'No, I mean, in the village.'

'Easy again,' said Becca. 'Ollie Axford.'

Mac's face dropped as at last the fire took hold. Although he says he's not into relationships, I reckon he's got a thing for Bec. I saw him staring at her before, when she was combing out her hair. Her hair's her best asset although she doesn't think so. She wants blonde straight hair like Gwyneth Paltrow but she looks more like a Pre-Raphaelite princess with her long Titian coloured mane and perfect alabaster skin.

'Are you honestly telling the absolute truth?' he asked.

I couldn't help but laugh. Typical boy. Just because Becca didn't say she fancied him, he thinks she must be lying.

'Yeah, the absolute real, double honest truth,' said Becca. 'Ollie Axford.'

Mac shrugged his shoulders. 'Don't know what you see in him. He's a right flash git.'

'Exactly,' said Becca. 'That's why I like him. He's different.'

I handed round the Cokes and gave Squidge the sausages to cook. I was thankful I hadn't been asked. I'd have had to say Ollie as well and Squidge wouldn't have liked that, never mind Becca. Squidge has been my boyfriend since junior school but lately, it's all felt flat, I want a bit more excitement. Squidge is so familiar; we grew up together. And it's not that I don't like him. I do, but he's become more of a mate, like family, a brother even. And who wants to snog their brother? *Ewww.* There has to be more. Becca's not the only one who's seen Ollie. Full name Orlando Axford. Son of Zac Axford, famous American rock star who lives out at Barton Hall. Everyone in the village is always on about them, they're *soooo* glamorous. They live in this fab house, more like a mansion, in acres of land with horses and dogs and they've even got a Vietnamese pot-bellied pig. I saw it once by the gate, when I went out there with my dad to deliver their groceries. Mrs Axford is totally gorgeous. She used to be a model and Ollie is the best-looking boy I've ever seen. I haven't ever spoken to him, but I've seen him around when he's been down from school in the holidays.

'OK, your turn, Cat,' said Squidge, putting a sausage on a fork and holding it over the fire. 'Truth, dare, kiss or promise.'

I stared out at the ocean in front of us while I considered which to choose. It was the beginning of September and term started on Monday. Another summer in Cornwall gone and here we all were, the gang, having a beach party before the sun went down. Nothing wrong with any of it, I thought. It is beautiful here and we do have a laugh, it's just, is this is it? Me and Squidge going together until we leave school? No. I want more. And I want it soon.

'Dare,' I said.

Squidge grinned. 'Er, let me think of a good one. Now who we can get you to moon at . . . ?'

Typical. Even the dares are predictable: show your bum to some unsuspecting person.

'No, *no*,' said Becca. 'I have a *much* better dare.'

'You butted in,' I said. 'Show your bum. Butted in. Bum, butt, geddit?'

Mac, Squidge and Becca stared at me as though I was mad. Maybe I am. I have been feeling a bit strange lately. Probably hormones. Mrs Jeffries, our form teacher, puts everything down to that, like when anyone goes off on a wobbly, 'Oh hormones,' she says. We all have a laugh about it, like if anyone acts even slightly weird, we all go, 'It's mi hormones playing me up something rotten.'

'Butthead,' said Becca, 'but I do have a brill dare.'

'Go on then.'

'I dare that the next time you see Ollie Axford, you have to go and talk to him.'

'*Talk* to him. Why?' I asked, fearing for a moment that Becca had sussed my secret.

Becca looked to the heavens. 'For me of course. Oh go on Cat, pleeease, you know how good you are at chatting up boys. And they always like you. Talk to him. Find out if he's noticed me. Find out if he has a girlfriend. That sort of thing, and maybe mention, kind of casually, that you have a friend who'd like to meet him.'

'No way,' I said. 'No, *no* way.'

I looked to Squidge for support.

'Oh go on Cat, if Becca has such a crush, the least you can do as a mate is help her out.'

Astounding. He's not even jealous, threatened. He's so sure of our relationship that he would send me out to chat up the most divine boy in Cornwall, if not the country, and I have his full go ahead.

'No, forget it. I'm not doing dare,' I said. 'I'll choose another one instead.'

'You can't change your mind because you don't like the dare,' objected Becca. 'That's against the rules.'

'Yeah, but what you want me to do is a dare that you should do yourself,' I said looking round at everyone, hoping that one of them would back me up. I could see that Mac had gone into a sulk. Shame, as I really like him. He's been living down here a year now and still hasn't quite landed. He's always going on about London and how he misses his old school and his mates. His mum and dad are divorced, and he lives for the times when he gets to go back to visit his dad who still lives up there in a flat in Islington. Having Becca as a girlfriend might help him settle, and I'm sure she would have been interested if it wasn't for Ollie Axford.

I decided to help him out.

'Truth, dare, kiss or promise, Mac?' I asked.

He shrugged. 'Don't care.'

'Then I'll pick for you,' I said. 'Kiss.'

'I'm not kissing you if that's what you think,' he said, and for a moment his face lightened. 'Squidge would kill me.'

'I never said *who* you have to kiss yet,' I said. 'No, you have to kiss Becca.'

'*Cat!*' said Becca looking shocked. Usually when we played the kiss option, it was to kiss someone geeky at school or one of the ancient locals. One time when we couldn't think of anyone, Becca made Squidge go and kiss a dustbin.

'OK, it has to be at a time when it feels right,' I said backtracking fast.

'That'll be never, then,' said Mac settling back into his sulk. 'And anyway, you haven't really had a proper go, Cat.'

'OK. Truth then,' I said.

'Tell us your biggest secret,' said Becca.

'Wouldn't be a secret then, would it?' I said playing for time.

'Rules are rules and you ducked out of the dare I gave you,' said Becca. 'Come on, spill.'

'OK,' I said, 'but how about I only tell you? There's nothing in the rules that says I have to tell everyone.'

'Fair enough,' said Squidge. 'I know all your secrets anyway.'

Mac shrugged. 'Whatever,' he said turning away and looking out to sea. I think he was pleased that I'd opted out of the dare.

Two packs of sausages, burgers and Cokes later, we set off on the long climb back up the cliff.

'Shouldn't have had that last sausage,' panted Becca after we'd been going ten minutes.

'Almost there,' I said coming up behind her on the path. We stopped for a moment to catch our breath and look at the view stretching out in front of us. Miles and miles of coastline as far as Rame Head. Even though I was born here, I still love watching the sea down below as it breaks on the sand making patterns like white lace.

Squidge and Mac had gone on ahead and had almost reached the top so I decided to tackle Becca while I had her alone.

'Don't you like Mac?' I asked.

Becca pulled her hair up into a ponytail and set off again. 'Yeah, course. But not like that. Besides he's not into having a girlfriend and certainly doesn't fancy me. I could kill you doing that kiss thing on me. Why would you want to set me up with him?'

'I thought you'd like it. I mean, he's your type. Blond, cute smile and he's a laugh most of the time.'

'Ah, but I've set my sights higher,' she said dreamily. 'Ollie Axford. He's The One.'

'That's this week. Last week Phil was The One.'

'Phil Davies? *Ew*. No way,' said Becca. 'Phil was a minor blip in my game plan.'

I had to laugh. No half measures for Becca. She was always in love. Every new boy she had a crush on was 'The One'. I wasn't sure how seriously to take this new infatuation with Ollie. Was it one of her whims or was she for real this time?

As I set off again another thought occurred to me. Why *was* I trying to get her off with Mac? Was it because I wanted the way free, so I could talk to Ollie for me not her?

'Bec.'

'What?'

'I'll tell you my secret now.'

'What?' said Becca stopping again.

'Promise you won't say anything?'

She nodded.

'I think I want to finish with Squidge.' Actually it wasn't my biggest secret. My biggest secret was that I fancied Ollie. But I was careful to omit the word *biggest* and hoped she wouldn't notice.

Becca turned. 'You're kidding. No wonder you didn't want to say in front of the others. But why? I mean you two have been an item since . . . for ever.'

'Exactly. Before the dawn of time, etc.'

'So why now? Has he done something to upset you?'

I laughed. 'Nah.' Squidge would never do anything to upset anyone. He's the nicest person I know. Kind and considerate. Wouldn't harm a fly. Always the first to offer help. Generous. Cool. Cute even. The perfect boyfriend. 'I want a change.'

Becca stared at me. 'Is that why you cut all your hair off?'

'You don't like it do you?'

'I *love* it. It's loads better. It makes your hair look really dark and glossy.' We walked on for a bit then Becca turned again. 'Do you fancy someone else? Is that why you want to finish with Squidge?'

I really wanted to tell her, yes, yes I *do*: Ollie. But I couldn't do it. 'Nah,' I said, 'there's nobody else. I just want to move on.'

Becca glanced up at the top of the cliff where the boys were waiting.

'He's going to be devastated. He adores you.'

I followed Becca's glance and Squidge waved down at us. Squidge, lovely lovely Squidge. My pal through thick and thin. He's been there for me in all the good and bad times. Times like when my mum died when I was nine. I've known him that long.

'So when are you going to do it?'

'Don't know,' I said.

'And how? What on earth are you going to say?'

'Double don't know.' I felt awful. I didn't want to hurt him. How was I ever going to find the right words?

2   Storm in a Teen Cup

'THE TOOTH fairy's not been,' blubbed Emma, as she scrabbled about under her pillow and found the tooth she'd left wrapped in tissue the night before.

I jumped down from the top bunk and went to look for Dad.

'Go away,' snuffled Luke from under his duvet when I poked my head in the boys' room. 'Dad's gone to the market.'

I went to Dad's desk, found a piece of card, scribbled an 'I Owe You' note, then sprinkled it with glitter.

Emma wasn't convinced when I handed it to her.

'The tooth fairy's a bit broke at the moment,' I explained. 'So many children to get round. When she's paid her overdraft off at the Fairy Bank, no doubt she'll be in touch.'

Emma looked like she was going to start crying again, so I found my bag and handed her the Smarties I'd bought yesterday.

'She left you these as well.'

She looked suspiciously at my bag as if to say how come she left them in *your* bag, but she took them, then stuck a couple up her nose. It's her latest game. She sticks sweets up her nose, then snorts them across the room. D'oh thanks, Emma, I thought as I flicked a sticky red one off my arm.

I went downstairs and laid the table for breakfast. That was when Joe (brother number two) decided to experiment with his juice by standing on his head and trying to drink upside down.

Course Emma had to try it as well, but couldn't get up on her head so started doing her whiney act.

At that moment, we heard a loud thump from upstairs. It was Luke, who appeared minutes later rubbing his arm. He'd tried to fly off the top bunk bed. Luckily nothing was broken.

It was then I spied Mogley the cat looking anxiously out of the window of the spin-dryer.

'Eeep!' I squeaked.

'It's her house,' said Emma. 'She likes it.'

As Mogley was frantically scratching to get out, some-how I doubted that. I opened the dryer and pulled her out from amongst the damp laundry and she purred happily in my arms. I was thankful that I'd got to her before anyone had switched it on.

There was peace for about ten minutes as we tucked into rounds of toast and honey, then I sent them off to get dressed. Or so I thought. It wasn't long before Joe came mumbling into the kitchen. He'd glued his back teeth together. He was sticking something down for his science project and put the glue tube in his mouth while he used his hands.

I gave him a glass of milk to swill round his mouth and, thank God, his teeth unlocked, but when Dad came back, the house was pandemonium. Emma wanted to do the glue trick to try and pull more of her teeth out, the laundry was all over the table where I'd been trying to remove the cat hairs, there was juice all over the floor from Joe's upside down drinking experiment and, next door, Luke had the telly on full blast.

'I can't leave you alone for five minutes,' said Dad taking in the scene before him. 'And look at you Cat, you're not even out of your pyjamas yet and it's already nine o'clock.'

'But . . .' I started.

'No buts about it,' said Dad. 'It's about time all of you learnt to behave properly.'

Sometimes I give up. But then, it's nothing new. It's only another typical Saturday morning in the Kennedy household.

'Cat, I need you to go into Kingsand and pick up a few things,' said Dad giving me a list later that morning.

'But Dad, I was going to go over to Becca's,' I began.

'You can go this afternoon, morning's for jobs.'

I couldn't argue as the others were all busy with their chores. Chores that no doubt I'd have to do again for them when I got back. Joe and Luke's idea of tidying their bedroom is to hide everything under their duvets. I'm forever clearing out old sweet wrappers, video games and assorted bits of clothing when they fall into bed at night.

I set off to the village and bought the items Dad wanted from the shop. There weren't many people about, only the occasional tourist strolling through the lanes admiring the coloured sandstone cottages and pots of flowers displayed everywhere. Kingsand prides itself on its appearance and has won the 'Best Kept Village' award many times.

I made my way down the narrow pavement towards the bay at the bottom. I wouldn't like to live here, I thought, as I gazed into some of houses lining the lane. It must be like this all the time – having strangers pass by and stare into your living room. In one window, a family sat around the table as their mum gave them breakfast. I turned away. Sometimes it still hurts seeing cosy families with a mum. I wonder if they know how lucky they are.

I decided to walk through the village to the next bay at Cawsand. Kingsand and Cawsand are twin villages, right next to each other, both with sandy bays that are easy to get to. Before she was ill, Mum used to bring us to Cawsand Bay as it's safe for swimming. We'd sit for hours watching the boats and people playing on the beach.

I made my way through the village, then down into the square at Cawsand, then turned into the bay. There were only a couple of people: a woman having a coffee at the café and a boy at the far end of the beach.

I went and sat by the rocks on the left and stared out at the sea. Some days I really miss mum. Most of the time I'm OK. I'm fourteen and I know she's gone and not coming back. But some days I don't feel so grown up and I wish she was here and I could cuddle up and feel looked after. Being grown-up can be confusing sometimes and I don't know what I want. I'm sure she'd have understood. Must be mi old hormones playing me up, I thought, as I brushed away a tear.

Suddenly the boy from the other end of the beach plonked himself down next to me on the sand. I'd been so caught up in my thoughts that I hadn't heard him approaching.

'It is lovely here isn't it?' he said, indicating the bay with a sweep of his hand.

I looked round at him and my chest tightened.

Ohmigo-o-o-od. It was Ollie Axford. Ollie Axford sitting right next to me in a black T-shirt and shorts. He stretched long tanned legs out in front of him. Totally, totally gorgeous. Jet black hair, denim blue eyes and a cute dimple on his chin.

'Cat got your tongue.' He was smiling.

I realised I must have been staring at him. Ogling, more like.

'Actually that's my name.'

He looked puzzled.

'Cat. Short for Catherine, but everyone calls me Cat.'

'Nice,' he said looking me up and down in a way that made me blush. 'That's a nice name. Suits you. You look like a cat sitting here on your own. You don't scratch do you?'

I laughed. 'Only if provoked. Then I bite as well.'

He grinned and raised an eyebrow. 'Oh really. Sounds dangerous. So I'd better be nice. Will you purr if I stroke you?'

And he began to gently stroke my arm. Ohmigod, ohmigod, *ohmigod*.

'We have cats up at the house,' he continued. 'They're very independent, aren't they? Are you like that?'

'Suppose I can be.'

He leaned close. 'But they can be very affectionate as well if they like you.'

I laughed. 'Yeah, but you have to be deserving.'

I couldn't believe it. I was flirting with him and he was flirting back. Ollie Axford. And me. On the beach. On our own. *Arghhhh*.

'Then I'd better be extra nice, hadn't I? Because I like cats,' he said. 'I'm Ollie by the way. Ollie Axford.'

'I know.'

He turned his head and looked at me quizzically causing my chest to tighten even more. I could hardly breath.

'How?'

'Oh, everyone knows who you are. You live at Barton Hall, don't you?'

He nodded. 'Yeah. How do you know that?'

'My dad owns the shop over in the next village. Um, your mum comes in sometimes.'

He seemed to be happy with that. 'So Cat. What do you do around here?'

'Do like what? What do you mean?'

He settled himself back against my rock so that his arm was touching mine. 'Tell me everything. Who you are. What you're doing here all on your own.'

'Er . . .' What could I say to make it interesting? He seemed to be enjoying my discomfort.

'OK, start with where you go to school.'

'Near Torpoint. Everyone round here goes there pretty well.'

'Oh yeah, Torpoint. My sister's going to go there.'

'Your sister?'

'Yeah, she starts on Monday. She was at school in London but hated it. She wanted to be closer to home, so Mum and Dad got her changed.'

Now this *was* interesting. I'd heard that he had a sister but I'd never seen her. Maybe he was going to change schools as well. That would cause a stir. Ollie Axford at our school. I couldn't wait to tell Becca. She'd think she'd died and gone to heaven. Ohmigod. Becca. I remembered the dare that I'd turned down, but now I had the perfect opportunity. I had to mention her or she'd kill me when I told her that I'd bumped into Ollie. I sat up so that we weren't touching any more.

'And, er, are you going to change schools as well?'

'No way,' he said. 'I like my school. But look out for Lia, will you? That's my sister. She's a good kid and you know, starting a new school can be a bit daunting sometimes.'

He seemed nice. I liked that he was watching out for his sister.

'I'll make a point of it,' I said. 'How old is she?'

'Fourteen, so she'll be going into Year Nine.'

'That's my year. So yeah, I'll watch out for her.'

Ollie leaned up so that he was touching me again. 'But what about you? You haven't told me much yet.'

I shrugged. 'Not a lot to tell. I grew up here. I've got two stupid brothers and a sister who I think may be an alien.'

'Older or younger?'

'Younger. Luke's ten, Joe's eight and Emma's the baby, she's just turned six. You?'

'Two sisters. One older, Star – she's up in London. And Lia.'

'Two? Bet they spoil you being an only boy.'

'I wish. And are you married, single or divorced?'

'Divorced,' I said. 'He got the kids, I kept the houses.'

He laughed. 'Seriously, though.'

'Um . . . there's a gang of us that hang out, you know.

Like mates . . . you know . . .' Why wasn't I telling him the truth? That I had a steady boyfriend.

'So what are you doing sitting down here all on your own?'

I looked down at the sand. 'Oh, nothing.'

'Looked like you had something on your mind to me. Come on, spill. I'm a good listener.'

'I was . . . I was thinking about my mum.'

'Why? Had a barney?'

'No. She used to bring me here when I was little. She died five years ago. I . . . I miss her and this place kind of brings her back.' I didn't know why I was telling him this. I hadn't told anyone this was my special place when I want to feel close to her. I learned pretty quickly after she died that some people feel uncomfortable when they hear about death. Like they don't know what to say, or they come out with something stupid and it's obvious that they're embarrassed and feel sorry for me, and I hate that.

But Ollie was looking at me kindly. I made myself smile. 'Sorry. I'm not usually like this. I was just thinking of her today and felt a bit sad.'

'Understandable,' he said. 'It means you loved her a lot.' He leapt to his feet. 'Come on, let me buy you an ice cream and we'll go for a paddle.'

I looked down at the shopping at my feet, then up at the vision standing only a foot away, grinning at me. Sorry Dad, I thought. You'll have to wait. Opportunities like this don't come along every day, not down here they don't.

And I still had to mention Becca.

We spent the next hour gabbing about everything. He was really nice. No, not nice, gorgeous, gorgeous, *gorgeous* and he made me feel the same. Like I was the most interesting, scintillating person on the planet.

'Eep!' I said looking at my watch. 'Got to go.'

'Eep?' he laughed. 'What kind of word is that?'

I laughed back. 'It's the noise our computer at home makes if I make a mistake on it. Eep. Eep. It's kind of got into my brain and now if I ever do something wrong, out it comes as a warning.'

He took my hand. 'And are you doing something wrong now?'

Eep, eep, eep, went a voice in my head as a delicious, warm sensation flooded through me. 'Er, no, just . . . should have been back ages ago.' I'd been on the beach with him for a long time. I still hadn't mentioned Becca and he was holding my hand. Eep, double eep.

'Er, um, Ollie?'

'Yes,' he said linking his fingers through mine.

'Um, er, I've got a friend, that is, have you ever noticed anyone about the village?'

Ollie began playing with my fingers and I felt like my brain was going to fuse.

'I've noticed lots of people round the village. The lady in the Post Office, the –'

'No, I mean, any girls.'

Ollie grinned. 'I notice all the girls.'

'But, see this one in particular.' It wasn't coming out right. I made myself think straight. 'See, I have this friend.'

'Ah,' said Ollie looking right into my eyes. 'A friend. OK. So what about this *friend*?'

'Well, she's noticed you and . . .' I didn't know that someone just looking at you could cause such chaos inside. It felt like time had slowed down yet my heart had sped up. I could hear it thumping in my chest.

Ollie put his other hand up to my neck and ran his fingers softly through my hair. 'Oh, has she now? So tell me more about this . . . friend.'

Eep, eep, eeeeep. 'Well, I think she kind of likes you and . . .'

He pulled me towards him and kissed me. A lovely soft kiss that went right down to the tips of my toes and back.

'I've been wanting to do that since I first saw you,' he whispered nuzzling into my neck.

EEEEEEP. I pulled back.

'What's the matter?' he asked.

'Nothing. Just got to go. Um, thanks for the ice cream. And . . .'

I began to walk backwards away from him. 'Bye, thanks, sorry.'

He stood there grinning. 'Any time, Cat. Hope to see you and your *friend* around.'

I ran all the way home feeling exhilarated. Just before I reached our house, I stopped to catch my breath. Ollie Axford had kissed me and I was floating on air. But he was Becca's. She'd bagged him first. And I already had a boyfriend. I should have told Becca the truth, my biggest secret, while I had the chance. What was I going to do? What was I going to say to Becca? She'd kill me. Never speak to me again.

I set off again more slowly. Got to think this through. Becca's been my friend for years. My best friend and she's more important than any boy. And I'd tried to do her dare for her even when I'd been let off the hook. It wasn't my fault that Ollie misunderstood about my 'friend'. Got to think this through.

As I put the key in the lock and braced myself for the telling off for being late, there was one thing that I knew for certain. That fabulous sensation was how I wanted to feel when I was kissed. I had to tell Squidge it was over. There were other boys besides Ollie. So maybe I couldn't have him, but there were others. There could be others. I'd blank Ollie out. Put him in a box in my head and lock the door. History. Pretend it never happened.

But as Dad went into his inquisition, all I could think about was how it felt when Ollie's lips touched mine. And how I felt when he held my hand. I couldn't stop it. He'd escaped from the box and a part of my brain had gone into action replay, action replay, action replay. And with each time, the feeling when he kissed me came back.

Oh, eep.

Fifty Ways to Leave Your Lover 3

Dear Squidge,
   I really like you but . . .

I RIPPED up the paper. Pathetic.

'Oh, how am I going to do this, Bec? *Help* me.'

'Only if you tell me again about Ollie,' said Becca staring dreamily out of her bedroom window.

'I've *told* you six times already,' I said getting up from her desk and going to lie on her bed.

'I know, but I love hearing. Tell me how he looked again.'

Divine, I thought. Sexy. Gorgeous. Stunning.

'He looked all right, I suppose.'

'All right? You must be blind. But you did really mention me, didn't you? You're not making it up?'

'No I *really* mentioned you. First I asked if he'd noticed

anyone around the village and he said loads of people . . .'

'Then you said about me?'

'Yeah I told you already. He said he noticed all the girls.'

'So maybe he has noticed me?'

'Maybe he has.'

'Did you describe me or anything? Say anything nice about me?'

'I did try, Bec, honestly, but it wasn't easy. I had a load of shopping with me and I had to get back with it and . . .'

'I know,' said Becca, 'and I am grateful. Going up and just talking to him out of the blue. I could never have done that. You're such a pal.'

I am a cow. A cow, cow, cow, I thought. I'd told her what I could. Not about the kiss of course. Or the holding hands. Or the flirting. I'd just told her the bits in between.

'And Lia's starting school on Monday?' she asked.

'Yes. He said she was. I told you.'

'And you have to watch out for her. And I will too. And hopefully get to meet him.'

'Yeah. Now *please*, help me come up with a way to finish with Squidge.'

'You could text him.'

I shook my head. 'Couldn't. Too cold. Like what would I say?'

'U R dumped.'

I threw a pillow at her. 'Heartless.'

'OK by e-mail.'

'Oh, very funny. Not.'

'By phone, then you have some security in case he wants to kill you.'

'And I wouldn't have to see his face. Oh Bec, this is awful, I really, really, really don't want to hurt him.'

'Then stay with him.'

I went back to my letter. 'Maybe this is best as he'll have time to read it in private and get used to the idea.'

'Isn't there a song about ways to leave your lover?'

'Yeah. "Fifty Ways to Leave Your Lover" by Paul Simon. Dad's got it on a CD in the car. But try naming one.'

Becca looked thoughtful. 'You could move abroad.'

'Get real.'

'You could get him to finish with you.'

'How?'

'Behave horribly. Like always be late and in a bad mood. Pick your nose and eat it.'

'Urrghhh Becca. *Gross*. Besides if I did act horrid, knowing Squidge and what a sweetie he is, he'd be all understanding and try and make me feel better.'

'Join the Foreign Legion.'

'Thanks, you're being really helpful.'

'Tell him you've had the God call and are going to be a nun.'

'Yeah, like he'd believe that.'

'Say you've gone lesbo.'

'Then you'd have to pretend to be my girlfriend.'

'*Ewww*. Get lost. No listen, if you want my real and honest opinion I think you should just go round and tell him face-to-face. You owe him that much seeing as you've been together so long. And it shouldn't be so difficult as you know each other so well.'

She was right. I did owe him that much. I'd bite the bullet, take the bull by its horns, all that sort of thing. I could do it.

So why was I feeling so terrified?

'Jack,' Mrs Squires called up the stairs, 'Cat's here. Come in, love.'

I followed her through into their kitchen. I usually feel so comfortable here, it's like my second home. The Squires family have lived in Cawsand for generations in the same little cottage in one of the lanes at the back of the village. Their ancestors were fishermen, but now his mum and dad are The Most Important People In the Village, as his dad runs the local garage and his mum is a hairdresser. Mr Squires fixes my dad's old van, which is forever breaking down, and Mrs Squires cuts my hair and colours Squidge's. This month his is dyed white blond like Spike's in 'Buffy the Vampire Slayer'. Squidge has even got a three-quarter length leather coat to complete the look. Mr and Mrs Squires are really nice. Normal. I like going there and hope I still can when I finish with Squidge. I hope we can still be mates.

'You're looking a bit peaky, Cat. Are you all right?' asked Mrs Squires.

'Yeah, fine,' I said going over to play with Amy, who was sitting in her high chair. 'Can I pick her up?'

'Course you can,' said Mrs Squires going back into the hall. 'JACK, Cat's here.'

It always sounds strange to hear him called Jack as everyone calls him Squidge except his mum and dad. He doesn't look like a Jack. He looks like a Squidge. We call him that partly because of his surname, Squires, but mainly because ever since he was tiny, he's been obsessed with cameras. He was always looking at the world through a lens and forever squidging up his eyes to focus. Still is.

'Come up,' called Squidge from upstairs.

'Next time,' I said to Amy and she acknowledged my presence by putting her bowl of mashed banana on her head and gurgling happily.

I took a deep breath and headed up the stairs. I still wasn't sure what I was going to say, but I was determined somehow or other to find the words.

Squidge was lying on his bed. 'Hey,' he said.

'Hey. What are you doing?'

'Nothing.'

This wasn't like Squidge. He was always doing something. Full of ideas or working on something.

'What's up?' I asked.

He showed me a letter and a brochure. 'This. It's that

course I wanted to do in London in half-term, you know, about story structure.'

I took the brochure from him. He'd been talking about this course for ages. Apparently all the film people do it and as Squidge's thing is to write and direct his own films, he'd been looking forward to it eagerly. He's been getting up at the crack of dawn to do a newspaper round over the summer to save up.

'Costs three hundred and something pounds. No way can I afford that.'

'Have you asked your parents?'

Squidge shook his head. 'Nah, with Amy, Mum can't work as much as she used to. And Will's starting secondary school, so . . . you know . . .'

I sat on the end of his bed and squeezed his foot. 'Sorry.'

'I thought it would be about forty quid or something. I've saved a hundred for my train and stuff, and Mac said I could stay at his dad's, but no way can I afford the course.' He sighed. 'Just as you think everything's working out, something like this comes along and ruins it all.'

He looked so sad. This isn't the time, I thought. I couldn't finish with him today. It would be the last straw.

'Want to play aeroplanes?' I asked.

Squidge forced a smile. 'Sure.'

I climbed on to the end of the bed and he raised his legs into the air while I balanced my abdomen on his feet.

'Ready,' he said.

'Ready,' I said.

Squidge raised his feet with me on them, held on to my shoulders and I flung my arms wide as his feet flew me through the air. That's aeroplanes. At least it got him to laugh.

Mr Squires popped his head in the door and found me in mid-flight.

'Honestly you two, you never grow up, do you?'

4 Sex Education

'HOW MANY times do you have to have sex to have a baby, Cat?' asked Joe as we finished wiping the supper dishes.

'Only once as far as I know,' I said.

Joe looked thoughtful. 'So that means Mum and Dad had sex four times.'

'How do you work that out?'

Joe counted on his fingers. 'You, me, Luke and Emma. Four of us.'

'I guess,' I said trying not to laugh. 'But maybe you'd better ask Dad about that sort of thing.'

Joe went into the living room where Dad was watching the news and Emma got up from the table to follow him.

'Private conversation,' I said. 'Leave them alone.'

She went and lay on the floor in the hall and was clearly doing her best to listen in.

'He's telling about how babies are made,' she whispered back to me.

A short while later, the door opened and Joe came out shaking his head. 'Yuck,' he said. 'Disgusting. You don't want to know.'

Dad followed him out and saw Luke doing his homework at the kitchen table.

'I've just been talking to Joe about the facts of life, Luke. Is there anything you'd like to know?'

Luke went scarlet and buried his head in his geography book. 'Go away Dad,' he muttered into the book.

Dad shrugged, went back to watch the news and that was the end of that. Or so I thought.

I was in the local Spar on Sunday morning with Emma doing some shopping when it happened. I'd just put some eggs in the trolley when Emma piped up.

'Better not let Dad or the boys near those or we'll have babies and there's not enough room for them at our house.'

'What do you mean?' I asked.

'I heard him telling Joe the other night. You need an egg and a willie and then you get a baby.'

I laughed. 'Not these kind of eggs, Emma. The eggs that make babies are already inside of you.'

Emma looked at her tummy. 'Where?'

'Um, in your ovaries. They're tiny and there's loads and loads of them. Oh, you'll understand later. Ask Dad when you're older.'

'But I am old,' she said. 'Six. That's *really* old.'

I quickly wheeled the trolley to the checkout and my stomach did a double flip. There was Ollie Axford with one of his mates.

He turned and smiled when he saw me. 'Cat,' he said.

Before I could say anything, Emma had caught me up and tugged on his hand. 'How many willies have you got?'

Ollie looked faintly surprised while his mate giggled behind him. 'Er, only one last time I looked.'

'My dad's got *four* willies,' said Emma in a loud voice.

I wanted to die.

'This is Emma,' I said, 'the alien I told you about. Why on earth do you think Dad has got four willies, Em?'

'You need a willie and an egg, I told you. There's four of us in our family so Dad must have four willies.'

By now, half the shop was listening in and Ollie's mate was holding his sides laughing.

'Aw . . . cute.' Ollie was smiling.

The checkout next to us opened up and I quickly wheeled my trolley there, paid my money and ran.

When I got home, Luke called me into the boys' room where we kept our family computer.

'There was an e-mail from Squidge for you,' he said. 'He's coming over.'

Good, I thought. No time like the present and this time I'll be ready. Seeing Ollie again had double convinced me that it was time to finish with Squidge. Not because I was after Ollie, but he'd reminded me what it could feel like to really fancy someone. I wished I could talk to Becca about it all truthfully, but I knew that was a no-no. This was the first time in all our years of friendship that I hadn't told her the whole story. But at least I could come clean with Squidge. It was a new term tomorrow and I wanted to start with a fresh slate and all that. A new beginning all round.

This time I'd planned exactly what I was going to say, complete with the obligatory 'can we still be friends?' at the end. And I'd mean it.

Squidge arrived as I was putting away the groceries. He had a big grin on his face, so he'd clearly got over his disappointment of yesterday. Fantastic, I thought. Squidge never stays down for long.

I took a deep breath and plunged in, 'I'm really glad you came, because I have something I want to talk to you about.'

'OK, he said, 'but me first. I've also got something I want to say.'

'OK.'

He rummaged around in his rucksack and pulled out a small package wrapped in purple shiny paper. 'I went over to Plymouth yesterday after you'd been over and I got you a wee prezzie,' he said handing it to me.

'Oh, Squidge, you shouldn't have,' I said. Oh, Squidge you *really* shouldn't have, I thought.

'Go on, open it.'

I ripped off the paper and opened the box inside. It was a jeweller's box and inside was the most perfect silver bracelet.

Squidge's grin stretched from ear to ear. 'The shop girl told me it's from a place in New York called Tiffany. See, I wanted to get you something really special to say I think you're the best friend anyone could ever have. Not just yesterday, but all the time we've known each other. Look on the inside, see it's engraved.'

I turned the bracelet over and there in tiny letters was, 'To Cat with love'.

'Squidge, this must have cost a fortune.'

Squidge shrugged. 'You deserve it. See, I know how hard it is for you sometimes, and yesterday kind of made me realise I'd been a bit selfish lately, obsessed with doing my film course and saving money and here's you having to be like a mum to Joe and Emma and Luke. You haven't had anything new for ages and I thought, what a pig I am, I've neglected you. So this is to say I do appreciate you.'

'You . . . you haven't spent your course money on this, have you?'

'Might have done,' he smiled. 'But you're worth it, Cat. So what's a stupid film course?'

'But Squidge, all those paper rounds . . .'

Squidge took my hand and looked into my eyes. 'What's important is having a mate like you. You've always been there for me when I needed you, making me laugh, listening to all my mad ideas. I wanted to do something nice for you. Now come on, put it on.'

He fastened the bracelet on my wrist. 'Looks fab,' he said turning my wrist over to admire it then gently kissing the palm of my hand. 'Now. Your turn. What was it you wanted to say?'

I looked at the bracelet and Squidge's smiling open face.

'Oh nothing important. Stuff like, you ready for school tomorrow?'

5
Back to School

'SUNITA AHMED,' read Mrs Jeffries.

'Here, Miss.'

'David Alexander.'

'Here.'

'Mary Andrews.'

'Present.'

'Ophelia Moonbeam Axford.'

A titter went round the class.

'Here, Miss,' said a stunning-looking girl a couple of desks away. 'But please, everyone calls me Lia.'

As Mrs Jeffries continued calling the register, everyone turned round to look at the new girl. All through assembly everyone had been wondering who she was. Course Bec and I had guessed. It was Ollie's sister. She looked so like him, the same denim blue eyes in a perfect heart-shaped face, the only difference was that her long hair was white blond whereas Ollie's was dark.

Mrs Jeffries had reached the Ks.

'Mark Keegan?'

'Yes, Miss.'

'Catherine Kennedy.'

'Here, Miss, but everyone calls me Cat.'

I smiled cheekily over at Lia and she smiled back. Not Mrs Jeffries, though.

'Anyone *else* want to be known by a name besides the one they were born with?'

Half the class put up their hands.

'Yes. And you can call me Madam,' she said wearily. 'Now where was I? Ah yes. *Catherine* Kennedy.'

'Here, Miss,' I said. Best not start the new term on the wrong foot.

At break I saw that Lia was hanging back as the rest of the class charged for the door. Ollie had been right. It was hard starting a new school, especially in Year Nine when everyone already knew each other. I felt for her, as she looked a bit lost and lonely.

'Do you know where to go?' I asked.

'Not really,' she said.

'Come with me and I'll show you round. This is Becca,' I said as Becca ambled over to join us.

As we gave her the grand tour of the essentials – the loos, the library and the best places to hang out without being hassled by teachers, I noticed that Becca had gone quiet. Unusual for her, as most days she never shuts up.

In the playground I spotted Squidge and Mac in a corner by the bike sheds, so I took Lia over to meet them. And *they* were quiet and shy. What was going on?

'What year are you in?' asked Lia.

'Year Eleven,' chorused Squidge and Mac, then stood there all gawky and gangly. Then it dawned on me: they were intimidated.

Lia was beautiful and somehow her presence had turned them stupid.

'Let's go and sit over there,' I said pointing at an empty bench. 'See you later, boys.'

Becca stayed behind with them for a moment and, as Lia and I sat down, I could tell they were talking about her.

'Do you always have that effect on boys?' I asked.

'What do you mean?' said Lia.

'They're gobsmacked.'

Lia looked over at them. 'Why?'

'Gorgeous girl turns them into jelloid,' I laughed.

'Who me? You're kidding.'

Becca came over to join us and sat awkwardly on the end of the bench. This is silly, I thought. I have to break the ice.

'Ophelia Moonbeam. Is that really your name?'

'I know. It's awful isn't it? I *hate* it.'

'But it's so romantic,' said Becca finding her tongue at last. 'Like Ophelia in Hamlet and in all those Pre-Raphaelite paintings.'

Lia nodded, 'Yeah, we did them in art at my old school.

But have you seen that painting of Ophelia by John Millais? All tragic-looking and drowning in the river. Apparently she had to get into a bath to be painted and got pneumonia after. Not so romantic.'

Becca looked miffed. 'I think it's a beautiful painting. I've got a poster of it on my wall. People say *I* look like a Pre-Raphaelite.'

Eep, I thought. Better step in, but Lia got there first.

'You do,' she said 'but you're more of a Burne-Jones princess than a trago-queen.'

Becca tossed her hair and seemed appeased.

'So why Moonbeam?' I asked.

'Mad parents. They're stuck in another era and have given us all weird names,' replied Lia. 'Like my older sister, she's called Star, my brother's called Orlando, then me, Ophelia Moonbeam. How naff it that?'

Becca perked up. 'Orlando. That's a nice name.'

I caught Becca's eye. I'd wondered how long it was going to be before she brought *him* up.

'We call him Ollie,' said Lia.

'Oh really,' said Becca going into her wide eyed and innocent act. 'And how old is your brother? . . . Oh, *and* your sister?'

'Star's twenty. She lives up in London. She's a model. And Ollie's seventeen. He goes to school in London. I used to go as well but I didn't like it. I like being at home, so Mum got me a place here.'

Becca wasn't to be distracted. 'But don't you miss Ollie when he's away? Oh, and Star, of course.'

I had to laugh to myself. She was being so obvious, but Lia hadn't cottoned on. She had no reason to know that we already knew who Ollie was.

'Yes I miss them, but Ollie comes down a lot at the weekends. At least once a month. And Star whenever she can.'

There was no stopping Becca now. 'What's he like?'

'He's OK. You know, usual brother stuff.'

'Does he look like you?' asked Becca, who had happily settled herself on the bench by now.

'Sort of, only he's got dark hair. Anyway, why are you so interested in him?'

Becca sighed and indicated the groups of boys in the playground. 'Take a look around. This is it. The local talent. Not up to much.'

'Mac and Squidge look nice,' said Lia.

'Oh Squidge is Cat's boyfriend. Or was. Or is. Have you done it yet?'

'Done what, Cat?' asked Lia.

I really didn't want to get into all this. I'd only just met Lia and already I was to be known as Cat and Squidge. Exactly what I didn't want.

'Ended it. We've been together for years and er, well, I think it's time to finish with him.'

'Look what he bought her,' said Becca pointing at my bracelet.

'It's beautiful,' said Lia. 'So why do you want to finish with him exactly? He looks kind of cute to me.'

'Yes, why *do* you want to finish with him exactly?' echoed Becca. 'I can't say I really understand. He's *sooo* nice. I mean, you get on, he buys you lovely presents, he's good looking, good company . . .'

I wanted to kill her. It was hard enough as it was. Even a voice in my own head kept asking, are you doing the right thing? Maybe I was about to make the biggest mistake of my whole life and I'd never meet anyone as lovely again. Never have another boyfriend. Ever. Both Lia and Becca were looking at me waiting for me to answer.

I remembered a line from telly the night before. 'The magic's gone,' I said.

Lia nodded. 'I had a boyfriend up in London like that. He was perfect in every way, but it was like there was no excitement left. I got bored.'

'So what did you do?'

Lia blushed. 'I'm afraid I took the cowardly way out and got my friend to tell him.'

I looked hopefully at Becca. 'No way, Cat. Don't look at me. You're on your own here. So Lia, when's Ollie down again?'

'A few weeks,' said Lia. 'He only went back last night. Why, do you want to meet him?'

Becca's face lit up. 'Yeah, maybe.'

'Then I have to warn you,' said Lia, 'Ollie may be my

brother, but he's a legendary heartbreaker.'

'In what way?' asked Becca, who had given up all attempts at being cool and was literally hanging on to Lia's every word.

'There's a trail of girls after him up in London, always phoning him. His longest relationship lasted about three weeks. His idea of commitment is to ask for someone's e-mail address. He strings girls along, makes them fall in love with him, then drops them.'

'Maybe he's not met the right one,' said Becca dreamily.

'That's what they all hope,' said Lia as Becca's face fell. 'He's even started down here. The other day, he said he'd snogged some girl on the beach. Poor girl I say, another one bites the dust.'

Eep. My heart began to thump in my chest. Did she know it was me? He had asked me to look out for her and maybe he'd told her. Then Becca would *know* it was me.

'Who?' demanded Becca.

Lia shrugged. 'Don't know. Some local girl, I guess. He said he liked her, though, and that they had a really long talk.'

Ohmigod. Ohmigod.

Becca was looking daggers at me.

'Er, excuse us for a mo Lia, I have to talk to Cat about something.'

Lia looked puzzled as Becca got up and beckoned me to follow her. 'Er, come on Cat. You know that, er, project we were working on. We need to go over a few things.'

I got up to follow her. Eep. Eep. I wished I'd told her the truth in the beginning.

Once inside the school, Becca hauled me into the science lab and turned on me. 'So you were there. Did you see him with anyone?'

I sighed with relief. She hadn't automatically thought it was me. 'Er no. But I was only there a short while, I told you.'

Becca's eyes were drilling into me. Tell the truth, I thought. Tell the truth.

'So was there anyone else around?' she asked. 'Anyone he could have got talking to after you left.'

'No. Only an older lady having a coffee.' I felt as if I was being interrogated by police on 'The Bill' or something. Honest, guv, it weren't me.

Becca looked thoughtful. 'It could have been anyone. Probably that tart, Megan Wilson, from Year Ten. She's always hanging about in Cawsand.'

'Yeah. Maybe. It could have been anyone.'

Oh argh. Double argh.

6 *White Lies*

WHEN I got home the following Friday, there was a delicious aroma of garlic and onions wafting from the kitchen. Oh fab, I thought, Jen's here.

I followed the smell and found her busy chopping peppers. It looked like she'd just come from work as she still had her air hostess uniform on underneath Dad's Homer Simpson apron. She works over in Plymouth and does the local flights up to Bristol or London and back.

'Hungry?' she asked, smoothing a stray tendril of hair back into place. She always looked so smart. Slim and blond with her hair twisted back into a neat French plait.

'Always am when you're here.' I smiled.

I liked Jen. Dad's been seeing her for over a year now and when she comes over, she likes to cook for us. It's a real treat, as Dad's not quite mastered the art of cooking. His idea of culinary delight is to put cheese in with the mash, which is usually served with burgers or sausages. And my specialities are pasta, pasta or pasta – anything that's quick and easy, so Jen's cooking is a welcome change.

'I'm doing a chicken casserole, that OK?'

I nodded. 'Need a hand?'

'You could chop those leeks for me,' she said pointing to the vegetable basket.

As we busied ourselves in the kitchen, Jen proceeded to do the usual adult interrogation. 'So how's school?'

'OK,' I said.

'You've gone into Year Nine, haven't you?'

I nodded and started setting the table.

'You seem subdued tonight,' she said. 'Not like you.'

I shrugged, then I guess I must have sighed, because she picked up on it in a second.

'School trouble?'

'No, school is fine. In fact it's nice to be back in a strange way. There's a new girl started called Lia. She's been hanging out with me and Bec all week. I think we're going to be friends. She's Zac Axford's daughter.'

'Oh, from Barton Hall?'

I nodded then rummaged in the cupboard for glasses.

'So what's up, then?' persisted Jen. 'Boy trouble? Friend trouble?'

I hesitated. I really needed to talk to someone about all the strange goings on in my head lately and Becca was off limits at the moment, and Dad, well Dad was never the easiest person to have a real conversation with.

'Both,' I said. 'Promise you won't tell anyone, not Dad or anyone.'

'Promise.'

'I've been thinking a lot lately about truth.'

Jen laughed. 'Oh, philosophical trouble.'

I smiled. 'Sort of. See, sometimes you don't tell the truth to protect someone, right?'

Jen nodded. 'Right.'

'Sometimes to just keep the peace and sometimes not to hurt someone. But it's not easy. Like what would you do if you knew if you told someone the truth it would upset them. But truth and lies, both can hurt can't they?'

Jen looked at me with concern. 'I guess. But it sounds serious. You going to tell me what this is really about?'

I hesitated again then decided I could trust Jen. She was OK for a grown-up. 'Well, it's about Squidge mainly. You know we've been going together for ages now?'

Jen nodded.

'Well, I've been trying to finish with him and it's really difficult. It never seems to be the right time and I don't want to hurt him. That's where telling the truth is hard, you know what I mean?'

Jen nodded again. 'It's always difficult finishing with someone.'

'So what do I do?'

Jen stopped her preparations. 'In a situation like this, honesty is always the best policy. Trying to protect someone from the truth can prolong the agony.'

'Tell me about it,' I interrupted.

'But for him as well as for you. If the situation was the other way round, say he wanted to finish with you, you'd want to know, wouldn't you?'

'Yeah. Definitely.'

'You've got to be cruel to be kind sometimes. It's only respectful if you care about someone, and you clearly do about Squidge. Be straight with him. Take a deep breath and tell him where you're at. Otherwise you're giving him false hope that everything's all right when it's not. He needs to be able to move on as well as you.'

She was right. I owed Squidge the truth, it wasn't fair otherwise.

Jen was looking at me kindly. 'It will be all right, Cat. Life goes on.'

I nodded. 'I know. You're right. I'll tell him.'

At that moment Emma burst in, 'Tarzan in the jungle, had a bellyache, couldn't find a toilet. Thwup, too late.'

Jen and I burst out laughing. 'Lovely,' said Jen. 'And where did you learn that? School?'

'No,' said Emma. 'Joe.'

At supper, Emma and Joe insisted that Jen serve dinner like an air hostess. Poor Jen. I felt sorry for her. On her few days off, she comes here and they make her do her work routine.

'After dinner,' she said into the soup ladle that she was using as a pretend microphone, 'I'll be coming down the corridor by the fridge serving dessert. On tonight's menu, we have a choice of chocolate chip ice cream or . . . or nothing. After that we'll be showing a film in the living room and turning the lights out so that passengers who wish to, can sleep.'

Dad laughed and looked at her appreciatively. It was good to see him happy and he always was when she was around.

After supper I went upstairs to start my weekend home-work. It's a difficult task seeing as we only have one proper table in the house where you can spread your books out, and that's in the kitchen. As Dad and Jen were having a drink and chatting in there, I didn't want to disturb them. Dad doesn't get to spend enough time with Jen as it is.

I looked around the tiny bedroom I shared with Emma and thought, I suppose I could put my books on the bottom bunk and sit on the floor to work. I wished Dad would buy the fold-down desk he'd promised, but he never seems to get around to it. Maybe I could work at Becca's instead, I thought. She's so lucky being an only child. She has a bed-room all to herself, plus her own computer and a desk unit with shelves. Maybe I'll give her a ring.

'I've been working on a song,' said Becca when she picked up the phone. 'It's a love ballad. Why don't I ring Jade and see if she wants to do some band practice and we could maybe put some music to the words?'

I wasn't really in the mood for Jade. She's Mac's younger sister and can be mega snotty. She's in Year Ten and thinks she knows it all as she's lived in London most of her life and tends to look down her nose at us as though we're country yokels. However, when Mac told her that Becca and I had a girl band, she asked if she could join us and I have to admit, she has got a brilliant voice.

In the rest of the house, there was a battle of sounds between Em banging on the piano downstairs, the telly blasting out and Luke playing hip hop next door. I looked at my books strewn all over the bed. No peace here, I thought.

'Good idea,' I said. 'I'll meet you at yours.'

I put my school stuff away and quickly got changed into my combats, T-shirt and leather jacket then headed downstairs for the back door.

'Where do you think you're going?' said Dad.

'Um, Becca's. We've got a school project we're working on.'

Luckily, Dad was in a good mood so didn't object. 'Make sure you're back at a reasonable hour,' he said as I shut the door behind me.

As I cycled over to Becca's, there was a strange feeling in the pit of my stomach. Jen's words from earlier that evening were nagging me. Honesty is the best policy she'd said and, although she was applying it to Squidge, I couldn't help but think I hadn't been honest with Dad just now. I'd told a lie. He wasn't too enthusiastic about the band idea, so lately, whenever we got together, I didn't give him all the details. A white lie. That's what I'd told. Was that OK? It wasn't harming anyone. Or was it? This truth versus lying business is beginning to get to me, I thought, as I peddled furiously up the hill to Becca's house.

As soon as I got to Becca's, she took me up to her room and insisted on reading me her latest song. She fancies herself as a songwriter and I've haven't the heart to tell her that her lyrics are truly, spectacularly *awful*.

'Ready?' she asked as I took off my jacket and flopped on her bed.

'Ready,' I said, bracing myself for inevitable. Then I thought, no, give her a break, maybe this time she'll prove me wrong.

She rummaged around the usual debris on her desk and found her piece of paper and began to read.

I met a boy around about, Ollie is his name.
The way he looked so cute and cool crawled right into
*   my brain.*
I'm sure that since that moment I've never felt quite right,
And when someone called him a flash git, I got
*   into a fight.*
When I see him I'm happy and squishy and warm,
'Cause I think Ollie's the coolest boy ever to be born.
One day I'll walk right up to him and tell him who I am,

Then he'll say that he fancies me without a doubt,
And how about next Friday, can we go out?

'What do you think?' Becca said expectantly.

'Um, maybe the end needs some polishing?' And the beginning and the middle, I thought.

'There's more,' she said. 'There's a chorus.'

Oh no, I thought. Like I'm ever going to sing this. In public.

'Ollie, Ollie, you're my brolly,' she read. 'My cover when it rains. Ollie, Ollie, I'm off my trolly, You've scrambled up my brains.'

I was dying to laugh but made my face go straight. 'Hmmm. Interesting,' I said as a voice in my head questioned, now was that a half-truth, white lie, or an outright fib?

Just at that moment the doorbell rang downstairs. 'That'll be Jade,' I said. 'Let's see what she thinks.'

Jade burst in a moment later. As always, she was looking fab in a mini hipster denim skirt and a short asymmetric T-shirt which showed off her flat tummy and the diamante stud through her belly button.

'Don't you ever tidy up?' she asked as she cleared a space on the floor where she could sit.

'I like it like this,' said Becca. Her room was always a mess and, this evening no less than usual, there were books, magazines, clothes and shoes all over the place. 'Us creative types haven't time for being anally retentive about tidiness.'

Hah. That put her in her place, I thought, as Jade moved a sock and pulled a face like she'd touched a piece of dog poo.

'I've written a new song,' said Becca, ignoring Jade's expression and beginning to read the lyrics.

Poor Becca, I thought, she's in for it now.

'Is that Ollie as in Ollie Axford?' asked Jade when Becca had finished.

'Yes,' said Becca. 'Why, do you know him?'

Jade smiled coyly and tossed her long blond hair back over her shoulder. 'Might do.'

Becca looked freaked. 'Er, you weren't with him the other day down on Cawsand beach, were you?'

'No,' said Jade. 'Why?'

'Nothing,' said Becca.

'So why ask? What's going on?'

I picked up one of Becca's books from the floor and made like I was really interested in it, but the words on the page were swimming before my eyes. Please don't ask me anything, I prayed. I don't want to go through it all again.

'Nothing,' said Becca. 'Just his sister Lia is a friend of ours and she said he was snogging some local girl on the beach last week.'

'Really? We must find out who it was,' said Jade. 'But it doesn't necessarily mean anything. A boy like Ollie is bound to have girls queuing up for him.'

'And are you one of them?' said Becca looking daggers at her.

'Might be. Why, are you?'

'Might be,' said Becca.

Oooch, I thought. This is getting more and more complicated.

7   *Cinders*

LIA PHONED on Saturday morning just as I was cleaning the bathroom.

'Do you want to come over?' she asked. 'Mum's got a few friends down and they've all gone off horse-riding and I'm bored.'

'Can't,' I sighed. 'Saturday's for doing chores.'

Lia sounded disappointed. 'But Becca's coming. See if you can come later.'

I put the phone down and saw that Jen was standing behind me. 'Who was that?' she asked.

'Lia Axford,' I said. 'Invited me over. But I haven't finished the bathroom yet, then I've – '

Jen put her hand on my shoulder and squeezed it. 'Leave it with me, Cinders. You shall go to the ball.'

Half an hour later I was on my way over to Lia's. Jen had been brilliant. She had a word in Dad's ear and, amazingly, he agreed to let me go. A whole day without jobs. Hurray.

I wish she'd move in permanently, I thought – life would be fantabulous. I can tell Dad's worried about how I and the others would take it, but we'd love it. I tried to talk to him about it a couple of weeks ago, but he changed the subject mucho fast. It's a shame because we all really like Jen and want him to be happy but, when I tried to tell him, he murmured something about us being his responsibility, then he went off to the shop.

All this thinking I've been doing about truth and being honest lately, it applies to me and Dad as well. It's not that we're dishonest with each other exactly, more like we don't tell the whole truth. One day we need to sit down and have a proper talk about things, I decided. Some day when I can get him on his own.

It was a cloudless blue sky as I peddled up and over towards Millbrook and it felt like the clear air was blowing away some of the cobwebs in my head. There's the truth, I thought, then white lies, then half-truths, then fibs. Then there's good and bad lies, some to protect, some to keep the peace and some that are plain cowardly, I suppose. Like when I've told Dad I've been somewhere I haven't so he won't be mad – like saying I've been at an extra class at school when actually I've been out spacing with Bec. Which is best, I wondered, and what do I do? Am I an honest person or a fibber?

I decided to keep an account over the next week of every fib or white lie that I told, starting tomorrow.

After ten minutes, I'd left Millbrook behind and reached Barton Hall. But how was I going to get in? The imposing wrought iron gates in front of me were firmly shut. I spied a small intercom box on one of the adjacent pillars and pressed the buzzer.

A camera whizzed into action and took a look at me. I smiled hopefully.

'Hi Cat, come on up,' said Lia's voice through the intercom, then I heard a buzz and, as if by magic, the gates began to open.

As I cycled up, down and around the bends of the long drive, I began to feel apprehensive. Although I'd been here before with Dad, someone had come down to collect the box of groceries at the gate. This time I was going inside as a guest. At least Ollie wasn't there. That *would* have been too much.

It seemed to take ages cycling up to the house, past stables, outhouses and an endless wood. I was just starting to think I was lost when suddenly the trees opened up and I saw Lia and Becca waiting for me at the top of the drive with two red setters running around their feet.

The house was very grand, like an old hotel, nestling in amongst a wooded area at the back and sides and, in front, there was a terraced lawn lined with huge palms in ginormous pots.

'Wow, Cat, you have got to see this place,' beamed Becca as I got off my bike and was immediately accosted by the dogs, who greeted me like their oldest, dearest friend. 'It's totally amazing. They've got their own tennis courts and a swimming pool *and* a billiards room.'

'This is Max and Molly,' said Lia. 'Down, good dogs, down.' Max jumped down, but Molly seemed to have taken a liking to me and had my sleeve firmly in her teeth. 'Down, Molly, down. Sorry Cat, she's still young and gets over-excited when people arrive.'

'Er, no prob,' I said as Lia prised her off. I leaned my bike against the porch and looked at the cars parked to the side of the house. A gleaming silver Mercedes, a black BMW and a Range Rover. 'Chauffeur was busy so I came on my own transport,' I laughed.

Lia smiled shyly. 'Do you want to come in? I'll give you the grand tour. That is, if Becca doesn't mind seeing it all again.'

'No, course not,' said Becca.

We followed her into the porch and through a door, which opened up into a hall with high ceilings and large mirrors and a wide staircase.

'This is the drawing room,' said Lia leading me into an elegant room with an enormous bay window and lovely thick curtains right down to the floor. Through the window was the most stunning view of the lawns in front leading down to the sea.

'They have their own private beach down there,' said Becca, who was clearly enjoying herself immensely. 'And boats.'

As I followed them round room by room, I began to enjoy myself as well. I felt like a tourist going round one of those National Trust stately homes. I'd never seen anything like it except for a hotel last year when my Auntie Brenda got married. Every downstairs room (four living rooms!) had lovely comfortable furniture, open fireplaces with baskets of logs next to them, and everywhere there were what looked like expensive antiques. Best of all, though, each room had its own television. Upstairs, all of the bedrooms (eight!) had their own bathroom and even some of *them* had televisions.

'It must be a dream to live here,' I said. 'Not having to share a bedroom or a bathroom and having your very own telly must be heaven.'

'Well I hope you'll come and stay some time,' said Lia. 'Mum loves having people over.'

'Yes please,' I said as she led us down a corridor and into another bedroom.

'This is where our Cornish Casanova lives,' she said.

'Ollie's room,' said Becca and gave me a wicked grin behind Lia's back.

It felt strange looking at his private things. There were loads of photos of him and his friends and family and seeing them made my insides go funny. Get back in your box, I told the thoughts in my head. I wasn't going to hang about in there, but Becca was busy scanning his shelves, his books, his CDs.

She grinned. 'Research'. Then looking at Lia, she said to me, 'It's OK, I told her I've seen Ollie about and really fancy him. Lia knows all my secrets now.'

Typical Becca. She wears her heart on her sleeve and can never keep anything to herself for long.

Lia smiled back at her. 'Don't say I didn't warn you, though.'

For a moment I felt a twinge of jealousy. Not because of the beautiful house or anything. I was jealous because it used to be so open between Bec and I. No secrets. And now she was sharing secrets with Lia. I hated not being able to tell her everything that was happening to me. It was like an invisible wall had gone up and I was stuck behind it.

We spent the rest of the afternoon doing the 'grand tour', but even after two hours, we still hadn't seen all the grounds.

'You must come and do *le grand tour* of our house one day,' I laughed. 'It'll take less than five minutes. Three up, two down and a small bathroom.'

'You don't mind, do you?' asked Lia as we stopped at the top of the lawns.

'Mind what?' asked Becca looking puzzled.

Lia indicated the estate with a sweep of her hand. 'All this.'

'Mind it? I *love* it,' I said.

'It's just, sometimes people are a bit funny about our family having so much, you know . . .'

'You mean jealous?' I asked.

Lia nodded. 'I hope it won't stop us being friends.'

'Course not,' I said. 'I mean, course I'm a bit jealous, who wouldn't be? But I was hoping you'd ask me and Bec to move in. No one would even notice we were here. We could camp out in one of the stables with the horses.'

Lia laughed and looked relieved. 'Good, then let's go and ask Meena to get us something to drink.'

'Who's Meena?' asked Becca.

Lia looked embarrassed. 'Our housekeeper. Sorry.'

As we followed her back into the house and into a kitchen that was bigger than our whole house put together, I couldn't help but think that people are strange. Here's Lia, who has everything: looks, glam parents, an enormous house and housekeeper, her own bedroom, bathroom, telly and goodness knows what else, and yet she's worried that *we* wouldn't want to be friends with her. Then I realised the one thing she *didn't* have down here was friends and that's what makes anywhere more enjoyable, whether you're in a huge place like this, or in a tiny place like where I live. You learn fast when someone like your mum dies that it's people that count. Friends. I looked at her with increasing admiration. She had it all but wasn't the least bit stuck up, unlike Jade, who acts as though she's God's gift. Friends. That's what's important, I thought, and Lia obviously knows that. I hoped we would be friends. And I hoped Becca and I would go back to the way we used to be. If only I could tell her the truth.

8

Liar, Liar, Pants on Fire

Sunday: Fibs (1)

Went to Plymouth with Squidge, Lia, Becca and Mac.
Lied that I was fifteen to get into the movie. Well *everyone*
does that, don't they? Lia and Becca did as well so don't
feel too bad.

Monday: Fibs (2)

Was late for school. Said bus didn't show up, when actually
I missed it because Emma refused to go to school in her
polka dot knickers, as she said you could see the dots
under her pink trousers. She made such a fuss that I had
to find her another pair, which made me late. Not my
fault and no way I'm explaining all *that* to Mrs Jeffries.

Becca asked if a spot on her nose was obvious. Said no,
when actually it was ginormous.

Tuesday: Fibs (3)

Ohmigod! Lied to Becca again, as she'd rewritten her love ballad and it was worse than the first version. Didn't want to hurt her feelings, so said it was cool.

Lied to Dad. He was working late and we got out a horror film from the shop, but told him we'd watched Disney's *Aladdin*.

Lied to Squidge when he asked if he could come over. I said I had homework to do, when actually I'd finished it and wanted to watch the horror movie with Luke, Joe and Emma. Felt mean after, because Squidge loves horror movies.

Wednesday: Fibs (0)

Hurrah.

Thursday: Fibs (5)

Eep. Eep.

Lied for Luke. A drippy girl at his school called Josephine Talbot has got a crush on him and he can't stand her. When she phoned, he asked me to say he wasn't in. And I did.

Lied to some Bible bashers who came to the door and asked if I was at peace with my God. Told them we were all Devil worshippers in our house to get rid of them. Joe and Luke thought it was hilarious and would have put on last year's Hallowe'en masks that drip blood and followed them down the street if I hadn't stopped them.

Lied to someone who phoned while we were having supper. He wanted to drop in next week and redesign our kitchen for free. Could *not* get him off the phone, so told him we were a hippie family and lived in a wigwam and cooked on a barbecue. Dad thought it was hilarious, so now I'm getting support on all sides for fibbing.

Lied to Becca, as she asked me about Ollie *again*.

Lied to Becca, after she saw Jade talking to me on the way into school. Jade was slagging Becca off and saying she never stood a chance with Ollie. When Bec asked what we were talking about, I said, 'Oh about herself as usual'.

Friday: Fibs (3)

Half-lied to Mr Ford in physics and said that I hadn't done my homework because our computer had run out of cartridge ink and I hadn't had time to go to Plymouth to get any. Was a half-lie, because the real reason was that Dad couldn't afford it this week and I didn't want to say that in front of the whole class and have everyone feeling sorry for me.

Lied to Moira Ferguson when she invited me to her party on Sunday. Said my cousins were coming to stay for the weekend. I can't stand her – she's so bossy.

Lied to Dad that I had done my music practice, when actually I haven't even looked at the piano in weeks.

Saturday: Fibs (1)

Lied when my gran phoned and asked if I liked the
sweater she'd sent that she knitted herself. Told her I
loved it, but really it is hideous.

I am appalled at myself. I always considered myself to be
an honest person, but I am the Fibbing Fibster of Fibville.
I wished I could talk to someone about it, but most people
would think I was mad or a criminal or something. I
wished Mum were here. I went into my wardrobe, found
my secret box and unlocked it. I kept all my special things
in there: old photos, cards Squidge had sent me and some
stuff of Mum's – a letter from her, bits of her old jewellery
and a bottle of Mitsouko by Guerlain. When we finally
cleared her stuff out of the cupboards in Dad's room, I
found the perfume and hid it. Whenever I smelt it, it
brought her back like she was in the house somewhere. I
took the cap off and did a spray on to my wrist and sniffed.
As always the soft flowery scent made me think of her.
What would she have made of all this and her daughter
qualifying for the Teenage Fibber of the Week award? She
was always so honest herself. All through her illness, she'd
insisted on knowing exactly how she was and also on
telling us the truth about her condition. I heard her telling
Dad once that she didn't want to give us false hope and
that death was a part of life and not to be shunned. She was
so brave about it all and I'm glad I knew how bad things

were because I think she was right: it would have been even worse if she'd just disappeared one day and I hadn't known how ill she'd really been.

Dad popped his head in the door. 'Supper's ready, Cat.'

I quickly stuffed my box back in the wardrobe as I didn't want him to see me getting upset, but he didn't go straight away. His eyes had misted and he seemed to be looking for someone else in the room. I think he'd smelled the Mitsouko. Maybe now was the time to have that talk about things, I thought. We'd never really sat down and talked about Mum's death, just the two of us.

'You all right, Dad?' I asked.

He coughed then sort of sniffed the air again. 'Yes fine. Just . . . I thought . . . oh, nothing.'

Then he left before I could say anything else.

Before I went down to supper, I got out Mum's letter to me. She'd written it a few weeks before she died and asked Dad to keep it and give it to me the day I started secondary school. It said:

My darling girl,
    All grown up and ready to start a new school and how I wish I was going to be there to see it. I wanted to write to you and tell you how proud I am of you. You have been a strength to me over the last year and the light of my days. Be strong, Cat. Be true to yourself

and always be brave as I know you will be.
God bless. My love will always be with you

Your mum.

That's it, I thought. From now on I am going to reform and be brave just like Mum was. From now on, I'm going to tell the Absolute Truth.

9 The Absolute Truth

I STARTED the new week feeling bright and optimistic. Pure as the newly fallen snow, that was going to be me.

Monday: Truths (2)

On the bus going to school, Becca asked what I thought of her latest song. I told her to stick to dancing.

She's not speaking to me.

At home after school, Josephine Talbot phoned for Luke. He was in front of me waving his arms madly and mouthing, 'No, *nooooo*.' But being a truth teller, I told her he was there and handed him the phone.

Luke's not speaking to me.

Tuesday: Truths (1)

At school, when Mr Ford asked where my homework was, I told him I hadn't done it. Then he asked why not, so I told him that *Dawson's Creek* was being repeated and after that I felt tired and couldn't be bothered as it was *sooo* boring.

Got detention. But am the class hero.

Wednesday: Truths (2)

Bec's speaking to me again, but the spot on her nose has grown even bigger than last week. When she asked if I was sure it wasn't noticeable, I told her that actually, it looked like it had taken over half her face.

She's not speaking to me again.

Bit of a do at home this evening. Dad was going down the video shop and asked what we wanted. Emma said, '*Jeepers Creepers*'. Then Dad said, 'But we don't watch horror in this house *do* we?'

I didn't have to tell the truth this time as Emma reeled off a whole list of films that we've watched when Dad's been out.

Am in the doghouse.

Thursday: Truths (2)

At school break, Mac asked if I thought he stood a chance with Becca. I said, no as she's so in love with Ollie Axford that no one else even gets a look in. It's the truth.

Mac went off in a sulk.

In second break, Lia asked if I fancied Ollie. Didn't know what to say at first, but as it's my truth week, I knew I had no choice and admitted I did. Turns out she knew I was 'the girl on the beach'! I was amazed because I thought he hadn't ever mentioned my name, but apparently he'd phoned from London and asked Lia if she'd met me and told her that I was the girl he had been with in Cawsand. She also said she had guessed I liked Ollie because I go mega-quiet whenever anyone talks about him. Interesting. Seems that sometimes you can't hide what you really feel.

V. glad I told her the truth. She'd never have trusted me again if I'd lied. I had to beg her not to tell Becca, though, as I want to pick my moment and don't want to hurt her. She agreed and said that Ollie has asked after me and she thinks he really likes me!! Plus he's coming down next weekend and he's going to go to Rock with a few mates. Arghhh.

So far this week, thank God, thank *God*, Becca hasn't asked about him.

Friday: Truths (4) Excellent!

On the school bus, Moira Ferguson asked how last weekend went with my cousins. Tricky one, but I was brave – I was the Truth Teller of Torpoint. I told her that they didn't come and, anyway, I wasn't in a party mood.

Later, Moira told the whole class that I am a liar. Phff. She obviously doesn't realise that I am She Who Is Honest.

At home in the evening, Gran phoned and asked if I'd

worn my new sweater. I finally admitted I hadn't as it just wasn't me. It was awful, as she went very quiet and asked to speak to Dad. He gave me a lecture about being diplomatic. It's not easy to be diplomatic *and* tell the truth.

In the doghouse again.

Later that evening, the Bible bashers came back to ask if I was at peace with my God. I said I didn't know and invited them in for a half-hour of debate. Got told off for letting strange men in the house by Dad and told off by Joe and Emma for giving them the last of the chocolate chip cookies.

At supper that night, someone phoned to ask if we needed a new bathroom. I told him truthfully that yes, we did. Desperately. Then he said that his company would have a designer in our area next week who could come and give us a free quote and design. I told him that that would be great, but there's no way we could afford a new bathroom so it might be a waste of time. OK, he said, good night then.

Well *that* one was easy!

Saturday: Truths (1)

At the cinema in Plymouth, when the lady behind the kiosk asked how old I was, I told her: fourteen. Course she wouldn't let me in. Then she looked at Becca, who promptly lost her nerve and now Becca's not very happy with me. She phoned an hour after I got home and said

I'd been acting really weird and what was the matter with me this week. I told her that I'd decided to tell the truth, the whole truth and nothing but the truth, so help me God. She said not to bother and that she wanted the old Cat back.

By the end of the week, I felt more confused than ever. Telling the truth is supposed to be the right thing to do, I thought, but it doesn't always work out. However, I wasn't ready to give up yet.

On Sunday Mr Squires drove me and Squidge to Rame Head, as he had to fix a car that had broken down in the car park up there. While he worked, I went up to the Head with Squidge. To tell The Truth.

Rame Head is my favourite place in all the peninsula, a little hill jutting out over the sea with a tiny Druid church on top. The local hippies all say that very powerful lay lines converge there. Don't know about that, but it does feel good up there. All you can see for miles on either side is sky and ocean.

'Squidge?' I said after we'd sat for a while gazing out over the view.

Squidge looked over and smiled. 'What?'

I was determined to do it this time. Absolute Truth. Being brave, that was me.

'Just, er, do you think, maybe it's time we moved on . . .'

He leapt up. 'Yes, it is getting chilly, quite a wind has blown up. Here, have my fleece.'

He picked up my bag and set off down the hill.

Try again, I thought as I followed him.

'Er, Squidge. You know I really like you, don't you?'

He grinned. 'And I like you.'

'Well I was thinking maybe we could reassess our relationship.'

'Already have,' he said cheekily. 'I get five stars, you get three.'

I had to laugh. 'I mean, don't you ever fancy other girls?'

He shook his head. 'Nope. Though that Lia's pretty stunning.'

D'oh? That wasn't part of the script and it threw me for a minute. 'So are you saying you fancy her?'

'No.'

'But you find her stunning?'

'Yes.'

He came back up a few steps and put his arm round me. 'You never need to feel insecure with me, Cat. You and me have something special. Must be your old hormones playing you up.'

I smiled at the familiar line as Squidge took my hand and, looking at me earnestly, said, 'What we have, it's on another level.'

I giggled, as we were halfway down the hill by now – another level.

'Like we can always be straight with each other, you know?' he continued.

I nodded, determined to see it through, 'Yeah, mainly. Best of friends. Though sometimes it's hard to find the right words to say what you mean.'

Squidge ran down the last steps ahead of me and into the field that led back to the car park. Then he did a sort of mad Indian dance. 'The right words? What like I'm the best-looking boy in the school. And brilliant. And cool. And *soooo* modest.' Then he ran the rest of the way back to the car.

Yeah, I thought, all of that. 'Plus I want to finish with you,' I said, but he was too far ahead to hear and the words got blown away in the wind.

'N.O. NO.'

'But Dad,' I said, 'I've done all my jobs *and* my home-work. Everyone's going. Pleeease.' I really *really* wanted to go. I wanted a day out with the girls. A day off from truth and lies. A day away from it all.

'Who's everyone?'

'Becca, Lia, Jade.'

'Is Squidge going or Mac?'

'No, they have footie on a Saturday afternoon. But Becca's dad is going to pick us up.'

'And how were you going to get there? I can't take you.'

'Bus. There's one leaving at three.'

Dad shook his head. 'I've heard about Rock. Teenagers get up to all sorts there. Sex, drugs, drink.'

'Dad, I'm *fourteen*, not a little girl any more. You can trust me. We only want to go and have a look around. And Becca's dad . . .'

'I heard you the first time. He'll pick you up. I don't know, Cat. There may be lots of older boys there just waiting for girls like you lot to turn up.'

Oh I *hope* so, I thought.

'If Squidge was going to keep an eye on you, I might think about it,' continued Dad.

No way was I inviting Squidge. This was to be a girls' day out, but then I remembered that Lia had said that Ollie was going.

'Lia's brother will be there.'

'How old is he?'

'Um, seventeen, I think.'

Dad seemed to be weakening. 'And will he be with your lot or off with his own crowd?'

'Oh, let her go, Peter,' said Jen who had been listening in from the hall. 'If this older boy's going to be there, they'll be fine.'

The bus got into the car park at Rock just after four. We'd all put on our make-up on the bus and were in major project mood – finding some boys. Luckily, Becca had put my behaviour of the last week down to hormones and had forgiven me for telling her the truth. She looked stunning. This was her 'big day'. She'd been looking forward to meeting Ollie for weeks and she'd spent the whole morning blow-drying her hair straight until it shone like red silk. She and Lia looked like Rose Red and

Rose White as they gave their long hair a final brush, then got off the bus.

'Do I look all right?' asked Becca, pulling down her tank top. 'Maybe I shouldn't have worn this. I look enormous. I should have worn my blue top.'

'Becca,' I said. 'You look fab. Relax.' She was always the same. Ever since I've known her she's had a thing about being too big. As if. She's a typical case of wanting to be Kate Moss when actually she's more like Kate Winslet. No one's ever happy, I thought. I wished I was tall and curvy like her, she wished she had straight hair like mine.

'Right, let's assess the situation,' she said looking around at the mass of cars. 'Beach or café?'

'Beach,' said Lia. 'Best make the most of it before it gets dark. I said we'd meet Ollie at the Mariner's Arms at about six-thirty.'

'Ollie. Cool,' said Jade and started off along the narrow path that led through gorse bushes down to the sea. Becca made a face behind her and Lia and I laughed. This was going to be interesting, I thought. Jade and Becca fighting over Ollie. Not me, of course, I was completely cool about him. Sort of.

We decided to wander down the beach, then pick a good place to sit and watch the world go by. It was crowded for October but then, I suppose, everyone wanted to make the most of what might be the last nice day before autumn set in. There were people having picnics and watching the boats, others playing frisbee, kicking balls about, and others walking dogs. A ferry had just arrived from Padstow on the other side of the bay and groups of teenagers made their way down the gang plank on to the beach then surveyed the scene, like us, looking for the talent.

Lia smiled. 'I think I may have to go and have a swim.'

'Are you mad?' I asked. She was fully clothed and even though it was a bright day, there was a chill wind, far too cold for stripping off.

'Ah gotya,' said Jade. 'A *definite* ten out of ten.'

I looked over to where they were staring and there was a gorgeous boy in a wet suit, sitting with a pair of binoculars.

'I may have to go and drown,' laughed Jade. 'That life guard is divine.' She minced up the beach near where he was. 'Oh save me, *save* me, I'm drowning.'

'I wish she would,' said Becca, as the boy looked over at Jade then turned back to sea with a bored expression as though he'd seen it all before.

After our walk up and down, Jade spotted a group of lads sitting beside one of the boats.

'They look like a laugh,' she said. 'Let's go and sit near them.'

Lia glanced over, then shook her head. 'I don't think so.'

But Jade ignored her and went and sat down near the boys. She went into her hair tossing routine interspersed with flirty looks in their direction.

There were four boys and they seemed to be playing

some sort of game. They had loads of cans of lager and a plump boy was counting on a stopwatch then, every thirty seconds or so, he'd fill everyone's glasses and they'd all knock back their drinks.

As he gulped down the liquid in his glass, he noticed Jade doing her routine.

'The idea is to drink as much as possible without going for a whaz,' he said in a very posh but slurred voice.

'Oh very clever,' said Becca.

'We're Rupert, *hic*, Baz, Henry and Patrick,' said a blond boy pointing at each of them in turn.

'Which one's hic again?' I asked Lia.

'Jade, Lia, Becca and Cat,' said Jade, who seemed blind to the fact that these boys were drunk out of their skulls.

'What school do you go to?' asked Rupert.

'Ignore them,' said Lia as Baz got up and came to sit in front of her. His eyes were completely out of focus as he gazed at her. 'Hey, you're *gorgeous*,' he dribbled. 'Up for a bit of snoggage?'

Henry got up and came over to sit next to me. As he leaned close, his breath stank of booze and I had to lean back to get away from the fumes. He propped himself up against me and pointed upwards. 'The stars are in the sky, Cat,' he drooled. 'Lie back, put your head on my shoulders and I'll show you Uranus.'

'Let's go,' I said, pushing him off then getting up and walking towards the slope that led to the cafés.

'Cat, *Cat*,' called Henry. 'Don't go. Be my honey.'

'What a load of plonkers,' said Becca, getting up and coming over to join me. 'Let's get away from them.'

Lia got up but Jade seemed reluctant to move. In the end she had no choice but to get up as well, as we were all walking away.

'Come to our beach party later,' called Baz as we backed off. 'Polzeath Beach, you only need some alcohol or a pair of breasts to get in.'

They all started sniggering, then Rupert suddenly looked as if he was going to be sick. He crossed his legs and dashed behind a boat. 'Have to whaz, have to whaz *now* . . . ahhhhhh.'

'Boys can be *really* stupid,' said Lia. 'Sometimes I wonder why we bother.'

'Ah, but then a special one comes along,' said Becca. 'What time did you say we're meeting Ollie?'

'Six-thirty-ish,' said Lia.

'You lot are such a load of killjoys,' said Jade catching us up. 'They were only having a laugh.'

Lia looked back at them. 'Nah. I know boys like that from my old school. They're all the same, like cardboard cut outs. They even dress the same, like some kind of uniform: brown loafers, brown belt, chinos and a Ralph Lauren or Tommy Hilfiger top.'

I glanced back. She was right. They were all dressed the same.

Jade had gone into a sulk. 'I thought they made a refreshing change from the usual pond life at our school.'

'You were wasting your time,' said Lia. 'Their motto is, Life and Lager.'

We walked along the road towards the pub. There was a group of older boys sitting on a wall and I couldn't help but notice that they all had the same uniform on as well. Brown shoes, brown belt, chinos. One of them shook his head as we walked past.

'Too young, too young, too young,' he said sadly. He looked like he was drunk as well and a moment later, he fell backwards off the wall.

Outside the Mariner's Arms the pavement was heaving with teenagers. There must have been about fifty standing about, laughing, drinking, eyeing each other up.

'Paradise,' said Jade perking up again as she surveyed the many groups of boys in the crowd. 'I'm home. Um, going to do a wreckie. Back later.' And with that, she disappeared.

Becca got out her mirror to reapply her lipstick. 'Ohmigod,' she shrieked. 'My *hair*. It's gone curly.'

Poor Becca. Her hair is the bane of her life. Personally I think it suits her curly, but she hates it and is forever buying new products and dryers to keep it straight. It's never any use, as the moment she steps out, especially if there's any moisture in the air like there is here, it coils back into its natural curls.

'Got to go and sort it before we see Ollie,' she said. 'I'm just off to find the Ladies. Don't do anything without me.'

We reassured her that we wouldn't, but already we could see boys eyeing us up and nudging each other.

'Excuse me,' said a dark haired boy sidling up to Lia, 'would you by any chance have a pair of knickers I could borrow?'

Lia looked taken aback, but I was intrigued; I hadn't heard this as a chat-up line before.

'Sorry,' said Lia. 'None spare.'

'Would you swop the ones you've got on with mine, then?' he asked as he began unzipping his fly.

'Get lost,' said Lia turning her back on him.

Then a boy came up to me. 'Have you got a twenty pence piece?' he asked.

I looked in my purse. 'Er, no . . . I've only got a pound coin.'

'Has to be a twenty pence,' he said, grinning.

'Why?'

'So I can call your dad and tell him you won't be home tonight.'

'Cat!' said a stern voice behind me. 'You *know* you're not allowed out of the detention centre without a guard!'

I turned and there was Ollie. 'You can leave now,' he said to the boy, 'before she has one of her turns and has to kill you.'

The boy scarpered and I laughed as Ollie smiled down at me.

'Hi Cat,' he said.

As always, he looked gorgeous. There were some pretty good looking boys in the crowd, but Ollie still stood out amongst them. Suddenly the atmosphere felt soft, like reality had melted at the edges. 'Hi,' I said.

At that moment, Becca reappeared on the steps of the pub. She went a brighter red than her hair when she saw Ollie and made her way through the crowd blushing like a bride walking towards the altar.

'Ollie, Becca, my friend,' said Lia. 'Becca, Ollie.'

Ollie smiled ravishingly at her. 'Anyone ever told you that you look like Nicole Kidman,' he asked.

He couldn't have said anything better. Nicole looks thinner than Kate Winslet. Becca was gone. Smitten. Knocked for six. Seduced.

'And I'm Jade,' purred Jade reappearing from nowhere and linking her arm through Ollie's. '*You* must be the *famous* Ollie Axford.'

11
White Lies and Barefaced Truths

THE JOURNEY back from Rock was a nightmare. Becca's dad picked us up at ten as arranged and Becca sat in the back and didn't say a word all the way home. She was furious with Jade, who had hogged Ollie from the moment she set eyes on him. He didn't seem to mind, though, in fact, he seemed to enjoy the attention. Later, when Bec's dad arrived, Jade declined the lift and cadged a ride back with Ollie instead.

Becca was almost hysterical at leaving them and we had to push her into the car, much to her dad's confusion.

Lia came with us although she was supposed to have gone back with Ollie. She didn't want to desert Becca and did her best to reassure her. Didn't do much good, though, as once we got in the car, Becca's lips were zipped.

The silence in the car was so uncomfortable I made an effort to lighten the atmosphere by chatting to Mr Howard, but underneath I couldn't help but feel jealous as well. Jealous that Ollie had played along with Jade. And jealous because he hadn't made more of a fuss of me. Some friend I am.

'It will all look better in the morning,' my mum used to say. After a while I decided to take her advice and snuggled up in the back of the car and fell asleep.

The phone was buzzing on Sunday.

'And did you *hear* the way she made her voice go all husky and deep when she was talking to him?' asked Becca.

'Probably nothing happened,' I said. 'They weren't totally alone, Ollie's mate was there and those other girls from London.'

'I know,' said Becca. I think that one called Tassie fancied Ollie as well.'

'So no worries. Jade had competition.'

'You've *got* to find out what happened, Cat. I can't bear to speak to her and have her gloat.'

'Haven't you spoken to Lia? She probably knows.'

'I'll phone you back,' said Becca. 'I'll call her now.'

Five minutes later Lia called.

'Bec's in a real state,' she said.

'I know. What happened? Did Ollie come home?'

'Yeah. About half an hour after us, so they can't have got up to much.'

'Didn't he say?'

'He's not up yet but, honestly, I don't think Jade's his type. Comes on too strong and Ollie prefers a bit of a challenge.'

'Do you think he liked Becca?'

'Hard to tell Cat. He flirts with everyone. I told you what he's like.'

'I know. Becca's really upset.'

'But what about you, Cat? How are you feeling about Ollie these days?'

'Dunno, really. More confused than anything.'

'Finished with Squidge yet?'

'No, but I'm going to do it soon.'

'Good. And Cat?'

'Yeah?'

'I want to talk to you about something. Not on the phone. One day at school when we're on our own.'

I was intrigued. What did she want to talk to *me* about?

At school on Monday, Jade was strutting round like the cat that got the cream. Not giving anything away, she smiled smugly over at us in assembly.

I cornered her at break in the playground.

'Um . . . what time did you get back on Saturday?' I asked, trying to keep my voice casual.

'Oh, Ollie dropped me off at about one.'

One? Lia said he got in not long after she did. Jade was clearly telling a fib.

'Had a good time, did you?' I asked.

Jade couldn't contain herself. 'He's asked me to the party.'

'What party?' I asked before I could stop myself.

'The one at the Axfords'. It's going to be the do of the year. Their dad's fortieth or fiftieth or something. Why?' And now she *was* gloating. 'Didn't *you* know about it?'

'Er, I think Lia may have mentioned something.' I said. Stick to half-truths, I thought. Lia *had* mentioned wanting to talk to me about 'something', it was probably about the party. This was my new philosophy after last week's 'tell the truth' championships. A half-truth didn't cause half as much trouble and sometimes saved face. In this case, my face.

'I don't know why Becca even thinks she stands a chance with him,' continued Jade. 'In fact, he asked more about you than he did her. Are you sure you haven't met him before? You seemed pretty pally when he first came over.'

'Might have seen him about,' I said, though I was longing to ask what he'd said about me.

'Anyway, Becca's far too young for him. He clearly wants someone a bit more mature like *moi*.'

'You're only a year older than Bec,' I said, as I thought back to that day on the beach when I first met Ollie. He didn't seem to be bothered about age.

'Anyway, how do you know?' I asked. 'I actually know from a good source that age wouldn't put him off.'

Jade looked at me closely. 'What good source? Lia?'

'No, just someone I know.'

Jade nodded her head slowly as if something was dawning in her brain. 'Oh, I get it. I *thought* it looked as though he'd met you before Rock. You were that girl he was with in Cawsand weren't you? *Weren't* you? How else would he have known your name?'

I felt my cheeks colour. Bugger.

I didn't answer.

'And do Becca and Squidge know about your little adventure?' asked Jade.

'There's nothing to tell,' I blustered.

'Not by my book,' she laughed. 'I think there's a lot to tell and they'll be more than interested to listen.'

The Cat Is Out of the Bag 12

'WHAT ARE you going to do?' asked Lia as we made our way out of the school gates later that day.

'Don't know,' I said. 'Double don't know. Becca's still not got over Saturday night. This is all she needs.'

'Has Jade spoken to her?'

'Don't think so. Bec was with us all through lunch and her mum picked her up early from school to take her to the dentist, so I don't reckon Jade's got to her yet. Squidge though, I don't know about.'

There were loads of cars and parents blocking the road outside the school, but no sign of Lia's ride, so she came with me to the bus stop while I waited. In the traffic queuing to get out of the road, I noticed Jade and Mac in the back of their mum's battered old Daimler. Jade was gabbing on her mobile. She looked up as they drove past and she did a sort of royal wave then pointed at her phone. Oh bugger, I thought. I wonder who she's talking to. Squidge, Becca or taking out an ad in the local paper. I wouldn't put it past her. *Cat Kennedy caught in love scandal on Cawsand Beach.* Have you heard the latest?

'What do you think I should do, Lia?'

'Two things. You *must* talk to Squidge and Bec before Jade does. Call her bluff. And second, I think you should think seriously about what you want.'

'That's obvious isn't it? Not lose my two best mates. And not have them think that they can never trust me again.'

'I didn't mean that,' said Lia. 'I meant what do you want? *You.* Cat Kennedy.'

'What I want is last on the list at the moment.'

'Exactly,' said Lia, then she was quiet for a few minutes as if chewing over what she was going to say next. 'I know I've not known you long Cat, so tell me if you think I'm out of order . . . but this is what I wanted to talk to you about. It just seems to me that you *always* put yourself last on the list.'

'What do you mean?'

'I'm not saying it's a bad thing, in fact I really like the way you consider others and what they're going through. But I can't help but feel that you've got lost along the way somewhere. Like you think that you don't matter and everyone else does. I mean, who considers *your* feelings? What *you* want? Or need?'

Much to my surprise, my eyes filled with tears.

'Oh God, I'm sorry,' said Lia. 'Now I've blown it. Sugar. I didn't mean to make you . . . oh sugar sugar . . . I mean . . . what I meant is . . . you're stuck in a relationship that's gone stale. You want to move on, but you don't want to hurt Squidge, so you haven't told him. And you like Ollie, but you don't want to hurt Becca, so again, you sacrifice your feelings, so that everyone else can have a jolly time. I . . . I just think that sometimes, maybe you need to think about being true to *your* feelings instead of trying to protect everyone else's.'

She was right. I'd been so busy thinking about how the others would take the truth that I hadn't even thought about being true to myself. I blinked back the tears that threatened to spill down my cheeks. 'Must be mi old hormones playing me up,' I joked as I brushed my eyes.

'All I was trying to say, Cat, is that *you* matter too. You spend your whole life keeping the peace and making sure everyone else is all right, but it's always at your own expense.'

I felt my eyes filling up again. 'Sorry. Sorry. Don't be nice to me, don't be nice to me,' I said, covering my face with my hands.

Lia put her hand on my arm. 'But I *am* going to be nice to you, Cat. You've been a real mate to me since I came down here. And mates look out for each other.'

Just at that moment a silver Mercedes honked and Meena waved from the driver's seat.

'Here's my ride,' said Lia. 'Can we drop you? I'd feel rotten leaving you like this.'

I shook my head. 'Bus'll be here in a sec. Honest. You go.'

Truth was, I wanted some time to think about what Lia had said, and work out what I was going to say to Bec and Squidge before Jade got to them.

'When I got home I picked up the portable phone from the hall and ran upstairs. Emma had arranged all her dolls on the lower bunk bed and was feeding them digestive biscuits.

'Oh Emma,' I said, 'there are crumbs everywhere. Can't you play with them downstairs?'

'Luke and Joe are down there,' she replied as she tried to force-feed one of the dolls. 'Open your mouth, bad doll.' When the doll wouldn't eat, she pulled its head off, crammed the biscuit in the body, then put the head back on. 'There, good girl, now your tummy's full.'

'You can't do that, Emma,' I laughed in spite of my misery. 'You wouldn't like it if someone tried that on you.'

'No. But that's because my head doesn't come off,' she said with a serious face. 'Joe tried to get it off, but it's stuck down.'

'Look Em, I need the room for a bit,' I said.

'S'my room too,' she said.

'But I need some privacy. I want to make a phone call.'

'I don't mind. I won't tell anyone.'

'Emma, pleeease.'

'Then use Luke and Joe's, they're watching telly,' said Emma.

Oh, what wouldn't I give for my own room, I thought, for the umpteenth time as I went into the boys' room.

Joe wasn't downstairs, he was doing his homework on the floor, so the boys' room was no good for a private conversation either. I turned around and headed for the bathroom.

'What's after space, Cat?' Joe called after me as I locked the bathroom door.

'More space,' I called back as I put a couple of towels in the bath, climbed in, then dialled Becca's number.

There was a knock on the door. 'What's after more space?' asked Joe's voice. 'I mean at the end of the universe?'

'I don't know. Go *away* . . . oh hi, no not you, Becca. It's Cat.'

'Uh-huh?' said a thick voice.

'You all right? Fillings? Bad? How was the dentist?'

'OK. Mouth's a bit numb.'

'Well that's OK,' I said, 'because I need to talk to you. All you have to do is listen. It's about Jade. You know that time in Cawsand with Ollie . . .'

'Oh, I know everything,' said Becca. 'She phoned already . . .'

My heart began to beat faster. 'Already . . . ?'

'Yeah. Still trying to stir it,' continued Becca. 'She's such a two-faced cow.'

'What did she say?'

'That you were with Ollie on Cawsand Beach a few weeks ago.'

'And what did you say?'

'That I already knew. Hah. That shut her up. She thought it was some big secret or something, and I was going to be really shocked. I told her to mind her own business and that I knew all about it because you'd already told me. I didn't tell her you were there chatting up Ollie as a favour though.'

'Was that all she said?'

'Yeah.'

I sighed with relief. So now Jade thought Becca knew it all, so hadn't mentioned that I was the girl Ollie had snogged. Phew. But maybe I'd better fill her in on the rest and hope she wouldn't hate me forever. At least half the truth, that being my new way of dealing with things.

'Becca?'

'Yeah?'

'About Ollie. I feel I wasn't altogether honest with you because actually, er, I do think he's attractive.'

'Yeah,' said Becca. 'You'd have to be blind or stupid not to. You're not saying you're after him are you?'

It was time to come clean. I took a deep breath and launched in, 'No, I'm not Becca. You bagged him first and I would never –'

'Oh, hold on Cat, there's someone on the other line. I'll call you back . . .'

I sat up and decided to tidy the shampoo bottles and jars around the bath while I waited. Luke, Joe and Emma always leave the tops off everything. It drives me mad. And they never put the soap back in the soap dish, so it turns to slime. Uck.

I was just rinsing Em's plastic duck when Becca rang again.

'Did *you* know about this?' she demanded.

'What, Bec? Know about what?'

At first she didn't say anything but, being Becca, she couldn't hold it in for long. 'I don't believe it . . .' she began.

'What? *What?*' Oh no, I thought, it must have been Jade on the other line and she'd told Bec the whole story about me and Ollie. Just as things were going so well and I was about to tell her myself.

'Jade phoned again,' said Becca.

Prepare to die, Cat Kennedy, I thought.

'Did *you* know about this party?' she continued.

'*Party?* Oh, yeah, sort of, Lia's dad's. Jade said Ollie had asked her.'

'Exactly,' said Becca. 'So why hasn't Lia asked *us?*'

'Well it's not her party, Bec. It's her dad's party,' I began in Lia's defence though I had to admit that the thought had occurred to me that maybe we would be asked. Especially now that Jade was going.

'She phoned just to rub it in that Ollie had invited her,'

said Becca. 'So I told her we already had invites.'

'You didn't.'

'I did. I'd *love* to go, Cat. And I'm sure it's only a matter of time. Lia's bound to invite us.'

I remembered what Lia had said earlier about being mates and stuff, so why hadn't she mentioned the party?

'OK, but maybe we should wait until we're asked properly before we go spreading it around that we're going.'

'OK,' said Becca, 'but she's bound to ask us.'

'Yeah,' I said. 'Bound to, and Bec?'

'Yeah?'

'I just wanted to say . . .'

'Oh. Hold on,' she said and the line went silent for a moment. 'Got to go, Cat. Mum's calling me down for supper.'

Then she hung up.

Cats in the Cupboard

13

AFTER SUPPER I went to find Dad in the back garden. When it was warm, he often went out in the early evening for a bit of quiet and to smoke one of his roll-ups. He was sitting on the bench under the apple tree at the bottom of the garden, so I decided to take him out a cup of coffee and keep him company for a while.

'Thanks, Cat, that's really kind of you,' he said taking the coffee.

I sat next to him on the bench and wondered how to start a conversation. Lia's questions had started me thinking. Now I wanted to know what *he* wanted: if he felt that he didn't matter because everyone else had to come first on his list. It can't be easy having four kids, I thought, and no wife to talk it all through with. At least when you have a partner, you can share the responsibility and you have each other to sympathise with and support when the going gets rough. I decided it must be quite lonely being my dad.

'What you thinking about, Dad?'

'Oh, nothing important. Shop stuff.'

'And, er . . . are you happy?'

'Happy? What kind of question is that, Cat?'

'It's a "how are you" type of question. I mean, do you ever get lonely?'

Dad sighed. 'Everyone has times when they're a bit lonely, Cat, but you just get on . . .'

'Well, I just wondered if you had anyone to talk to. I suppose there's Jen but she's only here once a month.'

'What's this about?'

'I just wondered how you were feeling about things. Mum's been gone over five years now and well, do you think Jen'll ever move in one day?'

'Well that's really not your business is it, Cat?' he said standing up. 'Not your concern at all.'

And with that he stomped off inside as if I'd said something really bad. I felt like I'd been shoved aside when I was only trying to be friendly. If I couldn't have a real talk with my own dad, then who could I talk to? Not my business he'd said. We'd have loads to talk about if only he'd open up, but he obviously didn't want to. Not my business.

We have a strange relationship, I thought, as I sat and watched the sky turn from blue to lavender to navy. We both skirt around what's really going on with half-truths that don't reveal the whole story. We keep it safe and on the surface, but there's a whole load of stuff underneath, I know there is, if we could only both be brave enough to open up and let what we really think and feel out. The real truth.

Eep! Let the real truth out! I remembered Squidge. Had Jade got to him yet? I better call him *quick*.

I ran back up to my private office in the bathroom and dialled Squidge's number.

'He's on his way over to see you, love,' said Mrs Squires. 'He had a phone call then left in a bit of a hurry.'

Oh sugar, I thought. This is it. Jade's called him and he's on his way over to confront me. The last thing I wanted now was a showdown. I felt like hiding away. My attempt to talk to Dad had made me feel rejected and I wasn't in the mood for more upset.

As I went into the landing hall, I heard someone knock on the back door. I flew down the stairs and found Luke.

'Luke, *Luke*. Squidge is at the door. Tell him I'm out.'

'Where are you going to be?'

'Er, when the going gets tough, the tough, er . . . hide in the cupboard under the stairs,' I said, diving into the cupboard and hiding behind a coat. I felt such a hypocrite. One minute thinking that Dad and I had to be brave enough to tell each other the truth. Then a moment later hiding because, while being brave is a good idea in theory, it's another thing in reality.

Squidge knocked again.

'Out. *Out*. Tell him I'm out,' I whispered through the coats.

'Yeah, yeah,' said Luke. 'I heard you.'

'Is Cat in?' I heard Squidge ask when Luke opened the door.

'Er, no,' said Luke.

'Well, do you know where she is? I have to speak to her.'

Luke hesitated then called back. 'What should I tell him now, Cat?'

I could *kill* him. I should have known he'd get me back for letting him down when Josephine Talbot phoned last week. Thirty seconds later the cupboard door opened, Squidge pulled aside the coats and burst out laughing. 'Cat! What on earth are you doing in here?'

I pulled him into the cupboard with me. 'No peace anywhere in this stupid house. Emma's in the bedroom, Dad's in the living room, Luke's in the kitchen and Joe's upstairs. I, er . . . came in here to get a bit of peace.' Half-true, I thought, as there's no way I'm telling him that I'm in there hiding from him.

Squidge didn't bat an eyelid. 'Cool,' he said and settled himself on the floor at the back of the cupboard next to the electric meter. 'I see Mogley likes it in here too.'

I hadn't noticed, but there was the cat curled up in an old shoebox.

'I came straight round as soon as I heard . . .' said Squidge, giving Mogley a stroke.

'Oh, so you've heard . . . ?'

'Yes . . . I guess Lia told you . . .'

'No, Jade told me. I was trying to tell you, Squidge . . . you know that day . . . What do you mean, Lia? Why should she tell me? Tell me what?'

'I'm so chuffed,' he said, his face lighting up.

'Chuffed?'

'Yeah. Lia called. You know . . . about the party?'

'Party?'

'Yeah.'

We were clearly having two separate conversations and I was getting confused. Had Lia invited him and not me or Becca? Why? I made myself take a deep breath. Get a grip, Cat.

'OK. You're chuffed. Chuffed is good. Now what about the party?'

'My first job, Cat. I have my *first* job. I've been asked to make a video of the party up at the Axfords'. Apparently Mrs Axford didn't want a stranger doing it as there will be loads of famous people there. And she didn't want to ask one of her friends as they wouldn't be able to just chill and enjoy themselves. Lia knows I'm into film and she thought of me and told her mum about me. But best of all, I'm to be paid.' His grin grew from ear to ear. 'Good money, Cat. I mean *good* money.'

'Ah.' The penny was beginning to drop. 'Enough to go on that film course?'

'Added to what I've saved, yes, enough to go on my film course.'

I sat down next to him and gave him a hug. 'Oh Squidge, that's top. I'm really, really pleased for you. And er, did Jade call?'

'Oh yeah, some crapola about you being on Cawsand Beach with Ollie. She was mega-miffed when I told her that it was history and I already knew.'

'How? How do you already know?'

'D'oh, Cat. I was *there*.'

'*There*? On Cawsand Beach? When I was with Ollie. I never saw you.' Ohmigod, I thought. What did he see?

'Keep up, Cat. No, not on *Cawsand* Beach. When we played Truth, Dare on *Whitsand* Beach. Remember? Last beach party of the summer? Becca dared you to go and chat Ollie up for her.'

'Oh right,' I said.

'You OK, Cat?'

'Yeah. Sort of. Why?' I laughed.

'I get the feeling that you've not really been listening.'

'Oh I have. Honest. But have you ever thought that people only ever hear what they want to hear no matter what you tell them?' Amazing, I thought. Jade had tried her darnest to stir it for me, but Becca and Squidge had only heard what they wanted to hear.

'Yeah. And see what they want to see,' said Squidge finding a torch in Dad's toolbox on the floor. He switched it on under his chin so that he looked like a ghoul. 'Wuh uh uh uh.'

We sat there under the coats seeing who could do the scariest face with the torch and chatting about everything the way we always have done. He was full of ideas for the video and what music he'd put it to and how he'd edit all the footage he planned to shoot, so that it would tell a story about the party.

So I don't feel mad passion for him, I thought, but I still care about him and we do have fun. I felt a pang of anxiety about having to have The Conversation when I finally say it's over. Watching him sitting there so comfortably, legs stretched out, stroking Mogley, I thought, he's been a part of my life for almost as long as I can remember. I don't want to lose him and I'm certainly not going to ruin the mood by finishing with him tonight. Once again, it wasn't the right time and, looking around, nor did the floor of the cupboard under the stairs seem the right place!

14 Cat-astrophy

'BECCA, CAT, wait up,' called Mac as we headed back through the school gates the following day.

'Have you heard about this party?' he said.

'Yes,' I said. 'Are you going?'

'Yeah. Sort of. In fact, my mum asked me to speak to you both. Remember I told you she used to do posh dinners and stuff for rich people when we lived in London.'

'Yeah,' said Becca. 'So what?'

'She's doing the catering. She's been asked to do the food for the Axfords'. For two hundred people! So she needs staff. She asked me to ask if you and Becca would be waitresses for the night. I'm going to do it. Fifty quid each. What do you think?'

'*Whadttt*?' Becca's jaw dropped. 'Does Jade know you're asking us?'

'Yes, in fact it was her that suggested you to Mum. Mum offered it to her as well but then, you know Jade. She's such a princess and waiting on people would be way beneath her. Besides I think she's got an invite. But hey, fifty quid for a night's work isn't bad and we'll get to see who's there and what's going on and everything.'

Becca looked as if she'd just found out she'd picked the winning lottery numbers but lost her ticket. 'Yeah. It will be great fun watching Jade swan round with Ollie and everyone having a top time while we slave in the kitchen. NOT.'

Mac looked puzzled. 'What's the prob? Fifty quid and it'll be a laugh. Jade said you'd be really into it.'

'I bet she did,' said Becca. 'She must have known I was fibbing when I told her that we had invites. And now, I can just see it, she'll be all, "Oh, I've been invited and oh, *poor* you, having to work as a waitress. Just fetch me another drink will you?"'

'I could use the money, Bec,' I said. 'And perhaps I could accidentally on purpose throw one of the drinks all over Jade at some point.'

'I know how you feel sometimes,' Mac laughed. 'At least you don't have to live with her. So what shall I tell Mum? I said I'd let her know. Do you want to do it?'

'*We're* going to get *proper* invites,' said Becca. 'Lia is *our* friend.'

'So what shall I tell Mum?'

'Don't know yet,' I said watching Becca storm off to assembly. 'It's just going as waitresses wasn't quite the invite we'd been hoping for.'

* * *

Murphy's Law – Lia wasn't in assembly. Nor in class. Nor answering her mobile when Becca called for the fifth time when we got off the bus after school.

We went and sat on the wall at the top of Kingsand and Becca dialled again.

'Leave a message,' I whispered as Becca mimed, 'Voice mail', then hung up.

'Don't want to seem desperate,' said Becca. 'It would be awful if I went, so Lia where's our invites? And she had no intention of giving us one.'

'Maybe we have to let it go,' I said. 'It's not the end of the world.'

'Yes it is,' said Becca.

'You're right, it is. Two hundred people. It's going to be mega. Oh stinkbombs. Why is it never easy when you want something?'

Becca nodded. 'I think we have to face facts. I mean Jade's been asked. And Squidge has been asked. If Lia was going to invite us, she'd have called us, wouldn't she?'

'I guess. Maybe she only has a limited number and has invited mates from her old school.'

'Maybe she doesn't want us as mates after all. I mean, I suppose she does live in another world doesn't she? Maybe she thinks we'd show her up or something and are only fit to be there as waitresses. What do you think?'

I shrugged. 'I'd be disappointed. I really thought we

were friends, but hey, as Dad says, you get on . . . I've done waitressing before at do's in the village and it can be a bit of a laugh.'

'Well *I've* never been so insulted in my life,' said Becca. 'I don't think I could do it, not with Jade there.'

'OK, bottom line. No invite and go as a waitress? Or, no invite and miss the whole thing?'

'Well if you put it like that,' said Becca. 'I suppose those waitress outfits can look kind of sexy.'

Just at that moment, a loud honk attracted our attention. We looked up to see a turquoise metallic Ka slow down at the kerb in front of us. Ollie rolled down the window and waved.

'Here they are,' he said to Lia who was sitting in the passenger seat.

She leapt out and came over to where we were sitting.

'I've just come from your house, Becca,' she said. 'And I was just on my way to yours, Cat. I've been delivering these.'

She shoved a white envelope into my hand. It had my name written on it in beautiful handwriting. 'Yours is waiting at home for you, Becca. Invites to my dad's party. I was going to bring them to school today, then my horse had a fall this morning and I had to go to the vet with him to check he was OK . . .'

Ollie parked the car and got out to come and join us. 'I designed them,' he said proudly. 'Sorry yours are late, but

Mum's invited so many people we ran out of invites and had to get another lot done. They didn't arrive from the printers until today.'

I ripped open the envelope and laughed at what was inside. It was a card. On the front was a photo of a crystal whisky tumbler, but instead of there being whisky and ice in the glass, there was a pair of false teeth and ice. Underneath it said, *'Help me celebrate my birthday'*. On the back were all the details and the date and address.

'And your dad approved this, did he?' I asked.

Ollie nodded. 'I'd like to do design or advertising when I leave school.' He stood behind me and looked over my shoulder. 'S'cool isn't it?'

I nodded, lost for words. I was only aware of the proximity of him, breathing softly on my neck.

'So will you come?' asked Lia.

'Course,' said Becca looking straight at Ollie, who went over to her and put his arm round her. She went bright red and, like me, suddenly looked lost for words.

'And you, Cat. Will you come?' he asked.

'Course,' I said. 'If my dad will let me.'

'Oh, practise a song,' said Lia. 'We always have a talent hour when anyone who wants can get up and do whatever they want. I thought it would be a brilliant chance for your band to show off.'

'What band?' asked Ollie.

'We're called Diamond Heart,' said Becca.

'Nice name,' said Ollie.

'Cat thought of it,' said Becca suddenly finding her tongue. 'We mainly sing to backing tracks but sometimes I write lyrics.'

Oh God, I thought suddenly remembering the last lot she wrote: *Ollie, Ollie, you're my brolly, my cover when it rains*.

'Diamond Heart,' said Ollie. 'I'll put it on Mum's list. She's doing a sort of programme so everyone knows when they're on.'

Then he looked deeply into my eyes. 'I look forward to seeing you perform,' he said meaningfully.

15 Fairy Godmother

'WHAT ARE you doing?' asked Emma, on finding me with my head in the wardrobe and every item of clothing I owned strewn across the floor.

'Disaster, Em,' I said. 'I've been invited to a party and haven't got anything to wear. I need something really special.'

Emma curled up on the bottom bunk. 'You need a fairy godmother. Like Cinderella.'

'Don't happen to know one, do you?'

Emma shook her head, then went to one of her drawers and picked out a tiny blue leotard. 'You can borrow this if you like.'

'Thanks, Em, but I think it's a *bit* small.'

Both Becca and Lia had offered to lend me something of theirs and I'd had a session at both their houses going through their clothes, but nothing fit. When I tried their things on, they looked borrowed. Becca's five foot six and

I'm five foot two. Her dresses hung on me. Same with Lia, she's five foot five, willowy with hardly any chest, so her clothes were too tight on my top and too long on the bottom. I was beginning to think it would be easier to go as a waitress after all.

'What about your sparkly silver top?' asked Emma. 'That's pretty.'

'Bit tatty since Luke put it in the washer with the footie things. Besides I'd need something to go with it. I always wear it with jeans for the school disco and this isn't a jeans type do.'

'Ask Dad for something new.'

'Did. He told me to wear the dress I wore to be bridesmaid at Auntie Brenda's wedding last year.'

Even Emma pulled a face at that suggestion. The dress was a candy pink meringue with puffball sleeves and I felt like I belonged on top of a Christmas tree when I wore it. Sexy. Not.

Emma went back into her drawer and pulled out her Barbie savings bank. She opened it up and handed me two twenty pence pieces. 'Here you can have all my money.'

I gave her a hug. 'Thanks, Em. You're a star.'

She can be so sweet when she wants to be.

I put all my clothes back, then went downstairs to watch telly with the others. I felt miserable. This was the first time I'd ever been invited to anything so glamorous. Lia's sister Star was coming down from London with all her model friends, half the rock music industry was going to be there, then there was Mrs Axford who always looked like she stepped out of *Vogue* and, of course, Ollie. And Jade. No doubt she'd have some fabulous little number planned and I, I was going to look like the back end of a bus. I'm sure Mum would have understood if she'd been here. Dads don't understand the importance of looking your best on occasions like this, not my dad, anyway.

'Why do you want money to buy an outfit you'll only wear once and put back in the cupboard?' he'd said.

It wasn't fair.

It was all right for Lia and Becca. They had mums to take them shopping. Lia had been up to London with hers and come back laden with designer carrier bags full of gorgeous things wrapped in tissue. Her mum had got her the works: mucho sexy high heels, a diamante choker that looked like it cost a bomb and a powder blue lace mini-dress. She'd even got new sexy underwear and make-up. She looked a million dollars when she tried it all on.

Becca's mum had also let her have something new. She'd taken her up to Exeter and Becca had chosen a black sleeve-less top with a feather trim, tight black satin trousers and really high black mules. She looked eighteen and really sophisticated.

I could just see me turning up in my candy pink brides-maid dress. I'd be the laughing stock. There's no point, I thought, as I tried to concentrate on the telly. I'm not going to be able to go.

Dad must have been feeling guilty, because he kept glancing over at me. 'Cheer up, love.'

'Uh,' I said.

'Honestly, Cat, with your looks, you'll be the belle of the ball. You don't need fancy clothes to stand out in a crowd.'

'Yeah right.' I said. You really *really* don't understand, I thought.

Just at that moment I spotted something on the bookshelf behind the telly. Stacked in with the photo albums and gardening books. That's *it*, I thought. My fairy godmother. Of sorts.

I waited until Luke, Joe and Emma had gone to bed and Dad had gone to make a cup of tea, then pulled the catalogue off the shelf, ran upstairs and locked myself in the bathroom.

I flicked through the pages until I found the teen evening wear section. A treasure trove of seriously cool clothes, sequinned tops, beaded dresses, silky fabrics, velvet trousers. Fab, *fabtastic.*

I checked the terms.

You pick what you want.

You phone up.

They deliver within forty-eight hours.

You return the item if it's not right.

It would be *so* easy. The party was in four days. I just had time. And after the party I could return the item as 'unsuitable'. No harm done. Dad need never know. He'd bought a lawnmower from them in the summer and a statement with his account number was in the front of the catalogue. *So* easy.

I flicked back through the pages. There was so much to choose from. Gorgeous colours, glittery, glamorous, girlie. I wished Lia or Becca were here to help me, but I decided there and then not to tell them. On one page there was a one-shouldered dress in purple silk. The business. That would do it.

Then a thought struck me. Was it bad? It wasn't *really* stealing as I'd return the dress the morning after the party. But a shadow of doubt crept in after all my efforts to be truthful. *Would* it be wrong? Dishonest? Dad need never see it, so I wouldn't have to lie about it and I'm sure that Lia and Becca would understand. I would just be borrowing the dress. Surely that was OK?

The dress was staring back at me from the glossy page. It would look *soooo* good. I could just see myself in it. No harm done, I told myself, no harm done. And I'm sure my mum would have let me have it if she'd been here.

I unlocked the bathroom door, crept down the stairs, picked up the portable phone then crept back up again.

I dialled the number before I could change my mind.

Party On

'YOU LOOK top,' said Lia, when I came out of her bathroom.

I went to look at my reflection in her wardrobe mirror. The dress looked great.

'Not sure about the sandals though,' I said. I hadn't dared to order shoes from the catalogue as well, so I had to wear my strappy black ones from the summer. They didn't go with the dress and looked a bit cheap next to Lia's and Becca's sexy mules.

'You could go barefoot,' suggested Becca, 'like that singer from the sixties.'

'Sandie Shaw,' said Lia. 'I think Dad sent her an invite, but I don't know if she's coming.'

'Barefoot at five foot two,' I laughed. 'I don't think so, people will think I'm about nine years old.'

Lia's bedroom door opened and in walked one of the most beautiful girls I'd ever seen. Like Lia, she was blond and willowy, but her hair was cut spiky short showing off

123

her cut-glass cheekbones perfectly.

'You must be Cat and Becca,' she smiled at us. 'Lia's told me all about you.'

'And you must be Star,' I said. 'Do people say that they're star-struck when they meet you?'

'Yeah,' she laughed as she took in our outfits. 'Particularly naff men who think that they're the first one to come up with it. So. *Look* at you three. Watch out boys, three stunning girls to choose from – a blond, a brunette and a redhead. ' Then she saw my feet and sighed. 'What size shoe are you, Cat?'

'Thirty-six.'

'Ah. Perfect,' she said and disappeared only to reappear a minute later with a shoebox. 'Here, try these,' she said getting out the most divine pair of shoes. 'Rule one of any outfit, make sure your shoes don't let you down.'

She handed me a pair of purple suede shoes with a kitten heel and a little suede flower on the toe.

'They're from Emma Hope,' she said as I nodded like I knew who Emma Hope was. 'Sexy, but unlike some high heels, you can actually walk in them.'

'So what's rule two of any outfit? I asked as I tried the shoes on.

'Make sure your underwear doesn't let you down,' she replied.

'I thought that was for when you had an accident,' said Becca. 'My gran was forever saying that when we were little. Make sure your underwear's clean in case you get run over.'

'Not what I was thinking of,' laughed Star, then winked at me like I knew what she meant.

The shoes looked gorgeous. The exact shade of my dress and suddenly the whole outfit came together.

'You shall go the ball,' said Becca.

'Story of my life,' I explained to Star.

After Becca had done her usual 'does my bum look big in this?' routine and we'd assured her that it didn't, we applied few squirts of perfume, a slick of lip gloss and we were ready to make our entrance.

The party was in full swing when we got downstairs. My stomach felt all fluttery with excitement as we took in the atmosphere – people chatting and laughing, the clink of glasses and sound of champagne corks being popped. Mrs Axford had lit the house with candles and it looked wonderfully romantic bathed in the soft honey light.

'What's that divine smell?' I asked Lia.

'Jasmine. Mum bought scented candles. It's heavenly isn't it?'

I nodded. Heavenly was the word. Everyone looked *sooo* glamorous in little cocktail dresses and gorgeous shoes. I was glad I'd bought my dress as, looking at all these guests, I'd have been way out of place if I hadn't made an effort. I could see Squidge, busy going from room to room videoing, and he gave us a little wave when he saw us, then pointed the camera at us for a few seconds before moving off again. He looked like he was in his element.

'I'm just going to check on a few people,' said Lia. 'Back in a mo, so help yourselves to drinks and whatever.'

Becca and I both felt shy and star-struck at all the famous faces in the crowd. We stood near the banisters, at first, doing our best not to look too gobsmacked as stars we'd only ever seen on MTV walked past. And here they were in the flesh. At the *same* party as us.

'Oh my God,' said Becca. 'Isn't that the guy from that band, The Heartbeats?'

I turned to look. 'Yes, it is. Oh Bec, I don't think I'm going to have the nerve to get up and sing in front of this lot.'

'Rubbish,' said Becca. 'It's only one number and we couldn't have practised it more. By the way, have you seen Jade yet? She was bringing the backing track.'

A few moments later I saw Jade coming towards us through the crowd. She looked fabulous as well, in a short white leather mini and studded jacket.

'Very rock chick,' I said.

She was in a good mood. 'Thanks. And I like your dress. Actually, I was looking for you. We're on soon in the green room.'

'Have you got the CD?' I asked.

'No,' she said. 'You were bringing it.'

'No I wasn't,' I said. 'I gave it to you.'

'You did not.'

'Did.'

I wasn't going to ruin the evening by arguing. 'Look. It's a popular song so we need to find Lia and ask if, by any miracle, she's got a CD with the track on it, so at least we can sing along.'

'Good plan,' said Becca, who was looking daggers at Jade.

'You go that way Bec,' I said pointing right. 'Jade, look upstairs and I'll go that way. Meet you back here in ten minutes. Then perhaps we could have a run through in Lia's bedroom.'

I felt a bit shy walking about on my own, but it was flattering in a way, as I was getting quite a lot of looks from the men there. So they were ancient, but it was still nice to be noticed.

'Looking good.' Mac grinned as he passed by with a tray of drinks.

'So are you,' I said. 'That waiter's outfit suits you.'

'So it does,' purred a middle-aged blond lady as she took a drink. 'I *love* a man in uniform.'

Mac went behind her and did me an 'arghhh' face.

I wandered into the green room where the talent hour had already begun. A woman who looked familiar from Cable TV was singing and playing the piano. She was brilliant and the crowd applauded like mad when she finished. I stayed to listen for a moment whilst scanning the room for Lia. Ollie was on the opposite side and, when he saw me, he put his hand on his heart then blew me a kiss. I felt really chuffed. It was going to be a great party.

Next up on stage was a woman who sang a Madonna song. She was awful, truly awful and I tried not to catch Ollie's eye because I knew I'd laugh. After she'd finished, the crowd applauded madly again and as she got down I heard people saying, 'Well done,' and, 'Brilliant show'.

We're all fibbers, I thought, and sometimes it's right to be. If anyone had said, 'God you were awful', it would have ruined her night. The guests' reaction confirmed to me yet again that there definitely was a time and place to be kind with a small lie. As Mrs Axford announced the next act, I remembered I was supposed to be looking for Lia so dragged myself away.

I looked in two of the living rooms on the left but there was no sign of her. No sign of Jade or Becca back at the banisters, so I decided to try Mr Axford's study. When I opened the door to look in, it was empty, but I paused to take in the atmosphere.

Like the rest of the house, it was bathed in candlelight and someone had lit a fire in the grate. It looked so cosy, like an old gentleman's club on a film set with its wood-panelled walls, dark leather sofas and tall bookshelves full of books. I couldn't help having a peek at some of the framed photos of Mr Axford when he was on tour with his band, Hot Snax. Suddenly two hands slipped round my waist and gently pushed me further into the room.

Ollie shut the door, took my hand and led me over to one of the sofas. 'Come and sit by the fire, Cat.'

I perched on the sofa and he sat next to me and leaned back. He looked so sexy, and sitting there in the mega-romantic atmosphere, all the feelings I'd been pushing away came flooding back.

'Alone at last,' he said, taking my hand again.

'But you're not alone,' I joked nervously. 'I'm here.'

He laughed and put his arm around me. 'I can see that. But we haven't had a chance to catch up properly for ages. Not since the beach that time.'

I slid a few spaces away from him, but he moved close up again.

'Relax,' he said, 'I'm not going to pounce.'

I smiled. God I was nervous. I felt stupid, like an immature little girl. I didn't want him to think I was inexperienced or a Miss Prim, so I didn't move away again. Anyway, it felt nice. I liked the sensation he caused whenever he was near. Calm and chaotic at the same time.

'Has anyone ever told you that you have the most gorgeous mouth?' he said staring at my lips.

I shook my head and tried to think of something witty to say back, but too late, he'd leaned in and was kissing me.

At first I was going to push him away, but it felt so

good. He was a top kisser, soft yet firm at the same time. He pushed me down further into the sofa at the exact moment that the door opened.

'Oh, er . . . sorry. *Oh!* It's you!' said a white-faced Becca when she saw us. Then she ran out leaving the door open.

'Oh sugar, got to go,' I said to Ollie, who looked taken aback as I shoved him off and ran after Bec.

Frantically I searched everywhere for her, but she seemed to have disappeared into thin air.

'Have you seen Becca?' I asked Lia, who was chatting to Mac as he refilled his tray in the kitchen.

'I saw her heading upstairs,' said Squidge, who I suddenly noticed lying under the table.

'What are you doing down there?' I asked.

'Mrs Axford asked me to film all angles of the party,' he replied. 'The good, the bad and the ugly.'

'Hmmm,' I said as I headed for the door, 'talking of bad, you haven't seen Jade have you?'

'Saw her go into the study,' said Mac.

I couldn't resist. I had to see if Ollie was still in there and if Jade was doing her 'I'm anybody's but especially yours' routine.

I crept down the corridor, opened the door a fraction and peeked in. My heart stopped. Ollie *was* still in there. And he was snogging Jade. I felt like someone had hit me in the stomach and I reeled back in shock. Oh *God*, this is how Becca must have felt. And all over a stupid boy who doesn't care who he snogs as long as he *gets* snogged. Sugar! He was a quick worker. *How* could I have been so naive to think that I was special. Lia had warned me. She'd told me what he was like. About all those silly girls who thought that they'd be the one to make the difference.

I ran back to the kitchen and found Squidge who was now perched on top of the fridge filming down.

'Has that camera got instant replay on it?' I asked.

He nodded.

'Can you film something, or rather someone, for a mo? But don't let them see you.'

Squidge nodded again and jumped down. 'I like a bit of secret filming, makes the result more interesting. Lead the way.'

We tiptoed back down the corridor to the study and again, I opened the door a fraction so Squidge could get his camera round.

'Ah, see what you mean,' he said as he saw that they were still going at it on the sofa. He filmed for a few moments then drew the camera out.

'Please will you show that to Becca? I want to prove to her that Ollie is after anyone and it's not worth being in love with him.'

Squidge looked at me closely. 'OK. But are *you* OK, Cat? You look kind of upset.'

'I'm fine,' I said remembering something I'd heard a girl in Year Eleven at school say once. 'Fine,' she'd said. 'F.

Foolish. I. Insecure. N. Neurotic. And E. Exhausted.'

Lia beckoned to us from the stairs. 'Bec's in my bathroom,' she said. 'Do you want to go up?'

I turned back to Squidge. 'Let me have a word first, OK?'

'OK.' He shrugged. 'If you're sure you think this is a good idea.'

I ran up the stairs and into Lia's bedroom. I knocked on the bathroom door. 'Bec, it's me. Can I come in?'

'Go *away*,' she said.

'Please, Bec.'

'GO AWAY. I don't want to talk to you.'

'I thought you might like to know that Ollie is now snogging someone else downstairs.'

Silence.

'He's snogging Jade.'

Silence.

'Becca. I just want you to know he's not worth it. I didn't *mean* to snog him. I was looking for Lia and he pushed me into the study and kissed me, then you came in.'

Silence.

'He made the first move.'

Double silence.

'Oh please, Becca. He's not worth falling out over.'

I heard the door unlock.

'How do I know you're not making it up?'

'Wait here.'

I went out into the hall and called Squidge in.

'Play back the video, Squidge.'

Squidge did as he was told and showed the scene he'd just filmed. Becca watched then looked at me.

'Does Squidge know about what happened earlier?' she asked.

I felt my heart begin to beat madly in my chest. Oh, please don't say anything, I thought. Not now. Not like this. It wouldn't be fair to Squidge.

'She's been after Ollie for ages,' continued Becca, 'when we went to Rock and God knows how long before.'

I wanted to die.

'Jade's such a cow. She knew I fancied Ollie, but wasn't even going to give me a look in. I say good luck to them.'

Suddenly she put her arm through mine and smiled at me. 'They deserve each other.'

'Cool attitude,' said Squidge. 'Good on you Becca. You're right, if he hasn't noticed anyone as fab and fun as you, then forget him. Anyway, got to go, got people to film.' He put his camera up to his eye and filmed the bedroom for a moment. 'See you later.'

After he'd gone I glanced over at Becca. 'I *am* sorry Bec.'

Becca shrugged. 'Was he a good kisser?'

I wasn't going to lie about this, so I nodded.

Becca shrugged again. 'You win some, you lose some. I've been obsessing about him for weeks and he's hardly given me a second glance. And Lia did say he's a love rat.

Phff. I'm not going to let him ruin my night. And to be honest, I was beginning to get tired of thinking about him. Unrequited is not my scene.'

I gave her a huge hug. 'You are my bestest, bestest friend, Becca. Top, top, top. And I'm *so* sorry about snogging Ollie.'

'So am I. But you're right, it isn't worth falling out over is it? I've been miserable sitting there in that bathroom.'

I hugged her again. 'We've been friends for years, Bec, it's important not to let *anything* get in the way. Boys are going to come and go in our lives, but true friends are always there for you.'

'Yeah. And Lia told us what he was like. I guess it's not your fault he fancies you.'

'Me and Jade and half the world,' I said.

'Yeah maybe. But no way I'm singing with Jade tonight.'

'Fine by me. I was dreading it anyway. Though . . . we could do a knife throwing act instead.'

Becca smiled. 'With Jade as the target?'

'Exactly.'

Becca combed her hair which for once had stayed straight and sleek, then she turned to me. 'Let's forget him, shall we? Boys just *aren't* worth the agro.'

'I agree,' I said. 'Friends are much more valuable.' I joined her at the mirror then began to sing: '*Love hurts, love scars . . .*'

'*Love wounds and mars,*' she sang back, then we both laughed.

Lia came in to find us collapsed on the bed laughing.

'What's going on?'

'We just decided boys stink,' said Becca.

'My brother included,' said Lia.

'They break your bloomin' 'art,' I sighed in my best 'EastEnders' voice.

'Too right,' said Lia. 'So let's get down there and break a few of theirs.'

We redid our make-up and hair and set out for round two.

We headed for the kitchen which is where most of the boys seemed to be, all stuffing their faces with vol-au-vents and little canapés like they'd never eaten before.

Phew, I thought, as I watched Becca get talking to Mac, then laugh at something he said. Everything's going to be all right. It certainly couldn't get any worse than half an hour ago.

'I'm just going to get some fresh air,' I said opening the back door and stepping out on to the terrace.

Once outside I leaned against the cool wall and looked up at the stars. I felt sad. Although I'd done my 'I don't care' act, I was still smarting from finding Jade with Ollie. I'd thought that we had something special and that he felt the same way about me. Hah.

Big lesson, I thought. *Big* lesson. Not all boys are like

Squidge, dependable and faithful. If you put your trust in the wrong boy, you get hurt. I'd been so naïve.

It was then that Max and Molly noticed I was there. They must have been put out in the garden so that they didn't bother the guests. They bounded up to me with their usual enthusiasm and I tried to get away before they leapt up with muddy paws. I opened the door to get back inside, but too late: Molly caught the hem of my dress in her mouth and, as I tried to get inside, I heard an almighty rip.

Telling the Truth 17

'I AM *not* a liar,' I said. 'A liar is someone who tells lies. A lot. And I'm not like that. Am I? Oh, I don't know. I've tried telling the truth, the whole truth, and nothing but the truth, and that got me nowhere . . . Actually it got me detention, but you know what I mean. And now this. I feel like I'm being punished again. I can't win.'

'What are you on about Cat?' asked Mac. 'Lia told me to bring you a drink and cheer you up. What's the problem?'

I was up in Lia's bedroom wearing her dressing gown and frantically trying to mend the tear in my dress. I pointed at the rip. '*This* is the problem. No, *I'm* the problem. No. *Everything's* the problem,' I said. '*Life* is a problem, Mac. First this stupid dress. Then Squidge and Ollie and Becca and . . .'

'What about Becca?'

'She fancied Ollie, but he got off with me, then Jade. By now, he's probably been through half the girls at the party.'

'Er. Stop there a mo. *Fancied* Ollie?' asked Mac. 'Fancied as in past tense? Are you saying she doesn't any more?'

'She's seen the light, I think.'

'Really? Excellent!' Mac smiled, punching the air. 'Er, sorry, what were you saying? What's the prob?'

'*Me*. I'm the problem. I'm a liar.' I didn't care who knew any more. I was sick of living in a shadowland of my own making. I wanted to be able to talk to my friends like I used to. Tell them everything. Have a laugh. Talk about what was happening.

'You're a liar?' said Mac looking puzzled. 'About what?'

'How long have you got?'

Mac looked at his watch. 'Five minutes,' he laughed. 'I'm on my break.'

'OK. Here's the problem, or part of it. Ollie. I fancy him. I do. I know it's stupid and he's Mr Ratfink and breaks hearts all over the place, but I feel what I feel. And I know I have to get over it. But it's not that so much that's bugging me. Well it is, but it isn't.'

'So what is it?'

'I hate not being able to tell Bec everything. I'm tired of dealing with everything on my own. Bec and me, we've never had any secrets and this is the first time I've ever held back. All because of a stupid boy. Ollie. Who's down there snogging *your* stupid sister.'

'Typical Jade.' Mac grinned. 'Actually he's not any more. He's in the kitchen talking to some girl from

London and Jade's hanging about looking really miffed.'

'Serves her right,' I said. 'Now she knows how we felt. Becca got upset because he snogged me earlier. Bec's got over it because she said she doesn't do unrequited and she's sick of thinking about him. But me. Me? I'm not over it. I feel like crapola. Becca's my best mate. You confide in best mates. I want to tell her the truth.'

A cloud passed over Mac's face. 'The truth can really mess things up. Believe me, I know. You know why my mum and dad split up?'

I shook my head as I continued sewing.

'Truth. That's why they split up. Dad had an affair when we lived up in London. He told Mum the truth about it and the next thing I knew, Mum, Jade and I were packed up and moving down here. He says it was a stupid thing. One night. Meaningless, he said. He doesn't even know why he did it. He felt he had to be honest with Mum and look where it got us. She won't speak to him. So, so much for the truth. I reckon if he'd kept his mouth shut, we'd all be happy still living up in London and I wouldn't have had to leave my school and all my mates.'

'Oh, I am sorry, Mac. I never knew what happened.'

'What Mum didn't know wouldn't have hurt her.'

'Maybe,' I said. 'But something like that, it's a tough call. I mean, if I was married I think I'd want to know if my husband was cheating. Wouldn't you, if you loved someone?'

'I guess,' said Mac wearily. 'But it wasn't as though he was a serial cheater, if you know what I mean. Believe me, he really regrets it. Every time I go up there, he's always asking if she has forgiven him yet.'

'It must be really hard for you, Mac,' I said. 'Awful being in the middle.'

'He should never have told the truth,' he said bitterly.

I thought about it. I didn't want to say too much as I could tell it had taken a lot for Mac to open up and I didn't want him to think I didn't understand.

'I know you think that him telling your mum the truth ruined everything for you, but it wasn't really that, was it?' I asked.

'So what was it?'

I hesitated. 'The fact he cheated in the first place.'

'So what are you saying?'

'It was *that* that caused the trouble. Not him telling the truth. If he had been faithful, he wouldn't have had to confess.'

Mac looked thoughtful. 'Yeah. Maybe.'

'Oh I don't know, Mac. Relationships are a complicated business. Believe me, I know. You want to be truthful, but you don't want to hurt people. I don't know your mum except to look at and I don't know your dad at all. Maybe things weren't right in the first place if your dad had an affair.'

Mac nodded. 'Maybe. I don't know, Cat. All I'm saying

is that, seeing what happened with my mum and dad, you've got to be prepared. If you do decide to tell the truth, it may have repercussions.'

I looked down at my ruined dress. 'Yeah, but so does being dishonest. Like for your dad. Having to tell the truth was a repercussion of being dishonest. He obviously felt bad about it, guilty, and decided to take responsibility for his actions. At least if you tell the truth, you can sleep at night.'

Mac looked sad again. 'Yeah. But you might have to sleep in separate houses.'

The next day I decided it was time to get my life back in order. I got up, got dressed and headed straight out.

'Won't be long, Dad,' I said. 'Got a few things I have to do.'

First I went to the newsagent's and signed up to do a paper round until Christmas. So it meant getting up at six in the morning, I didn't care. I had to earn enough money to pay for the dress. Lia had offered to cover the cost, saying that it was her problem as well as mine as they were her dogs, but I refused. I wanted to take responsibility for my actions and the repercussions. All of them.

Next I cycled over to Squidge's house. On the way, I thought about Mac's mum and dad. Poor Mac. He'd lost out because of honesty *and* dishonesty. They were like two sides of a coin. But on balance I decided, I think I'd rather know the truth. Holding back on the truth is dishonest too. I'd really learned that it only prolongs the agony and I wished I'd told Squidge it was over weeks ago.

Squidge grabbed his jacket when I called for him and we headed down towards Cawsand Square.

I wasn't going to wait for the right time or the right place. If I did I'd be waiting for ever. Dive in, I told myself.

'Squidge. You know I think the world of you and I hope we can be mates for ever. I'll always be there for you when you need a friend, but the boyfriend/girlfriend thing isn't working for me any more.'

'OK,' he said.

'*OK?* Did you hear what I said?'

'Yeah. You want to finish.'

I looked at his face. He seemed OK. No shock. No tears. *Nada.*

'Well, er, how do you feel about it?'

'Cool. Good idea, I think,' he said. 'It's a fact. Life is about evolution. Things move on. Change. Evolve. I think you're right – we should move on.'

I was *gobsmacked* at his reaction. *Double* gobsmacked. 'I thought you'd be upset.'

'Not if we can stay friends, Cat. I'd be upset if you didn't want to be friends any more.'

I took his hand. 'Friends for always, Squidge.'

'Well that's OK, then.' He grinned. 'I've been thinking the same thing. See if I'm going to be a film director and write my own scripts, then I need to experience life. New challenges and that means new relationships. I think it will be good for both of us to move on.'

'How long have you been feeling like this?'

'Since summer, really.'

'Why didn't you say anything?'

Squidge shrugged. 'It's hard letting go. Didn't want to upset you. And part of me wondered if it was a mistake. I mean, you are pretty special. Maybe I'll never find anyone like you ever again.'

All the stuff I'd been thinking! 'So you've wanted to tell me for weeks?'

Squidge nodded sheepishly. 'I was going to tell you that time I gave you the bracelet. I wanted it to be a kind of memento of our relationship. But I couldn't find the right words.'

'I know what you mean,' I laughed. 'So we're OK?'

He nodded again.

'Squidge. No matter what happens. Where we end up. Who we end up with. We will always be each other's first love. No one can ever take that away.'

'Yeah,' said Squidge, then gave me a huge bear hug. 'Cat Kennedy, my childhood sweetheart. Maybe I'll write a film about you one day. Now. Let's go and get a pasty. I'm starving.'

18

Cat-harsis

I WOKE up the next morning feeling brilliant. Full of hope. Everything was going to be all right.

'Cat. Can you come downstairs?' called Dad.

I could tell by his tone of voice that something was wrong. I pulled on my school clothes and ran down to the kitchen. He was sitting at the table with a pile of mail.

'Can you explain this?' he asked holding up an invoice from the catalogue company.

I hung my head. My plan had been to intercept the post-man and take care of the bill, so no questions asked. But after my wonderful day with Squidge yesterday, I'd slept better than I had done in weeks. And I'd overslept. Missed the post.

'Um . . .' I racked my brain as how to best put it.

'See,' continued Dad, 'it says here that a dress was sent last week. I rang to say I hadn't made an order, but they assured me that someone from this address phoned last week.

I took a deep breath. 'It was me. I'm sorry. I had nothing

to wear for the party and when I saw the catalogue, I . . .'
I decided to omit the part about the original plan to return
the dress. 'And I . . . I've got a job with Mrs Daly delivering the newspapers to pay for it.'

Dad was quiet. There are silences and silences, I
thought. And this ain't a good one.

'I can explain . . .'

'I don't want to hear explanations, Cat. Frankly, I'm
disappointed in you. I thought I'd raised my kids to be
honest.' And then he looked sad. 'Go, Cat, get to school.
I'll talk to you about it this evening.'

School passed in a blur. I felt numb all day, like I wasn't
quite there. Lessons went by, but God knows what the
teachers said. I tried to read my school books, but the
words swam before me on the pages.

'What's up, Cat?' said Becca on the bus home.

'Nothing,' I said. I didn't want to talk to anyone. Not
even to Becca. I'd let my dad down and I felt dreadful.
'Must be mi old hormones playing me up.'

'Is it because of Squidge?'

'No. I told you. That couldn't have gone better. I feel
like a huge weight has been lifted off my mind.'

'Doesn't look like it,' said Becca.

I smiled weakly. 'Just feeling a bit low.'

'Want to come back to mine? We could hang out, play
some music?'

'No thanks. Dad told me to be straight back.'

'Call you later then.'

After I'd left Becca at the bus stop, I set off to go home. Then I turned round and headed down to Cawsand Beach.

The light was fading, it was cold and beginning to rain when I got there. There wasn't a soul on the beach as I made my way over to my favourite spot and, as I sat down, the skies opened and it began to pour. Buckets. I didn't care. No one was about and I was going to have a good cry.

Once I started I couldn't stop. So much had happened since the summer. Feeling cut off from Becca. Not being able to tell her my secrets. Having nothing to wear for the party while my two best mates got fab new things. Then the dress from the catalogue being ripped. Becca finding Ollie snogging me. Ollie snogging Jade. Trying to tell the truth and getting in trouble with everyone. Trying to stay sane in an overcrowded house. *No one* appreciates me and how I try, I thought, as great gulps of pain poured out. Being poorer than all my friends. Having to share a bed-room with a mad midget. Finishing with Squidge. And he'd *agreed* it was a good idea. Maybe he knew I was bad underneath and that's why he was happy to finish. Maybe *no one* would ever want me ever again as long as I lived and I would die alone, lonely and unwanted. I didn't want to be me any more. Everyone always thought I was so strong and brave, so good at coping but I wasn't. I couldn't cope any longer. I felt pathetic. And Dad thought I was no good.

It was as if a dam had burst deep inside me and all the things I never dared to let myself think about, rose to the surface.

My thoughts turned to Mum and a memory came flooding back. It was after the funeral and the house was quiet after all the relatives and friends had packed up and returned to their homes. Dad had made us cheese on toast, then gone up to put Joe, Luke and Emma to bed. Not wanting to be on my own downstairs, I'd followed them up and gone into the bathroom. There was the bottle of Mum's perfume on the shelf by the window and I lifted the cap and squirted the scent into the room. It brought Mum's presence flooding back, but I realised the scent would fade. As Mum had.

Then I realised that in all the rushing and pandemonium of the funeral arrangements, Dad had forgotten to buy any loo paper and there wasn't any. That had been Mum's job.

It was at that moment that I realised I hadn't got a mum any more. No one to look after us. My mum had gone.

I sat on the loo and sobbed my heart out.

So much of what had been familiar disappeared with her – Sunday lunches, the fuss she made on birthdays and at Christmas, her words of encouragement on mornings of exams, the smell of cooking, Radio Four playing in the background as Mum got everyone sorted when I returned at night.

After that memory, there was no holding back.

I thought of all the people in the world who have lost someone as well and I cried for them.

I thought about all the bad news lately, fighting in distant places, and hatred, and people losing their families and homes and jobs.

This world is *soooo* horrible, I thought. There's so much *paiiiiiin*.

When I seemed to be running out of things to cry about, a voice in the back of my head said, *and* you're short. Cry about that as well, why don't you?

I *will*, I thought. Might as well while I'm at it. It's true, I *am* the smallest girl in my class. *And* I've got a spot coming on my chin. And the only boy I really *really* fancy is King of the Love Rats.

It felt right to be there, sobbing in the rain, staring out as the black waves swelled and broke angrily on the beach. I don't know how long I sat there, but it felt like I was one with the sea and the rain, one gushing torrent of salt water.

An Honest Woman 19

I DON'T know what the time was when I became aware of a figure to my right by the café. A man in a weatherproof with a torch.

'Cat,' he called. 'CAT.' His words were blown away by the gusting wind.

It was Dad.

As he cast his torch over the beach, the light fell on me and he came running over.

'Cat. Thank *God*. I've been looking everywhere for you.'

He picked me up in his arms and he felt so warm and safe that I started crying again.

'Dad . . .' I sobbed. 'I'm not dishonest. Honestly I'm not. I try to be good.'

'There, there,' he said as he carried me back to the car.

Once inside the car, I began to feel a bit stupid. And very wet.

'What were you thinking of going down there on your own in the dark?' asked Dad.

'Are you still mad at me?'

'No, Cat,' he said gently. 'I'm not mad at you. Worried. But not mad. I phoned everyone. Becca said she'd left you at the bus stop and you were coming home. Then I phoned Lia and she didn't know where you were. I've been out of my mind.'

'Mum used to bring us here when we were little.'

'I know,' said Dad. 'I remember.'

'How did you know I might be here?'

'Lia phoned back after I called her. She'd been talking to her brother Ollie and must have told him you were missing. He said to look down here.'

We sat in silence for a few moments, then Dad asked, 'Ready to come home now?'

I nodded. 'But can we talk first. Just for a few minutes.'

'Sure,' he said. 'Course we can.'

'I'm really sorry about the dress, Dad . . .'

'So am I. I should have known how much it meant to you to have something nice to wear. I'm sorry. I've not been much of a dad lately, have I?'

'No. *No*. You're the best dad in the world. It's just, I really need you to know that I didn't mean to be bad. I've been thinking about so much in the last few weeks. You wouldn't believe it. It's so hard. Sometimes when you're honest, it hurts people. But it doesn't work when you're not honest. Causes all sorts of trouble. And then sometimes it does work. I've been so confused.'

'What about, Cat? Are you in trouble? Is there something you want to tell me?'

'Yes. No. I mean I'm not in trouble. Except with you. I . . . I think it's really important that we talk to each other. About what's going on and stuff.'

Dad smiled sadly. 'Do you know how like your mother you are?'

I shook my head.

'You remind me of her in so many ways. Not only in looks, you have her spirit too, Cat. Big-hearted. She was always looking out for others, like you. And like you, she was always reminding me to be honest, talk stuff through as you say.' He paused a moment as though hesitant. 'Remember when she died?'

I nodded.

'Remember how she always said she wanted to know the truth? No lies? Well I'm going to tell you something I've never told anyone before. About when she died. It was the most difficult choice I ever had to make. See, I knew how ill she was. Only a matter of months. Weeks. I wanted to protect her and you from the truth . . .'

'So what did you do?'

Dad hesitated as though it was painful for him to remember. 'I agonised over it, but one day she asked me to be completely honest. She wanted to know exactly what her condition was so that she could prepare herself. I felt so helpless, frustrated, there was nothing I could do. But, in the end, I had to honour her wishes and I told her. She was so brave, Cat.'

'I know. I remember.'

'I couldn't give her false hope and I couldn't stop what was happening. At the very end, I tried to be there night and day, but one day I'd left her, not for long, just to get a few things from home. Change of clothes and that. The nurses told me afterwards that she was slipping away and they thought it was her time, but she came round for a moment. She asked the nurse where I was, the nurse explained I'd be back in about half an hour. Then she slipped back into unconsciousness. When I came back, I knew she didn't have long, they didn't think she'd regain consciousness. Then all of a sudden, she opened her eyes and turned and looked right at me. She took my hand, then she died.'

Dad brushed a tear away from his eyes and I reached over and took his hand in mine.

'It was like she'd waited for me. She wanted me there as she passed away. And Lord knows, it was important for me to be there. I realised afterwards that if I hadn't told her the truth, and she hadn't known that she was dying, then she might have slipped away when I wasn't at her bedside and I couldn't have lived with that, Cat. It meant everything that I was there, you know, by her side, holding her hand when she went.'

'I was glad I knew as well,' I said. 'It gave me time to get used to the idea. If she'd just gone one day and I hadn't understood how ill she was, it would have been even worse. She wasn't afraid of the truth, Mum. And I'm not going to be either.'

'You're right, Cat. As she was right then. And now, the most important thing is for us to keep talking about whatever. We're family and there's so much untruth in the world, we shouldn't have it at home.'

'I understand,' I said. 'That's why you were so disappointed in me.'

'Only for a moment, Cat. If you only knew how proud I am of you really.'

I felt choked. 'Thanks Dad and I'm glad you told me about Mum. You've been brave too. I'm proud of you.'

'So how about I take you home? We get you into some warm clothes, make a mug of hot chocolate and then I'll cook you one of my specials.'

I suddenly realised I was starving. 'Er, seeing as we're being honest here . . .' I smiled. 'How about we skip the home cooking and get some chips?'

'Excellent idea,' Dad said, grinning as he started up the car.

As we drove home, I felt closer to him than I ever had in my life. And we didn't stop talking. We talked about accepted lies, like telling kids that there's a Santa and a tooth fairy. Cowardly lies, compassionate lies, lies to make you buy things, political lies, false promises and we both agreed again that with us, with family, there was no room for any of them.

'In the end,' said Dad as we pulled up in our drive at the back of the house, 'honesty is best but it's important to be aware of people's feelings when you have something to say. Sometimes you have to adjust the truth. More important, though, is to be true to yourself.'

'OK,' I said turning to him before I got out the car. 'So, er, one more thing. Um . . . Jen. Don't you think it's time you made an honest woman out of her?'

Dad laughed. 'Maybe. Maybe I just will. You'd like that, would you?'

'I'd love it. So would Luke, Joe and Emma. We know that no one will ever replace Mum, but . . .' I remembered what Squidge had said to me the day before, 'life moves on. Evolves. There's good times and bad. Joy and pain. Mum's not coming back and I think she'd want you to be happy.'

'My little girl.' Dad smiled at me. 'Not so little any more, eh?'

Options are Open

IT WAS three weeks later when we got the news.

I was doing my homework up in my bedroom when Luke came in. He looked a bit worried.

'Dad wants to see us all in the kitchen now,' he said.

'Is someone in trouble?' I asked.

Luke shrugged. 'Dunno. Jen's with him. He looks pretty serious.'

Oh dear, I thought, as I followed him down the stairs. Since my epic wailing on the beach, everyone had been getting on better than ever.

When I got to the kitchen, Dad, Joe and Emma were already seated around the table. Jen was making tea.

'Want a drink before we start, Cat?' she asked.

I nodded and tried to gauge the atmosphere. Something was going on, but I couldn't tell if it was good or bad.

'Right,' said Dad as we all settled down. 'I have something I want to say to you all.'

We all looked at each other wondering who had blown it this time and why we'd all been gathered to hear about it.

'Don't look so worried. It's good news,' Dad assured us. 'At least, I think it is.' Then he smiled over at Jen. 'Two things. First, I've asked Jen to marry me and she's said yes.'

'Hurray,' shouted Joe as Jen smiled shyly.

'We'll probably have the wedding in the spring . . .'

'Fantastic,' I said, then sang, '*Congratulations* . . .'

The others joined in, '*And celebrations* . . .'

'I hope Cat and Emma will be my bridesmaids,' said Jen looking at us both.

'You bet,' said Emma, then looked worried. 'We won't have to wear pink meringues like Cat's horrible dress, will we?'

'No,' said Dad and gave me a wink. 'You can go up to London with Jen and pick out your dresses yourselves.'

'*London!*' I said. 'Fantastic. I've never been. So what's the second thing, Dad?'

'Well, it's not definite yet,' he said, 'but we were thinking of moving after the wedding. With two incomes coming in, we could maybe afford to buy something with a bit more room.'

In front of him, he had a pile of papers. 'We've been looking at a few places just to get an idea of prices.' He handed round the papers.

There were a number of properties. One showed a white

semi-detached house on the outskirts of Millbrook, near Becca's. I quickly read the details. 'Oh my God. This one's got a large garden at the back and oh, it's got *four* bedrooms, Dad. Could we really afford something like this?'

'We'll see.' He was grinning. 'We've got to do all our sums yet. But I thought it was about time you had your own room at last, Cat.'

My *own* bedroom. I couldn't believe it.

'That's not fair,' cried Luke taking the sheet of paper. 'Four bedrooms. One for you and Jen. One for Cat. One for Emma. What about *us*? I can't stand sharing with stinky feet . . .'

'Ah,' said Dad. 'We've thought of that. If, or rather, *when* we move, we thought we'd get you a tent for the garden.'

'Brilliant!' said Joe.

'But . . . but . . . it will be cold,' said Luke.

'Only joking,' beamed Dad. 'I wouldn't put you in the garden, you daft nonce. Anyway it's early days, but you never know, in a place like that, all you need is planning permission to build in the loft and we could put an extra bedroom up there.'

'Bagsy me,' said Joe.

'No me. I'm older than you. Me. Tell him, Dad,' said Luke.

Dad looked to the heavens. 'Fighting already and we've only just started talking about it. We'll sort out who has which room when we get wherever we're going to.'

'I have some news too,' announced Emma.

'And what's that?' asked Dad, turning to her.

'I've got nits!' she exclaimed proudly.

Luke and Joe scraped their chairs back and moved away from her. Jen went and had a look through Emma's hair and grimaced at Dad.

'One of the joys you're taking on, Jen,' said Dad.

Jen smiled back. 'Can't wait . . . Combing through nit-infested hair, mmm, can't wait!'

'When will we move, Dad?' I asked.

'Not sure yet, Cat. Moving house costs money, so we'll have to save up a bit. But I wanted to talk to you all about it first and if everyone's happy, we'll go ahead with working out finances in the next few months. So. Any objections?'

No one said a word.

'Excellent,' said Dad. 'In the meantime, all options are open.'

My very own bedroom. It may be months away, but already my head was full of ideas for paint and fabric. Lia and Becca could help me. I couldn't wait.

After the family conference I ran upstairs to phone Becca.

'That's fantastic,' she said. 'Oh, I hope you buy the one near me. We could walk home from the school bus together.'

'I know. Want to come round and celebrate?'

Becca went quiet, then giggled.

'What, Becca? What's going on?'

'Um. I've got a date.'

'Who with?'

'Mac.'

'Mac! When did all this happen?'

'At Lia's party, sort of. He was so kind when I was all freaked out and I realised that I really like him. He's OK when he drops the 'I don't care about anything' act and is himself. He's called a few times and he just phoned now to ask if I wanted to go and hang out this evening.'

'So Ollie's history?'

'Well he is for me, Cat.'

'What do you mean?'

Becca went quiet on the other end of the phone. 'I know I liked him, but what's true one moment can change.'

'Tell me about it! I almost blew a fuse trying to work out how I felt about him and Squidge. It changed every day, so don't get me started on all that again.'

'OK. But just one thing I have to tell you. I could tell Ollie liked you as soon as I saw you with him at Rock, the way he looked at you. I feel rotten because I was jealous and even though I said I fancied him first, I should have said something, but I was too mean. I'm sorry, I've been a crapola friend . . .'

'No you haven't. I've been a crap friend. I always fancied Ollie, but didn't want to get in your way. But I should have told you in the beginning . . .'

'Yeah, you should. But it wasn't your fault he fancied you not me, so I'm the crap friend.'

'No, I am.'

'No, *I* am,' she insisted.

'No, I am.'

'OK. We both are. Totally crapola. But best friends are for ever and as you said at Lia's, that's worth more than any stupid boy. But if you want to go out with him, I won't mind. Honest.'

'Nah . . .' I began.

'Do you *like* him?'

'Yes. But I don't know if I'd want to go out with him.'

'Well, as long as you know that whatever happens, I'm cool.'

After I'd finished talking to Becca, I called Lia and told her all the news. She was as delighted for me as Becca had been.

'And Cat, you know Ollie still keeps asking after you?'

'Does he?'

'Want me to say anything to him?'

'Nah,' I said. 'Not really.'

'Keeping your options open?' she asked.

'Exactly. I want to enjoy being free for a while. No secrets, no lies, no truths I have or haven't to tell. It's great. So much has changed since the summer, it's like a whole new chapter beginning. Dad's getting married, we may be moving. I'm not in a relationship any more. Who knows what might happen.'

'Who knows,' said Lia. 'But Ollie did ask for your e-mail address. Can I give it to him?'

'Why not?' I grinned down the phone. 'Options are open.'

Pop
Princess

Truth Dare
Kiss
Promise

Pop
Princess

Cathy Hopkins

PICCADILLY PRESS • LONDON

Thanks as always to Brenda Gardner, Yasemin Uçar and the lovely team at Piccadilly. To Rosemary Bromley at Juvenilia. And Becca Crewe, Alice Elwes, Jenni Herzberg and Olivia McDonnell for all their emails in answer to my questions.

Grease Mania

1

'ARGHHHHHHHHHHHHHH,' I groaned as I walked into the living room at Cat's house. 'Not you as well. I can't stand it.'

Cat looked up from the sofa. 'What? What's the matter?'

I pointed at the TV screen. 'That. That DVD of Grease. Everywhere I've been today, everyone's got it on – Lia, Mac's watching it at Squidge's . . . I can't get away from it. What is wrong with everyone?'

Actually, I thought, that should be: what's wrong with me? All my mates were excited by the prospect of our school putting on Grease as the end of term show. The whole school was, in fact. Everyone except me. But I had my reasons.

Cat sprang up and went into a dance routine. 'Summer loving, had me a blast,' she sang along with John Travolta on the TV. 'Oh, come on, Becca. It's the first time ever that we're doing something decent for the end of term show. Makes a change from all those boring fairy stories we usually do.'

I flopped down on the sofa. 'I suppose this means that you're going up for a part?'

'Yeah,' said Cat, sitting next to me and flicking off the video. 'I thought about going for the part of Rizzo. What do you think?'

'Perfect,' I said. She would be. She looks the part exactly – small, with dark hair like Stockard Channing in the movie. And she can sing as well. 'Yeah. And Rizzo has the best song, I think.'

'I could flirt with all the guys,' sang Cat.

'Tease and tantalise,' I joined in.

'What about you, Bec? Don't you want to be in it?'

I shrugged. 'Haven't really thought about it.' Actually, that was a lie. I had thought about it. We've got this new drama teacher at school called Miss Segal and she's really cool for a teacher. It was her idea to put on something more contemporary and suddenly everyone in the school wants to be in the show. Secretly I do as well, but I'd like to play the lead, Sandra Dee. She was played by Olivia Newton-John in the film, though, so they'll be looking for someone skinny and blonde. And that's the problem. I've got red hair and nobody in their right mind would ever use the word 'skinny' to describe me. Curvy is what Cat says. Fat is what I say. My secret fantasy is that I lose half a stone miraculously overnight, go for the audition and get picked from the crowds for my astounding talent. Ha! Dream on, Becca.

'You could play one of the Pink Ladies,' said Cat. 'Frenchy. You know, the one who goes to beauty school – she has red hair like you.'

'Er, she does in the beginning, then she has pink hair, then yellow hair later. Remember the scene where one of the boys says she looks like a beautiful pineapple?'

'Ah, so you *have* been watching it,' said Cat.

'Can't avoid it,' I said. 'I told you, Mac and Squidge are watching it round at Squidge's. That's why I came here, to get away from it. Squidge wants to be one of the T-Birds, you know, John Travolta's sidekick.'

'He's called Kenickie,' said Cat.

'Mac and I were supposed to be going out, then Squidge talked him into going for a part. I think he wants to be a T-Bird as well.'

'He probably wants to because they'd get to wear cool leather jackets, jeans and shades. But Squidge can't sing for toffee and I don't think Mac can either.'

'Nor can Lia,' I said, 'but she can dance. I think she's hoping to get into the chorus. And Jade – well, we all know what Jade wants to play.'

'The lead.' said Cat. 'What a joke. Whoever plays Sandra Dee will have to be all wide-eyed and innocent in the first half of the show, and sorry, but I just can't see Jade singing lines like, "I'm wholesome and pure, oh so scared and unsure". Er, Jade? No way. You should go for it, Bec. Your voice is just as good as hers.'

'I'm not blonde like Jade,' I said.

'You could wear a wig.'

I shook my head. 'Nah. I don't think so. Anyway I'm too fat.'

'No way you're fat, you idiot. Oh, come on, Becca, it will be fun. And you have to go public some day. You can't spend your whole life singing into a hairbrush in front of the mirror or in the shower.'

'I sing in our band.'

'Yeah right,' said Cat. 'And when did we last have a rehearsal? Months ago. Anyway, I don't think Jade wants to be in it any more. I think she wants to go solo.'

'No loss,' I said.

Jade is Mac's younger sister and she's in the year above us at our school. At first our band was just me and Cat, then we let Jade join as she has a great voice and we thought it would be good to have three. All the girl bands seem to have three . . . But Jade can be a bossy cow and she took over, always telling us what songs we should do and how we should move and what we should wear. The band was called Diamond Heart but it was turning into Jade and the Diamond Hearts.

Cat switched the DVD back on.

'Oh no. Please, Cat, let's go out for a bit. It's Sunday. Call Lia and ask her to meet us at Cawsand Beach. Please. You can work on your part later.

In the end, everyone wanted to come. I couldn't believe it when we got to the square down near Cawsand Beach – Lia and Squidge were acting out the dance routine to 'You're the One That I Want', with Mac singing the ooh, ooh, ooh's in the background. Actually, it was funny, as Squidge and Lia are both completely tone-deaf and it sounded dreadful. It's a shame that Lia can't sing, because she has the looks to play Sandra Dee – slim, with long blonde hair and a beautiful angel face.

A man walked past on the way to the pub and laughed when he heard the singing. 'I'd stick to the day jobs if I were you,' he called out, putting his fingers in his ears.

'Yeah, give us a break,' I said to Lia and Squidge. 'You've already frightened the tourists away.'

Cat laughed. In the summer, it's heaving with tourists around here, but as the autumn sets in, there's nobody but the locals to be seen.

'The auditions are tomorrow after school,' said Squidge and started jiving with Lia. 'And Kenickie doesn't have a solo song, so I've just got to get the moves right and dye my hair back to its normal colour.'

Squidge's mum, who's a hairdresser, dyed his hair blond at the beginning of term, as he was going through his spiky phase and wanted to look like the guy in *Buffy the Vampire Slayer*.

'Becca, do you think I should dye my hair?' asked Mac, running his hand through his blond hair. 'Most of the guys in *Grease* have dark hair.'

'It won't matter,' I said, beginning to feel left out. 'And anyway, we came out here for a break. From now on, this is officially a *Grease*-free zone. Let's do something else, at least for half an hour.'

'I can't believe you're not going in for it,' said Squidge. 'You've easily got the best chance of getting a role, apart from Cat. Isn't there anything we can do to persuade you?'

'Nope,' I said and headed off towards the bay.

'Chicken!' Squidge called after me.

'Stick and stones Squidge,' I called back. 'I've made up my mind.'

I turned to look at them as I walked away and noticed that Squidge was whispering something to the others, who all looked at me then nodded. What were they up to? A moment later, they came after me and we all walked down together to the café on the beach. When we got to it, we saw that it was closed for the season, so we went and sat on the wall to watch the boats. There weren't many at this time of year, but it was still good to sit there, watching them bobbing up and down on the waves and breathe in the salty air.

Mac stood behind me and put his arms around me. He felt solid and warm, which was nice, as even though it was bright, there was a chill wind.

'So Becca . . .' said Cat, with a sly look at the others.

'What?' I asked, looking at her suspiciously.

'Mates,' said Lia. 'Mates do things together, don't they?'

'Yeah. Course,' I said.

'Together through thick and thin?' asked Squidge.

'Yeah,' I said.

'So you wouldn't leave any of us to go through a nerve-wracking experience on our own?' asked Cat.

'No, course not,' I said.

'Excellent,' she said. 'So that means you'll be auditioning with the rest of us tomorrow.'

'No way. I told you already. I'm not going up for it.'

'Oh, come on,' said Lia. 'I'm giving it a go and I can't even sing. Please. As mates, moral support. Then we'll all be in it together.'

Mac squeezed my shoulders. 'Yeah. Come on, Bec. One for all and all for one and all that.'

'But . . .' I began.

'No buts,' said Mac. 'We think you should go for the part of Sandra Dee. Someone needs to give my sister a run for her money.'

'And if I don't?' I asked.

Squidge looked out to the sea then back at the others. 'It's *awfully* cold in there at this time of year . . .' He grinned, then nodded at Mac. Mac moved his arms from my shoulders and slipped them under my arms as Squidge picked up my feet. Suddenly, they'd hauled me up between them and were running with me, heading towards the sea.

'If you don't . . .' Mac laughed as they started swinging

me over the waves lapping up on to the sand. They were ready to chuck me in!

'*NOOO!!!*' I screamed, half laughing, half panicking. 'No. OK. *OK*. I'll *do* it.'

Auditions

2

'T-BIRDS NEXT,' called Miss Segal, sticking her head out into the corridor outside the assembly room. 'Then we'll see the Pink Ladies.'

A group of boys in fifties gear got up and trooped in after her. They looked great, especially Mac and Squidge who had dressed the part exactly. Both of them had slicked their hair back with gel, turned the collars on their leather jackets up and looked really cool in their shades. I gave them the thumbs-up.

Most of the school had turned up for the auditions. It was one of the few days in the school calendar when there wasn't a rush for the gate to go home as the bell went at the end of the day. The corridor looked like a scene from Rydell High, the school in the movie. So many people had changed from their school uniform into costumes, and some of the girls were even wearing pink bomber jackets with 'The Pink Ladies' sprayed on the back. There was an air of excitement as everyone buzzed about talking about what they were going to sing and who were the favourite contenders for the parts. The lead role of Danny Zucko was bound to go to Jonno Appleton, a complete dish from Year Eleven, and he was strutting up and down making everyone laugh by doing the 'Travolta' walk.

For a moment, I let myself fantasise about playing the female lead opposite him. It would be brilliant and everyone would be dead jealous. All the girls fancy him; he's cute and tanned, with dark hair and even has a dimple in his chin like John Travolta's. My mum and dad would come to the opening night and clap like crazy whenever I came on and everyone would admire me for my amazing performance . . .

I began to wish I'd made more of an effort. I hadn't even thought about dressing for the part and I still wasn't sure which of the songs I was going to do. Still, it should be OK, I thought, as long as Miss Segal didn't want to hear a *whole* song. Last night, I'd learned the opening bars of 'Hopelessly Devoted to You' and the chorus to 'Summer Loving', enough to show that I could actually sing in tune (unlike some of the others). What I hadn't realised, though, was that everyone was going to take it so *seriously*. Relax, I told myself as we heard various voices blast out the chorus of the T-Birds' song 'Greased Lightning' from the assembly room. I could wing it.

The boys came out a short while later. Mac and Squidge

had been told there and then that they didn't have a part, but they both looked quite happy.

'Don't you mind?' I asked Squidge.

'Not at all,' he said, grinning. 'I didn't really expect to get in, and anyway, Miss Segal asked if I would video the show. Much more my scene.'

We call him Squidge because he videos everything and his eye is always squidged up to look through his camera. He wants to be a film director when he's older, so I reckoned Miss Segal had picked the best person in the school to record the show.

'What about you, Mac?' I asked.

'She's asked me to get involved in painting the scenery and stuff,' he said.

'Good idea,' I said as I watched the next group of girls, including Cat and Lia, go in to try out for the Pink Ladies parts.

She's smart, this Miss Segal, I thought. She seems to have sussed everyone's talents already and she's only been at the school a short while. It really got me thinking. All my mates are *really* good at something, I realised. Lia's an excellent dancer, Cat's top at singing, Squidge is a really good photographer and Mac is ace at drawing. But what about me? What do I shine at? I might be OK at a lot of things, but the truth is, I don't stand out at anything.

Then a shiver of anxiety went through me when I realised that the 'Sandra Dees' would be next to be called.

I sat down and mentally went through my lines. It didn't seem long before Cat and Lia came back out to join us in the corridor. Cat looked flushed with excitement and punched the air.

'Got the part?' I asked.

She nodded. 'Think so, though it's not official until it's on the notice board tomorrow. And it's pretty definite that Josie Donaghue is going to play Marty, Kimberley Coleman's playing Jan and Chloe Barker is Frenchy.'

'So that's all the Pink Ladies. What about you, Lia?'

'She said I could be in the chorus.' She grinned. 'As long as I don't sing too loud. I'm cool with that. I just wanted to be in it.'

At that moment, a posse of Sandra Dee lookalikes lined up for their turn to audition. Some had dressed in white nighties with Alice bands in their hair, like Sandra Dee in the sleepover scene where she sings 'Hopelessly Devoted', and a couple were in tight PVC pants for the 'You're the One That I Want' song at the end. Suddenly I felt hopelessly unprepared, especially when Jade wafted past in a fifties-style gingham dress and looked at my jeans and trainers with disdain. She was just about to say something when we heard Miss Segal calling for the 'Sandra Dees.'

'Go get 'em, girl,' whispered Cat.

Jade was third up and I have to admit, she was good. She wasn't wearing any make-up, except for a slick of natural lip-gloss, and if you didn't know her better, you might have said she passed for innocent. She sang brilliantly, not a word wrong.

Before I knew it, it was my turn and I made my way up on to the stage. As I stood there, I felt very small and wobbly inside, and everyone in the assembly hall turned to watch. The pianist played the opening notes of 'Hopelessly Devoted' and I opened my mouth to start, but I missed my timing and the pianist glanced up at me.

'Can I start again?' I asked.

Miss Segal nodded and the pianist started up again.

This time I managed the opening lines and Miss Segal nodded and turned to say something to Mr Walker, who was sitting next to her.

'OK good, Becca, but we just want to hear a bit more,' she called. 'Can you do the next verse?'

'Um, I'm afraid I only learned the first one,' I said as Jade sniggered to one of her mates behind the teachers. 'I could do some of "Summer Living" . . . I mean "Loving".'

'Right, off you go,' said Miss Segal with a nod at the pianist.

This time I forgot the words after the opening bar. It was like my mind went blank. Everyone was staring. I wanted the ground to open up and swallow me. Miss Segal was looking at me with concern, as though willing me to go on, but I couldn't. The words had gone. My head was empty.

'OK, you can get down,' she said. 'Next.'

Next up was Dee Hackett, and after her, Susie Richards, but I didn't really take in their performances. I felt mortified. This wasn't anything close to my fantasy. This was my worst nightmare. Of course I wasn't surprised when I wasn't called back at the end with the final three.

I stumbled out into the corridor, made a dash for the door and ran home.

I read on the notice board the next day that Jade had got the part.

Parents' Evening

3

'BECCA, CAN you come down please?' Mum called up the stairs.

Should I pretend to be asleep? I thought as I eyed my duvet. Say I fancied an early night? I looked at my watch. It said eight-thirty. They wouldn't buy it. I took a deep breath and prepared myself to face the inevitable. It wasn't long now until the end of term, and Mum and Dad had just returned from Parents' Evening at our school.

Mum and Dad were waiting for me in the dining room with sheets of paper spread in front of them. Oh *no*, I thought, they've taken *notes*! Parents' evenings can be mad, with so many people milling around, so many teachers to see. I was hoping that they'd have got confused and not remembered it all or got mixed up about who said what. But no, they'd taken notes.

I tried a smile as I sat down opposite them at the table, but neither of them smiled back. It didn't bode well, so I decided to try Tactic Number Two: break the ice with a joke.

'So, you must have felt very proud when they all said I'm the school's star pupil. Top in maths, top in English, astounding at science . . . er, probably going to be prime minister.'

They didn't laugh.

'So,' Mum began, 'I think we need to talk, Becca.'

I decided to try Tactic Number Three: mental retreat and admit to nothing.

'Uh,' I said.

Dad looked encouragingly at me. 'It's OK, Becca, it wasn't *all* bad.'

'So what did they say?'

Mum shook her head. 'Well, it's interesting. They all seemed to say the same thing in different ways.' She looked at her notes. 'Mr Walker said, "lacks focus and is a bit of a dreamer". Mrs Jeffries said, "needs to develop staying power if she is to get anything but average". Mr Riley said that you need to focus as you could be good at a lot of things, but at the moment, you're more a jack of all trades, master of none. Mr Nash said you have a good brain and could be a high achiever if only you'd concentrate more.' She looked up. 'You see what I mean.'

I sat on my hands and looked at the carpet. 'Er . . .'

'Miss Segal said the same thing. "Has great potential but unless she knuckles down to some hard work, it's all going to drift by her."'

There wasn't anything I could say in my defence as I knew I hadn't been working as hard as I could. But, I mean, I'm only fourteen and it's ages before we have to do any important exams.

'Oh,' said Dad as he read one of the sheets of paper, 'and Miss Segal also said you could have been in the show at the end of term, in the chorus, but you didn't turn up for rehearsals. What was that all about? You told us you didn't get a part.'

'I didn't. Not the one I wanted anyway. I went for the part of Sandra Dee.'

I didn't want to tell them how awful it had been. I knew I could have been in the chorus with Lia, but I felt I couldn't join in and pretend I didn't care that I hadn't got the lead role. I couldn't handle seeing Jade swanning in every day, star of the show, and gloating because I was at the back in the chorus line.

I'd decided to ignore the whole thing and pretend that it hadn't happened. It hadn't been easy, though, as everywhere I went at school, it was *Grease* mania. And all my mates were up to their eyes in it. Cat and Lia were always busy rehearsing. Squidge insisted on videoing behind-the-scenes so that he had a story to tell about the production. And Mac – Mac who I was *supposed* to be going out with – didn't have a moment to spare now that he was painting scenery. I felt like I'd spent most of the term alone.

'Well, young lady . . .' Mum began.

I winced. I always knew I was going to get a lecture when she called me that. 'I think you need to change your attitude. Get down to some serious study.'

'Yes,' said Dad. 'Show them what you can do, Rebecca. You're a smart girl. Next term we want to see some good grades on your report and none of this dreamer nonsense.'

I had to bite my lip. Mum was always berating him for being a dreamer and I almost said, 'A dreamer like you then, Dad?' But I knew that it wouldn't have gone down very well and I didn't want to spark off an argument between them. Lately rows had been getting more and more frequent, always about the same thing. And secretly I was starting to get worried that they might split up like Mac's parents did.

When we had lived in Bristol about four years before, my dad had a proper job in advertising, then he was made redundant. Instead of getting another job, we moved down here where it's cheaper to live and his plan was to fulfil his life-long dream of writing a novel. His only sources of income were his savings and an allotment where he grows organic vegetables to supply to Cat's dad's shop. But his savings were running out and that was mainly what the arguing was about. Mum had become the main bread-winner, teaching English to foreign students in Plymouth and Dad spent his days tapping away at his computer. But so far, he hadn't had any success. He had a file of rejects from agents and publishers and Mum kept telling him he had to go out and get a 'proper' job. Dad kept saying that there weren't any jobs down here in advertising and anyway he wasn't ready to give up on being a writer yet. That's when Mum would call him a dreamer. I felt sorry for him in a way, as I knew his writing meant a lot to him.

'Becca, are you listening?' asked Mum.

I nodded. 'Yes, work harder. I will. I promise.'

I went straight upstairs to commiserate with Cat on the phone.

'They don't understand what it's like,' I said.

'I know,' said Cat. 'I mean, my report was OK except

hard enough at it. I *would* if it was any fun and he'd stop picking on me, but anyway, Dad has been going on and on about it and hasn't said anything about all the good stuff.'

'Yeah,' I said. 'My mum and dad didn't say anything about any of the good stuff either.' I didn't tell Cat that I didn't think there *had* been any good stuff.

'It's rotten, isn't it?' said Cat.

'Yeah, rotten. Have you spoken to Lia?'

'Yeah. Hers was OK. She said she reckons the teachers were going easy on her as she's the new girl.'

'Maybe. They probably think that if they're too tough on her she'll want to go back to her old school in London. She only started in September, so I guess they're giving her time to adjust. But she *is* clever. She probably always does well.'

'Yeah.'

'Yeah,' I said. 'Ready for tomorrow night?'

'Just about. Bit nervous. In fact, I don't think I'll get any sleep tonight, my stomach's in a knot. Tickets are sold out, apparently. Dad's coming, and Jen. Are your mum and dad coming?'

'Nah. They're economising as usual and weren't bothered about seeing the show as I wasn't in it.'

'You could have been.'

'Couldn't.'

'Could.'

'Couldn't, couldn't, couldn't. OK, 'night Cat. I'm going to call Mac now.'

'Hey, have you read about this competition?' he said before I could ask him about Parents' Evening.

'What competition?'

'It's in the paper. Apparently it's going to be nationwide, for all those who felt they missed out on the *X Factor*-type competitions.'

'Oh, not another,' I groaned. 'There are so many of them now. Every kids' programme on telly has a load of hopefuls of all ages trying to be the next superstar idol.'

'Yeah,' said Mac, 'but this new competition is for fourteen to sixteens. The entry age for those TV shows was over sixteen.'

'So what is it this time? Are they looking for a band or just one star>'

'A girl and a boy. A Pop Princess and a Pop Prince.'

'Oh well, good luck to them,' I said. 'I don't know why people put themselves through that sort of thing. Some of the judges on those programmes were ruthless. I felt really sorry for some of the contestants. How could they take it?'

'But look at what happens if you win,' countered Mac.

'Yeah, but I don't know if it's worth it. Sorry, better go. I need to wish Lia good luck.'

'Hi Lia. You all ready for the opening night tomorrow?'

'Yeah,' said Lia. 'Sort of. Mum and Dad are coming. And Ollie's coming down from London.'

'Really?' Ollie is Lia's divine elder brother. Cat and I both had a crush on him at the beginning of term but he was more interested in Cat at the time and I decided that 'reject' wasn't a role I wanted to play. And then I got together with Mac, so it was all cool in the end. Cat still sees Ollie when he's down from school but doesn't really know where she stands with him. She says she doesn't mind as she just came out of a long relationship with Squidge and doesn't want to get into anything serious just yet, but it's obvious that she really likes him.

'Does Cat know?'

'No. And don't tell her. She's nervous enough as it is and

if she knew Ollie was sitting there watching her, I think she'd die. Oh, I hope it all goes OK. I feel so nervous.'

Suddenly I felt glad I wasn't in the show. It would be much more enjoyable sitting in the audience watching everybody else sweat.

Show-Time

4

I MADE sure I was sitting behind Mr and Mrs Axford and Ollie at the show. I wanted to watch Ollie's reaction when Cat was on so that I could tell her about it afterwards. I knew she'd want all the details. Everyone was taking sneaky looks at Mr Axford, otherwise known as Zac Axford, from the famous rock band Hot Snax. With his long hair and leather jacket, he really stood out amid the straight dads dressed in Marks and Spencer's casuals. Mrs Axford looked fab as usual. She is stunning, with shoulder-length blonde hair, and even though the family is dead rich, she always dresses simply, in jeans and a T-shirt. It must be great having parents that cool.

As I sat waiting for the show to start, I felt conspicuous as the only person in school who wasn't involved in the production in some way. There were people from all years rushing about, acting important, ushering, fixing the lights, adjusting loudspeakers, selling programmes. The hall was packed with parents and friends and there was an excited buzz in the audience as the lights went down and the music to 'Love Is a Many Splendored Thing' struck up off stage. The curtain rose and there were Jade and Jonno, going into the first number on a beach set painted by Mac. After that, we were transported to Rydell High and I had to stop myself standing up and applauding when Cat came on as Rizzo. Ollie looked well impressed; in fact, everyone looked impressed when she started to sing. I felt a twinge of jealousy, just for a moment. I wished I'd worked harder to get a part; then everyone would be watching me with the same admiration. The feeling didn't last long, though, as I knew in private that it was my own fault that I didn't have a part.

As the show got going, I was pulled in and really began to enjoy it. Apart from one scene when Kimberley Coleman got her dance steps mixed up, it went without a hitch, and at the end, the audience gave them a standing ovation. It was only then that Cat caught sight of Ollie who was standing, cheering with the rest of them. She looked shocked for a minute and I was glad she hadn't seen him before as he might have put her off. But he gave her the thumbs-up and she grinned back at him.

After the curtain had gone down and people got up to leave, I went backstage. Of course Squidge was there film- ing away and Mac was busy carrying out bits of scenery.

'Brilliant, weren't they?' said Mac.

I nodded. 'And so was your scenery. It looked great.'

'Thanks.'

'And Cat and Lia were fab.'

'They were, weren't they?' said Mac. 'In fact, having seen her tonight, I'm going to tell Cat she should go in for that competition – you know, for Pop Princess. She's easily good enough. Jade's been on about it for days. Course she's already got plans to enter, but I think Cat should as well. She was great tonight. I reckon she could win.'

I waited for him to suggest that I went in for it as well, but the thought didn't seem to have occurred to him, and for a moment I felt miffed. Why didn't he think that I'd stand a chance?

'Hey Becca,' called Cat as she came out of the dressing room with the other girls.

I gave her a big hug. 'Well done! I was so proud of you.' Then I caught sight of Ollie coming towards us with a bunch of freesias. 'And I don't think I was the only one.'

Cat blushed when she saw Ollie, so I decided to make myself scarce for a moment and went to find Lia. I popped my head around the dressing room door and there was Jade, surrounded by her mates. She caught my eye and gave me one of her 'What are you doing here?' looks, but I decided to be generous. She *had* been good, after all, and I would be friends with her if she would just be a bit nicer.

'Fab show, Jade,' I said. 'Well done – you were really top.'

She looked like she was going to faint with shock. 'Oh,

right, thanks,' she stuttered.

I laughed to myself. I may have felt a bit jealous but I believe in giving credit where it's due.

'Thank God that's over,' laughed Lia, coming up behind me with Squidge in tow. 'Now we can all relax.'

'No,' said Squidge. 'I think we should move on. Today Torpoint, tomorrow the world.'

'What are you on about, Squidge?' I asked.

'We have to think big,' he said. 'So Becca, truth, dare, kiss or promise?'

'What, *now*?' I asked.

'Yeah. *Now*. Come on. Quick.'

'OK. Dare' I said.

'Good,' said Squidge. 'I was hoping you'd pick that one.'

'Lia, truth, dare, kiss or promise?'

'Promise,' she said.

He called over to Cat, who was deep in conversation with Ollie. 'Truth, dare, kiss or promise?' he asked.

She looked flirtily at Ollie. 'Dare.' She smiled up at him.

'Excellent.' Squidge grinned as he pulled a piece of newspaper out of his back pocket. 'I have *un grando* dare for Becca and Cat. You know this competition for Pop Prince and Pop Princess? Well I dare both of you . . .' He looked pointedly at me, '. . . and I mean, *both* of you, to go up for it. Lia, you picked promise, so you have to promise to go as well. Mac and I have already decided to give it a go. Auditions are in Plymouth next Saturday.'

You Got to Have a Dream 5

MUM BROUGHT the post in and put one of the envelopes in front of Dad.

'What's that?' He looked up, smiling, from his breakfast of toast and Marmite. 'Not another rejection, I hope.'

'No,' said Mum.

He scanned the letter. 'Oh.'

'Yes,' said Mum. 'The building insurance renewal. Three hundred and eighty pounds and it's due by the end of the month.'

I started to get up to go. I didn't want to witness another of their rows.

'We'll find a way,' said Dad.

Mum folded her arms in front of her. 'You mean *I'll* find a way. Where are you going to get that kind of money?'

As I was leaving, Dad glanced up at me with concern, then focused on his toast. I felt really sorry for him. He looked so helpless when she started on at him.

I crept upstairs to my bedroom and got out the newspaper cutting that Squidge had given me the night before.

'Are you the next best thing?' it said. *'Rocket Productions are looking for a new Pop Prince and Pop Princess. Auditions in Plymouth Town Hall on Saturday 14th and Sunday 15th December, 9 a.m. to 8 p.m. Come prepared with a song of your choice. Entry age: 14–16 years. Prize £5000 each for our Prince and Princess, and a recording deal to make a single.'*

I leaned back and closed my eyes. First, I imagined myself handing the cheque over to Mum and Dad. That should stop them rowing. All the press would want to know me, I'd be given a top makeover, my photo would be on the front of all the magazines. Everyone at school would be so jealous when my single went straight to number one. I'd win an award at the Grammys; in fact, I'd present an award with my new best friend Kylie Minogue. I'd be a stone thinner and wearing an amazing sparkly designer dress and shoes, my hair would be perfectly straight for a change and afterwards I'd go to an all celebrity party with Robbie and Eminem and Madonna. Ohmigod, I thought as I folded the paper away, here I go again. The teachers were right – I *am* a dreamer.

At that moment, Dad stuck his head round the door. 'You in there, Bec?' he said, then came in and sat at the end of my bed. 'What you up to?'

I showed him the newspaper cutting. 'We thought we might go in for it.'

Dad read the cutting. 'Who's we?'

'Me, Lia, Cat, Mac and Squidge. Squidge dared me. Squidge, Mac and Lia know that they won't really stand a chance because they can't sing, but Mac says it will be a laugh. Squidge wants to do it for experience, he said. You know what he's like, always going on about how a film director needs to have lots of different experiences in life.'

Dad laughed. 'And you and Cat? Reckon you're in with a chance?'

I shrugged. 'Dunno . . . Dad, do you think I'm a dreamer?'

'Well, your report –' he began.

'But what I mean is, is it a bad thing to be?'

Dad looked at me closely. 'Yes and no. Yes if it's affecting your schoolwork. It does help to know where you're going and to focus. But otherwise, no. Everything has its good and bad side, and the other side to being a dreamer is having an imagination and that's an excellent thing. No, I think you have to have a dream and you have to follow that dream.'

'Your dream is to get your novel published, isn't it?'

Dad nodded. 'It is but it can take years to become successful. I'm not going to give up.'

'Even though . . .'

'Even though,' said Dad, then patted my hand. 'Things aren't so bad, Becca. I've still got some savings left and I'm not going to let you or your mum down. Don't you worry. And one day, my work will land on the right desk. The main thing is you have to believe in yourself, even when it seems like nobody else does.'

'You mean Mum?'

'Mum believes in me in her own way. It's just . . . sometimes she doesn't show it. I know she worries when the bills come in . . . But enough about me. Let's talk about you. This competition. I think it's a great idea you go up for it. Squidge is right about having experiences, and not only if you want to be a film director. But you mustn't be disappointed if you don't get through. You mustn't take it personally. When I get those rejects from the publishers, of course I feel disappointed for a day or so, then I put the letter in the file with the others and send my stuff off to the next one. Success is fifty per cent talent and fifty per cent perseverance.'

'So I can go in for it?'

'Of course you can. In fact, I'll drive you over.' He grinned, then he began to sing, 'You got to have a dream. If you don't have a dream, how you gonna have a dream come true?'

I gave him a hug. 'I believe in your dream, Dad.'

Cat and Lia came over later in the afternoon to do some homework for social science. The week before we'd had a lecture from a visiting social worker who'd given us a lesson in political correctness and we were supposed to think of some terms that could be seen as offensive to some people and think of another way of phrasing it.

'This is too boring,' I said, putting down my pen, 'I can't think of anything. Why don't we go through my CD collection and decide what songs we'll do at the audition?'

I spread all my CDs on the floor and we sat down and began to sift through.

'I got Whitney, Mariah Carey, Janet Jackson, Atomic Kitten, Destiny's Child, All Saint's, Kylie . . .'

'Actually, I think I'd like to do "Hero" by Mariah Carey,' said Cat. 'I listened to it this morning and wrote out all the words.'

Lia picked up a Britney Spears CD. 'Maybe I could do "Baby One More Time".'

'Good idea,' I said.

'What about you, Bec?' asked Lia.

'Not sure yet,' I said, looking at the CDs. 'Maybe "Crazy For You" by Madonna or maybe an Anastacia number. Dunno.'

'How long do we actually get to perform?' asked Lia.

'Oh, only a couple of minutes, if that,' I said. 'They'll either like you or not.'

'They'll be able to tell with me in the first ten seconds.'

I looked at Lia with admiration. If I couldn't sing, you wouldn't catch me anywhere near the competition. She must be very secure, I thought, like she doesn't feel she has to prove anything. Then a thought flashed through my mind. So what am I trying to prove?

'I think you're amazing, Lia,' I said. 'Putting yourself up for this.'

'Not really,' she said. 'I mean, I know I don't stand a chance so I don't have any expectations – it'll be fun. But it will be harder for you and Cat because you do stand a chance.'

'I know. I'm feeling nervous already,' I said.

'You'll be great,' said Cat. 'You look good.'

'No, I don't!' I interrupted. 'I need to lose a ton of weight.'

Cat sighed. 'You're blind, Becca. You look perfect and you sing well. You should do a ballad, something to really show off your voice.'

She's such a good mate, Cat. We're going to be competing against each other and yet, here she is, being really encouraging. She's so supportive of her friends. Jade, on the other hand, has apparently been practising in secret for weeks. Mac told us that she knew about the competition before any of us and didn't mention it to anyone. He said that she's really miffed that we're all going in for it as she thought it was her special thing. What cheek. The competition's open to anyone.

'Most important, though,' said Lia, 'is what are we going to wear?'

'Yeah, course,' I said. 'There might be some decent boys there.'

'*Becca*,' said Cat. 'You have a boyfriend, remember? Mac?'

I grinned. 'No harm in looking.'

'Oh, don't say you've gone off him already,' said Cat.

'What do you mean?'

'Well, you know what you're like.'

'No, I don't know what I'm like. Tell me.'

The atmosphere in the room suddenly felt tense and I sensed I was being got at.

Cat looked at me anxiously. 'You know, with boys . . .'

'What are you saying, Cat?'

'Um, nothing . . . not really, just, er, well . . . OK what you *were* like before you met Mac. Always changing your mind, in love with a different boy each week.'

'I *never* was.'

'OK, what about Laurence Grant, Robin Barker, Phil . . . Ollie . . .'

I suddenly saw the funny side. 'D'oh. Oh yeah – Mark Jones, Dave McIntosh . . . Yeah, I suppose, but I never did anything with any of them, I never got off with them or anything, it was only in my head . . . oh no!'

'What?' said Lia.

'In my *head*.' I looked at both of them. 'Do you think I'm a dreamer? You know, like always fantasising and never doing anything about it?'

Cat gave me a hug. 'That's why we like you, Becca. You make life interesting with all your dreams and ideas. But you're not going to mess Mac around, are you?'

I shook my head. 'Nah, no, course not, but it's not as

though we're married or anything. I mean, we're having a nice time and that, but it's not like, well, what you and Squidge were like, Cat. I mean, you went out with him for years.'

'Yeah, like an old married couple we were,' said Cat, then she laughed. 'So what you're saying is, it's not that you're not into commitment, but rather you are monogamously challenged.'

I laughed. 'Yeah, that's brilliant,' I said, getting my homework out again. '*Now* I get what the social worker was on about. And I got one.' I put on my best snotty voice. 'One mustn't say, "stop nagging"; one ought to say, "stop being verbally repetitive", as it is less offensive.'

We all got our books out again and for the next ten minutes, there was no stopping us.

Lia giggled. 'You mustn't say drunk, you must say chemically inconvenienced,' she said. 'And you can't say male chauvinist pig, you have to say, a man with swine empathy.'

Cat cracked up. 'OK, here's some of mine. You can't say someone's a tart, rather you should say she's sexually focused. You can't say someone has big boobs, rather she is pectorally superior. Becca, you got any more?'

I nodded. 'Someone isn't bald, he's in follicle regression. A woman doesn't have a big tummy, she has developed a chocolate storage facility.'

'Excellent,' said Lia, putting her books away. 'That

should keep old Jeffries happy. Now back to more important things. What are we going to wear to Plymouth – glitzy or casual?'

I felt relieved. The atmosphere was light again.

Cat considered the question. 'Hmmm . . . I don't think we should dress up too much; it might look like we trying too hard.'

'And all the serious performers always turn up for auditions in working clothes,' said Lia, 'like leggings, torn T-shirts and scuffed trainers, to show that what's important to them is their art.'

'Oh yes, my art . . .' I laughed. 'Oh, luvvie darlings, tear me a T-shirt, will you? Then run out and get me an Evian. Evian mind, not Perrier, or any other brand. I *must* have my Evian.'

6   Pop Idol

'LOOK WHAT I got,' said Mac, waving a DVD at us when we arrived at Squidge's the next Friday after school. 'I nicked it from Jade's room when she wasn't looking.'

It was the New Talent DVD, a compilation of all the wannabe celebrity episodes that were on telly.

'Brilliant,' said Cat, following Squidge into his living room. 'Put it on.'

Wow, Jade's really been doing her homework, I thought as Mac put the DVD in the player and we settled down to watch. Hah, just you wait Jade Macey, because this time *I've* been practising too. I'd decided to do 'Not That Kind' by Anastacia and had gone over and over it until it was perfect. I wasn't going to let Saturday be a repeat of the *Grease* audition where I dried up. This time I'd be ready.

As the DVD started and we watched the crowds waiting to go in for their auditions, I felt a surge of excitement go through me. Tomorrow it would be us out there among the hopefuls.

'Ohmigod,' said Lia as the DVD progressed to showing the actual auditions. 'Are we really going to put ourselves through this?'

'We are,' said Mac, but he was starting to look a bit worried as well as we watched one of the judges tear to shreds yet another contestant's performance.

Squidge noticed and punched his arm. 'You're not going to bottle out now, are you, mate?'

'Um, no,' said Mac. 'Course not.'

Suddenly my heart sank. Someone on screen was singing 'Not That Kind'.

'But that's my song,' I said.

Not long later, another contestant sang Britney's 'Baby One More Time'.

'That's *my* song,' said Lia.

Then someone did 'Hero' and Cat cried, 'And that's my song!'

'You sound like the three bears out of "Goldilocks and the Three Bears",' laughed Mac. 'And the little bear said "and that's *my* porridge".'

As the DVD progressed, it got worse. A whole load of people did songs by Anastacia and one of the judges actually said that if anyone else did one by her, he would hit them.

'No wonder Jade didn't want to share this,' said Lia. 'She

asked me on Monday what songs we were doing, but when I told her she didn't say anything.'

Cat put her head in her hands. 'We've got to pick new songs, guys. Songs that haven't been done to death on other shows.'

'Oh no. How?' I said, looking at my watch. 'The competition's tomorrow.'

'Chill, you guys,' said Squidge. 'I don't reckon it matters. Whatever you choose, there's bound to be someone else doing it as well. It's whether you can impress the judges or not that counts. Want to see what I'm doing?'

I nodded and Squidge got up and went into an ear shattering, rocked up version of the Talking Heads number 'Psycho Killer'. What he lacked in vocals, he certainly made up for in enthusiasm and the rest of us split our sides laughing.

'I'm going to wear one of my dad's suits,' said Squidge, 'like David Byrne from the Talking Heads. What do you think?'

'Different,' said Cat.

'Don't give up the day job,' I said.

Squidge smiled. 'I won't. But look, it's going to be a laugh, an *experience*. If we take it seriously, then we won't enjoy it.'

'Right,' I said. But I was beginning to have doubts. The judges on TV had been ruthless in their criticisms and some of the contestants were in tears afterwards. And suddenly I didn't feel so confident about *anything* – my hair, my weight or my choice of song.

'At least this DVD has given us an idea of what to expect,' I ventured.

'Yeah,' said Mac. 'Assassination.'

'Yeah,' sighed Lia. 'But at least you and Cat can sing.'

'That doesn't seem to make much difference,' said Cat. 'Even some of the good ones got thrown out because the judge didn't like their face or clothes or something. I think Squidge is right. We go for a laugh – no expectations. That way there'll be no disappointments.'

'Right,' said Lia. 'So what are you going to do, Mac?'

He started tugging at the fly on his jeans. 'I got something to show you.'

'*Mac,*' said Cat as Mac started taking off his jeans, '*what* are you doing?'

Mac stripped off to his boxers then he turned round and bent over. On the back of his boxers, he'd written, 'Vote for Mac.'

We all cracked up.

'Are you honestly going to do that?' I said.

Mac nodded. 'Well, I know my voice isn't memorable, but my boxers will be.'

'But what song are you going to do?' asked Cat.

'"Hang the DJ" by the Smiths.'

'Don't know that one,' I said.

'The song's actually called "Panic", but the chorus goes,

"Hang the DJ, hang the DJ, hang the DJ . . ."' said Mac.

'But are you *sure* you want to do a song with those words? What if one of the judges is a DJ?'

Mac grinned. 'Then I'll have the sympathy of the contestants.'

'I think it's brilliant,' said Squidge.

'But what are *we* going to do now?' I asked, looking at Cat and Lia. 'Maybe I shouldn't go.'

'Oh come on, Becca, don't back out now,' said Squidge.

'But I don't know what to do now that I've seen that DVD. I spent *ages* practising my Anastacia song. But having seen what that judge said about wanting to hit the next person who sang one, I'll have to do something more original.'

'Not necessarily,' said Mac. 'They'll be different judges tomorrow, won't they?'

'God, I hope so,' said Cat. 'I don't think I could face that panel from TV.'

'Why learn a new song, Cat?' asked Squidge. 'Why don't you do Rizzo's song from *Grease*? It showed off your voice. You know it inside out, so if you get nervous, you probably won't forget the lines.'

Lia and I nodded.

Cat beamed. 'Good idea. You're right, I do know the words backwards and if I do it, I won't have to stay up half the night learning a new one. In fact, Lia, why don't you do one of the songs from *Grease*? Saves you all the hassle of learning something new as well.'

'Yeah and I could do the dance steps we learned at school. That way, I can at least show them that I can do *something*.'

'So that leaves you, Becca,' said Squidge. 'Fancy another go at "Hopelessly Devoted"?'

'My version didn't include the devoted part,' I said. 'It was just hopeless. So no way. Once was more than enough. No . . . Oh God, so what am I going to do?' I cast my mind over all the songs we'd done in our band. None of them seemed right for a solo. 'The only other song I know all the way through is "You've Got a Friend" by Carole King. I know it off by heart because my mum always plays it in the car whenever we go anywhere.'

'So let's hear it,' said Cat.

I stood up and took a deep breath. I felt really nervous. This is mad, I thought. I have to do it, but if I feel this bad with my mates, how on earth am I going to feel at the audition? Come on, Becca, I told myself. You can do it and it's only for a laugh. I took another breath, then launched into the song.

After I'd finished, I took a quick look at the others. They all had wide grins on their faces.

'You're really good, Becca,' said Cat. 'And your voice suits that song. I think you're in with a real chance, even more than if you did the Anastacia one.'

'Really?' I asked.

Mac nodded. 'Definitely. In fact, I can just see you going up to get your Golden Globe Award. The cameras will be flashing. You'll be in an off-the-shoulder Versace number, looking fab. I'll be somewhere in the crowd, trying to get your attention – "Becca, Becca, remember me? I knew you when you were nobody. Spare a moment for an old friend?"'

I laughed. 'No way, José. You'll be on my *arm*, my escort. And Cat will be going up to receive her award, just in front of me with Squidge and Lia.'

Maybe it was OK to have mad fantasies, I thought, as long as you didn't take them too seriously.

Round One 7

DAD DROPPED Lia, Cat and I off outside the hall in Plymouth, where already there was a long queue waiting for the doors to open.

'Knock 'em dead,' said Dad as we got out of the car. 'I'll go and do some jobs in town, so ring me on your mobile when you're ready to be picked up later this afternoon.'

'Right Dad,' I said as I scanned the queue. There were all sorts there – cute, glam, hippie, small, tall, fat, skinny . . . Some with their parents, a few boys with dreadlocks, a girl with pink hair, one with a shaven head and loads of earrings, lots of girls in tiny tops showing pierced navels even though the weather was freezing. Cat, Lia and I had come well prepared for a long wait in the cold, with jackets, scarves and gloves. I'd worn my black jeans, a black halter top under-neath my jacket and a black baseball cap that Dad had bought me with the word 'Princess' written on it in sequins. Lia had her baggy jeans on, a tiny top and a Mulberry handkerchief on her head. Cat was in faded jeans and an off-the-shoulder top. The boys had arrived already. Squidge looked like a star in his dad's suit and tie with black shades and Mac wore his jeans and Converse sneakers. I thought we looked pretty cool, not mad like some of the others.

'Fab cap,' said one of the girls as we joined the queue. 'I should have thought of that.'

'Thanks,' I said as I watched a tall black girl in front begin to do stretching exercises.

'Shall we make a run for it now or later?' asked Lia as a couple of girls in front burst into song and were absolutely pitch perfect.

'Later,' I said. Even though the size of the crowd was daunting, I felt excited, and now that we were there, I wanted to be part of it. It was hysterical – Squidge had borrowed a digi-cam to film everything and because he looked like an executive in his suit, everyone thought he was from the telly. Some girls were flirting openly with him and singing their songs for him. I guess they were hoping that they'd be put in a programme showing edited highlights later. Little did they know that they probably would, but the video would only be seen by an audience of five teenagers.

The doors opened at nine on the dot and the line slowly moved through the entrance. When we got inside, there were a number of people at tables taking our details as we filed past, then each of us was given a sticky label. The boys' labels had 'Pop Prince' written on them with a number, and the girls' had 'Pop Princess' and a number.

'Hi, I'm Tanya,' said a lady with red spiky hair when we reached the registration tables. 'Put the label on your top so that we can see it, and go into the hall down the corridor, on the right, then wait until your number is called.'

Once inside the hall, I forgot my nerves as there were so many people to look at. But then I caught sight of Jade and a couple of her mates from Year Ten and my heart sank.

'Oh *no*,' I said. 'Jade's got a cap on exactly like mine and she'll go in before me. Pants.'

'Stick your label over the sequinned princess on your cap,' Cat suggested. 'Then it won't look the same, and yours will say "Pop Princess" not just "Princess".'

'Good idea,' I said and took the label off my top. Loads of other people had done similar things. Some had stuck their labels on their trousers or on their abdomens and one guy had even stuck his on his forehead.

As we settled ourselves in a corner on the floor, Tanya came in and called for the first fifty to go and wait in a corridor outside the audition room.

'We're in for a long wait,' said Mac, pointing at his number. He was Number 223, Squidge was 224, Cat was 225, Lia was 226 and I was 227. 'Did anyone bring anything to eat?'

I shook my head. I hadn't even thought about food and suddenly I realised that I was starving. All around us people were eating sandwiches and crisps and my stomach started gurgling.

'Ohmigod,' I said. 'If I can't remember the words of my song, my stomach will sing it for me.'

I quickly forgot about my hunger when the hall started buzzing as the first person came out of the audition. He was followed by another then another, then another. News of the judges spread through the hall like a Mexican wave.

'There's three judges,' said Cat, after she'd eavesdropped on a couple of boys by a radiator. 'Two blokes and one woman.'

'And one of them is a DJ from a London radio station,' said Mac, coming back in from the loo. 'Eek. He's gonna love my song.'

I was beginning to get butterflies as we continued to wait. A few people came back in, or rather leapt in, telling people that they'd got through. Others looked downcast and disappointed and came back shaking their heads, or in tears.

'Oh God,' I said to Cat. 'People are crying already. I can feel my stomach tightening into a knot. I'm so nervous.'

'I know,' said Cat. 'And I have to go to the loo *again*.'

'We'll come with you,' Lia and I chorused.

As we set off for the loo for the third time that morning, it was amazing to witness all the mini-dramas unfolding in the corridors. One girl was weeping on her mum's shoulder, another guy was mouthing off about one of the judges, loads of people were doing warm-up exercises, some were practising their songs. Even in the loos, girls were leaning on the sinks singing into the mirrors.

On our way back to the hall, I noticed Jade dancing about with a mate.

'Looks like Jade's through,' I said to Lia.

'I thought she would be,' Lia replied. 'She may be a top bitch, but she can sing.'

Eleven o'clock went by, twelve o'clock, one o'clock . . . Then, thank God, a couple of lads appeared and set up a table selling sandwiches and juices. As we lined up to buy something, we started chatting with some of the other contestants and it became apparent that some of them were taking it deadly seriously. There was a group from a drama school in Bristol and they clearly saw the competition as their big chance to break into show business.

'There's some real talent here,' said Cat as one girl in the line rehearsed 'Killing Me Softly'.

'I know,' I said. 'Some of them are . . . like, really professional. I was chatting to one girl over there and she's been singing since she was five, in shows and stuff.'

'And everyone's talking about the latest wannabe pop star programmes,' said Mac, 'and wondering if one of the judges is going to be nasty.'

'Bound to be,' said Squidge. 'If they film any of this, it makes better telly if there's a bad guy and some tears. Then you get everyone reacting to him and what he says. That nasty judge is probably a nice bloke, really, but that was the part he had to play.'

'Do you think?' I asked. 'I thought he was just plain horrible and so insulting sometimes. He destroyed some contestants.'

'It all makes good telly,' said Squidge. 'And see? It worked. It got everyone talking about the show.'

'I guess,' I said, but I hoped there wouldn't be a judge like that on our panel.

Mid-afternoon, Tanya came back in. 'Two hundred to two hundred and fifty,' she called. 'If you could go and wait in the corridor.'

'*Aargghhh*, that's us,' said Lia. 'Whose stupid idea was this anyway? What am I doing here? I must be mad.'

'You'll be fine,' I said. 'And you look great.' Secretly, though, I felt the same – I must be insane to put myself through this.

Even Squidge looked a bit nervous. 'It's a laugh, it's a laugh, it's a laugh,' he chanted as we trooped out with the others.

Once in the corridor, we sat down on the chairs lining the walls and waited.

'I'm not being bitchy,' whispered Cat as a skinny-looking boy with round shoulders and bad spots got up to go into the audition room, 'but you can tell just by looking at some people that they're not going to get through.'

'I know,' I said. 'Poor guy. He looks terrified.'

'Well, good on him for trying,' said Squidge. 'But in the end, I guess they're going to want a Pop Prince or Princess to look the part as well as be able to sing.'

'That's me out as well, then,' I said.

Squidge punched my arm. 'Do you have one of those fairground mirrors at home? – the ones that distort your image? Because you just don't see it, do you? You look fab!'

I didn't feel fab, but it was nice to hear it anyway.

Along with the others waiting in the corridor, we strained to hear the skinny boy's performance. He was completely flat and came out only moments later, shaking his head.

'How was it?' Lia asked as he walked past us.

'Nightmare,' he said. 'They said it was the worst audition they'd ever heard.'

Lia smiled at him. 'Ah well, they haven't heard me yet, have they?'

Some went in and sounded fantastic, and others were like the skinny boy and sounded awful. One girl came out in floods of tears.

'I couldn't remember the words,' she sobbed. 'It was awful with all them sitting there staring at me.'

'That happened to me once,' I said. 'You'll get another chance some other time.'

'Do you think?' she said hopefully.

'Sure,' I said.

Then we got chatting to a guy who looked like a real laugh. He was wearing a grass skirt and a Hawaiian shirt.

'I can't sing,' he said, 'so I'm going to do an instrumental version of "Hawaii Five-O".'

'Can I film you?' asked Squidge.

'Yeah,' he said and went into his routine, complete with Hawaiian dancing. 'Da da da da daaah da, da da da da.'

We all fell about laughing and Tanya came out and told Squidge to put away his camera, then told the rest of us to 'pipe down'. Hawaiian boy made faces behind her back and it was good to know that there was at least one person there who wasn't treating the situation like it was life or death.

Tanya reappeared moments later and looked up and down the corridor.

'Two hundred and twenty-three,' she called.

'Oh God, that's me,' said Mac. He went white and stood up, looking as though he was going off to see the dentist for some very nasty root work. After the door closed behind him, we all shot over to the door and strained to hear. We heard him say something, then could just about make out the words 'Hang the DJ'. He was back out in a flash.

'Phew,' he said. 'Don't remind me to do that again in a hurry.'

'Two hundred and twenty-four,' called Tanya, and Squidge got up to go in.

'How was it?' I asked as Mac slumped down on the floor next to us.

'They just look at you,' he said. 'No expression. No nothing.'

'What did they say?' asked Lia.

'They asked why I saw myself as the next Pop Prince.'

'What did you say?' I asked.

He grinned. 'Because I have blue blood. They didn't laugh, though. Then the woman said, "Do you realise that you can't sing?"'

'What did you say?' I asked.

'I said yes, but that one ought to be positive in life,' said Mac. 'Then they did smile and one of the blokes said, "Well sorry, mate, this isn't your competition and we won't be asking you to London."'

'You should have said that saying you can't sing is offensive,' I said. '"Vocally challenged" would be much more sensitive.'

'Did you show them your boxers?' asked Cat.

Mac shook his head. 'Nah, bottled out. You'll see what it's like when you get in there. I couldn't do it.'

Squidge came out a moment later. He was grinning from ear to ear.

'Two hundred and twenty-five,' called Tanya, and Cat got up to go.

'Eep,' she said.

'You'll be fine,' I said, squeezing her arm as she went past. 'Remember to breathe.'

'Oh yeah,' said Cat and took a deep breath.

'Are you in?' I asked Squidge as Cat disappeared behind the door.

'Nah,' he said. 'But they said I may have a good career ahead of me, frightening young children.'

As he reached into his rucksack to get his camera, I stuck my ear to the door to hear Cat. She was singing the opening bars of Rizzo's number and sounded really good, confident. Then it went quiet then I could hear them talking. Oh, please don't let them say anything horrible to her, I prayed.

She came out a moment later with Tanya.

'Two hundred and twenty-six,' said Tanya as Cat grinned at me from behind her and gave me the thumbs-up.

'You're in?' I whispered to Cat as Lia got up to go with Tanya.

She nodded, still grinning. 'Yeah,' she said. 'Good luck, Lia.'

Poor Lia. She sang "Summer Loving", but stopped after a few lines. Then all we could hear was the murmur of voices.

She was back out a moment later, shaking her head. She didn't look too freaked, though, just relieved that it was over.

'Two hundred and twenty-seven,' called Tanya.

'You're on, kid,' said Squidge as he pointed his camera at me.

Oh God, I thought, as I followed Tanya into the room. This is it.

The room was smaller than I expected, like a conference

room in a hotel. The three judges were sitting at one end, behind a table with glasses and bottles of water on it. The woman looked in her thirties – pretty, with short dark hair. One of the men was plump and looked older, maybe as old as fifty – balding, with mousy hair. The other man was dark, with glasses, and good-looking in a Tom Cruise kind of way. They were talking amongst themselves and one of them said something that made the other two laugh. I stood at the door, wondering what to do. My hands were sweating and I felt numb, like time was standing still.

The woman finally looked over at me and gave me a friendly smile. 'Well, come in,' she said, pointing to the floor about six feet away from their table, 'and stand on the circle.'

In the middle of the floor, there was a white circle, so I walked over to it and stood there, trying to stop my knees from shaking.

'Shall I begin?' I asked.

'First, tell us your name,' said the older man.

'Becca Howard,' I said.

'Where are you from?'

'St Antony, Cornwall.'

'Ah, come with your mates, have you?' said the woman, looking at her notes. 'The last four?'

I nodded.

'Age?'

'Fourteen.'

'And why do you think you might be our Pop Princess, Becca?'

The words 'because it's my dream' were out before I could think about it.

'OK, then, away you go,' said the woman.

Imagine you're in the car with Mum, I thought as I took a deep breath and started: 'When you're down and troubled . . .'

Halfway through the song, the older man held up his hand. 'OK, that's enough.' He then turned to his companions and said something.

Prepare to die, I told myself as all the awful things the judges had said to the contestants on every wannabe pop star programme ever shown flashed through my mind – 'You're no singer', 'You think you're a Ferrari when actually you're a Skoda', 'You're an insult to the song' . . .

'OK, I'll start,' said the woman to the other two judges. 'Yeah, good. I think you were a bit nervous in the beginning, but that's understandable. But you got going and your voice has a nice throaty quality. So, yes. A yes from me. Martin, what did you think?'

The older man looked me up and down and nodded. 'Hmmm,' he said. 'Not sure. We're looking for star quality here. The X-factor, something that hits you the minute the person walks through the door. Not sure that's you, Becca. You looked more like a timid mouse when you first came in, not a confident pop star, so I'm afraid it's a no from me.'

He turned to the last judge. 'Looks like you have the deciding vote, Paul.'

'I think it was a good choice of song for your voice,' he said, 'and I think you did it justice. We're looking for genuine talent here and no doubt, you can sing. Confidence? Well, that can always be worked on so, yes, I'd like to give you another chance.'

I think I felt my jaw drop, and I stood there for a minute gawping at them.

'OK then, out-voted,' said Martin, with a grin at me. 'So, you can go now, Becca, and you're through to the next round.'

I wanted to rush forward and hug them all. 'Thank you, thanks, thank you . . .'

I stumbled out into the corridor where the rest of the gang were waiting expectantly.

'I'm *through*!' I cried. 'I can't *believe* it. I'm through and they were so nice.'

Cat gave me a huge hug and we jumped up and down on the spot. Then Mac, Squidge and Lia put their arms around us and we jumped about in a circle.

'Knew you would be,' said Mac.

'Arghhh,' said Cat.

'I know!' I replied. '*Arrrghhhhhh.*'

8

Roller-Coaster Ride

MR WALKER, our English teacher at school, says that life is a roller coaster – up, down and round and round we go. I sat in my bedroom thinking about it later that day. Down I'd gone with the audition at school for Sandra Dee in *Grease*, then up, up, up, I'd gone today in Plymouth. It was one of the best feelings in the world to be picked. I'd remember it forever. I was through to the next round! Only a hundred people were chosen from four cities to go up to London the following Saturday and I was one of them. It had been totally top. Cat was over the moon too, and Lia also got her moment, even though she wasn't through for the next audition. The telly crew had turned up in the corridor when I was auditioning and made a beeline for her. They interviewed her for the programme they're doing on the competition, then filmed all of us jumping up and down when I came out after my go.

Dad was thrilled when he came to pick us up, genuinely

chuffed. But then we got home and I told Mum.

'No,' she said and turned away to put the kettle on.

'But *Mum*,' I pleaded, 'this is the chance of a lifetime. I *can't* not go.'

Mum turned back and looked uncomfortable. 'Look, Becca, don't get me wrong. I'm really happy that you had a good time today . . .'

'It wasn't exactly a good time,' I objected. 'Well, it *was* in the end – it was brilliant – but God, if you'd been there when we were all waiting . . . it was *nerve*-wracking. Much worse than waiting for exam results.'

'I know,' said Dad. 'It took a lot of guts to do what you did today. I'm really proud of you.'

'So why can't I go to London, then?'

Mum sighed. 'A number of reasons, Becca. One: this wanting to be a pop star has just come out of the blue –'

'No, it hasn't. You *know* it hasn't. I've always wanted to sing. What about my band with Cat – Diamond Heart?'

'You abandoned that weeks ago. And you know what you're like, Becca. In the summer you wanted to be a vet, last month it was an air hostess, before that a TV presenter. If I thought you were serious about any of it, you know you'd have my full support.'

'But I *am* serious about this. I really am. You *have* to believe me. Before I didn't know what I wanted to do and that's why I could never make up my mind. But I know now. Oh please, Mum, I have to go.'

'Chances like this don't come round often, Meg,' said Dad. 'A great experience, even if nothing comes of it.'

Mum got up from the table and started stacking dishes irritably, then she turned to us. 'It's not fair. Why do I have to be the bad guy in all of this? Always the one who says no. Honestly, Joe, you know the real reason.'

'What?' I asked.

Mum looked at Dad. 'London!' she said. 'And where do you think she's going to stay? How do you think she's going to get there? These kinds of trips cost money, never mind some kind of chaperone. I can't take time off and you can't go, Joe.'

'But it's at the weekend.' I looked pleadingly at Dad, but he had his defeated look on. Money. Same old story. He didn't have a leg to stand on.

'You'd have to go up on the Friday. You'd need money for travel,' said Mum wearily. 'Money for a place to stay. Money for food.'

Oh, not this again, I thought. How I wished I'd done a paper round, like Squidge and Cat did. Then I could have saved some of my own money. Maybe it wasn't too late.

'I'll get a job,' I said.

'Be practical, Becca,' said Mum. 'London's next Saturday. I don't think any job would earn you enough in that time. I said no, Becca, and that's my final word on the subject. You had a good time today. Enjoy that, then put it behind you. It's not as though you were really serious about it before today anyway. You were only going into it

224

because of a dare as I remember. A laugh, you told us.'

'But today's changed everything,' I said, getting up to leave. 'And I worked hard on that song. You just don't understand, do you?'

Neither of them said anything.

'Thanks for the support,' I said and stomped off.

Upstairs I rang Cat. She sounded down as well.

'My dad says I can't go,' she said. 'No money and he can't leave the shop, blah, blah, won't let me go alone, blah, blah.'

'Tell me about it,' I said. 'I've just had the "and that's my final word on the subject" talk downstairs.'

'It's not fair, is it?'

'No, it really stinks. Haven't you got *any* money, Cat?'

'Thirty quid and that's really for getting Christmas presents.'

'We could do the lottery.'

'I guess,' said Cat. 'I feel really rotten. Today was so great and now, it's like a huge anti-climax.'

'I know what you mean. Like being given something really fab then told to give it back.'

'I know,' said Cat. 'Life sucks. I think I need chocolate.'

'Yeah, me too. Still at least we break up on Thursday.'

'I guess,' said Cat.

'I guess,' I said. 'Christmas.' But even the thought of that didn't cheer me up.

* * *

225

The next morning, I grabbed my bike and headed out before the Miseries came down to ruin my life some more. I'd arranged to meet Cat and go to Lia's where at least we could commiserate in style. Lia's house is so fab and posh, it's like a fancy hotel. It has its own grounds, tennis courts and a swimming pool. Amazingly, Lia isn't spoiled or stuck-up at all about being so well off and her mum always makes Cat and me feel really welcome. I love going there, so it was just the job for today.

On the way, I couldn't help thinking what it would be like if I could go for the next round. It occurred to me that all the big stars had to start somewhere; that they were all ordinary people once, but they made it happen. Like Dad always says, because they kept trying. I bet they had obstacles to overcome, I thought as I peddled furiously up a hill.

Cat was waiting for me at the top and we rode the rest of the way together.

'You know what, Cat?' I said after we were let in the gates, as we were cycling up the long drive to the house.

'What?'

'I think we should practise new songs for the auditions anyway.'

'Why?' she asked. 'What's the point?'

'We shouldn't give up. We'll pray for a miracle. You never know what might happen. My dad's always saying that when he gets a rejection for his novel – it's not over until it's over and you must never give up. Like we were watching the World Cup once when my grandad was at our house – I can't remember who was playing – and it looked like one team had won. Then it went into extra time and in the very last ten seconds, the losing team scored a goal. Grandad was really fed up because he missed it. He thought his team had lost, so got up to make a cup of tea. He'd missed the best moment in the whole match.'

'Yeah, I see what you're saying,' said Cat, 'but . . .'

'No buts,' I said, 'and that's my final word on the subject.'

'Oo, er, get *her*,' said Cat. But I'd got her smiling again.

Lia was waiting for us at the top of the drive and waved when she saw us.

'I've had a brill idea,' she said, beaming at us.

'So have I,' I said as Cat and I leaned our bikes against the wall and followed Lia inside.

'Come upstairs and I'll tell you mine,' she said.

We bounded up the stairs two at a time and into her gorgeous princess's bedroom – enormous, with a bay window that has a seat in it so you can sit and look out over the fields to the sea down below, and a huge bed with a turquoise canopy.

'OK, you first,' she said as she flopped on the bed and Cat and I sat in the window seat.

'Well, I think Cat and I should learn a song anyway,' I

said, 'even though Cat's dad and my stupid parents have said we can't go. Then we pray for a miracle. I don't know what, but you never know. Something might turn up, even if we have to hitch-hike and sleep on the street.'

Lia grinned at us. 'I may have your miracle. I was thinking about it this morning after you phoned. No place to stay, you said. Then I thought, of course – my sister Star.'

Cat and I looked at each other and smiled. Star is Lia's elder sister. Star's a model in London. She has a *flat* in London.

'You could stay with her,' said Lia. 'I'm sure she wouldn't mind.'

I leaped off my seat and gave Lia a hug. 'Oh, do you think she'd let us? God, that would be so fab. I bet she lives somewhere amazing.'

'She lives in Notting Hill Gate. It is pretty good there,' said Lia. 'I could phone her, but first I'd better tell Mum, even though I'm sure she'll agree. I told her all about your parents saying you couldn't go and she felt really sorry for you.'

The roller-coaster ride suddenly changed direction and my hopes soared. 'Ohmigod, Cat, maybe we can go after all.'

Lia got up. 'I'll go and ask Mum, then I'll be right back and we can phone Star. OK?'

'OK,' we chorused as she left the room.

Cat and I had a look through Lia's CD collection while she was gone.

'I think I'd like to do the Britney Spears song,' I said. 'You know, the one she sings in the movie *Crossroads*, "I'm Not a Girl, Not Yet a Woman".'

'Oh, good choice,' said Cat. 'I think I'd like to do Atomic Kitten, "Whole Again". I know a few people did it yesterday, but I don't think that matters, does it?'

'Nah. I lost count of the number of people who did "Rock DJ" or Kylie's "Spinning Around".'

The door opened as we were engrossed in the CDs. We looked up expectantly, but Lia shook her head.

'I'm so sorry, guys; I didn't know. Apparently Star's going to Bermuda for Christmas with some new bloke she's met and she's already said a couple of her friends can have the flat. I'm so sorry.'

Down, down, down, my spirits sank. But then I had a flash of inspiration.

'Mac!' I said.

'Mac what?' asked Cat.

'*Mac*. Why didn't I think of it before? His dad lives in London, doesn't he?'

'Course! Let's ring him,' said Cat. Then her face dropped. 'Oh, but there's Jade. Jade's bound to be staying there, isn't she? She's not going to want us along.'

'Yeah,' I said, 'But Mac's my *boyfriend*. Let's phone and see what he says.'

Lia picked up the phone, dialled and asked for Mac.

'Not there,' she said as she put the phone down.

'Oh no,' said Cat. 'I can't stand this suspense. Where is he? Bec, haven't you got his mobile number?'

But I was already on the phone and this time I got through and explained our idea.

'I was about to ring you,' he said. 'Mum's driving us up on Friday – Jade for the competition and me to spend some time with Dad before Christmas. I was going to tell you so that we could meet up or I could come to the audition with you. Let me ask Dad if you can stay.'

'What about Jade?' I asked.

'Oh, stuff her,' said Mac. 'I'm sick of her at the moment. She's obsessed with this competition and in a really bad mood all the time. I don't care what she thinks. It's if Dad says yes or no that counts.'

He hung up then called back a few minutes later. 'The man from Del Monte says yes,' he said. 'Pack your bags.'

'Mac, you are *top*,' I said. 'Now all I've got to do is persuade the Miseries.'

Practice Makes Perfect

9

'LET ME GO and have a quick word with your mother,' said Dad, after I'd explained the plan, the minute I got home. 'You wait here.'

We were sitting in his study and I could see he was weakening. 'Make sure you tell her *exactly*, Dad,' I said. 'Mac's mum said that Cat and I could have a lift up with them, so *no* travel expenses, and we could stay at Mac's so *no* accommodation to pay for. All I need is a bit of pocket money for the tube and, as for food, I'll starve. It's only two days. I can do it. And Cat's dad has already said that she could go as long as I was going as well and I can't let her down, not now. OK? Make *sure* you say that Cat's dad has said yes.'

'Don't worry,' said Dad, getting up from his chair. 'I think I've got it all.'

As I waited for Dad to come back from talking to Mum, I had a mooch round the study. Everything I saw echoed the way I was feeling. Dad had reminders on sticky notes on his walls to inspire him. One was by a bloke called Hannibal: 'We will either find a way, or make one,' it said. That's right, Hannibal my man, I thought. My sentiments exactly. Another said, 'The darkest hour is just before dawn.' Too true. 'No failure except in not trying,' said another. I was beginning to feel more and more fired up as I read them.

Dad came back a few minutes later and smiled when he saw me reading the notes.

'There's some really good quotes here, Dad,' I said.

'I know. Some days I need all the inspiration I can get.' He walked over to his desk. 'This is one of my favourites. It's by Robert Browning: "A man's reach must exceed his grasp. Else what's a heaven for?"'

'Exactly. You got to have a dream. So? What did Mum say?'

Dad sat at his desk. 'She'll be here in a moment. I'll let her tell you.'

I tried to read his face for signs of the verdict, but he wasn't giving anything away. Oh please, *please* let her say yes, I prayed, as Dad rummaged in his drawer and pulled out a sheet of paper.

'Look at these,' he said. 'It's a list of novels that were rejected by publishers. *Day of the Jackal, Tess of the D'Urbervilles, Catch 22, Animal Farm, Lord of the Flies, Wind in the Willows . . .*'

'*Wind in the Willows?*' I asked. 'But we did that at junior school and Mac is doing *Lord of the Flies* in English.'

'Exactly,' said Dad. 'I keep this list to remind myself that even writers who have become household names had their fair share of rejections. But they persevered and got accepted in the end. Even *Harry Potter* was rejected by publishers at first.'

'I think you're amazing, Dad,' I said. 'You've had so many rejections and you still keep at it.'

'Well, believe me – there are days when I feel like packing it all in, but, well, what I wanted to say, Becca, is that you have to believe in yourself. There's a lot of competition out there, there can be a lot of obstacles to overcome on the way.'

Oh dear, I thought. Is he trying to tell me that Mum's going to be an obstacle?

At that moment, the door opened and Mum came in to join us. I looked up at her hopefully. 'So? Can I go?'

'If it really means so much to you, Becca,' she said, 'yes, you can go. But you mustn't be disappointed if nothing comes of it. I'd hate you to get all your hopes up then be let down.'

I ran over to her gave her a huge hug. 'Oh *top*, Mum. Thanks, thanks so much.'

She smiled then got out her purse. 'We've been having a chat, your dad and I, and we've got something to put to you. It's your choice, but, well, it's Christmas soon and of course we've put a bit aside to get your presents. If you like you can have the cash to take with you up to London. But it will mean no presents on the day.'

'Oh *fantastic*. No, Mum, Dad, this is the *best* Christmas present in the world. This is what I want more than anything. And it means I won't have to starve.'

Mum laughed. 'We'd never let you starve, Becca. Don't be daft.'

The rest of the week was brilliant. It felt as if my whole life had gone up a gear. I felt really alive. On Tuesday, Cat and I both got letters confirming our places in the next round and asking us to bring casual clothes and be prepared to stay in London if we were picked for the third round on Sunday. At school, everyone was talking about the competition and when news got out that three of us had got through, we were treated like celebrities. People whispered when we walked past and one girl from Year Seven even asked for my autograph. Of course Jade was a bit sniffy with us and kept to herself. Shame, because if she'd only been a bit friendlier, Cat and I would have been as supportive of her as we were of each other. Part of it all being so fantastic was sharing it with Cat.

Cat and I practised at every available moment. I'd never worked so hard at anything in my life – sometimes at her house, sometimes at mine, sometimes at Lia's. And Mac and Squidge came over to watch and lend their support.

'So what happens on Saturday?' asked Squidge as he filmed us rehearsing in Lia's bedroom.

'Don't know exactly,' I said. 'We've just been asked to come prepared with another song.'

'But are they going to get the numbers down again?' he asked. 'How many get through this time?'

'I think it's down to fifty next,' said Cat. 'Twenty-five boys and twenty-five girls. Oh, I wish you could come as well, Squidge.'

Squidge shrugged and pointed at Mac. 'Ah well, I have my man here to report back, and besides, that Tanya told me I had to stop filming when the real TV crews arrived last week so I couldn't have done much anyway.'

'I wish I was coming as well,' said Lia, 'but Mum wants me here to help her get ready for Christmas. Maybe next time.'

'Next time?' I asked.

'Yeah, dummy,' she said. 'You don't think it's all going to stop this weekend, do you? What about the next round?'

I hadn't thought about that. I'd been so focused on this weekend, I hadn't thought about what would come after that. I'd better be careful with my Christmas money, I thought. I may need it to stretch to two weekends.

'Ohmigod. What if one of us actually won? What if we do get through into the final rounds?' I asked Cat.

'I know,' she said. 'It's so exciting isn't it? Today Torpoint, tomorrow . . .'

'The world,' said Squidge, grinning.

'Let's look up what your horoscope says on the Net,' said Lia. 'There's a brilliant site my sister told me about. Maybe it will tell us if you're going to win or not.'

'Brill,' said Cat. 'Switch your computer on.'

A few minutes later, Lia had printed off our horoscopes. Aries for Cat and Pisces for me. Cat and I quickly read the sheets of paper Lia handed us.

'Ohmigod,' said Cat, 'December twenty-first . . . Does it say anything on yours, Becca? Mine says there's a new moon on that day and that can signify the start of a new chapter. Then it says that Aries is the sign of individuality and I should be ready to shine. I'll be getting attention from some 'higher-ups'. That probably means the judges, don't you think? It doesn't say if they're going to like me or not, though. What does yours say, Bec?'

'Same. The twenty-first is a star-studded day and time of new beginning. Oh, and Venus is conjunct with the moon, meaning romance is in the air for those who are single. A meeting with new friends . . .'

'Hmm,' said Mac, 'don't like the sound of that. Maybe it's a good job I'm coming along to keep an eye on you.'

I went over to Lia's window seat where he was sitting and put my arm around him. 'Not worried about me running off with Robbie Williams, are you now?'

Mac took my hand. 'Nah, course not. He's way too old for you.'

I laughed and went back to my horoscope. It did sound promising and I had to admit to myself that there had been some very cute boys at the last audition. It would be nice to at least get talking to some of them and I hoped Mac wasn't going to hold me back from getting to know them by being possessive or jealous or anything. No harm in making a few new friends, I told myself.

'Well, bring a few of those boys home for me,' said Lia. 'I could do with a bit of romance.'

'No prob,' I said. I noticed that Cat wasn't saying anything. I was sure she wanted to meet new people as well, as things with Ollie weren't serious, and besides, he'd gone skiing with a bunch of mates for the Christmas holidays. But I guessed that she was being sensitive to Squidge as they'd only broken up recently. Even though they were both cool about it, she probably didn't want to hurt his feelings by being too eager about other boys.

After we'd run through our numbers a couple of times, Lia's dad popped his head around the door.

'Hey,' he said, 'sounds good. Lia's been telling me all about the competition. Want to show me what you're going to do?'

At first, I didn't want to. I mean, he's not just any dad — he's Zac Axford, rock singer extraordinaire. Then I thought, No, if anyone can give us a few tips, it's him. So I nodded. 'If you can give us advice, that would be great.'

I went first and Cat and Lia clapped afterwards.

'Good,' said Zac. 'Yeah, you have a good voice, Becca. OK, a few tips: posture – you look terrified. Stand up straight, but try and relax. You were standing too rigidly there. Loosen up – don't hold your arms so tight to your sides, and bend your knees a little.'

'I think I look rigid because I'm trying to stop my knees from shaking,' I said. 'It was awful in the first round.'

'Ah, classic case of jelly knees,' Zac said, smiling. 'We all get it when we start out. OK, I want you to sing the song again, but this time, I *want* you to shake. Shake on purpose. Sing the song and tremble, shake your arms . . .'

I started singing and did as he told me.

'Good,' he said, 'let those legs wobble and tremble, give in to it. Come on, really get into it, shake, shake, *shake* . . .'

I continued singing and shaking, and in the end, I couldn't help laughing as well.

'OK, good,' he said. 'Now do it again. This time without the exaggerated shaking.'

I did the song again and it did feel better – more relaxed, and my knees seemed to behave themselves this time.

'Good,' he said when I'd finished. 'See, what you resist, persists. Don't resist it. Before you go in on Saturday, have a good shake and tremble. Let rip, wibble wobble like mad. Shake it all out of your arms, your hands, your legs. That way, you'll get it out of your system.'

Cat sang next and he had some good advice for her as

well. 'OK, Cat, you sing well too,' he said. 'But try and put a bit more emotion into the words. Really think about what you're singing. Feel it.'

By the time, he'd finished with us, we both felt way better. Loads more confident.

'This time, I feel ready,' I said to Cat as we cycled home together. 'I can't wait.'

10 Moaning Minnie

TALK ABOUT sulky! Jade insisted on going in the front on the way up to London. Mrs Macey wanted Mac to go in the passenger seat, because he was the tallest and needed the leg room, but he said he didn't care. So Mac, Cat and I had to squash into the back seat. Then Jade hardly said a word the whole way, except to complain.

'Could we open a window? It's too hot.'

'Could we close the window? It's too cold.'

'I'm hungry.'

'I'm thirsty.'

'I need a wee.'

We didn't mind too much, though, as we had a really good laugh in the back, singing daft songs at the top of our voices. I felt great. Term was over and we were off to the big city.

'Do you mind?' said Jade at one point when we were singing our own version of 'Reach for the Sky' in Scottish accents. 'Some of us are taking this competition seriously. I can't think with you lot caterwauling in the back.'

Mac made a face at the back of her head and began to sing his version of 'Hang the DJ' in an Indian accent.

'Mum, *Mum*, tell them, will you?' Jade whined to her mother.

'Keep it down,' said Mrs Macey, but I could see in the car mirror that she was smiling.

We tried to be quiet for a bit after that, then Cat got a fit of giggles which started me off, then Mac.

'*Mac*,' moaned Jade.

'Oh shut it, prissy-pants,' said Mac.

'Nappy-bucket,' said Jade.

'Marsupial,' said Mac. 'Moaning Minnie.'

'Mac, cut it out,' said Mrs Macey.

'But *Mum*, she started it,' Mac objected.

'And you're going to finish it,' said Mrs Macey. 'Both of you, act your ages.'

Mac pretended to dribble in the back and that set Cat and I off laughing again and Jade looked even crosser and folded her arms and legs tightly. She looked really miserable. Oops, I thought, she *really* wishes we weren't here. I used to think it would be nice to have brothers and sisters; it can be lonely being an only child sometimes. Not after today, though, after listening to Mac and Jade wind each other up like crazy. I thanked my lucky stars I was an only child.

All Jade's moaning was soon forgotten when we reached the big city. I had come up on a school trip to London from Bristol when I was about seven, but I didn't remember much. Now it looked awesome, as different to Cornwall as you could get. Like another country, I thought as I took in the traffic, the buses, the crowds hurrying home from work, the shops . . . and the *shops*. Wow. I was tempted to go and cruise them for something special to wear for the auditions, but then I reminded myself that I might get through even further in the competition so I'd better hang on to what money I had.

After a while, the heavy traffic petered out and we reached some lovely tree-lined streets with big old houses.

'This is Hampstead,' said Mac. 'We're almost there. Dad moved last month to a flat near Highgate tube, so it will be easy in the morning if he can't drop us.'

When we reached Mr Macey's flat, Mrs Macey didn't get out of the car. Mac's mum and dad had only been divorced for a year or so and it was still a bit weird between them. Mac got out and fetched the bags from the boot and Cat and I helped him carry them in. Mr Macey came out as we unloaded and said something to Mrs Macey while she sat stony-faced in the car. I couldn't hear what he said, but I could tell by his body language that he wasn't comfortable. Mac glanced over at them a few times. I knew he wished that they'd never got divorced because it meant he'd had to leave London and all his mates.

'You OK?' I asked as I hauled a bag on to the front steps.

He shrugged. 'Yeah. Same old, same old.' Then he carried the bags inside. 'I'll take our stuff into our room in a mo.'

I'd told Mum and Dad that Cat and I were going to sleep on the floor in Jade's room. I don't think they'd have agreed to let me sleep in Mac's room. But he'd insisted he'd behave so we'd arranged that Cat was going to sleep on Jade's floor in her sleeping bag and Mac was going to sleep on his floor and let me have his bed.

However, as soon as we got inside, Cat came over to me and pleaded. 'Don't make me sleep with her, please. Can't I come in with you and Mac?'

'Sure,' I said. I wouldn't have wanted to share with Jade either. 'She probably snores anyway.'

'I heard that,' said Jade, coming in the front door. 'And I do *not* snore. And I'm very happy to have my room to myself. It wasn't *my* idea to bring you two along. Mac, Mum wants to say goodbye.'

Mac went out and returned a few minutes later. His dad seemed nice and more relaxed after Mrs Macey had driven off. He looked a lot like Mac, same dimple on his chin, blue eyes and a friendly face. 'So, you lot, what would you like to do tonight?'

'Pizza,' said Mac.

'I have to rehearse,' said Jade, flouncing off upstairs. 'And I don't want to be disturbed.'

'No problem there,' said Mac.

'Pizza it is, then,' said Mr Macey. 'You know I can't cook. So we'll eat, then how about I get a film?'

'Great,' said Cat and I. We'd already decided we'd go over the songs once that night, then we'd relax so we were fresh for the morning.

Everything was going really well until bedtime. Cat and I went up and got changed and Mac stayed downstairs to catch up with his dad. When he came up half an hour later, he didn't look happy.

'What's up?' I asked.

'Nothing,' he said. But he looked really down. What on earth could have happened in half an hour? I wondered.

'Come on, Mac,' said Cat. 'Spill. We're your mates, you can tell us.'

Mac sat on the end of the bed. 'Oh, it's probably nothing. Just, well, Dad's gone and got himself a stupid girlfriend. He wants Jade and me to go out with him tomorrow night and meet her. I don't want to go.'

'Why not?' I asked. 'She might be really nice.'

'Nah,' said Mac. 'She's causing problems already. Like I've come up here to see my dad and already he's saying I have to make my own arrangements for Sunday night. Apparently she's an actress and he's going to some play and after-production party with her. I mean, what's the point of coming up to see him if he's not going to be here? Then it'll be Monday and Mum will be back to pick us up.'

'Well, we're here,' I said, snuggling up to him.

'Yeah, but you won't always be. And I can just see it. I know exactly what's going to happen. He'll start cancelling my visits. I'll be in the way. He'll probably marry her and have more babies and they'll take my room and then they won't want me around any more, ever.'

'You sound like Puddleglum the marsh-wiggle in the Narnia books,' I said. 'Only seeing the worst. Come on, Mac, it might not be so bad. You might like her.'

'Yeah,' said Cat. 'Like when Dad first started going out with Jen, I was all like, Ohmigod, I don't know if I like this, but it turned out to be the best thing ever. She's great and it's good to see Dad happy again. Parents have to get on with their lives as well.'

'Yeah but your mum died,' said Mac. 'My mum and dad got divorced so it's different. And what about Mum? Now she'll never have him back.'

'Does she want him back?' I asked.

'Well, not at the moment,' said Mac. 'But I thought it was only a matter of time. They used to get on really well. Now this has ruined everything.'

Sometimes advice is not what's required, I thought as I put my arms round him. Sometimes all you need is a hug and something to distract you. Poor Mac. It's not like him to be sulky and negative, but then I don't think I'd like it if my mum and dad split up and had new partners either. God, I hope it doesn't happen. Mustn't think those thoughts, I told myself. I have to be positive for the morning.

'Come on,' I said, climbing into bed as Mac struggled to get comfortable in his sleeping bag on the floor. 'Let's all sleep on it. Big day tomorrow. Now, who's going to tell the first ghost story?'

Round Two

11

'WHAT I said about the judges being nice the first time . . .' I said to Cat when we caught up at the lunch break the next day. 'I take it back.'

'Tell me about it,' she said gloomily.

Mr Macey had dropped us off at the hall behind Tottenham Court Road at nine o'clock. It was now twelve and the last three hours were possibly the most excruciating of my whole life.

After we'd arrived and registered, we were separated from the boys and split into groups of five. Then we were asked to go in, one group at a time, to see the judges. Sadly, Cat wasn't in my group; happily, Jade wasn't either. When we got in the hall, we all had to troop up on to the stage and stand there with the spotlight on us. It was awful – the judges didn't say anything, just looked us up and down like we were contestants at a pet show, then they all wrote stuff on pads of paper in front of them. I felt like doing something really stupid at one point, like flashing my chest at them, then I saw that a camera crew had set up at the back of the hall and decided that my parents wouldn't be too happy if they saw me doing something daft like that on telly.

When the judges had all had a good stare at us, they dimmed the lights, and one by one, we were called to sing our song, in front of each other as well as in front of the camera and judges. I was third up and was feeling intimidated, as the two girls before me were good, and I mean *really* good. The one after me was OK and the fifth one blew it all together. Worst of all, though, was that at the end of our performances the judges made no comment. I'd prepared myself for the usual insults, but total silence was much worse. Nothing. Not a 'good', a 'bad' or a 'you're ugly'. They just told each group, 'We'll let you know this afternoon when we've seen everyone.'

After that, everyone had to go and have lunch in a room on the first floor. It felt like we were at a funeral, not a pop competition. No one was popping here, not any more. We'd done our bubbly bit, now everyone looked anxious and deflated. Not surprising, really, considering what we'd been though.

Cat and I took a sandwich and an apple juice from the table and went to sit on a bench in a corner to talk over the events of the morning.

'Well, at least we get a free buttie this time.' Cat smiled weakly.

'Consolation prize,' I said. 'Not a Grammy, but a cheese and tomato bap. Yeah, at least we'll have something to show for our efforts. So how did you get on?'

'Crap, crap, crapola,' said Cat, shaking her head. 'It really threw me when we had to get up in groups of five.'

'I know,' I said. 'It felt weird to be compared to one another like that.'

'I guess they were looking to see if anyone stood out with star quality. I just wish I'd been in a group with smaller girls. I felt really conspicuous. All the girls in my group were tall with legs up to their armpits.'

'Kylie's tiny and Madonna's not much taller,' I said. 'They won't hold your height against you. Better to be tiny than enormous like me!' I said.

'Becca!' said Cat. 'You're not enormous. You may not be a size 8, but you're not enormous. You're normal.'

'Can I join you?' said a voice to our left.

I looked up to see a boy I'd noticed on the way in. He was dark, with spiky hair and he was very, very good-looking.

'Sure,' I said.

'Thanks,' he said, taking a seat next to Cat. 'I don't know anyone in this round and boy, I feel like I need to talk to someone.'

'Know what you mean,' said Cat. 'How were the boys' groups?'

'Tense. It's like the stakes have gone way up, you know.

If you don't cut it, then *kaput*. I'm Elliott, by the way.'

'Cat and Becca,' said Cat.

'How was your session?' he asked.

'About as much fun as having your arm ripped off,' I said.

'And being hit with the soggy end,' said Cat.

I started laughing then. 'So much for my fantasy about being on a *Top of the Pops* type show.'

'I dunno,' said Elliott. 'Who knows what they're looking for? Weren't they happy with your song?'

'Hard to say. It helped having the lights turned down,' I said. 'Then I couldn't see the three monkeys in front of me. You know, see no evil, hear no evil, speak no evil. They didn't say a word. I tried to imagine I was in my mate's room back home and that helped a bit.'

'So what happens now?' said Cat. 'They've seen half of us so I guess it's going to take as long again to see the next lot.'

Elliott nodded. 'Yeah. We wait. And we wait. And we wait. That's why I thought I'd come and introduce myself. Didn't want to sit here on my own, imagining the worst. So, anyone want another stale sandwich?'

We both shook our heads and he got up and went back to the food table. Cat nudged me. 'Cute, huh?'

'*Très* cute,' I said. I'd felt a bit rotten this morning when they wouldn't allow Mac to come in with us. He'd been sent away at the door with all the other friends and relatives and told to come back at four o'clock. So instead he'd gone off to catch up with some of his old mates. Now I was almost glad he wasn't there. I'd have a chance to get to know the gorgeous Elliott. Fickle is thy name, Becca, I thought to myself. But I'm only going to talk to him . . .

There's a saying that goes something like: Time is too short for those who rush, too long for those who wait. I looked at the clock again. I could have sworn it hadn't moved since the last time I glanced up. It was like the room was standing still and the moment had become eternal. We'd learned all that we could about Elliott. Fifteen years old, Aquarius, from Manchester, three sisters, both parents teachers, staying with his aunt in Crouch End. Hobbies: tennis, surfing the Net, movies, wants to be – what else? – a pop star, plays the guitar, fave film: *Road Trip*.

He got the same rundown about us. We talked endlessly about the other competitions and who we'd wanted to win. By mid-afternoon, I felt I'd known Elliott all my life.

Elliott seemed to know all about the judges. 'Martin Riley,' he said. 'He's the older one. He's a DJ and he's been involved in the music business for years. Rumour has it, he puts up a lot of money to sponsor new bands. The one with glasses is Paul Parker – he's a producer. He's got some brill bands on his list. And the woman is Sarah Hardman – she manages the bands on Paul Parker's list.

'So, which of them do you think is going to be the bad guy?' I asked.

'Martin,' said Elliott. 'He's already laid into a few of the boys for wasting their time.'

'Thought so,' I said. 'He wasn't going to let me through the first round, but the other two voted him out. Wonder what he wrote about me this morning.'

As the clock hit half past three, Cat sighed. 'No sign of Jade. She must be in with the afternoon groups. So what shall we do? How about we play I Spy?'

'I spy with my little eye, fifty worried-looking teenagers,' I said. 'It's weird, though, with all this waiting I feel like I've gone from anxiety to excitement to anxiety, and now I feel, oh so what?'

At that moment, Tanya came in and clapped her hands for silence. 'All the girls, please go into the main hall,' she said.

My 'oh so what?' feeling suddenly evaporated and my tummy tightened into a knot. It was back to 'oh God', 'oh argggh', 'oh yeah', 'oh *no*'. I think I may be cracking up, I thought as I followed the others in and wondered if they were all feeling as barking mad as I was.

All fifty girls went up on stage and I stood in a line at the back with Cat.

'OK, it's cut-down time,' said Paul, getting up. 'Some of you are going to go forward to the next round. Some of you, we won't be asking back. First, I'd like to say we've seen some great talent here today and you should all be very proud of yourselves . . .'

'Blah, blah,' Cat whispered. 'Get *on* with it.'

'So I'm going to call some names,' Paul continued. 'When I've finished, I want those girls to step forward and the rest of you to stay where you are.'

'Ohmigod,' I said. 'Here we go – prolong the agony.'

The roll-call began and girls began to step forward. It was deathly quiet as no one knew which group would be carrying on and which were finished – the girls being called forward or those staying put.

'Cat Kennedy,' called Paul.

Cat squeezed my arm. 'Nice knowing yus, *amigo*,' she said as she left to take her place at the front.

The roll-call continued and I realised they were doing it alphabetically. They got to the M's, but didn't call Jade Macey. She'd get through, surely. And the girl that hit the bum notes in my group was one of the ones called forward. Ohmigod, did that mean I was through again? I felt like my brain was going to fuse. Maybe? . . . Maybe not? . . . Maybe? It would be fantastic. But then that would mean that Cat didn't get through. Not so fantastic. The suspense was unbearable. When Paul had reached the final name, Martin got up.

'As Paul said,' he started, 'we've seen some amazing talent here today. It's been really hard coming to a decision. But after seeing you all today, it's become clear that some of you definitely are *not* our Pop Princess, some of you gave borderline performances, and some of you were terrific. But a Pop Princess can never be borderline. You could never describe Madonna, or Kylie Minogue as borderline. They've got the X-factor and you know it. So the group at the back . . .' He paused and looked towards the back of the stage. My heart sank. So I hadn't got through. Then Martin smiled and went on, '. . . well done. We're going to ask you to come back tomorrow, 9 a.m. sharp. The group at the front, I'm afraid we won't be asking you back, but thanks for coming and well done everybody.'

There was a huge sigh of relief from the back, then cheers as girls started jumping up and down and hugging each other. I went straight over to Cat and gave her a huge hug.

'God. Sorry, Cat,' I said.

She shrugged. 'I kind of knew I wouldn't get through. I knew I was crapola today. You know it in your bones when it's not your best. But *hey*, well done, you.'

'Yeah, I guess,' I said. But somehow it didn't feel like last time when we'd got through together.

Journey Into Hell

12

'WHERE'S JADE?' I asked early the next morning when I walked into the kitchen.

'In her room,' said Mac. 'She's about to leave, so I said I'd take you if you want to grab a bit of toast or something.'

'Yeah, best to eat something as you've got a long day ahead,' said Cat. 'I'll come with you as well. Mac and I are going to go down to Spitalfields Market.'

'God, I wish I could come with you,' I said. 'I'd love to go there.'

'And I'd love to be coming with you,' said Cat, putting a piece of bread in the toaster. 'Now do you want to run through the song they gave you one more time?'

'Nah, I've been thinking about it all night. I haven't slept a wink, hardly. I kept dreaming I was doing exams but hadn't done any revision. Then I dreamed I was standing on stage naked. Honestly, this was supposed to be fun, but it's turning out to be even worse than school.'

The twenty-five girls chosen to go back the next day had all been asked to stay behind for five minutes after the judge's verdict then we'd been given song sheets to learn overnight and have ready for the morning. I'd been given 'Wind Beneath My Wings' by Bette Midler and I felt over-whelmingly nervous.

'Well, what did you expect?' said Jade, coming in behind us. 'I don't even know why you bothered coming up this time, Becca. Mac told me you only did it because Squidge dared you. Some other girl who was serious about it could have had your place instead of you wasting the judge's time.'

'Oh, leave off, Jade,' said Cat. 'Loads of people entered, for all sorts of reasons. And Becca wouldn't have got this far if she wasn't good.'

'Well, that's a matter of opinion,' she said. 'Anyway, I'm off. See you there if you can be bothered to turn up.'

'See you,' I said, then thought, And thanks so much for all the support and encouragement. I'd been ready to be really sympathetic today, as I felt sorry for her, having to go out for dinner with her dad the night before. Not because he was going to be introducing his new girlfriend, but because I knew she had a song to learn as well. I'd been lucky, I had Cat to help me go over mine and an empty flat to practise in while Mr Macey, Jade and Mac were out. Jade went into her room to rehearse the minute she got back and I could still hear her every time I woke up from my bad dreams, so she can't have got much sleep either. Maybe that was why she was double ratty.

'Take no notice of her,' said Cat after Jade had left. 'She's probably feeling threatened because you *are* good and she knows it.'

'Thanks,' I said. 'At least you believe in me. I'd far prefer travelling with you two to getting slagged off by her for the whole journey.'

After a quick bite of toast and some tea, we set off for the tube station. I looked at my watch. We had an hour, plenty of time to get to Tottenham Court Road, as the journey only took about half an hour.

'So, new girlfriend?' I asked. 'Any more thoughts this morning?'

'I'll see how it goes,' said Mac. Last night he'd seemed reticent to say much when he got back, and I didn't want to push him. Mac wasn't someone you could make talk if he didn't want to. He opened up when and if he was ready.

'Well, I hope you were nice to her,' said Cat. 'I bet it was hard for her too, meeting your dad's kids.'

'I was polite,' said Mac.

'She probably just wants to get on with you,' I said. 'I think you should give her a break.'

'Hmphh,' said Mac.

When we got to Highgate tube, the next train wasn't for fifteen minutes.

'Bugger,' said Mac. 'I should have remembered. Trains

are always less frequent on a Sunday. That's probably why Jade went early; she must have remembered and didn't want to take any chances. Shouldn't be a problem, though. We've still got time.'

I tried to make myself relax and mentally ran through the words of the song as we waited. Then Cat made me do Zac's 'shake it out' routine which got a few funny looks from some of the people waiting at the station. Thankfully, the train arrived when it was supposed to and we all got on.

'We'll make it,' said Mac, glancing at his watch, 'so you can chill out now.'

Phew, I thought, at last we're on our way. I'll get there just in time.

Then the train stopped at Camden.

'Oh God, what's happening now?' I asked after we'd been sitting there for a few minutes.

'This train is no longer in service,' said an announcement. 'All change please. If you are travelling further south, go to the Charing Cross branch and continue your journey from there.'

'What does that mean?' I asked Mac as we got off the train.

'It means we run like hell through the tunnel,' said Mac setting off at a pace. 'The other line.'

He began to run up some steps so we followed him, then through a tunnel and down some more steps.

'Next train in eight minutes,' I said. I checked my

watch. 'Oh God, it's a quarter to nine. I'm going to be late.'

'We might just make it,' said Mac, but even he was beginning to look worried. 'The Northern Line. Londoners call it the misery line – now you know why.'

I arrived at the hall at twelve minutes past nine.

'We'll meet you outside later,' Cat called after me as I hurried inside.

The foyer was deserted, so I ran towards the hall. As I pushed the door open, everyone turned to look, including Martin Riley. And he didn't look pleased.

The boys and girls were in separate halls again and the judges split their time between the two.

By mid-afternoon, I'd had enough. Martin definitely had it in for me. After a dressing down for being late, in front of *everyone*, he'd taken every opportunity to slag me off.

10.00 a.m.: 'You sound like you're singing along with the radio.'

11.10 a.m.: 'It's all on one level, Becca. Start quietly, build. Put some emotion into it. You sound like you're singing, "I had eggs for breakfast". It's that boring.'

12.00 p.m.: 'Breathe, Becca, breathe.'

1.30 p.m.: 'Nah, not good enough, start again.'

2.15 p.m.: 'You're holding yourself too tight. Relax, let it come from your abdomen, not your throat.'

3.00 p.m.: 'Come *on*, Becca, impress me.'

I got worse and worse as the day progressed and by the

end I had the confidence of a timid amoeba. On the other hand, the real stars were beginning to stand out. Jade performed brilliantly, as did an Indian girl called Sushila, and a small blonde girl called Fizz.

'They're going to let another twenty go today,' whispered a blonde girl as we went to stand around a piano to sing with accompaniment for the fifth time that day. 'Ten boys and ten girls.'

'Good,' I whispered back. 'I hope I'm one of the ones they let go.'

She gave me a strange look, but I meant it. I could have been out having a good time with Cat and Mac all day, but instead I was locked in a strange hall with a load of people I didn't know, being put through physical and mental torture. We'd had to sing solo, sing in groups, sing solo again with the piano . . . I was tired and hoarse and my feet hurt like hell from a dance session with a choreographer in which we had to prance about to 'It's Raining Men'. It wasn't fun any more. I felt so alone. Although Elliott had got through, I didn't have a chance to talk to him, as the boys were shunted off into another hall to perform. I looked for him at the lunch break, but he was busy with a group of lads, practising for the afternoon.

At the afternoon break, I took an apple juice from the table, then I looked for Jade, in the hope that she'd have chilled out since the morning. She was at the back of the room with Fizz and looked like she was having a great time practising the dance steps we'd been taught in the morning. Of course, she had them down to perfection. I went and collapsed in the corner of the room to call Cat on my mobile.

'Hey, Pop Princess,' said Cat, when she answered her phone. 'How's it going?'

'Get me *out* of here,' I said.

Cat laughed.

'No seriously, it's awful here today. Torture. Where are you?'

'We're in Camden Lock,' said Cat. 'It's fantastic, amazing. We did Spitalfields this morning, and caught the tube back up here. You'd love it. It's buzzing.'

'I'll be there in half an hour. Where should I meet you?'

'Why? Has it finished already?'

'No. But *I* have Cat, I've had it.'

'You've been voted out?'

'No.'

'So why do you want to leave?'

'I told you, it's torture. I can't do it, Cat, and that Martin Riley's got it in for me.'

'Just a mo, Mac wants to know what's happening.'

The phone went quiet for a moment and I could just about hear Cat saying something to Mac. He came on the phone a moment later.

'You must be out of your mind, Becca,' he said. 'You've got this far – you *can't* give up now.'

I felt like crying. 'But you don't understand . . .'

Cat came back on the phone. 'Why do you want to leave, Becca? You were so into it all before.'

'I know, but there's loads of people here who are better than I am. And I'm having a horrible time. I know I won't win, so why not quit while I'm still ahead.'

I could hear Cat sigh heavily at the other end of the phone. 'Typical,' she said. 'This is so totally typical of you, Becca.'

'What do you mean?'

'Giving up the minute things get hard. Well, I think it's rotten of you. You've got a real problem — you know that, don't you? You can't see how good you are. It's only your fear that's holding you back. Fear of failure, fear of rejection. You'll never get anywhere if you give into it all the time.'

I was taken aback. I'd never heard Cat cross at me before. 'Well, it's not just that,' I said. 'I don't know any one here . . .'

'You know the gorgeous Elliott, go and talk to him.'

'Who's Elliott?' I heard Mac ask in the background.

'He's been busy all day,' I said. 'And it's like, me and you, we were in this together and it was all a laugh, but now you're out and . . .'

'Don't use me as an excuse, Becca.'

'I'm not, Cat, honest. It's not an excuse. And you don't know what it's been like today. Why put myself through more misery when I know I don't stand a chance?'

'You *do* stand a chance, Becca. You're good and you just might win if you stop this whingeing.'

I felt tears prick the back of my eyes. 'You just don't understand, Cat,' I said, then I hung up. I felt really miserable. I thought at least my *friends* would understand.

I reached into my rucksack to find a tissue and when I looked up, Elliott was coming over to join me. I took a big sniff and smiled so he wouldn't see that I'd been near to tears. He flopped down beside me. 'Rough day, huh?'

I nodded.

'I think loads of people are ready to drop out,' he said.

'Really?'

'Yeah. When the going gets tough . . . et cetera.'

'Yeah, the not-so-tough get going,' I said. 'Me included.'

'Feeling down?'

I nodded. 'This place is freezing and I'm so *tired*.'

'I don't think anyone slept. That's why everyone's feeling so fragile and it doesn't help that the judges are coming down really heavy on everyone today.'

'Tell me about it. That Martin Riley's been horrible to me.'

'Not just you, Becca. Everyone. See, I reckon what they're doing today is testing our staying power. I mean, this is for real. Whoever wins is going to have to be serious about it, not flaky. So I reckon that's why they're pushing everyone today, to see who will crack and who can go the distance.'

Suddenly I remembered what Dad had said. 'Success is fifty per cent talent, fifty per cent perseverance.'

'Right,' said Elliott. 'Anyway, got to go practise. Catch you later.'

I took a look around the hall. It was true. Everyone did look shattered, not just me. And it had helped talking to Elliott. I felt myself starting to get fired up again. So, they were testing everybody, were they? I'd show them who was flaky and who was not. I got up to go and splash my face with cold water.

In the loos, I found Sushila in tears.

'Hey,' I said and went over to put my arm around her.

'Sorry,' she sniffed. 'Just . . .'

'I know,' I said. 'Tough today. But don't let it put you off. I was just talking to a mate and we reckon that today's all about seeing who's going to crack. Don't let them get to you. You were great up there this morning. You really stood out. All you have to do is get through another hour and it'll get better.'

'You reckon? I'm just about ready to walk,' she said.

'I was too. But let's show them we're made of stronger stuff, eh? You're good – you can't give up now.'

She gave me a weak smile. 'Thanks. And I thought you were good as well – loads better than some of the others. I'm Sushila, by the way.'

'Becca,' I said and remembered another of Dad's inspirational lines. 'My quote for the day is "Fortune favours the brave." So come on, let's get out there and strut our stuff.'

The rest of the afternoon flew by. When the judges said something critical, I didn't take it personally – it spurred me on. I listened, but instead of thinking, Oh no, they think I'm crapola, I thought, OK, how can I use that to improve my performance? Ha, I *am* professional, I thought, not a dreamer, or a flaky flake. I *can* do it.

At the end of a group session around the piano, Sarah Hardman pulled me to one side.

'Well done, Becca,' she said. 'I've been watching you and you've done really well today. I know Martin's given you a bit of a rough time, but you haven't let it get to you. And don't be afraid of the criticism; it's to help, not to hinder. It's got to a lot of people today and they've gone under. Three people have dropped out already. Understandable, but I say there's no crime in falling, only in refusing to get up again. And I saw you get up a few times after Martin had his say. That's just what we're looking for. Being a Pop Princess isn't all about glamour. Whoever wins may get knocked by the press, the public . . . It can all turn from nice to nasty in an instant and we need to know that our winner can take it.'

When I heard later that I'd made it through into the last fifteen girls, I felt fantastic. Nothing is going to stop me, I thought. I'm going to go for this. I'm going to show them all. Cat, Mac, Jade, Mum, Dad, Mr Walker . . . I may be a dreamer, but I've got what it takes to make a dream come true.

Christmas Sulks

13

MAC HAD been in a sulk for days, partly because he knew Elliott had been phoning every day to see how things were going – no matter what I told him, Mac wouldn't believe that Elliott and I were 'just good friends' – and partly because he'd been in a funny mood ever since London. Meeting Sonia, his dad's new girlfriend had given him a bit of an abandonment complex, even though no one was planning on deserting him. Certainly not me and, I'm pretty sure, not his dad.

'I'm not going to go off with Elliott,' I tried to reassure him when he came over on Christmas Eve to give me my present. 'For one thing, he lives in Manchester, and for another, *you're* my boyfriend. But if you keep acting so jealous for no reason, you're going to drive me away.'

It was obviously the wrong thing to say because it made him sulk even more and he went off in a huff before I'd had time to open my present or give him his. Good job, really, because he gave me the latest chill out CD, *exactly* what I'd got him. At least it gave me the chance to swop presents and labels around, so he'd get the Eminem CD that I'd bought for Squidge instead.

Mac had written 'To my top Pop Princess' on the label of my present. It was a shame he was weirded out because he can be so sweet when he wants to be. I'm beginning to understand why mega-stars have difficulties with relationships. It's because their partners don't trust them when they're out meeting new glam people all the time. I hoped I wouldn't have to resort to buying a dog for company, like some celebs do in their 'lonely' phases . . . although, on second thought, maybe a dog is a good idea. They're always pleased to see you and are less trouble than boys, as you don't have to explain yourself to them all the time. But I wasn't ready to give up on Mac just yet. I decided I wouldn't let him sulk for long, I'd just give him a little space, then go to his place and win him over.

Mum was in a sulk with me too on Christmas day, because I wouldn't have roast potatoes with our Christmas dinner, nor any pudding, which she said she made with extra pecans and cherries especially for me.

'You're going to waste away if you don't eat properly,' she said.

No point in saying anything, I decided as I picked at my turkey. She just doesn't get it. If I want to win this competition, I have to lose half a stone at least. All the other finalists, except for one tubby girl, are stick insects. Pop icons are skinny and wear really tight jeans, often with their belly buttons showing. I knew I had to be skinny.

So far, I'd lost two pounds and I'd put all my Christmas chocolates away until the competition was over, when I could get together with Cat and Lia for a chocfest. At least Dad understands, I thought – not so much about losing weight, but about needing to be serious about the competition. No one could be more serious than he is about succeeding. He's still working away on his novel.

The rowing was still going on, though. It was awful. I could hear them sometimes when they thought I'd gone to sleep and it was always about the same thing. Money, money, money. Poor Dad. It was supposed to be the season of goodwill and Mum wouldn't get off on his case.

Cat came over in the evening. She was in a sulk with me too, but mainly because I'd been slightly in a sulk with her since that talk in London about never seeing anything through. It's hard staying mad at Cat, though. She was right, anyway. I made it one of my New Year's resolutions to take criticism on the chin, as long as it's constructive. And besides, Cat bought me a gorgeous black strappy top for Christmas, perfect for wearing at the next round of the competition and loads nicer than the glitter bath gels I gave her. I hadn't had much time to shop, as I'd been busy rehearsing. I'd gone to Plymouth with Mum on one of her grocery buying trips and done it all in one mad dash so I could get back to practise.

'Should I do one of the songs I've written for the next round?' I asked.

'*Nff-NO!,*' said Cat through a mouthful of mince pie.

'Why not?'

'Er, um, best to stick to songs that are well-known. Um . . . like, remember that guy – I think his name was Darius – anyway, he was on one of the earliest pop star programmes and he wanted to do his own thing and the judges didn't appreciate it, said he was corny. He got the message to "play the game" and he came back and did really well in another show. It was only later he had his number-one hit with his own song. No, Bec, you're better off singing songs they recognise.'

I decided to let it go and not take offence, but I had a sneaky feeling that Cat didn't think much of my lyrics. Perhaps she's right again, I thought. Best to stick to what the judges know, as there's standing out in a good way and standing out in a naff way, and I don't want to do that.

Lia and Squidge had both been really cool since London. They came over on Boxing Day and I was really touched by their Chrissie presents.

'Wow,' I said as I opened the envelopes they gave me and found two crisp ten pound notes. 'Cash.'

Lia smiled. 'I know it's a bit boring, but we knew that you probably need some money for your next trip to London.

Don't want it to be a problem with your parents again.'

'No, wow, *thanks*,' I said. 'No, this is top. exactly what I need, because I've spent all the Christmas money I had left from Mum and Dad on buying all my presents for you lot. Luckily my gran and grandad sent me some dosh, but with this as well, it shouldn't be a problem at all.'

'So when are you off next?' asked Squidge.

'Weekend after New Year.'

'Have you decided what song you're going to do?' asked Lia.

'I thought I might do "Endless Love" or "Total Eclipse of the Heart". What do you think?'

'"Endless Love",' said Lia.

'"Total Eclipse",' said Squidge at the same time.

I laughed. 'Thanks. Or how about I combine them into "Endless Eclipse"?'

'Sing both of them for us,' said Squidge, 'then we'll vote.'

I stood up and sang both songs for them.

They looked genuinely impressed. 'Wow,' said Squidge when I'd finished, 'you're getting really good. You're loads more confident now.'

'Yeah,' said Lia, '*really* good.'

I smiled, 'Thanks. So which one?'

'"Total Eclipse",' said Lia.

'"Endless Love",' said Squidge.

I laughed. 'Oh, that's really helpful.'

In the end, we went over to Cat's house and gave her the casting vote. I think she was quite chuffed that I did value her opinion. She decided on 'Endless Love'. And she lent me a pair of diamond stud earrings that her mum gave to her before she died, to wear for luck. Lia lent me a pair of strappy shoes to wear. 'More glam than trainers,' she said. I have the best mates, I thought, they're being really brilliant. I just wished that Mac would chill out and be happy for me as well.

For the rest of the week, I practised every spare moment I had. When the others were off somewhere hanging out or watching films, I stayed home and rehearsed. When I wasn't rehearsing, I jogged to get fit, so that I could keep up if they made us do any more dance sessions. I drank loads of water to make sure my skin was good. And I made sure I got to bed reasonably early every night, so I looked youthful and fresh. It's a full-time business, aiming for the top.

My parents didn't know what to think. I don't think either of them had ever seen me work so hard, but I knew the next round would be the toughest. There were fifteen girls and fifteen boys left in the competition and the judges were going to lose five of each.

'I think it's great that you're really going for this,' said Dad one afternoon when I took him a cup of tea in his study. 'But I'm worried that you're going to take it hard if you don't get through – you know, after having come so far.'

I read him the quote he had on his wall. 'A man's reach

should exceed his grasp. Else what's a heaven for? That's your favourite, isn't it?'

That silenced him and he gave me a hug. 'I'm very proud of you,' he said, 'and will be, whether you win or not.'

Actually we'd had a few brilliant conversations since London. He understood about going for what you want and I was feeling really close to him. I grew to admire him a lot. He'd had a lot of setbacks, like I did from Martin Riley, but he kept getting up and trying again and again.

On New Year's Eve, I went over to Mac's. I was determined to get him smiling again. It was freezing outside and even looked like it might snow, but I wrapped up warmly, then cycled over and threw a stone up at his window.

'I've come to serenade you,' I called up when he opened the window.

He laughed. 'Like *Romeo and Juliet*?' he asked. 'But isn't it supposed to be me down there and you up here on a balcony?'

'Hey,' I said, 'this is the twenty-first century. Things change.' Then I sang 'Endless Love' for him. It was hysterical, because Jade opened her window as well, but shut it as soon as she heard it was me, then the neighbour's dog came and sat on the lawn next to me and joined in, barking away with great enthusiasm.

Mac was killing himself laughing. 'Enough, enough,' he

said. 'I'll come down and let you in.'

He let me in and I followed him up the stairs to his room. 'So, do you think I stand a chance?' I asked.

'Always did,' he said, going into his bedroom and lying back on his bed. 'But I'd lose the doggy accompaniment. I tell you something, Becca. I've been thinking about it a lot. You *do* stand a chance. I always thought you had a cracking voice, but, well, if you *do* win, you might not enjoy it as much as you think you will. Like, already you've changed. I never thought you would, but you're getting like Jade lately. This whole thing, it's become more like an obsession than a dream, for both of you. You don't want to hang out any more, you're always rehearsing, it's all you ever talk about. The rest of us have still got lives and stuff going on, you know.'

I felt hurt. 'I know. And I know I haven't exactly been around. But this is important.'

'And we're not?'

'The others don't seem to mind,' I said. 'And it's only for a few more weeks.'

'Yeah, we'll see. And what if you win?'

'It'd be great.'

'No, it wouldn't,' he said. 'It'll be more and more of the same. You'll change, your life will change. Some old *Pop Idol*s were being repeated the other night and it was obvious to anyone with half a brain who came out as the real winners.'

'Yeah. The real winners usually stand out a mile.' I said.

'No,' said Mac. 'Think about it, Becca. They were just like pawns in a chess game. They have no control. They're being moulded and shaped, told what to sing, what to say and what to wear by the record companies.'

'Yeah. But a *professional* makeover. I'd love it. In fact, I think the stylists are coming in next time.'

Mac shrugged. 'If you want to be a puppet in someone else's show, then go right ahead. But the ones that make all the money and have all the say are the producers and the management team, not the artists.'

'It's not like that, Mac,' I said. 'You don't understand.'

Mac's face clouded. 'And Elliott does, I suppose,' he said.

'Yes, actually he does,' I said and headed for the door. I had been planning to drag him off to Squidge's to meet up with the others to see the New Year in. But come midnight, no way was I going to snog such a cynical old misery.

14 Complications

I THOUGHT it was all sorted. Got the song. Got the dosh.
Got a place to stay . . . or so I thought until Mac put a
spanner in the works.

'But I thought it was all arranged,' I said when he
phoned the Thursday before I was due to go up to London.
'I go up with you and Jade with your mum again and . . .'

'I know. But . . . well, it's got complicated. Apparently
Sonia has a daughter Tamara and she's going to be staying
at dad's. I told you this would happen. I've read about it.
Parents get divorced, one has a new family and they
become more important . . .'

'But you don't know that. Did your dad actually say you
couldn't stay?' I asked. I couldn't believe his own dad
would stop him from visiting.

'Not exactly,' said Mac. 'That is, well, he does want me
to go, said he wants Tamara to meet me and Jade. But he
can stuff it. I'm not going to go and be all pally and big

brothery with someone I don't even know. I don't want to hang out with some eight-year-old kid, or her mother. Hopefully this thing with Sonia will run its course and she'll clear off so we can get back to normal.'

'And what if she doesn't?' I asked. 'What if they, like, really make a go of it? You'll have to get to know them sometime.'

'Yeah, well, not going. Sorry. No way José,' said Mac. 'But I did ask if you could stay even though I won't be there, but apparently Jade has told some other girl from the competition – Tizz or Fizz or somebody, I think her name is – that she could stay, so there isn't room.'

I could feel myself starting to panic. What was I going to do? I had to get there, even if it meant sleeping on the streets.

'Maybe I could get a lift up with Jade and your mum anyway, then I'll try and find a B&B or something. Mum and Dad needn't know. If I told them I wasn't staying with you, they might stop me going, so . . . oh pants. I could still get a lift, couldn't I?'

'Er, well, that's the other thing,' said Mac. 'Mum's not driving Jade up. She's gone already; Mum put her on the train this morning and Dad's meeting her at the other end. God, I'm sorry, Bec. I know I was heavy the other night, but I didn't mean for any of this to happen. I didn't plan it or anything. I feel rotten for you.'

He did sound genuinely bad about it so it was hard to

be cross. I'd save that for Jade. I wouldn't put it past her to have invited Fizz to spite me and ruin my chances.

'Don't worry, Mac,' I said. 'I'll sort something out.'

'But you can't stay in a B&B on your own, Becca,' he said. 'You said your dad's been great. Ask if he'll go with you just this once.'

I sighed. 'Not after this morning, I don't think.'

'Why? What happened this morning?'

'I came down to breakfast and Dad was wearing a suit.'

'So?' said Mac.

'A *suit*, Mac,' I said. 'He's gone for a job interview. Some crapola job in a college that he doesn't even want. It's just to keep my mum happy and stop her nagging him. He looked so sad. I felt awful for him. It's not what he wants. He's given up. That's another reason I have to go and do this competition – to remind him of everything he's told me over the last few weeks. Don't give up, don't give up, don't give up.'

'OK then,' said Mac. 'I know it will be difficult, but call Jade this evening and ask if you can kip on the floor with Fizz. She can't possibly be so hard-hearted to say no. I mean, you are all in this together. Or do you want me to ring and try again?'

'No, no,' I said. 'I'll think of something and if I do have to ask Jade, better that it comes from me.'

At first I thought, No way I'm going crawling to Jade, but as the day went on, I realised it was my only choice. I'd have let her stay if I had a dad in London, even though we didn't get on. It was either call or not go, so I bit the bullet and dialled the number.

'Oh, but slight problem, Becca,' she said after I'd eaten humble pie. 'See, Fizz will be here and there's really not room for both of you as well as Sonia's kid.'

'But couldn't you just squeeze me in? Please. I'll sleep in a corner somewhere.'

'Er, just a minute, Becca. Just got to do something,' said Jade, then the phone went dead. Maybe she's changed her mind, I thought hopefully as I waited for her. A moment later, I heard a click and Jade came back on the line.

'I wanted to ask you something,' she said. 'Just between you and me. I don't really know this Fizz girl very well and she's coming here to stay and everything. You've seen her about. Do you think it will be OK? What do you think of her?'

'I don't really know,' I said, wondering why she was asking me of all people and why she was even having Fizz to stay if she was having doubts about it. 'I don't really know her.'

'Yeah, well what do you think of her chances, you know as, Pop Princess?'

It was the first time Jade had asked for my opinion about anything to do with the competition so I took a moment to think about it. Knowing Jade, she'd want me to say something about her standing more of a chance than her new friend. Maybe if I played along, she'd let me stay.

'I think she has a really strong voice,' I said. 'Yeah, I think she stands a good chance, but she's not as good as you.'

'But do you think she looks the part?' asked Jade.

That I could answer easily. I had noticed Fizz because of her voice, but she wasn't exactly gorgeous; in fact, she was a bit weird-looking in a Marge Simpson kind of way.

'I think she needs to make more of herself image-wise,' I said. 'I think they're looking for a Pop Princess in every way, you know . . .'

'What do you mean?' urged Jade.

'Well, I guess what I'm trying to say is that even though it shouldn't matter, I think it does, and she's not as good-looking as some of the other entrants.'

Suddenly a girl's voice came on the line and it wasn't Jade. 'Oh, and I suppose *you* are?' she said.

'Who's that?' I asked, thinking it might be Tamara who'd picked up the other line.

I heard Jade laugh. 'It's Fizz, dummy. She's been listening on the extension the whole time.'

I was aghast. 'That's *really* mean, Jade.'

I would never have said anything if I'd known Fizz was actually there. It was bad enough that Jade had it in for me, but another contestant hating me as well, that was *all* I needed.

I put the phone down and stared out of the window.

Now what? I thought. What am I going to do? Nowhere to stay, no lift and two contestants who would be more than glad if I didn't make it up there at all.

I picked up the phone again and dialled Elliott's number. Maybe I could stay with him.

''Fraid not,' he said after I'd filled him in. 'The whole family is down this time, to do the post-Christmas sales. Don't you know anyone else? You must know someone in London. You *can't* not come.'

I racked my brains after I'd put down the phone. Who? Then a thought struck me. Ollie went to school up there. Maybe I could sneak into his dorm and sleep under his bed. But no, he was away on his skiing trip and his school would be closed. Maybe Lia's sister. Would Star be back from her holiday in Bermuda? My hopes rose again and I picked up the phone to dial Lia's number.

Half an hour later, it was all sorted again. Phew. Lia's dad was going to drive up to London as he wanted to see Star, and even better, Lia was going to come as well. Once again I thought, Never, never, never give up.

Staying at Star's was the best thing ever. Her flat is exactly how I want mine to be when I leave home. It's on the first floor of an old house in Notting Hill Gate and although it's tiny, it's mega-glamorous, like walking into a luxurious Sheik's tent. She'd painted it all soft lavender and corn-flower blue and there were gorgeous Indian fabrics everywhere — soft muslins at the windows, silk cushions and throws. And on every wall were framed magazine covers with pictures of Star. She's worked as a model for all the glossies and is absolutely stunning. Like the rest of her family, she has a perfect heart-shaped face and amazing cheekbones — only her hair is cut short and spiky, unlike Lia's.

She made me feel really welcome. We sent out for Japanese food, including sushi, then drank mint tea. I felt really grown-up and glam sitting with her in her living room.

In the evening, Mr Axford went off to stay with one of his rock band friends and Star wanted to have a girlie night in. She insisted on dressing me for the competition, even though I told her that the stylists were supposed to be coming in to dress the final ten contestants. 'That's if I get through,' I said. 'There's fifteen boys and fifteen girls left, but it will be down to ten of each by lunch-time tomorrow.'

'Oh, you'll get through,' she said. 'A gorgeous girl like you.'

I was dead chuffed with the compliment, especially as she was a model and Lia had told me that Star never gives false praise.

'But don't wait for the stylists,' Star went on. 'They don't always know what suits you best, believe me — I've worked with enough of them. No, best to go with some idea of how you want to look or else they might put you in something you feel weird in. That can knock your confidence.'

She went into her bedroom and came back with a pile of amazing clothes that she'd been given on her photo shoots and Lia and I had a great night trying everything on and doing our hair and nails. When we settled down on the sofa-bed later, I couldn't sleep. I felt so happy, like a whole new world was opening up for me. So much had happened over the last few weeks. I'd met some brilliant people and now was staying in probably the most fabtastic flat in London. It was loads better than it would have been camping on the floor in two-faced Jade's bedroom. It made me think about how things don't always turn out the way you expect them to, but if you don't give up trying, then sometimes they can work out even better than you imagined. I must remember to tell Dad, I thought. He's obviously forgotten.

15 Round Three

ELLIOTT DID a long wolf-whistle when he saw me the next day. He was sitting on the steps outside the hall with a number of the other contestants waiting to go in. Jade and Fizz were there too and Jade looked surprised when she saw me. She whispered something to Fizz, who laughed. I decided that I wasn't going to stoop to their level so I purposely walked near them and smiled.

'Hi,' I said.

They both looked at me as though I was a bad smell under their noses, then turned away. Fine, I thought, be like that, and I went to sit with Elliott.

'You look great,' he said. 'Very rock chick.'

'Thanks,' I replied. I did feel great, despite Jade and Fizz. Star had lent me some top clothes, black Gucci jeans, which fitted like a dream, a handkerchief top and the most amazing black leather jacket by someone called Joseph. I felt a million dollars and ready for anything.

'So, all set for today?'

'Just about,' I said.

'What song are you doing?'

'"Endless Love". What about your lot? Do you think the winner stands out yet?'

He shrugged. 'I ought to say, Yes, *me*, but who knows? There are a few lads in there who are major-league talent.'

'Same in our group,' I said. 'I think just about everyone still in deserves to win.'

A moment later, the doors opened and, as we all got up to go in, I spotted the television cameras inside the reception area and felt a rush of adrenalin.

'Do the nerves *ever* go away?' I asked Elliott.

'Doubt it,' he said. 'But nerves are supposed to be good. They say that the day you don't have them, is the day you lose your edge.'

'Oh good,' I said, 'because my knees have just gone to jelly.'

Elliott grinned. 'You'll be OK. And good luck.'

'Yeah, like, break a leg,' sneered Jade as she walked past.

What is her problem? I asked myself as I followed her in. I've never done anything to her.

This time, all the girls and boys had to wait together in a small hall until we were called. One by one we were called in and Sushila was first up.

She gave me a smile when she came out and came over to sit with Elliott and me. Jade looked really peeved. I knew she was dying to know what went on, but she couldn't bring herself to come over.

'How did it go?' I asked.

'OK, I think. The cameras are in there, which is a bit unnerving, but I think I was OK.'

'And how were the judges?' asked Elliott.

'Not giving anything away,' said Sushila. 'Like stone statues. Very encouraging. Not.'

I was called in fifth and I made sure I walked in confidently and gave the judges a big smile.

'OK,' said Sarah. 'When you're ready.'

I started singing and Martin Riley stopped me about a quarter of the way through. 'OK, Becca, now start again, but this time do it with more conviction.'

'OK,' I said, determined not to let him unnerve me. I thought I had done it with conviction, but anyway . . . I started again.

'No,' said Martin, interrupting again. 'Now you're trying too hard. Take it back a bit. It's an emotional song so don't just belt it out.'

I know what you're doing, I thought. You're testing to see if I'm going to crack. Well, I'm not. I started again, and this time, he let me finish. I think I did as well as I could do – I sang in tune and tried to inject as much feeling as possible. When I finished, I glanced over at the judges. Paul and Martin were looking down at their writing pads and Paul was writing something, but at least Sarah gave me a smile.

'OK Becca,' she said. 'Not long to wait this time as there's only thirty of you to see. We'll let you know at lunch-time if you're going through.'

And then it was back to the waiting. I sat and chatted to Sushila while the others went in. She was really nice. It was good to know that I had one ally in the girl's group. One dark-haired girl called Olivia looked a bit shaken when she came out and went and sat in the corner, looking a bit lost. I decided to go and talk to her as I remembered how I'd felt when Cat was voted out and how lonely it can be.

'Hey,' I said, sitting next to her.

'Hey,' she said.

'How was it in there?'

'Awful,' she said. 'I don't think I'm through.'

I decided to share my new-found wisdom with her. 'You don't know that. It's not over until it's over,' I said. 'Thing is, we mustn't give up. My dad's taught me that. Keep trying. He says the cream always rises to the top of the milk eventually. Same if you have talent. It will win through. And we've got this far – that must say something.'

'God, you're so positive,' she said. 'But really, I don't think I was very good today.'

'Ah,' I said. 'But everyone feels the same. That's what you have to remember. We're all feeling nervous and have had our confidence knocked a bit. So we're all up against the same stuff.'

'I guess,' she said, then smiled. 'Yeah. It's not the end of the world is it?'

'Nah,' I said. 'We're only fourteen. This has been the most brilliant experience and it's not even over yet. Look at us, in the last fifteen girls and that's out of thousands.'

'Yeah,' she smiled. 'That is something, isn't it? I guess that I've been so intent on getting through today that I hadn't even thought about how far we've come.'

'Exactly,' I said.

The judges finished seeing everyone at about half past one and then Tanya divided us into three groups of ten, mixing girls with boys.

'Eek,' said Sushila, who was put in a group with Jade, Fizz and Elliott. 'Know what this means, don't you? One of the groups is out and that will leave the final twenty.'

'Oh God,' I said, feeling *another* rush of nerves and wishing I was with Elliott and Sushila. 'I hope I'm through.'

'You will be, Becca,' said Sushila, looking over at the third group. 'I reckon that group over there won't make it. See that guy with the blond crew cut? I can tell you he wasn't good when I heard him, so don't worry, I reckon your group is a goer.'

Tanya called for everyone's attention then asked Jade's group to stay where they were. After that, she led the remaining twenty of us into the corridor, then put ten in one room and the other ten in a second room.

'Here we go again,' I groaned to Olivia, who was in my group. 'I can't bear this tension.'

'I know,' she said. 'And it doesn't help with the cameras in the corridor, watching every expression.'

'I know,' I said. 'You can almost feel them cheering inside when they catch someone crying. My mate Squidge says they love it when someone breaks down as it makes good telly.'

After Tanya had left us, everyone was very quiet, straining to hear what was going on in the other rooms and waiting for the sound of footsteps. Every time we heard anyone walk past, everyone looked up expectantly, then when they didn't come in, people's shoulders would drop and it was back to waiting. After about ten minutes of excruciating silence, we heard a huge cheer from the room next door.

'One lot through, then,' said Olivia. 'Fingers crossed for us.'

Five minutes later, the doors opened and a cameraman came through and started filming our group.

'Come to catch the tears of success or failure,' said Olivia.

Sarah and Paul came through the door after the cameraman.

'Sorry to keep you waiting like this, everyone,' Paul said, 'as I know you're all eager to hear what's happening. First, I'd like to say how brilliant you've all been . . .'

He doesn't need to say any more, I said to myself as he

went on saying how good everyone had been. I know the dumping-you speech – the 'I'd like to say how much I like you and I hope we can stay friends et cetera, et cetera' speech. Anyone with half a brain knows what it means.

'. . . So,' Paul went on, 'I'm afraid we won't be asking you to go through to the next round. But don't be too disappointed. You've all done brilliantly to have come this far and I hope to be seeing some of you again in future competitions.'

Blah, blah, I thought. Dumped.

Chocfest Blues 16

LIA AND Star were lovely when I got back to the flat on Saturday afternoon. Star told me there would be other chances and that I could go and stay with her whenever I wanted. She even gave me her Gucci jeans, because, she said, they looked so good on me. I hardly took in anything they said. I just felt numb.

'I don't get every job I'm up for,' Star said the next day as we were getting ready for her dad to come and pick us up, 'but you soon learn in the modelling business that you have to take it on the chin – not take it personally, get on with the next thing. You'll get there in the end, Becca.'

And Mr Axford was so sweet on the journey back home. 'It's a tough business,' he said. 'You win some and you lose some. You mustn't give up. I had my share of setbacks in the early days, believe you me.'

Seems like everyone has their stories to tell, I thought as I sat in the back and stared out the window, but it's different when it happens to you. I don't know if I want to be involved in a business that knocks your confidence all the time.

Dad gave me a big hug when I got home and Mum bustled about making cups of tea, like that was going to help. In fact, people being nice to me only made me feel worse, like I was ill or something and had to be treated with kid gloves. I wasn't ill. I wasn't anything. I felt numb. Deflated. Disappointed.

'You were so right, Dad,' I said as I sipped my tea.

'About what?'

'To give up on your dream and go out and get a proper job,' I said. 'Save yourself a lot of pain.'

'Oh Becca,' he said. 'There'll be other chances for me *and* for you. And I haven't given up. I'll still be working on my book in the evenings and weekends.'

Mum stood behind Dad and put her hands on his shoulders. 'Your dad will get there in the end,' she said. 'But in the meantime, we have bills to pay. You have to be practical as well as having a dream.'

'Well my dream's become a nightmare,' I said.

Suddenly it was all too much, sitting there, chatting like the competition was in the distant past. I felt exhausted and I knew I was going to cry. I just wanted to get away, escape my parents' sympathetic looks and words of concern and consolation. I went upstairs and locked my bedroom door.

There was only one thing for it. Only one thing that would take away the pain . . . I rolled my desk chair over to the wardrobe, climbed on to it and hauled down the box I'd put away at Christmas. Chocolates. Five whole boxes of chocolates. I opened the first box and scoffed them down like I hadn't eaten for weeks. Actually, I realised, I hardly had. All that stupid dieting, and for what? What was the point? All that stupid stuff I'd told myself about never giving up. Idiotic. You put in all your best effort and where does it get you? Nowhere.

After ten minutes I decided I needed something more. I unlocked the door, sneaked downstairs and found the can of squirty cream Mum kept for special occasions and took it back upstairs. I put a squirt on every one of the chocolates and ate them, one after the other. Huh, I thought as I swallowed a toffee cream, that's to spite you, stupid Martin Riley. You had it in for me from Day One. Then I ate a hazelnut crunch. And that's for you, Jade Macey, who's got through to the next round with her ugly friend Fizz. Next was a strawberry cream, not my favourite, but topped with an extra squirt of cream — down it went, to spite *all* of them. I hate life, I thought as I went for gold and crammed in two chocolates at the same time. Just when you think everything's going your way, a great big bulldozer comes along and flattens you. I hate myself, I thought, for being so stupid, so full of myself. I winced when I remembered how I'd pratted around, giving everyone 'good advice'.

They must have thought I was a right plonker, I thought. Fat lot of good it did anyone. And I hate school and it stinking well starts tomorrow and everyone will be gossiping. Oh, there's that Rebecca Howard. She thought she was it, you know. Thought she had the makings of a Pop Princess, stupid idiot. We knew she'd never make it. What ever made her think she would?

Oh God. I have no future, no life, no hope.

After I'd finished three-quarters of the second box of chocs, I started to feel very strange. I groaned and lay back on my bed. Then there was a knock on my door.

'Are you in there, Becca?' asked Dad.

'No,' I said. 'Leave me alone. I don't want to talk to anyone.' I certainly didn't want to talk to Dad any more. It was *his* stupid fault I'd got so carried away, putting all those daft ideas into my head about never giving up. What a load of rubbish. If I hadn't listened to him, I wouldn't have had to go through all this. And I wouldn't be feeling so sick now.

'Cat's on the phone.'

'Tell her I've gone to Katmandu with the milkman,' I said. I didn't even want to talk to her. There was nothing she could say. Although to give her her due, she had tried. They all had. As soon as I'd got back to Star's flat, the phone had started going – Cat, Squidge and Mac, all wanting to know how it had gone.

Mac. Stupid git. I didn't even know if he was my

boyfriend any more. We hadn't been out on a date in ages and we hadn't snogged each other properly for weeks. Maybe it was all over and I'd been so wrapped up I hadn't noticed I'd been dumped by him as well as the competition.

Squidge. Stupid git. It was really all *his* fault. Him and that stupid dare. It was all right for all of them. They'd done it for a laugh. Squidge told me that Andy Warhol once said that everyone has their fifteen minutes of fame. The Pop Princess competition was mine. And now it was over. For ever.

But Mac is the *stupidest* git, thinking I was off with Elliott all the time. As if a boy like him would ever take an interest in me. He probably felt sorry for me.

And Cat, well, she's just a stupid git, because . . . because everyone is, especially me. I'm the most stupid git of all, stupid, stupid, *stupid*.

I felt tears pricking the back of my eyes again. And now I'm going to cry, I thought as tears started to spill down my cheeks. And I don't care. I am a loser, a failure. A stupid, stupid person. Then there was a sudden lurch in my stomach and, oops, better run for it. I'm going to . . . eeeew . . .

As I kneeled on the bathroom floor, I caught sight of my reflection in the mirror – mad hair, red eyes, deathly white and on my knees with chocolate smeared around my mouth. 'Hey, Pop Princess,' I said as I grimaced at myself. 'This is what happens when you try to exceed your grasp or whatever that stupid quote of Dad's is.' To have imagined I could have actually won Pop Princess. Hah. Never again. Never, never, never, never, never, never, never . . .

I went back into my bedroom and lay on the bed, ready for another good cry. Once again, there was a knock at the door.

'Becca,' said Mum.

'Go away,' I called. 'I need to be alone.'

'OK,' said Mum. 'It's just that someone from the competition is on the phone for you.'

'Who?' I said. 'Elliott?' I'd already spoken to Elliott on Saturday after the 'dumping'. He was lovely. He'd put his arm around me and hadn't come out with any of the clichés about trying again or getting another chance, et cetera. He just held me tight, like he understood.

'No,' said Mum through the door. 'It's someone called Martin Riley.'

I sat up like a shot. Martin Riley? Ohmigod, I thought. What does he want? . . . Probably phoned to check I haven't put my head in a gas oven. Probably checking that I'm OK. I don't know if I want to hear him come out with some claptrap about being a good loser.

But my curiosity had been aroused. It couldn't hurt to just hear what he had to say . . .

'Are you going to pick up your phone?' asked Mum. 'Or shall I ask him to call back later?'

'No, no,' I said as I smoothed my hair and wiped away

chocolate smears. 'I'll take it.'

I picked up the phone. 'Er, hello?'

'Becca,' said Martin. 'Sorry to call so late, but we needed to get in touch with you.'

I didn't say anything.

'So you got home OK?' he asked.

D'oh, *obviously*, I thought. 'Yes, thank you,' I said.

'Have you been crying, Becca?' he asked. 'Your voice sounds a bit funny.'

'Um no,' I said. 'Bit bunged up that's all. Um, hayfever.'

'Ah,' said Martin. 'Yes, hayfever. I always get hayfever in January. Anyway, I may have a cure for you. Reason I'm calling is, we've had a problem with one of the finalists, Fiona McPhilbin – I think you all know her as Fizz? Well, she lied about her age. Remember the entry age was up to sixteen? Well she was seventeen at the beginning of December and so we've had no choice but to disqualify her.'

My head started to spin. Why was he telling *me*? What did it mean?

'So Sarah, Paul and I put our heads together,' he continued, 'and decided that we'd like to ask you to come back. It was very close between you and another contestant anyway. I don't think you knew that. So, what do you say? Give it another shot?'

17 The Final

PROGRAMME FOR
POP PRINCE AND POP PRINCESS FINAL
Saturday, January 11th Starts 4.00 p.m.

Pop Princes

1) Jason Barker: 'Bridge Over Troubled Water'
   (Simon and Garfunkel)
2) Mark Bosman: 'Everything I Do (I Do It For You)'
   (Bryan Adams)
3) Ewan Hughes: 'Candle in the Wind' (Elton John)
4) David Keenan: 'Careless Whisper' (George Michael)
5) Scott Lewis: 'Every Breath You Take' (Police)
6) Martin McDonnell: 'Rock DJ' (Robbie Williams)
7) Jonathan McKeever: 'You've Lost That Loving
   Feeling' (Righteous Brothers)
8) Paul Nash: 'Waterloo Sunset' (The Kinks)
9) Rick Schneider: 'I'm Not in Love' (10 CC)
10) Elliott Williams: 'Suspicious Minds' (Elvis Presley)

Pop Princesses

1) Kate Anderson: 'Natural Woman' (Carole King)

2) Charlotte Bennie: 'Like a Prayer' (Madonna)

3) Jessica Harris: 'Baby One More Time'
   (Britney Spears)

4) Becca Howard: 'Nothing Compares 2 U'
   (Sinead O'Connor)

5) Alice Seymour Jones: 'I Will Always Love You'
   (Whitney Houston)

6) Jade Macey: 'My Heart Will Go On' (Celine Dion)

7) Heather Nicholson: 'Can't Get You Out of My Head'
   (Kylie Minogue)

8) Marie Oliver: 'Eternal Flame' (The Bangles)

9) Sushila Patel: 'Hero' (Mariah Carey)

10) Chloe Wilson: 'I Will Survive' (Gloria Gayner)

The final will be televised live and tickets will be available for friends and family. Please refrain from taking photographs during the performances. Thank you for your co-operation.

WHAT A top week. I phoned Cat, Squidge, Mac and Lia immediately and told them the latest news. They went wild, like it was happening to them. But the best bit of the week was bumping in to Jade at school and seeing her face. She looked like I'd looked after my chocfest. Classmates were fantastic. Of course news had spread that I'd been out then in again and I was amazed at the support I was given from everyone. Even people I didn't know. Even Jonno Appleton in Year Eleven.

Everyone came up to London for the final, as they were letting friends and family in to see the last performances. Mum and Dad stayed in a B&B around the corner from Star's. Cat, Lia and I slept at Star's and Squidge stayed with Mac at Mr Macey's. I'd gone up on the Friday and had spent the Friday night and all day Saturday going over my song with a voice coach and a guy accompanying on the piano. They were totally brilliant and gave me some excellent tips. Late on Saturday afternoon, a stylist came in for a session with all the contestants, but I wasn't that bothered with what she had to say because I had my own personal stylist back at the flat – Star Axford and her wardrobe of fantastic designer clothes. When I dashed back to the flat just before the final show, I found that Star had picked out a stunning dress for me to wear. It was royal blue – not a colour I'd normally choose, but it was low-cut, with a slit up the side and looked amazing with the pair of Jimmy Choo heels that she also lent me. She blow-dried my hair straight and loose and put the dress in a plastic carrier for me to change into when I got to the hall.

I felt so calm. It was weird, but having thought I'd lost

once and then to be given a second chance, I had no expectations, and as Mum always says, Blessed is she who has no expectations, for she is never disappointed. I was lucky to be going at all, and I knew it.

Loads of press were waiting outside the hall when we arrived and one of them called over to Lia.

'Hey, you one of the finalists?'

'No,' she replied, then pointed at me. 'But my mate Becca is.'

Suddenly I had a crowd buzzing around me and a bunch of photographers snapping pictures.

'So how's it been? What do you think of your chances?'

'What's the atmosphere been like? Any nastiness between the contestants?'

'How do you see your future?'

'Just say "no comment",' whispered Cat.

'Er, it's been fantastic,' I said. 'All the contestants have been great. We're all very supportive of each other. Um. Don't know about my chances – everybody's really good.'

Then we made a dash for the hall as the press swirled around one of the boy contestants who'd just walked in.

'God, this is so glamorous,' said Cat when we got inside. 'It's like you're a real star.'

'I know. It's amazing, isn't it?' I said. It felt like a dream come true.

Mum and Dad were waiting in the foyer and I gave them a wave.

'Just do your best, love,' said Dad, walking towards us. 'We'll be out there with our fingers crossed for you.'

Mum gave me a hug. 'My little girl,' she said. 'I'm so proud of you.'

'Thanks, Mum. Anyway, got to go and get ready.'

Elliott arrived a moment later, ran over and gave me a huge hug. 'How top is this?' he said. 'Both of us in the finals. You said it's never over until it's over and you were right.'

I gave him a huge hug back. 'I know. I still can hardly believe I'm here.'

He took my hand and led me towards the performers' door. Of course that had to be the exact moment that Mac arrived with Squidge, who was holding a kid I'd never seen before by the hand. I saw Mac's face light up when he saw me, then shut down when he saw Elliott holding my hand. It was awful.

Right, Mac Macey, I thought. I'm going to deal with you *this* instant. Being dumped from the competition made me do a lot of thinking, and a lot of it was about Mac. I'd neglected him horribly at a time when he really needed me – a time when you turn to your mates and hope they'll be there for you. I hadn't been there for him, because I'd been sitting on my Pop Princess cloud. But the semi-final had brought me down to earth with a thump, and boy was I glad I had my mates. Even though I hadn't wanted to talk to them at first, I *had* appreciated just how supportive they'd been through all of it, even Mac. He'd sorted it out so that I could stay with his dad, Lia had sorted it so that I could stay with Star, Cat and Squidge had listened to all my rehearsals and had been encouraging every time. Cat and Squidge and Lia had been totally top and not at all critical that I'd only been thinking about myself for the last few weeks.

I pulled Elliott over to Squidge and Mac.

'This is Elliott,' I said to the boys. 'He's been my best mate in the competition and I reckon he's going to win.'

Elliott smiled and shrugged. 'I wish.'

Squidge said, 'Hi,' and Mac sort of mumbled.

'Elliott,' I continued, 'these are my best mates from home. Squidge and my *boyfriend* Mac.'

I let go of Elliott's hand, took Mac's and gave him a big smacker on the cheek. 'We've been going out for about . . . How long has it been, Mac?'

Mac squeezed my hand and smiled. 'About three months . . .' Then he laughed. 'And one week, three days, nine hours . . .'

Elliott laughed. 'You're a lucky bloke, mate. You make sure you hang on to her.'

'Oh, I will.' Mac grinned at me. 'I *will*.'

I looked over at the little girl who had been holding on to Squidge's hand through all this. She looked about eight – a bit young, even for Squidge. 'And who's your new girl-friend, Squidge?' I teased.

'This is Tamara,' said Mac. 'Sonia's daughter. She wouldn't let us come without her, would you, T?'

Tamara smiled up at Mac like they were oldest, bestest friends. 'Not after I heard that Mac's girlfriend was in the competition,' she said, blushing.

'Yes . . . And I just need to have a private moment with him,' I said and took him aside. 'So, how's it going? At the flat. You know, with Sonia and her daughter and stuff?' This was something I'd promised myself I'd do from now on — take an interest in what was happening to him, even if there was something happening to me as well.

Mac smiled. 'OK . . . Tamara's cool. She's a kid.' Then he grinned. 'In fact, I think she's got a bit of a crush on Squidge. She asked if he had a girlfriend. I think she wants to marry him when she grows up.'

'And what about Sonia?'

'OK too. We get on all right, I guess,' said Mac. 'She's OK. And Dad does seem happier. I had a chat with him and he's not going to move in with her or anything. And he said she's not going to be there every time I go up. So yeah, I guess it might be OK.'

'It *will* be OK,' I said as I took his hand. 'And I wanted to say I'm sorry I've been such a pain all these weeks. You know, like totally self-obsessed.'

Mac squeezed my hand. 'Hey, no biggie. I'm sorry *I've* been such a pain. I could have been more supportive. I guess I got a bit jealous. I dunno, it felt like I was losing you or something.'

'I think I lost myself back there for a while. But after tonight, it's all back to normal,' I said.

Elliott came over and looked at his watch. 'Show-time folks.'

Mac put his arms around me and gave me a huge bear hug. 'Good luck, kiddo. Now go and show them what you can do.'

Happy, happy, happy, I thought as I headed for the dressing room. And here I go again. But this time it felt so different, in a really good way.

After we'd got ready, the girl contestants were allowed to sit in the audience with the others to watch the boys. My dad's eyes almost fell out of their sockets when he saw me walk in wearing Star's dress. I thought it was a good job I was sitting in a different section as he'd probably have made me go and change into something less revealing. Too late, Dad. Chances to dress like this don't come around very often and it wasn't as though I was out of place in my designer frock. All the contestants had really pulled out the stops and looked amazing. I was used to seeing everyone in their jeans and trainers, but now we all looked like we'd just stepped on to the red carpet at the Oscars.

The lights went down and Paul Parker walked on to the stage. He explained how the voting worked and what time the lines would close for each category. Then he began to introduce the male contestants. It was fantastic to sit there and watch them all. The girls hadn't had a chance to see what the boys had been up to because we'd always been in a separate hall. As each of them sang, I thought they were all really good, but of course, I was rooting for Elliott. I couldn't wait to hear him perform.

The audience cheered like mad after every performance. It was really obvious where the friends and family of each contestant were sitting as they went wild when their boy was up. Elliott was on last and when Paul announced his name and he walked out to centre stage I felt my stomach tighten with nerves on his behalf. He looked every inch a Pop Prince in black leather trousers, a black T-shirt and with spiked hair. It was clear he worked out as well, as he had great muscle tone. He'd even put some temporary tattoos on his arm to give him that 'Robbie Williams' look. The music struck up and he sang 'Suspicious Minds' by Elvis Presley. I thought, I might be biased, but he was easily the best. Confident, cheeky, and he had a great voice. I felt so chuffed for him at the end when the audience cheered madly, and I turned to see my mates, including Mac, standing and whistling with the others.

Before I knew it, Tanya was beckoning for the girls to go backstage. Shame, as I'd have loved to stay where I was and watch the other girls.

'You can wait here,' said Tanya as she led us behind the

curtains. 'You won't be able to see, but you will be able to hear. OK, Kate, you're on first, so stand over there. And good luck to all of you. You all look fabulous.'

I stood with Sushila as Kate got ready for her name to be announced. Suddenly my new-found calm deserted me and my knees started to go. Ohmigod, I thought, it'll be me in a moment. Live on television, in front of thousands of viewers. It's not just three judges any more, it's *thousands*. Ohmigod, ohmigod, ohmigod. Nervous, nervous, nervous.

Everything went into slow motion. Kate did her number, then Charlotte, then Jessica, and before I knew it, I heard Paul's voice saying, 'And our next performer is Becca Howard from St Antony, Cornwall. She's going to be singing 'Nothing Compares 2 U'.

Sushila pushed me forward. 'You're on. Good luck!'

My legs had turned from jelly to stone. 'I can't move,' I moaned.

Sushila pushed me again. 'Yes you can, go *on*.'

I took a deep breath and did a quick shake and tremble as Zac had taught me, then I walked out on to the stage and towards the microphone.

The spotlights were blinding. It all felt so unreal. Just breathe, Becca, I told myself. It's going to be OK. Oh God, please don't let me fall over or dry up or forget the words – please, please, please. I'd never felt so petrified. I looked at the audience and tried to find Mum and Dad and my mates. And there they were, all looking at me with so much hope and

307

anticipation on their faces that I felt myself start to smile.

The music started up and I began to sing the opening lines. Suddenly I got an amazing rush. Here I was, singing in front of an audience, cameras on me, my friends and family in the audience . . . This was my moment. It was going to be all right.

When I'd finished, the audience erupted into cheers and applause and I looked over to my support group. They were standing and clapping and whistling. It was so totally brilliant. And I swear I saw my mum put a handkerchief to her eye, like she was crying.

After that, it was over, and the next one was on. At last, I could enjoy the rest of the performances. I'd done my bit and I could relax. From now on, it was up to the audience at home to phone in and decide on the winner.

When everyone had finished, there was a break for the guests to go and have refreshments while the contestants were led into a green room to wait for the public's verdict. The atmosphere was bubbling, not like the other times – this was *it* and we all knew it. I felt on top of the world and I buzzed about, telling everyone how brilliant they'd been and how great they looked. I even tried to congratulate Jade, but she did her usual snooty look, then turned away to talk to one of the guys, so I decided not to bother. Why ruin the atmosphere with one of her snide comments, I thought. I'd done what I could with her and she was still being off with me so why waste energy? I didn't need her to like me. Why had I been so bothered about making someone I didn't even like, like me? I had enough real friends without her.

About half an hour later we were all called back on to the stage and the guests took their seats once more.

'The phone lines for Pop Prince have now closed and the votes have been counted,' said Martin. 'But before we announce our winners, I should say that I and the other two judges have been extremely impressed by the standard of the contestants. They've worked hard and taken a lot of criticism, mainly from me. But they've stuck it out and I'd like to stress that all the contestants here are winners tonight.'

'Blah, blah,' I said and grinned at Sushila, who grinned back.

'So, without further ado, I'll pass the microphone over to Sarah, who holds the results for our Pop Prince,' Martin said. 'Let's see how the public voted. Over to you, Sarah.'

Sarah took the microphone. 'In third place,' she announced, 'with eighteen per cent of the vote, we have . . . Martin McDonnell.'

The audience cheered madly as Martin stepped forward and stood beside her.

'In second place, with twenty-two per cent of the vote . . . Ewan Hughes.'

More cheering and I glanced over at Elliott. He smiled at me and gulped, so I held up my hands to show that my fingers were crossed for him.

'And finally, this year's Pop Prince, with thirty-eight per cent of the votes . . .

Dead silence.

'. . . Elliott Williams.'

Elliott gasped, went bright red, then stepped forward to shake Sarah's hand. The audience went wild. I glanced back at the seven boys who hadn't been chosen. I really felt for them as they must have been terribly disappointed, but they were all doing their best to keep smiling and look happy for Elliott.

Once the awards had been given and photos taken of the three boys, Sarah took the microphone again. 'And now, we finally get to our Pop Princesses. Tanya can you bring out the results please?'

I felt all ten of us stiffen in anticipation as Tanya walked over to Sarah. Who would it be?

Tanya seemed to whisper something in Sarah's ear, then Sarah nodded and turned to the audience.

'I'm sorry,' she said into the microphone, 'but there will be a slight delay in announcing the winner. The technicians are having problems with a couple of the phone lines and people haven't been getting through. Perhaps while we're waiting, we could ask our Pop Prince to come forward and sing for us again. 'I'll keep you informed and let you know as soon as we have some news.'

'Oh argghhh,' said Sushila, leaning against me.

'I know,' I said. 'Argh, argh, *argh* . . .'

18

Duchess

THE MORNING after we got back from London, I had a lie-in until eleven o'clock. Mum said that even though it was a bit naughty, I could have the morning off school. She and Dad were even taking time off. It felt like bliss to sleep in and not have to think about songs or rehearsals or what I'd wear or losing half a stone. Bliss, bliss, bliss.

When I finally got up and went down to breakfast, I found Dad grinning and waving an envelope at me.

'What?' I asked.

'Good news,' he said. 'Nothing definite yet, but it's a step in the right direction. It's a letter from an agent. A very good agent in London. She likes the outline and chapters I sent her and wants to see the rest of the book.'

'So does that mean you'll have a deal?' I asked.

'No,' said Dad, 'but it means someone is taking me seriously. These guys don't waste time if they're not really interested. If she takes me on, she'll try and get me a deal. So fingers crossed for me, Becca.'

'So will you give up your job?' I asked. Although I was glad he had received a positive response, I didn't want to go back to those nights lying awake listening to him and Mum arguing.

'No, I won't give up the job,' he said. 'In fact, I'm beginning to enjoy it. I missed being in a working environment, missed the stimulation. I'd only give up work if I made it on to the bestseller lists and stayed there for the better part of a year. I can write *and* work for the time being.'

'That's fantastic, Dad,' I said. 'You deserve a break.'

'Too right,' said Mum, coming in through the back door with a carrier bag. 'I'm going to cook your dad a celebratory breakfast. Scrambled eggs, smoked salmon and . . .' She pulled out a bottle of champagne, '. . . a bit of bubbly.'

Dad looked really chuffed. 'Oh Megan, you needn't have . . .'

'No bother,' she said and kissed the top of his head. 'I think it's important to celebrate the small successes in life as well as the big ones. And Lord knows, you've tried hard enough to get someone to pay you some attention. And of course, there's Becca's news . . .'

Mum put the champagne in an ice bucket, then found three glasses.

'Who else is coming?' I asked.

'It's for you, you daft nonce,' she said, then she popped

the cork and poured three glasses. 'You can have it with some orange juice.'

I took the glass she offered me and held it up the way people do at weddings. 'A toast,' I said. 'To my dad, the famous novelist.'

Dad lifted his glass. 'To my lovely family, without whom none of it means anything.'

'So you're not going to split up, then?' I asked.

Mum looked shocked. '*Split up*? Of course not!'

'Whatever made you think that, Becca?' asked Dad.

I shrugged. 'Nothing. Just heard you rowing sometimes.'

'All couples row sometimes, love,' said Mum. 'It doesn't mean they don't love each other.'

'You've not been worried about this for long have you?' asked Dad.

'No . . . Yeah, sort of. People *do* break up, you know,' I said. 'Like Mac's mum and dad.'

'Well, you don't need to worry about us,' said Dad. 'We're in for the duration. It would take a lot more than a few rows to break us up.'

Mum raised her glass. 'To us,' she said. 'Our little family. To you, Joe – wishing you every success. And to you, Becca – singer extraordinaire and our very own Pop Duchess.'

'Duchess?' I asked.

'Well, that lovely Indian girl won the title Pop Princess. You came third, so I reckon that makes you a Duchess.'

I laughed and gave a royal wave. 'It was top, wasn't it?'

'I've never felt so proud of you,' said Mum. 'You were brilliant.'

It had been brilliant. We only had to wait half an hour for the phones to start working again then the results came through. Sushila won, with thirty-five per cent of the vote, Jade came in second with twenty-one per cent of the votes, then . . . me. *Me*! With nineteen per cent of the votes. I was over the moon. Delirious. Ecstatic. Sushila deserved to win – she stood out a mile. And Jade – well, I've always known Jade was good. She wasn't too happy about coming second, though, and couldn't help showing it. Shame, because when the press pictures come, everyone's going to see what a sulky cow she really is.

I was gobsmacked that I came third. I really, really, *really* didn't expect it. I was hoping for sixth or seventh or something, so coming in third had far exceeded my expectations.

After a lovely morning with my parents, I finally got into school at lunch-time. Everyone in the playground cheered. It was fantastic. Loads of people came up and said, 'Well done' and 'You were fab' and 'We saw you on telly' . . . I felt like a real star. The press had put our school on the map for having two competitors in the finals. One paper said there must be something in the Cornish air that breeds talent. That should keep my teachers happy, I thought. Maybe they'll give me a better report next time.

As we were going into classes for the afternoon, Miss Segal waved for me to go over to her.

'Yes, Miss Segal,' I said.

'Well first, I believe congratulations are in order,' she said. 'I saw you and Jade last night. You were both fantastic. I felt so proud. That's why I wanted to have a word. It's about the Easter show. I don't know if you've noticed yet, but I put a notice up about it last week and I wondered if you'd like to take part this time.'

I felt really chuffed. To actually be *asked* this time.

'Of course Jade will be wanting a leading role, but I'm sure there will be room for both of you,' continued Miss Segal. 'We're going to be casting next week. So what do you think? Would you like to be in it?'

I glanced over at Mac, who was standing behind her. 'Um, yes, sort of, but I . . . I don't want a lead part. In fact, I don't even really want to be in it.'

Miss Segal looked puzzled. 'So what would you like, then?'

'How about if I get involved in the other side of things. – like producing?'

Miss Segal was obviously surprised. 'Why produce and not sing?'

'Couple of things. First: I've been thinking a lot about what I want to do when I'm older. I could carry on with my singing, but most singers, unless they're Kylie or Madonna or someone, they only have a short time at the top, and

316

then what? What would I do if that was me? It would be back to all the angst I felt throughout that competition.'

Miss Segal smiled. 'What a sensible girl you are, Becca. Most girls your age wouldn't have that kind of foresight. So what's the other reason?'

'Something Mac said to me ages ago. About managing and producing and the people who make it all happen. I think maybe I could go into producing or management when I'm older and the school show would be good practice to see if I'd like it.'

'Well, yes. And I'm sure your experiences from the show will stand you in good stead if you want to pursue producing. But that's my job, really.'

'Maybe you could use an assistant? I think I learned a lot doing that competition, about people needing encouragement and ways to relax, as it can all be pretty stressful.'

'It can indeed,' said Miss Segal, looking closely at me. Then she smiled again. 'This is a surprise, Becca. Very encouraging that you haven't got your head in the clouds and been carried away by it all.'

'No,' I said. 'I've seen how good the competition is out there. It won't be an easy ride for anyone, not even Sushila or Elliott, who won first prize.'

'So you'd rather be a big fish in a small pond?'

'For now, I guess,' I said. 'Until I know what I want to do. Then, well . . . you can achieve anything if you put your mind to it and work hard.'

Miss Segal leaned back against the wall in mock shock. 'I can't believe I'm hearing this,' she laughed.

'And with the Easter show, could I be involved from the beginning – with the casting as well?'

Miss Segal nodded. 'Yes, I don't see why not. You could sit in on that as well.'

Fab, I thought. It would be interesting sitting on the other side of things and I decided I wouldn't be mean to anyone, even if they were rotten. And I wouldn't be horrid to Jade, but I doubted she'd even want to be in it once she heard I was producing.

'And, um, you know what you just said about me being sensible and having foresight and stuff?'

'Yes, Becca?'

'Well, er, could you put that in my next report?'

Miss Segal laughed. 'Yes, of course I can. How about this: Becca shows great ambition, but her head isn't in the clouds; in fact, her feet are firmly planted on the ground and she seems to know exactly where she's going.'

I beamed back at her. 'Sounds excellent to me.'

Teen Queens
and
Has-Beens

Truth Dare Kiss Promise

Teen Queens and Has-Beens

Cathy Hopkins

PICCADILLY PRESS • LONDON

Thanks as always to Brenda Gardner, Yasemin Uçar and the ever fab team at Piccadilly. To Rosemary Bromley at Juvenilia. And to Georgina Acar, Scott Brenman, Becca Crewe, Alice Elwes, Jenni Herzberg, Rachel Hopkins and Olivia McDonnell for answering all my questions about what it's like being a teenager these days.

Valentine's Day

'POST IS HERE, Lia,' Mum called as she went past my bedroom.

I looked out of the window to see the post van zooming away down the drive to the left of the house. It was a lovely clear day and the view from my window was stunning. Terraced lawns, then acres of fields leading down to the sea and our private beach. Although I've been officially living at home for almost eight months now, opening my curtains in the morning is still a thrill and such a change from the apartment block that I looked out on when I was at boarding school up in London.

'Be right down,' I called back, then went into my bathroom to find my make-up bag. I wasn't in any great hurry to go downstairs. Not today. It was Friday, February 14th. Valentine's Day. That meant cards and I knew there wouldn't be any for me.

As I slicked on some lip-gloss, I thought back to this time last year when I was still a boarder. I'd got loads of cards then. I had loads of boyfriends too. Jason, Max, Elliott, Leo, Edward. None of them were major or soulmates or anything serious, just part of the gang that used to hang out together. But there had been dates. And cards. We'd send them to each other just for a laugh or so that no one missed out.

Life is so different since I moved down here to Cornwall. New school, new friends, new everything apart from romance. Not one single date since I changed schools. Hence the lack of expectation when it came to Valentine's cards.

I pottered around in my room getting ready for school, then my curiosity got the better of me. Maybe there'd be one card from some mysterious stranger who was secretly pining for me. An admirer who will later reveal himself to be the next best thing since pecan fudge ice cream. Yeah, and there's a yeti living in my fridge, I thought as I grabbed my rucksack and headed downstairs.

Mum was sorting through a pile of envelopes at the counter in the kitchen when I got down. She glanced up and by the look in her eyes, I could tell that I'd been right. Nothing for me.

'It's cool,' I said. 'I wasn't expecting any.'

Mum shook her head. 'They all need their heads examining, these boys down here.' She pointed at a jug on the counter. 'I've just made some juice. Beetroot, orange and raspberry. Help yourself.'

'Um, think I'll stick with plain orange,' I said going to the fridge and helping myself to a carton.

Juicing is one of Mum's passions – partly for health reasons, partly for beauty. She's forty, but only looks thirty, which she puts down to juicing. She says it takes years off people and improves their skin no end. Some of her concoctions are fab, but some of them are strange with a capital S. I looked over at the dark crimson liquid in the juicer. 'You're not going to serve that at the party tonight, are you?'

Mum laughed. 'No. Course not. We'll be having Bellinis as the theme is Venetian.'

'That's champagne and peach juice, isn't it?' I knew because my sister Star likes them. She always has a bottle of champagne and a carton of peach juice in the fridge in her tiny flat in Notting Hill. She makes me laugh as sometimes that's *all* she has in her fridge and, when I go to stay with her, I have to go and buy proper food myself. It's not that Star doesn't eat, she does, it's just that she eats out most of the time and is hardly ever home.

Mum nodded. 'There's a place near St Mark's Square in Venice called Harry's Bar. It's famous for its Bellinis.'

'Harry's Bar? Doesn't sound very Italian. Sounds more like a café in the East End of London.'

'I know,' said Mum. 'But then there's probably a famous café in the East End called La Dolce Vita that sells the best cup of tea in the city.'

I laughed. Mum was in her element planning parties. If she ever had to work, that would be her perfect job as she's always throwing a do or planning the next. Always over the top. Always with a theme and always no expense spared. This time, the party planners have been here for weeks recreating Venice for a masked ball to be held in a marquee in the top acre of the garden. I felt like I was living in a hotel with all the catering vans outside and people buzzing about carrying vast flower arrangements, swathes of fabric or lights.

'Any cards there for the Cornish Casanova?' I asked.

The Cornish Casanova is my elder brother, Ollie. He boards at school up in London, but he comes back about once a month and has a long list of admirers down here, including my mate, Cat.

Mum counted the cards. 'Three. But most girls know to send his to his school as he's there in the week.'

'I guess,' I said. 'In fact, the post office probably had to hire an extra van to cope with the load addressed to him.' Ollie's always been a girl magnet. He's got Mum's great bone structure and blue eyes but with dark hair like Dad, not blonde like Mum and me. As I drank my juice, I wondered if Cat had sent a card to him. She and Ollie have had a bit of a 'thing' since last summer. Nothing official, but you can see that they're really into each other whenever they're together. She knows that he's commitment-phobic so doesn't expect too much. I think that's one of the things that he likes about her and why she's lasted so long. She's cool about him, whereas other girls have virtually camped on his door to try and pin him down. Perfect way to get him to back off, which is why Cat is playing it just right.

'I got one from Dad.' Mum smiled as she put an enormous flowery card on the kitchen counter. 'And he's got his usual sack full.'

My dad is Zac Axford, lead singer of the rock band Hot Snax. They were big in the eighties and he still has a bunch of faithful followers who never forget him, even though most of them are in their forties now. I tease him that he's like Cliff Richard with his middle-aged fan club, but with his faded rock star looks, his tatty jeans, leather jackets and shoulder length hair, he's more Mick Jagger than Cliff.

I went out into the hall, grabbed my jacket and went to wait outside for Meena, our housekeeper, to bring the Mercedes round to take me to school. Max and Molly, our mad red setters, came bounding up with their usual morning greeting of licks and paws on the shoulder. At least you love me, I thought as Max almost knocked me off my feet.

I couldn't help but feel disappointed that there wasn't

one card for me even though I'd told myself that there wouldn't be. Get over it, it's no biggie, I told myself. So I haven't got a boyfriend down here, so what? At least I've made good mates – Cat, Becca, Mac and Squidge. They're really cool, though different to the London crowd in that their relationships seem to be more long-term. Becca has been going out with Mac for about six months, and Cat went out with Squidge for a few years until they broke up last summer, when she fell under the spell of the Cornish Casanova. The longest that I or any of my London mates ever lasted in a relationship was about three months. No one wanted to get tied down to one person.

Still, this new crowd have been brilliant and have made me feel really welcome. I felt petrified that first day of term last year and began to wonder if I'd made a huge mistake asking to change school. It wasn't that I didn't like my old school, I did, and I had great mates there – Tara, Athina, Gabby, Sienna, Isobel, Olivia and Natalie. It was after Mum and Dad bought the house down here that everything changed. I had to be a boarder and as my mates were all day pupils, it was a bit lonely some evenings. On top of that, getting home at the weekend was a long way to travel. I felt like I never saw Mum and Dad properly, as I was forever on a train going back and forth. It didn't bother Ollie. He wanted to stay as a boarder, but I told Mum I'd like to go to a local school and live at home. She didn't object or try and talk me out of it, not even for a second, as I think she missed me as much as I missed her. She spoke to the headmistress down here and it was agreed. I'd move after Year Eight.

When I got to the new school, everyone seemed to know each other so well, all chatting and catching up after the summer, all totally familiar with where classes were, who the teachers were, who their mates were. And then there was me, the new girl in Year Nine, wondering where I fitted, if anywhere. All the cliques and friendships had clearly been established long ago and I wondered if I was destined to be a loner for the whole year, standing on the outside looking in. Not my favourite time, plus I really missed all the old gang back in London. Cat was my saviour. She offered to show me around the school and we clicked immediately. She's one of the nicest, most genuine, unpretentious people I've ever met. Her mum died when she was nine and I think it made her grow up over night. Whatever, it's made her sensitive to people when they're a bit lost, maybe on account of feeling lost herself when her mum first went.

I heard the car toot outside the garages, so I took a deep breath and prepared myself for the inevitable inquisition at school.

2 Mystery Admirer?

EVERYONE WAS hanging out in the corridor by the assembly hall when I got in. All the talk was about the school Valentine's disco and cards, with lots of whispering, giggling and secret looks as people tried to guess who'd sent which card to who and who'd left which card in whose locker or rucksack.

'So, how many did you get?' asked Becca.

'Oh, way too many to count,' I replied, trying to laugh it off. I started to count on my fingers. 'One from Robbie

Becca's eyes widened. 'Really?'

Cat punched her arm. 'No, she's kidding you.'

I laughed. Becca was so gullible. She thinks that because Dad's in the music business that we know everyone. 'How many cards did you get, Bec?'

'Just one, I guess it's from Mac,' said Becca, as she pulled her long red hair into a ponytail. 'At least it better had be seeing as I sent him one. What about you, Cat?'

'One. Don't know who it's from. At first, I thought it was from Squidge as we've sent each other cards for years, but it's not his writing. I'd know his scrawl even if he tried to disguise it.'

'I think people ought to sign Valentine's cards,' said Becca. 'It would save a lot of grief knowing who they were from.'

'They do in some places,' I said. 'One of my mates at my old school was American and she said that sometimes they sign them there.'

'Yeah, but it would take the mystery out it,' said Cat. 'It's fun trying to guess.'

'Did you send Squidge a card?' I asked.

Cat shook her head. 'It's not like that with us any more.'

'Did you send Ollie one?'

'Nah. I reckon his head's big enough as it is and no doubt he'll get a sack-load despite me. But seriously, Lia, how many did you get?'

I made my finger and thumb into an O.

'I don't get it,' said Cat. 'I mean, look at you. You're *stunning*, tall, long blonde hair, silver-blue eyes . . . you're most boys' fantasy girl! Boys visibly dribble when you enter a room, and no, don't shake your head, I've *seen* them. By my reckoning, half the school is madly in love with you.'

'Yeah, but some of the boys here like to act really hard,' said Becca. 'You know, they think that they'd look like soppy Sarahs if they did anything remotely romantic like send a card. Pathetic, isn't it? Doesn't mean that you haven't got loads of boys interested in you, though, Lia.'

'So why haven't I had one single date since I got here then?'

'Beneath the hard act, most boys are chickens,' said Becca. 'They're intimidated. You're beautiful, a five-star babe and most of them know that they're not in your league. Boys hate rejection more than anything, so I reckon most of them daren't ask you out for fear of being turned down.'

'I agree,' said Cat. 'Anyway, you're not missing much. Our school isn't exactly Talent City.'

Becca punched Cat's arm. 'Er, excuse me. Mac?'

'Yeah, course,' said Cat. 'And Squidge, but I don't count them. They're mates.'

I didn't say anything, but privately, I think I could fancy Squidge if I let myself. But I don't go there seeing as Cat and he were an item for ages and they're still really close mates. I don't know how she'd feel about me being into Squidge and I don't want to mess up anything between us. So I'm happy to just be good friends with him. Besides, I don't think I'm his type. I'm tall and blonde and Cat is petite and dark, plus he's never given the slightest indication that he feels the same way about me.

'There's always Jonno Appleton,' said Becca glancing at a tall boy with spiky dark hair from Year Eleven, who was standing by the doors. 'He's a nine out of ten in anybody's book.'

'Yeah,' I said, 'I do fancy him, but who doesn't? Anyway, he's taken by Rosie Crawford, so it's hands off. Boyfriend stealing is against my rules.'

'What do we care?' said Cat. 'Isn't Ollie bringing that Michael guy down from London with him tonight?'

I felt my face flush. 'Yeah. Michael Bradley.'

'Does Ollie know that you like him?' asked Becca.

'No way,' I said. 'And you mustn't say anything. I'd die. No, I'd *never* tell Ollie as he might think he could do me a favour or something and try and fix us up. No, I want it to happen naturally.'

I've known Michael since I was knee-high and had a crush on him since I was seven. Not that he's ever noticed me, not in a big way. I'm just Ollie's kid sister, someone to thrash at tennis and throw in the swimming pool in summer. But tonight I intend to change all that. We haven't seen each other for nearly a year and when Ollie told me that he was bringing him down for Mum's party, my imagination went into overdrive. My plan was to persuade Ollie to come with Michael to the school disco with the rest of us. That way, I could show Michael off a bit and prove to the school that I am not *totally* repulsive to boys. Then later at Mum's do . . . well, who knows what a romantic night in Venice might bring?

When the last bell went in the afternoon, school emptied in a flash. Doubtless everyone had their plans. Home, shower, dress, make-up, back to school. Our plan was to meet at Cat's, get dressed there, go to the school disco for an hour or so, then up to my house for Mum's latest extravaganza. She said that I could invite anyone I liked from school, but I'd only invited Becca, Cat, Squidge and Mac.

It's funny, but since I came down here, sometimes I feel a bit awkward about how rich my family are. It's like I don't want anyone to think I'm showing off or flaunting it. All I've ever wanted was to be normal and be accepted and that was easy at my old school because most people's parents were loaded or famous. There was even a princess in Year Ten. Down here, though, people aren't as well off and sometimes all they see are the flash cars, the big house and my dad's fame. What they don't know is that Mum and Dad lead very quiet lives most of the time. Both of them are real homebodies. Mum loves nothing better than pottering in the garden growing herbs and vegetables and Dad is happiest in his studio listening to sounds or watching the telly. But that's not what the public see. They see Dad on telly whenever he does interviews, which is rarely these days. Or in videos on MTV. They think that he's the wild man of rock and roll. The Cornish Ozzy Osbourne. I can't help being his daughter, and down here, I want to be Lia Axford – not Lia, Zac Axford, famous rock star's daughter. There's a difference, and sometimes it gets in the way of people's perception of me at my new school. I guess that's why I try to keep my family history quiet and in the background, so to speak.

I raced home to pick up my clothes to take to Cat's. It was complete pandemonium when I got there with even more people dashing about than there had been in the morning. The Venetian theme had really taken shape. A trio of musicians were rehearsing in the hall and there were ornate candelabras in the corridor leading to the right of the house where the marquee had been set up for the party. It's going to look really fab, I thought as I spotted Mum giving a group of caterers some last minute instructions.

'Is Ollie back?' I asked her.

She nodded her chin towards the stairs. 'In his room with his friends, and oh, Lia, I'll leave a selection of masks in your room for you and your friends to put on when you're back from the school disco. Don't be back too late, OK?'

'OK. Thanks, Mum,' I said. Ollie's with his friends? Who else besides Michael, I wondered as I took the stairs two at a time. Never mind, the more, the merrier. I made a quick dash up to my room to brush my hair and spritz some Cristalle on before going to say hello and hopefully get Michael to notice me properly for the first time.

As soon as I opened my door, I noticed a blue envelope on my bed. My name had been written on it in beautiful handwriting. I ripped it open. It was a card with a red rose on it. Inside, it read: *To the girl with silver eyes, from a distant admirer who's waiting until the time is right to reveal himself. Happy Valentine's.* Then three kisses.

I felt a rush of excitement as I studied the envelope for clues. No stamp, so it must have been either delivered by hand or come from someone in the house.

Hmmm. Interesting, I thought as I heard Ollie and Michael's voices in the corridor outside.

Disco

3

'HEY, IF it isn't little Lia,' said Michael when I opened my bedroom door. Then he looked me up and down. 'Only not so little any more. You've shot up in the last year. You look great!'

'Thanks,' I said and gave him my best flirty look. So far, so good, I thought as he enveloped me in a huge hug. He looked as gorgeous as I remembered – tall and dark, with velvety brown eyes and amazing chiselled features.

'All ready for tonight?' asked Ollie. 'Is Cat coming?'

'Yeah. Later with me. First we've got to go to our school disco. In fact, I wondered if you and Mich . . .' At that moment, I heard the door of one of the guest rooms open and close behind us and as I turned, a girl with long dark hair was coming towards us. She was very pretty – Indian-looking, with lovely high cheekbones. Oh *no*, I thought. Ollie's brought one of his 'girlfriends' with him. I hope

Cat's not going to be upset. I felt a flash of annoyance. He *always* does this. Keeps himself surrounded with different girls, so that no one can get too close to him.

'Lia, this is Usha,' said Ollie as the girl came to join us. 'Michael's girlfriend.'

As she slipped her hand into Michael's, I tried to smile and look friendly, but inside, I felt like my chest was made of glass and someone had just shattered it. 'Oh . . . er, hi Usha.'

'So what were you just saying?' asked Ollie. 'Something about a disco?'

'Yeah. Got to dash. Disco at school. Going there first. Be back later. See you then.'

I ran back to my room, locked the door, dived on to my bed and put my pillow over my head. Girlfriend? He'd brought his *girlfriend*! Stinking finking. I never saw that coming. But, of course, someone as attractive as Michael was bound to have a girlfriend and Ollie wasn't to know that I fancied him. I lay on my bed for a while, stared at the ceiling and ran through all the swear words I knew in my head. I daren't say them out loud as there were too many people in the house and someone might be passing my room and think I'd gone mad. Suddenly I wasn't in the mood for a disco, or a party. I wanted to hide under my bed and come out when it was all over.

A moment later, Cat phoned to ask if she could borrow my red beaded choker and it all came tumbling out.

'. . . so, you see, I just can't come,' I said. 'I'd be lousy company and . . .'

'So what are you going to do? Hide in your bedroom all night? You know you can't do that. Your mum or someone's bound to come up and drag you out, then you'll have to spend the whole night watching Michael with Usha. No, come on, Lia, best get out of there. Take your mind off it. And you never know, we might have a good time at school, then later, at least Bec, Mac, Squidge and I will be there with you.'

The school disco was well underway by the time we got there. In the end, it wasn't me who held us up but Becca. She took six changes of clothes to Cat's and couldn't decide what to wear. She finally decided on black trousers and a black handkerchief top. She looked really sophisticated, more eighteen than fourteen.

Cat wore her short red dress and my choker and looked lovely as always. The name Cat suits her as she looks a bit like a cat – dark, glossy and serene. Mum and I had picked out a silvery coloured mini-dress with sparkles on it last time we were up in London, but it seemed a bit OTT for the school disco. I wasn't in the mood for dressing up, so I just put on my jeans and a pale blue halter-neck top instead.

'You'd look good whatever you wore,' said Becca as we

tried to apply lip-gloss beneath the glaring fluorescent lights in the girls' cloakroom at school. I couldn't help thinking how different it looked to back home where Mum had put jasmine scented candles, flowers and Floris soaps in all the cloakrooms. The only aroma here was the pong of disinfectant that the cleaners used to scour the loos with.

As we stood in front of the mirrors doing our hair, Kaylie O'Hara came in with one of her mates, Susie Cooke. Cat gave me an 'Oh, here we go' look as Kaylie is one of those girls who takes over a place even if it's only the cloakroom. It's as if when she arrives, no one else is important. She has to be the centre of attention and she's certainly very popular, especially with the boys. Becca says it's because boys are breast-fixated and she has the largest chest in our year. She always wears very tight tops that make her boobs look as though they're straining to escape. She's easily the prettiest of her group, in a baby-doll kind of way, and her mates are all clones of her. There are four of them. Kaylie, Susie, Jackie and Fran. Becca calls them the Barbies. Cat calls them the Clones. All of them are really girlie girls who have blonde highlighted hair that they flick around a lot. They all wear loads of shiny lip-gloss which they are always reapplying, even in the middle of maths. And lately, they've all started talking in this lispy breathy voice. Kaylie started it a few weeks ago and now they all do it. I guess they think it makes them sound sexy, but I think it makes them sound silly. Cat says Kaylie and her mates are as thick as two short planks. In her usual subtle way (not), Becca thinks that they will all probably marry some very rich but stupid men. 'The type that likes arm candy, but doesn't care that the candy is braindead.'

'Tonight's the night,' sang Kaylie as she headed for the mirror next to us and began to apply pink gloss to her lips.

'You look happy,' said Becca.

Kaylie winked at Susie. '*Indeed.* Just heard some interesting news. Some *very* interesting news.'

'Come on, then,' said Becca, who never held back when she wanted to know something. 'Spill.'

Kaylie smiled. 'Ah, well . . .' Then she began singing again. 'Tonight's the night . . .'

Becca shrugged and headed for the door.

'Oh, all right,' pouted Kaylie. 'You'll find out soon enough anyway.' She folded her arms and leaned back against the sink. 'Jonno Appleton's broken up with Rosie.'

'Is *that* all?' said Becca. 'So what's the big deal?'

'He's free, you eejit,' she said then raised an eyebrow, 'but not for long if I have my way.'

Cat shot me a look as if to say, Yeah right, then turned to Kaylie. 'But sometimes people need a bit of space when they've just split up with someone. He may not be ready yet.'

Kaylie tapped the side of her nose. 'Oh, don't worry. I

know how to play it. I have it all worked out, in fact. I have an ickle plan.'

I guess I must have let out a sigh when she said that, as she turned to look at me. 'You don't think I can do it?' she asked in a tight voice.

'No, I . . . it wasn't that . . .' I blustered. I didn't mean to dismiss her. I was just thinking that getting off with Michael had fizzled out despite all *my* plans. But I wasn't going to tell her about that. I felt intimidated by Kaylie. She's one of those girls who acts friendly, but you get the feeling that if you said the wrong thing, she could turn nasty. I've never crossed her, but I've seen her be really sarcastic to a couple of girls in our class. Luckily, she seemed to be in a good mood tonight.

'Whatever,' she said as she took out a can of hairspray and sprayed liberally around her head. Some of the spray hit me in the eye. 'Oh *sorry,* Lia, did I get you? Oops.'

'S'OK,' I said as I rubbed my eye. I swear she did it on purpose, but there was no way I was going to say anything.

Kaylie stood back and looked at her reflection. 'Tonight, Mr Appleton, you are mine, *all* mine.'

Susie laughed and flicked her hair back. 'He doesn't stand a chance, poor guy.'

At that moment, Annie Peters came in and stood next to Kaylie at the sink. I like Annie. She's in Year Eleven and is a bit of an oddball. She does her own thing, has her own hippie style and is brilliant at art, particularly photography.

'Hey, nice watch,' she said to Kaylie as she applied some moss-green kohl to her eyes.

Kaylie beamed. 'Thanks. It's a Cartier.'

'For real?' asked Annie, taking Kaylie's wrist.

'Yeah, course. My brother brought it back from Thailand for me. Cool, huh?'

Annie examined the watch and nodded. 'Yeah. Nice. There's one sure way to tell if it's real, though.'

'How?' asked Kaylie as I headed for the door. Now would be a good time to leave, I thought as I had the same watch on. My dad got it for me last Christmas and I've no doubt that mine's real, as I was with him when he bought it from the Cartier shop in London.

'Easy,' said Annie. 'My dad got my mum one for their twentieth wedding anniversary. She said that you can tell a real Cartier by looking at one of the numbers, I think it's the V, under a magnifying glass. If it's genuine, you can see the word Cartier written in minuscule writing.'

I gave Becca the nod to say let's go, but she clearly wanted to stay and watch what was happening. Annie rummaged in her bag. 'I've got a magnifying glass in here somewhere. Let's have a look.'

She pulled out her glass, held it close to Kaylie's wrist, then screwed her eyes up to look at the watch. 'Nope. Can't see any word.'

I thought it was a bit mean of Annie to humiliate Kaylie like that, as she'd obviously been chuffed thinking that she had a real Cartier. To me, it's no big deal. A watch is a watch, main thing is that it tells the time, but I wanted to say something to make Kaylie feel better. 'It looks real to me,' I said. 'It might just be on a particular model that the V has Cartier written on it.' Big mistake as all eyes turned to me. Eagle-eyes Annie spotted my watch straight away.

'Hey, same watch,' she said, before I could hide my arm behind my back. 'What a coincidence. Here. Let's have a look at yours, Lia.'

Quick as a flash, she had my wrist in her hand and was scrutinising my watch. 'Yep,' she said. 'Here it is. Tiny. Cartier. Want to look, Kaylie?'

'Think I'll pass,' she said sulkily as she flounced towards the door. 'Little things for little minds.'

'Good luck with Jonno,' I called after her, in an attempt to break the sour atmosphere.

'Yeah, whatever,' she said. Then she smiled back at me. But it was with her mouth not her eyes. She may be pretty, I thought, but there's something hard about her. She's clearly not someone to get on the wrong side of.

The music was thumping in the hall where the disco was being held. Already people were up, dancing and having a good time and the atmosphere was infectious. I soon forgot the incident in the cloakroom, as Becca and Cat pulled me out on to the floor and we began to dance. Mac and Squidge soon came to join us and after a while I began to really enjoy myself. Squidge is a brilliant dancer when he wants to be, but he was in the mood for looning about by doing Hawaiian dancing, then Greek, then Egyptian, then Russian – complete with knee bends and kicks. Then he fell over.

'And now, so that the teachers don't feel left out, we'll have a golden oldie session,' said the DJ. 'Here's a blast from the past for the wrinklies with an old Beatles number – "Can't Buy Me Love".'

The group of teachers, who were standing by the drinks table, smiled wearily then carried on chatting.

As we danced to the words, 'Money can't buy me love', I thought, that's so true. Money can't buy a good time either. Like there in the hall. The decorations looked really tatty. There were a few token balloons scattered around the walls and an old faded glitter ball catching light on the ceiling, and that was it, but it hadn't stopped anyone having a great time. Probably cost about five quid, I thought, whereas Mum's party must have cost thousands.

After a few dances, we went to get a drink and Becca nudged me. 'Over there,' she whispered. 'Kaylie gets her man.'

'Or not,' said Cat as she looked over. 'I think it's going to be a no score.'

I glanced over to where they were looking and saw Kaylie at the other end of the drinks table. She was desperately trying to get Jonno's attention, but he seemed more interested in talking to one of his mates from the football team. She was flicking her hair and sticking her chest out for all she was worth, but he wasn't taking any notice. When another Beatles track began to play, she pulled on his arm and tried to get him to join her on the dance floor, but he shook his head and turned away to get a drink.

That makes two of us let down by love today, I thought, feeling sorry for her for a moment.

Cat, Becca and I downed an orange juice then headed back on to the floor to join Mac and Squidge, who by now had moved on to sixties go-go dancing, *à la* Austin Powers style. We joined in and were having a real laugh when someone tapped me on the shoulder. I turned to see a handsome face smiling down at me.

'Want to dance?' asked Jonno Appleton.

Over his shoulder, I could see Kaylie watching from the drinks table. She didn't look pleased.

Party Time

4

WE LEFT the disco around ten o'clock and piled into Squidge's dad's van. He was great at ferrying us all around when we needed a lift.

'You don't mind roughing it, do you?' asked Mr Squires as he spread an old blanket that stank of petrol on the floor in the back.

I wedged myself in between a tool box and Becca. 'No, course not. Rough is the new smooth, don't you know?'

'Bet you never travelled like this up in London,' said Becca.

'Yeah, course I did,' I lied. I didn't want Squidge or his dad to think I was snobby about the van. I wasn't bothered at all, but the truth was, at my old school, everyone used cabs to get about. One night, my friend Gabby's dad even had his chauffeur pick us up and take us to the theatre in their Bentley. It was really cool. Her dad's a politician and

347

the car had tinted windows and was bullet proof, at least Gabby said it was. Either way, we felt like we were in a Bond movie.

Mac jumped in and sat back against Becca pretending that she wasn't there. 'Er, seats are a bit lumpy, mate,' he joked to Squidge.

'Gerroff,' said Becca, pushing him off and into Cat who was squashed up in the corner.

'Gerroff yourself,' she said, pushing him back at Becca.

Mac made his body go limp and lay over both of them. 'Ah, poor me. At the mercy of cold-hearted women again.'

'Get in the front beside me, nutter,' Squidge laughed.

Mac climbed out, then closed the back door on us before getting in beside Squidge in the front.

What a strange night, I thought. In fact, what a strange day. No Valentine's card, then a card appears on my bed. I still don't know who sent it, but I guess Michael is off the list now. Probably Mum. It's the sort of thing she'd do. No boy interested in me, then the most popular boy in school makes a beeline for me. I had one dance with Jonno and he was really flirty, putting his arms around my waist and stuff, but I was so aware of Kaylie's eyes boring into me that I couldn't let go and enjoy it. In the end, I made an excuse and went back to mad dancing with my mates.

'You're bonkers,' said Becca as the van reached our driveway and the gates swung open. 'Jonno's *gorgeous*.'

'I know,' I said, 'but I don't want any trouble. Kaylie bagged him in the loos. You heard her.'

'So what? It doesn't mean that they're an item,' continued Becca. 'Anyone could see that he wasn't interested in her. He only had eyes for you.'

I shook my head. 'Not worth the aggro. I don't want to get on the wrong side of her.'

Becca sighed. 'Tough for her, I say. You can't let girls like Kaylie O'Hara run your life. Look at what *you* want to happen, not what she wants.'

'Yeah . . . I will,' I said. 'In fact, at the disco, I invited a few boys from Year Eleven up to the party.'

'Really?' said Cat. 'Who? Jonno?'

'No. Not Jonno. Seth and Charlie from your class, Squidge.'

'Yeah. They're OK,' he said from the front. 'Do you fancy one of them?'

'No. But I thought I ought to at least make an effort to be friendly to some new boys. New start, new chapter and all that.' I'd decided back at the disco that it was time I got to know some of the local boys a bit better, especially as all my stupid dreams about Michael had fallen through.

'In that case,' said Mac. 'No better way to make a new start than with a quick round of Truth, Dare, Kiss or Promise . . .'

'Oh *nooo*,' groaned Cat. 'It always gets us into trouble of some sort.'

'Oh, let's play,' said Becca, then she grinned. 'Only, because it's Valentine's day, you only have one option: Kiss. Sorry.'

'So, who do we have to kiss, Cupid?' asked Cat.

'And don't say I have to kiss Seth or Charlie, please,' I said.

'Well, Mac, you have to kiss me and I have to kiss you,' said Becca. 'Um, Cat, I'll make it easy for you, you have to kiss Ollie.'

Cat smiled. 'No problemo.'

'Now. What about Squidge?' asked Becca.

'How about I choose for myself in my own time,' he said. 'I don't like to rush these things. Let me think about it.'

I was about to say, Me too, I want to choose in my own time as well, when Becca piped up. 'OK, but Lia *has* to kiss Jonno Appleton.'

'No, oh come on, don't be a wind-up,' I said.

Becca shook her head. 'Sorry, it's been decided. If you're going to be such a wimp as to be intimidated by Kaylie, then you need a push from us. All those in favour of Lia snogging Jonno, raise your hands.'

Mac, Cat and Becca raised their hands.

'You should let her choose herself,' said Squidge as we reached the top of the drive.

'Sorry, you're out-voted, Squidge. Lia, did you or did you not say that you fancied Jonno Appleton?' demanded Becca.

'Yeah, but pick someone else, please . . .'

'Well, who else do you fancy?' demanded Becca as Mr Squires slowed the van down and parked between a Porsche and a BMW.

There was no way I was going to admit that I secretly liked Squidge. 'No one, really.'

'So the only boy you think is fanciable is Jonno, then?'

'I suppose,' I said, then looked at Mac and Squidge, who are both very good looking in their own ways. Mac is blond, with fine features and Squidge has brown, spiky hair, an open and friendly face, and a gorgeous, wide, smiley mouth, 'present company excepted, of course.'

'So that's settled, then,' said Becca. 'Better to kiss someone you actually like than being dared to go and kiss some reject. It will be fine, Lia. Live dangerously.'

'OK, but I'll do it in my own time,' I said.

'Fine,' said Becca, then grinned. 'You've got ten minutes. No, only joking. In your own time.'

Cat gave me a half smile and looked at Becca as if to say, What can you do? I smiled back. Sometimes you can't argue with Becca. And it might not be so bad if I could get Jonno on his own some time.

Mum had laid out some amazing masks on my bed for us.

'And there's more downstairs in the hall,' I said. 'Mum put a basket of them out by the fireplace for guests who didn't bring one.'

'No, these are brilliant,' said Becca holding up a silver mask to her face in the mirror.

The girls chose the pretty ones. Becca opted for one with a full white face with delicate gold sequinned patterning on the cheeks, gold lips and gold curls made out of paper around the head. Cat also went for a full face mask with red and gold diamond shapes painted on the cheeks, green rhinestones around the eyes and a red feather plume. Squidge chose a black half mask with a hooked nose. As he was wearing his long black leather coat, the combination with the mask made him look pretty sinister. Not to be outdone, Mac picked a scary one as well – red with a bird's beak nose. It didn't look as effective as Squidge's, as Mac was wearing a fleece and jeans. I picked a Pierrot mask. White with sad eyes, red lips and a tear painted on one cheek. Somehow it seemed to fit the mood of the day. It seemed I'd never be with a boy I liked. The beautiful Michael was attached, getting involved with the lovely Squidge was way too complicated and to respond to Jonno would only cause trouble. Yes, the Pierrot mask would be perfect.

When we were ready, we headed down and out to join the party. Most of the guests had already arrived as it was almost eleven o'clock and as we made our way through them, it was hard to tell who was who.

'Woah,' exclaimed Mac as he took in the sumptuous

decorations in the marquee. It did look fabulous – like stepping into another world where everything was red and gold. Mum had really surpassed herself. Soft candlelight lit the tented room and the trio of musicians dressed in eighteenth century costumes were playing classical music in a corner. Swathes of silk were draped around pillars and huge arrangements of flowers and grapes adorned every table. The whole effect was rich and romantic. There was even an ice sculpture of a lion with vodka coming out of it's mouth.

The classical trio finished playing their pieces and it wasn't long before one of Dad's old hits from the eighties blasted through the speakers. Ollie appeared and swept Cat off to dance, then of course, Mac took off with Becca.

'You OK?' asked Squidge, who by now had his video camera out ready to film the proceedings.

Squidge wants to be a film director when he leaves school and, ever since I've known him, I've never seen him without his camera. He takes it everywhere and has a wall full of recorded material in his bedroom. Mum asked him to film our Christmas party last year and she was so pleased with the results that she asked if he'd do this one as well.

I nodded. 'Yeah, sure. You go ahead and start your filming.'

After Squidge had gone, I sat at one of the tables and picked at some grapes. It looked like everyone was having a great time. Cat with Ollie, Mac with Becca, Mum with

Dad, Michael and Usha, and Star, who was down from London with some new man. I felt like a spare part sitting there with no one to dance with, but it wasn't long before Dad spotted me and hauled me up on to the floor. After a few numbers, he had to go and greet some friends who had just arrived, so I sat down again. I was hoping Star would come and say 'Hi', but she looked too busy with her new boyfriend. Like Ollie, she's never short of admirers. I guess I'm the odd one out in our family, in fact Dad even has a joke about it. He calls me the white sheep because, in comparison to the rest of them, I'm quiet whereas they're all outgoing and mega-confident. Sometimes I think I must be a disappointment to them. They're all so sociable and popular. Ollie with the girls, Star with the boys and of course Dad, with his enormous fan club. And then me. It's not that I'm *not* sociable, it's just that I'm shyer than they are – until I get to know someone. That's part of the reason I liked hanging around in a large group at my old school. There were so many of us that people didn't notice that I was quieter than the rest.

I was just starting to feel self-conscious sitting there on my own, when I spied Seth and Charlie from school. At least they'd be someone to talk to, I thought. I was about to go over when someone tapped me on the shoulder. It was one of the magicians Mum had hired to circulate amongst the guests and do magic tricks. He was wearing a half mask and a cloak and produced a five pound note and a cigarette from his sleeve. He held up the note, lit the cigarette, then burned a hole in the money with the cigarette, only when I looked at the fiver, there was no trace of a hole. It was amazing.

'How did you do that?' I gasped. I *saw* him burn the hole in the fiver and I was so close, I would have seen if he'd replaced the note with another.

He grinned. 'Magic.'

Just at that moment, someone else in a full mask and cloak tapped him on the shoulder and said something. The first magician nodded and moved away.

'So, want to see another trick?' asked the man. I nodded. He got out a five pound note and a cigarette, then lit the cigarette.

'Er, your friend has just done that trick,' I said.

Too late. The magician was pushing the cigarette through the fiver, but this time, it didn't go through. It set the fiver on fire!

'Oh *no*,' he cried as he dropped the fiver on the floor and stamped on it. 'Looks easier than it is.'

I started to laugh as I recognised the voice. 'Jonno,' I said.

He peeled off his mask. 'Hi, Lia. I knew it was you under your mask. Um, Seth and Charlie said you'd invited them. They're over by the ice sculpture, in fact, I think Seth may have got his tongue stuck to it . . . Hope you don't mind me, er . . .'

'Gate-crashing?' I asked.

He looked sheepish. 'Yeah, and almost burning down the marquee.' Jonno gave me a cheeky smile. 'Er, maybe I'd better go . . .'

I glanced over at the dance floor where by now, everyone was slow dancing to one of Sting's ballads. Shall I, shan't I? I asked myself. Jonno was still looking at me as if to gauge whether I minded him being there. He was very attractive in a Keanu Reeves kind of way . . . Oh, why not? I thought. Kaylie's not here. Jonno is very cute, why shouldn't I enjoy myself with him? I got up, took his hand and led him to the dance floor. He pulled me close and put his arms around my waist.

'Bit different here to the school disco.' He smiled, then leaned in and kissed me gently on the lips. 'Happy Valentine's Day,' he whispered in my ear.

Over his shoulder, I could see Becca. She was standing with Mac and Charlie who were trying to separate Seth from the ice sculpture. She looked over at me and gave me the thumbs-up.

Picked On

5

IT WAS the following Monday at school that it all started.

I was in the corridor on my way to the art class and Kaylie was coming the other way with Fran. She was walking towards class and she steered off course and straight into me causing me to drop my books.

'Oh, *so* sorry, Ophelia,' she said with a fake smile. 'Wasn't looking where I was going.'

'S'OK,' I said as I picked up my things. 'And please call me Lia. No one calls me Ophelia.'

My parents christened me Ophelia Moonbeam. How naff is that? I never use that name as everyone calls me Lia and I certainly never tell anyone, but it was read out on the first day of registration last autumn. I didn't think anyone had taken much notice. Amazingly, Kaylie seemed to have remembered.

'But it *is* your name, isn't it?' insisted Kaylie.

'Yeah, but . . .' I started, then I decided to confront what I thought was probably really bothering her. 'Look, about Jonno. I didn't mean for anything to happen. He just kind of . . .'

'Yeah, yeah . . .'

'He came after me.'

'That's not what I saw. You were all over him at the school disco.'

'I *wasn't*. He came over to *me*. In fact, I purposely tried to stay out of his way, because I knew you liked him.'

'Yeah, so that's why you were snogging him later at your parent's do.' said Kaylie with a toss of her hair. 'Anyway, it's his loss.'

'Well, I just wanted you to know that I didn't set out to get him.'

'Yeah, right. That's not what I heard. Oh, don't worry, everyone knows you begged him to go to your party.'

'I didn't,' I said. 'He just turned up.'

'That's not what Seth said.'

'Seth? I did invite him and Charlie, but Jonno came along with them.'

Kaylie put a finger under her chin and feigned surprise. 'Oh and *what* a coincidence that they just happen to be Jonno's mates from the football team.'

'Honestly Kaylie, he just turned up.'

'Whatever,' said Kaylie again. 'That's your story. But

then we all know about you and your stories, don't we?'

'What do you mean?'

Kaylie shrugged and made a face at Fran. 'Why you had to leave your old school.'

'I don't know what you're talking about. What are you saying?'

Kaylie smiled one of her fake smiles. 'Oh, nothing, Lia. Come *on*, we're just teasing you. Lighten up. Honestly, you're like . . . *so* intense.' She put her hand on my shoulder and gave me a gentle shove. 'Don't take things so seriously.'

And with that, she flounced into class. I felt close to tears. And confused. Was I being oversensitive? Taking it all too seriously? It felt like she'd had a real go at me, but it was done with such a smile that I couldn't be sure. Maybe I was imagining things.

'Hey, Lia, everything all right?' asked a voice behind me.

I turned. It was Squidge.

'So what was all that about?' he asked. 'I saw Kaylie walk into you. What's her problem?'

'Bad loser, I guess. I don't think she's too happy about the fact that I got off with Jonno and she didn't.'

Squidge raised his eyes to the ceiling. 'Sour grapes, huh? Well, you take no notice of her and if she gives you any trouble, you let me know, OK?'

I nodded.

'So,' continued Squidge, 'you and Jonno? You going out with him now?'

I grinned. 'Well, it's still early days, but . . . so far, so good. We've got a proper date on Saturday. Going out somewhere, don't know where yet.'

Squidge looked at me with concern for a moment, then turned to go. 'Better get to class,' he said. 'Hope it all works out for you, Lia. You deserve a decent bloke, someone who really appreciates you. Don't let any stupid girl ruin it all for you.'

'Thanks, Squidge. You're a mate.'

As he took off down the corridor I took a deep breath and followed Kaylie and Fran into class. I hoped that they weren't going to make an issue of me going out with Jonno. It wasn't my fault that he'd chosen me and not Kaylie. And I didn't have any regrets. I'd had a great time with him at the party and we even saw each other again on Sunday. He came up to the house after breakfast and we talked for hours – about school and what music we like and what we want to do after we finish school. He wants to get into the music business, so he asked me loads of questions about what it was like having a rock star dad. He stayed and had lunch with us and was well impressed by Dad's gold records. Dad even showed him around his studio and that's not something he does with many people. I think he realised that Jonno was serious about pursuing music as a career. I really like him. He was clearly starstruck by Dad, but he still paid me loads of attention and seemed genuinely interested in what I was into.

No, stuff you, Kaylie O'Hara, I thought as I took my place at a table with Cat and Becca. I'm not going to let you run my life.

The next class was English and I made sure that I was out of the art room first and along the corridor so that Kaylie and the Clones couldn't 'accidentally' bump into me again.

'You're in a hurry,' said Cat catching up with me. 'What's the rush?'

'Oh nothing,' I said. 'Just wanted to go through some notes before the lesson starts.'

Cat gave me a look like she didn't quite believe me, but she let it go. I didn't want to tell her about the run in with Kaylie before art, because I hoped it would all blow over. If I told Cat and Becca about it, they'd take my side and stick up for me and maybe start something. No best ignore it, I thought, and it will all go away.

'Right,' said Mrs Ashton, our English teacher, once we'd all taken our places. 'First, I'll give you your essays back, then I thought we'd have a quick quiz to see who's remembered what from this term.' She began to walk up and down the aisles, putting people's work in front of them on their desks. 'Well done,' she said when she got to me.

Cat caught my eye and grinned, but behind her, I saw

Kaylie whisper something to Susie Cooke and they both looked over at me and giggled.

When she'd handed out the essays, Mrs Ashton went back to her desk. 'Some of the work has been to a very high standard and I was impressed,' she said. 'George Gaynor, well done. Sunita Ahmed, also good. Lia Axford, excellent. Nick Thorn, keep up the good work. Becca Howard, an improvement. I'm glad to see you're putting your mind to your work at last.' Then she paused. 'Sadly, there were a number of essays that . . . how can I put it . . . ? Needed work, would be being polite. What has happened to some of you lately? I won't mention names, but you know who you are by your low grades and I'll be keeping an eye on you for the rest of the term.' She gave Kaylie and the Clones a pointed look, but Kaylie just raised an eyebrow and looked away.

Mrs Ashton adjusted her glasses and began to read from a sheet of paper in front of her. 'OK. Question one. Finish this sentence: King Solomon had three hundred wives and seven hundred what . . . ? Frances Wilton, maybe you'd like to stop staring out of the window and give us the answer?'

'Um . . . seven hundred porcupines, Miss.'

The class cracked up laughing.

'OK, what did she mean to say?' asked Mrs Ashton looking around.

Laura Johnson raised her hand. 'Concubines,' she said.

Mrs Ashton looked over at Fran. 'Exactly. What on earth would Solomon have done with hundreds of porcupines?'

Frances went bright red and looked at her desk as Mrs Ashton went on to the next question. 'Caesar was murdered on the Ides of March. His last words were . . .'

Mark Keegan stuck his hand up this time.

'Yes, Mark,' said Mrs Ashton.

'Tee hee, Brutus,' said Mark.

Once again, the class started laughing and Mark smiled broadly, pleased that his answer had got a laugh.

'I get the impression that you're not taking this quiz seriously, Mark,' said Mrs Ashton, then she looked around. 'The attitude of some of the people in this class will have to change or else it will show on your end of term reports. So. Anyone like to tell me what Caesar's last words really were?'

She looked around the class. I knew the answer, but I didn't want to be a Norma Know-It-All. However, Mrs Ashton looked over at me. 'Lia?'

'Um, *et tu* Brute,' I muttered.

'Correct. Without the "um", though. Well done, Lia.'

Kaylie looked over at Fran Wilton and raised her eyebrows. I should have said I didn't know, I thought. Now they will think I'm a swotty nerd.

'Now,' said Mrs Ashton, going back to her quiz. 'Kaylie O'Hara. Here's one for you. Shakespeare . . .' She adjusted her glasses and began to read. 'When was William Shakespeare born?'

'On his birthday,' said Kaylie as if it was absolutely obvious.

Once again, the class cracked up and I glanced over at Kaylie and noticed that she was blushing slightly. Unlike Mark who had given his answer for a laugh, I got the feeling that Kaylie thought that she'd given the right answer.

'Of *course* he was born on his *birth*day, Kaylie,' said Mrs Ashton. 'Anybody like to give me the actual year?'

Joss Peters put his hand up. '1564,' he said.

'Correct,' said Mrs Ashton, who then turned back to Kaylie. 'OK, Kaylie. Here's an easy one for you. We've been doing *Romeo and Juliet* this term. What was Romeo's last wish?'

'To be laid by Juliet,' said Kaylie.

This got a huge laugh especially from the boys. Kaylie looked over at me with a hard expression in her eyes, as though daring me to join in the laughter. I kept my face straight.

'I think what you meant to say was that Romeo's last wish was to die alongside Juliet, Kaylie. Like Frances, try and pay more attention to how you express yourself.'

Kaylie nodded and looked bored. 'Yes, Miss,' she drawled.

'And now for the last question,' said Mrs Ashton. 'Jackie Reeves, I think you can have this one.'

Kaylie looked over at her mate and sighed as though Mrs Ashton's comments were all a great waste of time.

'The most famous composer in the world is?' asked Mrs Ashton.

'Um . . . Bach. Um . . . Handel,' drawled Jackie.

There was a snigger from the back of the class as Mrs Ashton sighed. 'Anyone like to tell us what's wrong with that?' she asked.

This time I kept my head down. Luckily, Sunita Ahmed put her hand up. 'It's got to be either one or the other, Miss. Either Bach is the most famous or Handel. Not both.'

Jackie gave Sunita a really filthy look and I could see that, like me, Sunita suddenly felt as though she wished she'd kept her mouth shut.

'Exactly,' said Mrs Ashton with a weary sigh. 'But I've heard worse. One pupil once told me that Handel was half German, half Italian and half English . . . Anyone like to comment?'

A few people tittered, but no one spoke. 'Come on class, it's not difficult. Wake up. Who can tell me what's wrong with that? Cat Kennedy?'

'Um, the maths aren't quite right. If he was half German, half Italian and half English, he'd be one and a half people.'

'Correct,' said Mrs Ashton. 'Now all of you, I don't want

to see any of you making these types of mistakes, not in my class. It shows you're not thinking. We have pupils like George, Sunita, Nick and Lia in the class setting a standard. Try and learn from them.'

The Clones all started sniggering at this and Mrs Ashton saw them. 'Seeing as you find the whole thing so amusing, Susie Cooke, you can answer the next question. Who was it Salome danced naked in front of?'

Susie shrugged her shoulders like she didn't care.

'Come on, Susie,' said Mrs Ashton. 'We only did it last week.'

I could see Kaylie mouthing an answer to her mate. Susie screwed up her eyes to try and read Kaylie's lips then she nodded.

'Harrods,' she said.

Mrs Ashton looked up at the ceiling. 'Herod, Susie. Not *Harrods*. Harrods is a shop in Knightsbridge.'

I glanced over at Kaylie and she was staring at me again with narrowed eyes. It was hard not to laugh at what her and the Clones had said, especially as most of the class was giggling away. Becca and Cat may be right, I thought. Kaylie and her mates may be popular and trendy, but they're not very bright. I stared back at Kaylie thinking, two can play at this game and I'm not going to be intimidated by you. After a few minutes, she leaned back in her chair and whispered something to Fran behind her. Fran glanced over at me and laughed. I turned away. She wasn't worth it and I didn't want to get into playing stupid games. All I wanted was to go to school, do my lessons and get on with everyone without any aggro. Sadly, though, by the look on Kaylie's face, she wasn't going to let that happen.

6
A Turn for the Worse

THE NEXT day, I went into school determined not to let Kaylie and the Clones phase me. I'd tough it out, be all smiling and friendly. But they decided to try a new tactic. They just plain ignored me. When I saw them in the corridor before assembly, I said hi, and they all turned the other way like they'd smelled a bad smell. It was weird, I felt like I was invisible or something.

'What's up with them?' asked Becca, when she noticed them give me the cold shoulder.

'Oh nothing,' I said. 'I think Kaylie's got it in for me because of Jonno.'

'God. How pathetic,' said Becca, giving them a scornful look.

Suddenly Kaylie came bustling over and stood between Becca and me with her back to me. 'I hear you're going to be helping Miss Segal produce the end-of-year show,' she said.

'That's right,' said Becca moving to the right to include me in the conversation.

Kaylie moved, obscuring my view again. 'Do you know what it's going to be yet?'

Becca nodded. 'Nothing official, but I'm pretty sure we're going to be doing *The Rocky Horror Picture Show*.'

'Oh, top!' said Kaylie then beckoned to her mates and began to sing, 'Let's do the time warp again.'

Fran, Susie and Jackie came over to join us. '*Rocky Horror.* Excellent. Can we be in it?' asked Fran. I moved to stand with them, but Susie stepped to the left once again keeping me out of the circle.

Becca glanced at me with a worried expression. 'Casting is in the main hall on Saturday afternoon,' she said.

'Cool,' said Kaylie, then she took a step back and stood on my toes.

'Ow!' I cried.

'Oh, *sooo* sorry, Ophelia. I didn't see you there.' Then she gave me a snooty look and turned back to Becca. 'I suppose *some* people wanting a part will be taking advantage of the fact that their mate is the producer.'

'I doubt it,' said Becca. 'Best man wins, as always.'

'Good,' said Kaylie. 'Because we don't want anyone getting in for the wrong reasons or because their dad is in the music business or anything.'

'Knock it off, Kaylie,' said Becca. 'You know people get

in because of their individual performances. Who's right for the part and so on.'

'Yeah right,' said Kaylie. 'Well, we'll see shall we?'

'What's going on?' asked Becca when they'd gone. 'They were, like, totally blanking you.'

'I know,' I said. 'They were a bit weird with me yesterday as well, to be honest, but I'm not going to let it get to me.'

'Good. They're not worth it. So you'll be at the casting session, won't you? I think it will be a total gas doing *The Rocky Horror Picture Show*. Mac will do the scenery and, of course, Squidge will film it, so it will be a laugh, all of us together.'

I hesitated. I had no illusions about my singing so wouldn't expect to get a lead role, but I can dance and had hoped that maybe I could be in the chorus. Plus, Miss Segal is my favourite teacher. It's like she's really tuned in to people and can bring out the best in them. But if Kaylie was going to be there making jibes at me at every rehearsal, maybe it wouldn't be much fun.

'Not sure yet,' I said.

Becca grimaced. 'If you let them put you off, I'll . . . I'll . . .'

'You won't speak to me either,' I laughed. 'Then *no one* will be speaking to me.'

Becca linked her arm through mine. 'I'd never do that,' she said.

I decided to confide in Becca. If anyone would understand how mean girls can be, it would be her. Recently, she'd had a run-in with Mac's sister, Jade, when both of them went up for a national singing competition to find a 'Pop Princess'. Jade can be a total cow when she wants and she acted really unfriendly and unsupportive. She even tricked Becca into saying something negative on the phone about one of the competitors when, unaware to Becca, the girl was listening in on an extension.

'Only reason I'm hesitating is that . . .' I started. 'Look, I know people gossip about my dad and our house and stuff locally, but I don't want that to affect things here at school. I just want to be normal. To fit in with everyone else and for now, until Kaylie's got over whatever's bugging her, that's more important than having a role in the school show. Do you understand?'

Becca nodded, then shook her head. 'I do, but don't let them walk all over you. I've seen them do it to girls in our year before. You have to stand up to them. Don't let them win. They don't bother me, I can tell you that. Do you want me to have a word with them?'

'No,' I said. 'Please. That would only make an issue of it, and they'll get all sniffy about me talking to you about them. No. Please, don't get into it. Let me sort it my way, OK?'

'OK,' said Becca. 'But you know that whatever they do, I'm on your side. Right?'

'Right,' I said.

On my side, she said. Though I appreciated the support, I felt sad. Already, it was about taking sides. Oh, why can't I just fit in? Have my mates and not be noticed? All I want is to be accepted.

In the changing rooms on Wednesday, things took a turn for the worse. The Clones all stood in one corner and were whispering and looking at me as I was getting changed for gym. It was awful. Everyone seems to have got boobs except me. I've shot up to five-foot-seven, yet still have the shape of a nine-year-old boy. Becca's really sweet about it. She says I'm the perfect shape to be a model and she wishes she was like me, but I think she's just being kind. I wish I was more like her. She's got a great figure – really curvy, although she thinks she's fat. I guess no one's ever happy with their body. Even Cat, who is perfect, thinks she's too short.

As the Clones continued staring, I began to think I'd grown an extra breast or something. Then I remembered what Becca had said about standing up to them so I turned around and asked, 'What are you looking at?'

Of course, they all turned away and looked at the floor or the wall – except Kaylie, that is. She leaned on her right hip, stuck her chin out at me and said, 'Think a lot of yourself, don't you?'

'No,' I replied. 'What do you mean?'

'Like, *why* would we be staring at you? You've a problem you know, Lia. You think everything is about you when it isn't. People do have their own lives you know.'

I didn't know what to say, so I looked away. I felt confused again. They *had* been staring at me, I'm sure of it, but Kaylie had managed to turn everything around and make out that it was me who had the problem. Maybe she was right. Maybe I *am* getting obsessive about them. I had certainly spent a lot of time thinking about them and how to handle them over the past few days. Maybe I do spend too much time thinking about myself and what people think of me. Maybe it *is* me. Maybe I do have a problem.

As the week went on, I tried to tell myself that it didn't matter, but by Thursday, I felt more confused than ever and I dreaded going into school for fear of what they were going to do or say.

I've always been happy enough at school, but suddenly, it felt like some ordeal I had to endure. All I wanted was just to get to the end of the day so that I could go home. I tried my best to stay out of their way, but it's hard when we have so many classes together. I was sure I wasn't imagining it. Every time I saw the Clones, it seemed like they'd been busy chatting to people, but as soon as I arrived, everyone would go quiet for a moment in a guilty sort of way and sometimes they'd laugh. I wondered what they were saying about me, but I daren't ask for fear that Kaylie would tell me that I was self-obsessed again and that people had other things to talk about besides Lia Axford.

Friday was the final straw. At break, I met up with Cat and Becca and both of them were holding little pink invitations cards.

'Invite to Kaylie's tomorrow night,' said Becca. 'Shall we go after the casting session?'

'Dunno,' said Cat. 'I mean, those girls aren't exactly our best mates and she's never asked us before.'

'All the more reason to go and see what it's like,' said Becca. 'I bet loads of people will be going and there's nothing else happening.'

'I think that may be another reason that Kaylie is jealous of you, Lia,' said Cat. 'Before your family arrived, the do's at Kaylie's house were legendary. I think your mum's parties have stolen her thunder a bit.'

'Understatement,' said Becca. 'I bet she's seething, mainly because you've never invited her. In fact, she's probably jealous of every aspect of your life. A glam rock star dad, an ex-model mum, a fab mansion to live in, latest clothes . . .'

'Gorgeous brother, gorgeous sister . . .' said Cat. 'The list is endless.'

'But it's not my fault,' I said. 'I didn't choose my parents or my family . . .'

'Yeah, but she would have, given half the chance,' said Becca. 'And she hasn't even got a look-in to any part of it.'

'How come she holds so many parties?' I asked.

'Partly because she likes to be popular and being "hostess with the mostest" gives her a chance to surround herself with people,' said Becca. 'Plus, her mum works night shifts in a hospital over in Plymouth, so she has a free reign of her house most evenings.'

'What about her dad?' I asked. 'Surely he's home.'

Cat shook her head. 'Disappeared years ago. Rumour has it he ran off with the barmaid from the Crown and Anchor. Anyway, it's an empty house at the weekend and where else is there for teenagers to go round here in the winter? Weekends, a lot of people hang out at Kaylie's.'

'I wonder if her mum knows that she uses the house,' I said.

'Doubt it,' said Becca. 'She probably gets her little clones to tidy up for her afterwards. So shall we go? It might be a laugh if we all go together. What do you think, Lia. You up for it?'

'She hasn't invited me,' I said.

'Are you sure?' asked Becca. 'Why would she invite us and not you? Look again. I saw her putting cards on everyone's desk. Maybe yours fell off, go back and look.'

I didn't have to. Not after the week I'd had. I had a feeling that she'd excluded me on purpose. It was weird, because she hadn't done anything major, not like when a boy bullies another boy. That might be simpler to deal with, I thought. If someone kicks or smacks you about, there's no doubt about it – you're being bullied. But this? I wasn't sure what was going on and wondered if it was all in my imagination. What had been happening was so subtle. Almost unseen. Secret looks between Kaylie and her mates, or whispers or sniggers, and now, no invite to her party. Plus, I felt there was no way I could go to the casting session. No big deal, not really. But inside, I felt like Kaylie had got it in for me and I felt miserable.

First Date

7

'PENNY FOR them,' said Dad, making me jump as he came up behind me.

'Oh, sorry, I was miles away.'

It was Saturday morning and I was sitting in the kitchen, gazing out of the window and going over the week in my mind.

'I could see that,' said Dad. 'So what's going on in that head of yours? How's your week been?'

'Oh . . . fine.'

'Hmm. You sure? You don't look your usual bright self and you've been quieter than usual this week.'

'No, honest. I'm great.'

'Everything OK at school?'

'Yeah.'

'Everything OK with Jonno?'

'Yeah, in fact, he's coming up tonight. We're going out somewhere.'

'You don't sound too excited. Tonight's a first date, isn't it?'

I nodded. He was right. I wasn't too excited. It was as if, in putting up a wall in my head to keep Kaylie out, I'd kept everything else out as well.

'So what is it, pet?' asked Dad. 'Come on, spill. You don't live in the same house as someone and not notice when something's going on.'

'Honest, Dad. It's nothing. Just . . . do you think I'm self-obsessed?'

Dad laughed. 'What kind of question is that? What do you mean?'

'You know, always thinking about myself?'

Dad laughed again. 'All teenagers are self-obsessed. It's part of the package. And, to a degree, so is everyone else. I mean, you live in your body, in your world. You're the only one who sees things through your eyes, so you're bound to be a little self-obsessed.'

I laughed.

'Maybe we need another word,' said Dad. 'Not "obsessed" . . . um, self-motivated. That sounds better, more positive. But why did you ask that, Lia? Is something worrying you?'

I sighed and tried to decide how much to tell him. Sometimes if you get parents involved, they worry. Then they end up becoming more of a problem than the problem itself. I decided to tell him part of the story.

'It's like . . . well, there's this girl and her mates at school, and I don't think they like me very much. I haven't ever done anything bad to them, but they seem to have it in for me.'

Dad pulled up a stool, took my hand and looked me directly in the eye. 'Are you being bullied, Lia?'

'*No*. No. That's exactly it. I'm not. But it almost feels like I am. But then, I don't know if it's me being paranoid or self-obsessed. Thinking too much about what other people think of me, when they're not even thinking about me at all . . . Oh, I don't know. It's OK, Dad, really. I know I'm not even making any sense. It's just, I want to fit in. You know, new school. But it's like some people won't even give me a chance.'

'Could be they're jealous,' said Dad, indicating our vast, top-of-the-range kitchen with his hand. 'We do live very well compared to most. And, you are a very pretty girl . . .'

'Yeah, yeah . . .'

'Seriously. It could be that.'

'I don't think these girls are jealous. I'm not sure. I mean, one of them was a bit miffed that I got off with Jonno, but these girls are popular and very pretty. The Teen Queens. It's not like I'm any kind of threat to their position in the school.'

Dad nodded. 'Yes, but you got Jonno and they didn't. They might think, first you get him, what's next?'

'Nothing. I just want to be ordinary.'

'Then sorry, Lia, can't help you. You'll never be ordinary, not with your looks and personality. And you're a clever girl. So you'll always do well at school if you keep working. And our life, well, no one can ever say that that's ordinary, can they? Sometimes you just have to accept your lot and get on with it.'

'I know. Sorry. I'm going on about nothing. And I may be imagining it all anyway.'

'So these girls who are giving you a hard time . . . How, exactly? Calling you names? What?'

My brain felt numb for a moment as I tried to think about it. There wasn't actually anything I could say that sounded so bad. So someone stared at me and didn't say hi back. Big deal. It sounds so pathetic.

'I'm pretty sure that they're all talking about me, but not in a nice way. Sometimes they ignore me, but sometimes, like when I go into a class, everyone shuts up like they've been talking about me . . . that sort of thing.'

Dad got up to fill the coffee grinder with beans. 'What do Cat and Becca think?'

'Becca says stand up to them and I haven't really talked to Cat about it much. To tell the truth, I don't want them to get into it. You know, they might feel that they have to take sides and all that . . . I just want it all to go away.'

Dad came over and squeezed my shoulder. 'I know just how you feel, love.'

'You do? How can you? Did someone give you a hard time at school?'

'Bully me? No way. I'd have thumped anyone back who tried. But it's different with lads. If someone's a bully and tries to kick your head in, it's pretty clear what's happening. No. It was later when I first began to make a name for myself in the music business that I got bullied, but in a different kind of way to what goes on in schools.'

'Who by?'

Dad went to the fridge and got some milk. 'The press,' he said with a grim expression. 'First, they're all, Oh, the new golden boy, and they can't get enough of you. But they can turn, and when they do, boy, do you feel it! I tell you, Lia, the press can be the biggest bullies of all and they can make or break someone.'

'So what happened?'

'I was on tour in the States and there was some story about a girl I was supposed to be having an affair with. All nonsense. I sat next to her in a club and the next day it was all over the papers over here. Course, your mum got to hear about it and was livid. Didn't know what or who to believe. The more I defended my position, the more guilty I looked. I had to learn fast, believe me. No, the best way to deal with them, or those girls at your school, is not to waste any energy on them. Don't rise to the challenge. Don't engage. Don't try to defend yourself as sometimes you can't win.'

'So what can you do?'

'Decide who's important in your life and be honest with them. Keep them close. But keep them out of it – gossip, rumour mongering, all of it. I've learned to keep my head down where the press are involved. But at the time, when I was younger, I used to get so mad at some of the things they'd write. Total fiction, but I had sleepless nights, thinking, What will people think? I must put the story straight, and so on. Dignified silence, that's the best. Now, I know who I can count on and they're the people who matter. They know the score and the rest of them can go to hell and believe what they want. Fame is fickle. The press are fickle. Sounds like these girls at your school are fickle. It sounds like you wouldn't want them as friends anyway, would you?'

I shook my head.

'So, there's your answer. Don't waste your energy letting them bother you. Enjoy your date tonight. And you have some great mates that care about you and they're the ones who matter. There will always be other people who won't like you, no matter what you do. Don't even give them the time of day. OK, pal?'

'OK,' I said.

'So how's about one of my cappuccino specials with extra chocolate on top?'

'Sure,' I said. I felt a lot better after talking to Dad. He was right. I'd been stupid letting it all get to me so much. In future, Kaylie and the Clones could do what they liked. I had my friends and my family, and they're the ones that counted. 'Thanks, Dad.'

Later, I went upstairs to have a bath and get ready for my date. I was really looking forward to it and wondered where Jonno would suggest going. There weren't that many places open nearby apart from pubs, so maybe he planned on going into Plymouth. I decided to make a real effort and spent ages trying on different outfits and doing my make-up. My first proper date since London. I couldn't wait.

Jonno arrived at seven o'clock, full of gossip about the casting session for *The Rocky Horror Picture Show* that had taken place at school in the afternoon.

'Did you get it?' I asked as I took him into the red sitting room. He'd played Danny Zucko in *Grease* in the Christmas show, so everyone was expecting that he'd play the lead again.

He shook his head and flopped on to a sofa. 'No, the role of Dr Frank N Furter went to Adam Hall.'

'Do you mind?'

'Nah. I'm cool with it. It can be a bit time-consuming playing the lead, and actually, I could do with some time to concentrate on other things.'

'So who got the other parts?'

'Do you know the story?'

'Vaguely. Some kids end up in a castle with a load of weirdos.'

Jonno laughed. 'That's about the gist of it. Dan Archer is playing Brad Majors and Jessica Moon is playing Janet. They're the geeky kids whose car breaks down and who end up at Frank N Furter's castle. Ryan Nolan is Riff Raff, the hunchback henchman, and Jade Macey is playing his sister, Magenta.'

'What about Cat?'

'I think she's playing the tap dancing groupie, Columbia. But where were you? I thought you'd be there.'

'Um, I decided to give it a miss this time. As you said, being in a show can be a bit full on. Did Kaylie and her mates get parts?'

Jonno nodded. 'Chorus, I think. Good job, because I doubt if they'd be able to remember their lines if they got bigger parts. They're not exactly the brightest coins in the collection, are they? Once when I was asked to coach the netball team, I said I wanted to discuss tactics. One of them, I think it was Jackie, thought I was talking about mints.'

I laughed, but wasn't quite sure if he was just joking.

'By the way, did you get the invite to Kaylie's?' he asked.

I shook my head. I hadn't thought of her party as an

option and hoped that Jonno hadn't planned on taking me there. 'No. But . . . but you go if you want.'

'No thanks,' he said getting up and going over to look at a painting on the wall opposite. 'Nice painting. Picasso, isn't it? My mum's got the same print.'

'Er, yeah, Picasso.' I didn't tell him that ours was the original, in case he thought I was showing off.

'Nah,' he continued, 'Kaylie's do's are not my scene. I find her crowd a bit too . . .' he mimicked a girlie-girl walking on high heels and flicking her hair. 'You know, lipstick, handbags and pointy shoes – that's all they think about.'

Yeah, I thought and how to ruin my life. 'So what shall we do this evening?' I asked.

Jonno came and sat next to me and took my hand. 'Ah well. I wanted to talk to you about this . . .'

At that moment, Dad came in. 'Watcha, Jonno,' he said as he turned on the television. 'Don't mind me.'

Jonno glanced at me, then looked longingly at the telly. 'Er, how about we stay here? Hang out. It's raining outside and I missed this afternoon's game . . . because of the casting session . . . and now, well, there's the . . .'

'Highlights of the Arsenal versus Man United game,' said Dad, rubbing his hands together, then bouncing on to the sofa.

***

Fifteen minutes later, Dad and Jonno were ensconced, shoes off, feet up, Cokes in hand, watching the football.

'*Woah*,' cried Dad as both of them rose in unison from the sofa when there was a near miss goal. As they settled back down again, Dad turned to look at me with one of his cheeky grins. 'Think we need another after that,' he said pointing at his Coke can.

This wasn't quite my romantic fantasy, I thought as I got up to go to the kitchen for fresh supplies. Mum was in the kitchen feeding the dogs when I went over to the fridge.

She smiled up at me. 'Not going out?'

'Arsenal versus Man United,' I said. 'I think Dad and Jonno have just discovered that they're soulmates.'

'Ah,' sighed Mum. 'Some things you just can't compete with.'

'Why did Dad have to watch in the red room? There's five other televisions in the house.'

'But that's where the biggest telly is. He got it specially for the footie. Digital sound, wide screen . . . he says he feels like he's actually there.'

'I just don't get it,' I said. 'How men can get so excited about kicking a bit of leather around a field.'

'Welcome to the club,' said Mum. 'Want to hear a joke about football?'

I nodded.

'What's the similarity between a boy and a football player?' she asked.

'Dunno.'

'They both dribble when they're trying to score.'

I laughed, then turned my head towards the door. I could hear singing. It sounded like the 'I–I–yippee, song'. Mum laughed. 'Better get used to it. Men tend to behave like kids when their beloved football's on. It can get very emotional.'

We went and stood in the hall by the red room door and, sure enough, they were both singing their hearts out. 'We're the best behaved supporters in the land, we're the best behaved supporters in the land, the best behaved supporters, best behaved supporters, the best behaved supporters in the land . . . when we win. We're a right bunch of bastards when we lose, we're a right bunch of bastards when we lose, we're a right bunch of bastards, right bunch of bastards, right bunch of bastards when we lose.'

'Hmm,' said Mum. 'Fancy a game of backgammon in the library?'

'Anything to get away from this,' I laughed, putting my hands over my ears.

I spent the evening in the library with Mum while Jonno bonded with my dad in the red room. At one point, I crept in to catch up, but they were deeply absorbed in conversation, analysing the game so far. As the second half of their programme started up, they burst into song again. This time it was to the tune of 'Glory, Glory Hallelujah'. 'Glory, Glory, Man United. Glory, Glory, Man United,' they sang. 'Glory, Glory, Man United. When the Reds keep marching on, on, on.'

'Ah, the famous rock star and the aspiring music student,' I teased from the door. 'I wish your fans could see you now, Dad.'

'I've had a *top* time,' said Jonno later when I saw him to the door. 'We must do it again soon.'

'Yeah, right,' I said as he leaned in to kiss me goodnight.

'Next week for Man United and Liverpool,' called Dad as he went up the stairs.

'Absolutely,' said Jonno, giving Dad a wave. Somehow the moment for snogging had been ruined, so I stepped back inside. Jonno didn't even seem to have noticed and went off smiling.

So much for my first date, I thought later as I wiped off my make-up.

Junk Mail?

8

THE FOLLOWING week at school, to my relief, the Clones seemed to have lost interest in me and life got back to normal. Sort of. At home, some rather strange things were starting to happen.

On Monday, when I got back from school, I had post. A catalogue advertising Tea Tree oil products for people who suffer from bad perspiration and BO. I didn't think anything of it, as so much junk mail comes through the door, so I chucked it in the bin.

Tuesday, I got a catalogue about padded bras for women who had flat chests. Quite useful, I thought, seeing as I'm as flat as a pancake. Again, I didn't think anything of it, only that our address must have gone on some mailing list somewhere. Although it was strange that it was addressed to me, as I wasn't the home owner.

Wednesday, a catalogue came for me from a company

selling gravestones. It couldn't be Kaylie, could it, I wondered? Surely she wouldn't go to all the trouble of getting these things sent to me? A shiver went down my spine when I thought over the things that had been sent. A catalogue for people with BO, a catalogue for padded bras and now one for gravestones. The insinuations were horrible. That I smelled, had no chest and soon might need a gravestone. No, *no*, I told myself, *no one* would be that horrible.

By the time the evening came, I had to believe that my earlier suspicions about Kaylie were right. At eight o'clock, two nettuna cheese pizzas arrived for me and I definitely hadn't ordered them. The delivery boy insisted that I had – he had my name, phone number and everything. Mum phoned the restaurant and, sure enough, they had all my details. She paid the boy, then turned to me in the hall.

'What's going on, Lia? Were you still hungry after supper and didn't want to say?'

'No. Course not. I'd tell you if I wanted pizza, you know that.'

'So who ordered these if you didn't?'

Kaylie O'Hara and her mates, I thought. And I'm pretty sure that they arranged for the catalogues to be sent as well. Mum saw me hesitate.

'Do you think you might know who ordered these?' she asked.

'Maybe . . .'

'Come on, let's go and sit down and try and get to the bottom of this.'

I followed Mum into the red room and we sat on the sofa. My mind was whirring round and round like a washing machine on spin. What to say? I couldn't be sure it was Kaylie. It might just be a mistake on the computer at the pizza restaurant. There was only one locally and we had ordered from there before, so I know they had our details on record. It was possible that they'd made a mistake. But a nagging feeling told me otherwise, although I couldn't prove anything. I felt miserable. If Kaylie was doing these things, she was doing them in a way that didn't obviously point the finger back at her. It could be her being vindictive, but it also could be me being paranoid and imagining things.

'So?' asked Mum.

'I'm not sure,' I said. 'Just at school lately, this girl has kind of got it in for me. I thought she'd dropped it as she's been pretty cool this week. Sort of back to normal, but maybe not.'

Mum nodded. 'Your dad did mention that someone had upset you. You do know that you can come to either of us don't you?'

I nodded. 'Yeah. I . . . I didn't want to make a big deal out of it.'

'Has anything else arrived out of the ordinary, Lia? I

noticed that there's been a lot of post for you this week.'

'Catalogues,' I admitted. 'At first I thought they were junk mail, but now . . .'

'What sort of catalogues?'

'One for people with BO, one for people with flat chests and one for gravestones.'

'Oh, Lia,' gasped Mum. 'Why didn't you say anything?'

'Because I'm not a hundred per cent sure, you know how much rubbish comes through the door – people advertising everything from windows to life insurance.'

'Yes, but all that stuff comes to me or your father. There's no reason why mail order firms would have your name. If it *is* this girl, then she has to be stopped. Do you want me to have a word with your class teacher?'

'*No!*' I cried. 'God *no*, that would be the worst thing ever. What if it wasn't her? Maybe it's just coincidence. She's already accused me of being self-obsessed . . .'

'One coincidence I could buy,' said Mum softly, 'but not this many.'

The thought of Mum going into the school filled me with horror. I imagined the teachers ticking Kaylie off, then she'd spread it around that I'd ratted on her, then there'd be even more talking about me behind my back and sniggering behind hands. No, Mum mustn't go in. I decided to try and make light of the situation.

'It's not a big deal, Mum. Not really. I thought it would

all blow over and maybe it has. But if it *was* Kaylie who ordered the pizzas and you went and talked to the teachers, then I'd be labelled as a sneak.'

'But Lia darling, you can't let her get away with this.'

'I know.'

'So what do you want to do?'

'Don't know,' I sighed. 'I really don't know.'

'Do I know this girl?' asked Mum, putting her arm around me.

I shook my head. 'Doubt it.'

'What's her name?'

'Kaylie. But please, Mum, don't do anything about it. I can handle it.'

'Well, you'll keep me informed as to what's going on, won't you?'

'Sure,' I said. It was good to know I had her support, but another part of me felt like I was letting her down. Star was so popular at school and Ollie is at his. And it's not that I wasn't popular. Lots of people thought I was OK, but I knew that could change if Kaylie carried on poisoning people's minds about me. Already, I was noticing that people in our class weren't being quite as friendly as they had been. God, I hate this, I thought. I really, really hate it. Why can't Kaylie just leave me alone? Heaven knows what people are thinking.

I had to make sure that Mum didn't make things worse.

'I'll talk to her. Please, Mum, let me deal with it.'

The next morning before school, Meena called me down into the hall. She was holding a huge bunch of tulips.

'Who are they for?' I asked.

'For you. See, here your name. No message, though.'

Oh, not Kaylie again, I thought, but then she wouldn't send me flowers. Must be from Jonno, I decided as I took the bouquet. How sweet. He must have felt bad about neglecting me Saturday. I went to phone him immediately.

'But . . . but they're not from me,' he said. 'Sorry. Should be, I suppose, I just didn't think of it. Looks like you have another admirer. Hmm . . . don't know if I like that. No message, you say?'

'Not an admirer,' I said. 'I think I might know who sent them and believe me, you've got no competition. Er, see you at school later.'

Just as I was about to leave for school, Mum called me into her room. 'I've just had a call from the florists, Lia. They say that you called yesterday and ordered some flowers. They called to ask if I wanted to change my usual weekly order of white lilies to tulips from now on.'

I shook my head. 'Sorry, Mum. I think it might be Kaylie stirring it again.'

Mum sighed. 'Darling, we have to do something.'

'I know, I know,' I said. I could kill Kaylie, I thought. But then that's probably just what she wanted – a confrontation so that she can deny everything and make me look like a fool. But now this was getting out of hand. She was involving Mum. I wondered what else she'd ordered in my name that Mum would have to pay for.

When I got to school, Kaylie, Jackie, Susie and Fran were all standing in their usual spot near the radiators in the hall. I saw them look over when I walked in and Kaylie said something and they all giggled.

How to play it, I thought. I guess they're waiting for me to be upset or mad. Well, I'm not going to be.

I smiled as I went by. 'Hi. Lovely day, isn't it?'

Ha. A puzzled expression flashed across Kaylie's face. She couldn't ask if I'd got the post or flowers, as that would identify her as the person sending things. And she'd never know if I got them or not if I didn't react. Yes, that was how to play it. She could deny sending me things and I could deny ever getting anything.

Sadly, though, my lack of reaction only made Kaylie react more. It was just after RE at the end of the day and most of the class had filed out. I asked Cat if I could borrow a book. 'Yeah, sure. In my bag,' she said, pointing to her rucksack. But then she suddenly tried to grab it before I did. 'Er, *no*, let me get it for you.'

I was instantly suspicious. There was something in her bag she didn't want me to see. Maybe another invite to one of Kaylie's little weekend parties. I didn't mind that, but I did mind Cat hiding stuff from me.

I looked into her bag before she could stop me and saw a piece of pink paper folded up next to the books. Kaylie always wrote on pink. I quickly pulled it out and began to read it.

'Oh no,' said Cat. '*Please* don't read that. I *so* didn't want you to see it.'

My face must have fallen, because Cat put her arm around me. 'Lia, she's not worth it. Nobody's going to believe what she's written.'

It said:

To Year Nine,
If you ever wondered why Lia Axford left her last school, this is why. She was expelled for lying and making up stories about classmates to try and make out that they were doing bad things. Be very careful what she says about anyone, as it will be lies. She twists events to make people think that everything is about her. Remember – Lia equals LIAR.

I felt tears sting my eyes. 'It's not true!' I blurted. 'I left my old school because I wanted to live at home. That's all.'

Cat put her arms around me. 'We know that, Lia. That's why I didn't want you to see the note.'

'*Why* has she got it in for me? I don't understand.'

'Because she's a mean, spiteful cow,' said Cat. 'And she's jealous because you've got everything that she wants.'

I glanced up and saw Susie peering through the glass pane at the classroom door. I didn't even bother to try and hide that I was crying. OK, result, I thought. You got me. Made me cry. Now go and tell your leader. Let her know Lia's in tears and I hope you'll all be very happy.

9 Negotiation Time

I DECIDED I had to take action. Put a stop to it. And there was only one way to do it. Cat had said that I had everything that Kaylie wanted, and that included Jonno. So the solution was simple.

'What do you mean you don't want to meet up later? Why?' he asked, when I saw him outside the gates after school.

'Look, it's not you, it's me . . .' I started.

'It's because I watched the game with your dad last week, isn't it? I *knew* it was a mistake. Girls always hate it when blokes watch the footie. Look, I won't do it again if you don't want me to.'

'It's not that Jonno. I didn't mind. Not really.'

'So what is it, then?'

This was proving more difficult than I'd thought. I couldn't come up with a logical reason. I did like him.

'It doesn't make sense, Lia. Come on, talk to me. We get on really well, so what's the problem?'

'Just . . . things are a bit awkward at the moment. Maybe we could go out at a later date. In a month or so?'

Jonno looked bewildered. 'Now you're really not making sense. Unless . . . is there someone else you've been seeing and you have to finish with him?'

'No. No one else.'

'So *what*, then? Come on. This is crazy.'

At that moment, Becca walked past. 'Phone me later, Lia,' she called.

'Sure,' I said.

Jonno waved her over. 'Hey, Becca. Lia doesn't want to see me any more and won't tell me why. You're her mate. Can you enlighten me?'

Becca looked surprised and glanced at me, then back at Jonno. 'Kaylie O'Horrible,' she said.

'What's she got to do with it?' asked Jonno.

Becca nudged me. 'I think you should tell him, Lia. She can't rule people's lives like this.'

'What is going on?' asked Jonno, who by now looked really confused. 'What do you mean, Kaylie can't rule people's lives?'

'She's been giving Lia a hard time,' Becca blurted out, 'because you're going out with Lia and not with her.'

Jonno narrowed his eyes and his expression turned to thunder. 'A hard time? Like how?'

'Telling lies about Lia, for a start,' said Becca. 'Spreading rumours.'

Jonno turned to face me. 'Why didn't you tell me?'

I felt at a loss to say anything. I felt so mixed up. Part of me felt relieved, as I'd been worried that he might have heard something about the note and wondered if it was true, if I really was a liar. Another part just wanted to escape from everything. It was all happening too fast. My head suddenly felt vacant, like someone had sucked all the air out of it. I saw Jonno glance behind Becca and me at a crowd coming out of school. Kaylie and the Clones were amongst them. Jonno took one look at them and went straight over.

'Oh hell, now what have you started, Becca?' I asked.

Becca looked hurt. 'Look, I told you I'm on your side. Girls like her can't be allowed to get away with it. I saw that note she sent round class. You – *we* – have to stand up to them.'

I strained to hear what Jonno was saying to Kaylie. Whatever it was, it looked heated and a small crowd gathered to see what was going on. Jonno is easily the most popular boy in school and Kaylie wouldn't like the fact that he was yelling at her in public. She was shifting about on her feet and looking at the pavement as though she wanted it to swallow her. Jonno finished what he was saying, then turned to leave. As he walked back towards us, he turned back. 'Just stay out of my business and grow up, Kaylie. I'll see who I choose and it wouldn't be you even if you were the last girl on the planet.'

'You'd be so lucky,' she called after him. But she looked upset.

Oh finking stinking, I thought as my stomach twisted into a knot. What now? I know Becca meant well. I know Jonno meant well, but now it was all out in the open, in front of the whole school. Jonno came back to me and put his arm around my shoulder. I glanced back at Kaylie as he began to lead me away and she gave me the filthiest look. If looks could kill, I thought, I'd be six foot under. It was awful. Everyone was staring and I knew it would be all around the school in half an hour. So much for fitting in and lying low, I thought. She's never going to let that happen now.

Jonno seemed to think that his 'conversation' with Kaylie had put an end to the idea of finishing with him. And quite honestly, it didn't seem to matter any more. Whether I was with Jonno or not, it was too late. Kaylie had been humiliated in public. War had been declared, and though not directly by me, I was in the front line whether I liked it or not.

Jonno and Becca stayed with me as I waited for Meena to pick me up. Only when they saw Kaylie and the Clones pile on the bus with the other school kids, did they go off on their various ways, Jonno to football practice and

Becca to a production meeting with Miss Segal.

This is ridiculous, I thought. Now they think I need bodyguards.

As Meena drove me home, I had a good long hard think. The situation couldn't continue like this. I didn't want to fight with Kaylie or any of her mates. Or argue with them. I just wanted to get on.

'What would you do if someone waged war on you, Meena?' I asked.

'Hmmm,' she said as she drove down the windy roads towards our house. 'I no like war. I think is big waste of time, money and innocent lives. Best not have war.'

'Yes, but if someone starts a war against you, even though you don't want it, what then?'

'Once I read book by Mahatma Gandhi. He leader of India for long time. He had good philosophy. He say that before resorting to war, one should always try the peaceful approach. Make effort to negotiate.'

I hadn't thought of taking that approach. I'd thought my only two options were to back off or fight. Hmm. Negotiate. Maybe I should give it a try. Plus, Mum's always saying that there's good in everyone. Kaylie must have feelings; she's only human. There's bound to be a heart in there somewhere. Maybe I could appeal to her better nature.

When I got home, I went straight to my room and

turned on my computer. I opened my Outlook Express and looked for the folder of old e-mails. There was one in particular I was looking for. It was from before Christmas, before everything went weird with Kaylie. It was one of those chain letters that tells you to send it on to ten people immediately or else something awful will happen to you. It had been sent around to just about everyone in the school and before you got to the actual message, there were about five pages of people's e-mail addresses. I vaguely remembered Kaylie's being on the list. It was blondebombshell.co.uk or something. I scrolled down the list. Bingo, there it was. Barbiebombshell@info.co.uk.

I opened a page for a new message and began to write:

```
Dear Kaylie,
I wanted to ask why you are being so horrible
to me. These last few weeks have been the worst
of my life and I've been really miserable . . .
```

I deleted that. It sounded too much like I was a victim.

```
Dear Kaylie,
Mahatma Gandhi said that in times of war, one
should try the peaceful methods of finding a
solution before resorting to fighting . . .
```

Definitely not. For one thing, Kaylie wouldn't know who Mahatma Gandhi was and would probably think that I was trying to be clever. Delete.

Dear Kaylie,
As you know these last few weeks have been rather strained . . .

Rather *strained*? Understatement! When did I get to be so polite? I sounded like the blooming Queen! May husboind and A have been rather strained lately . . . it has been my annus horribilis. No. Definitely the wrong tone. Delete.

Dear Kaylie,
You finking stinking cow. You're making my life hell — to the point that I don't want to come to school any more. But I suppose that would make you very happy, so you can stuff it. You're not going to win, you rotten bitch. I don't know why you've got it in for me, but LEAVE ME ALONE. You stink, your hair's dyed and . . . and you've got a big bum and short legs. And I bet that they're hairy.

Hmmm. I *knew* I couldn't send that, but it did make me feel slightly better writing it. I quickly deleted it. With my luck, I'd press the wrong button and send it off by mistake!

After about twenty more versions, I finally wrote:

```
Dear Kaylie,
I don't understand why you have been so mean to
me the last few weeks or why you sent that
blatantly untrue note around our year. However,
I'm prepared to put it all behind me if you are.
Can we start again, make an effort to get on and
be friends?
Li@
```

There, I thought. Simple, to the point, and not too emotional. I pressed the send button before I could change my mind and off it went. I felt lighter than I had in days.

Half an hour later, Cat phoned.

'Are you on your own?' she asked.

'Yes. Why?'

There was a silence. Then Cat said, 'I don't know how to tell you this . . .'

I felt my chest tighten and the knot in my stomach twist. 'What?'

'I was just on the computer and I got mail. From Kaylie. I think she's sent the same message to everyone.'

'*What?* What did she say?'

'I wanted it to come from me and not anyone else.'

'I understand. What did she say?'

'She's written: *Ha ha, look at this. How pathetic. Poor little rich girl's got no friends.* Then she's pasted an e-mail from you asking if you could be friends with her. Did you write that?'

I felt sick. 'Yeah. Yeah, I did. I . . . I thought . . . oh, I don't know what I thought.'

'I'm so sorry, Lia. She's such a cow.'

'Yeah.'

'You *do* have friends. *I'm* your friend – you know that, don't you? And Becca. And Mac and Squidge. You don't need people like her. Or her approval.'

I knew she was right, but her words didn't console me. I didn't understand. Why were some people so horrible?

Two hours later, Becca phoned to tell me about the message. Apparently Mac and Squidge had got it as well.

'It looks like she's sent it to everyone from our school that has a computer,' said Becca.

'And that's just about everyone.'

'I'm going to kill her,' said Becca.

'Be my guest,' I said. 'I can't deal with it any more.'

Teen Queens and Has-beens 10

I CRIED myself to sleep that night and the next day woke with the now familiar knot in my stomach. I didn't want to go into school, but I daren't tell Mum. She'd soon realise why and storm in and have it out with the teachers. Another person waging war on my behalf was the last thing I needed. But then, my methods of trying to resolve things hadn't worked either. I felt ill. I didn't want to eat, didn't want to do anything but hide under the duvet and come out when it was all over and someone appeared at my bedside to tell me that it had all been a bad dream.

I made myself get up and get dressed, and then hoped that Mum and Dad would go out somewhere for the day and not notice that I hadn't gone in.

At half past eight, the doorbell rang. It was Squidge.

'Hey,' he said.

'Hey. What are you doing here?'

'Thought you might like someone to go into school with,' he said.

'But you've come right out of your way.'

'No problem,' he said.

'And Meena usually drives me.'

'Cool. I'll arrive in style.'

'Not if Max and Molly have their way,' I laughed. 'They'll be covered in mud.' The dogs had just spotted us from one of the lawns below the house and were running as fast as they could towards us. Squidge and I made a dive for the car, which was waiting outside one of the garages, ready to take me to school. We only just made it in time and couldn't help laughing at the disappointed looks on their faces as they put their paws up to the windows.

A few moments later, Meena appeared and we were on our way, leaving Max and Molly behind on the drive. As we got closer to school, I asked if he'd seen the message that Kaylie had sent round.

'Oh that.' He shrugged. 'That's what the delete button is for.'

Then he asked about what I was doing at the weekend and filled me in on the film he was making about the school show. We talked about music, what movies were coming out . . . everything apart from Kaylie and the Clones. By the time we got to school, the knot in my tummy had loosened a bit. Only when we got out of the car, did he refer to it.

'Don't let them wear you down, Lia,' he said. 'And you know where I am if you need me.'

As I walked towards class, Jackie came up behind me.

'Hey, Lia,' she said.

'Uh,' I replied, wondering what nastiness she had in store.

'How are you?'

What does she mean, how am I? I thought. She must know the effect that they've had on me these last two weeks.

'Look, Jackie, I don't know what you want, but if you want the truth, I've been very freaked out. I don't know why you and your mates are being so horrid to me. I've never done anything to you and I've had about as much as I can take.'

Jackie shook her head. 'I know. I feel rotten about it.'

I felt shocked. 'You do?'

'Yeah, course. Not everyone agrees with Kaylie all the time and I think she's been really mean to you. I'm sorry.'

This was the last thing I expected. 'Oh,' was all I could say.

'Yeah, a few of us feel bad about it. She can be a Class A bitch, can Kaylie.'

'Really,' I agreed. 'A total bitch.'

She gave me a friendly smile, then took off down the corridor. Strange, I thought. Not at all what I expected, but then maybe some of the Clones have got minds of their own after all. I made my way to the girls' cloakroom to sit for a minute on my own before facing everyone who had no doubt got Kaylie's e-mail the night before. I'd only been in there a few minutes when I heard the door open and voices. One of them was Kaylie's. I quickly lifted my feet off the floor so that she wouldn't know that I was in there.

'And did you see the way she wrote her name? Lia with an "at" symbol, like you use on e-mail addresses,' Kaylie was saying. 'I suppose she thinks she's pretty cool, doing that.'

'You thought it was cool before,' said Susie.

'I never did,' said Kaylie. 'Who's side are you on?'

'Yours, of course,' said Susie. 'I've always thought that she was full of herself, so stuck up. She makes me sick.'

'Yeah, with her designer clothes and her private chauffeur,' said Jackie.

That's Jackie's voice! I thought. But she was just so friendly to me and now she's slagging me off with the rest of them. What's going on?

But they weren't finished yet.

'And I bet her hair is dyed,' said Fran. 'No one has hair that blonde without spending some serious money on it.'

'Which we all know darling daddy has,' said Jackie. 'She probably thinks she can buy friends as well.'

'And she's such a show-off,' said Kaylie. 'With her *real*

Cartier watch. Like who cares? And why does she have to get driven to school every day in a Mercedes? Just to rub our noses in it. Like, look what I've got and you haven't. I mean, she could get the bus with the rest of us, but oh no, she wouldn't mix with us, would she?'

'I don't think she's that pretty anyway,' said Fran.

'No, me neither,' said Susie. 'Only in a really obvious way. Honestly, Kaylie, I couldn't believe that e-mail she sent you. What a cheek. Let's be friends – like, who'd want to be her friend?'

'And she didn't mean it,' said Jackie. 'I spoke to her two minutes ago in the hall and she said she thought you were a total bitch, Kaylie.'

'Really?' said Kaylie.

'Really. Her very words. "A total bitch." She was trying so hard to be friendly with me and get me on her side, but course, I wasn't having any of it.'

I felt my shoulders sag and I hung my head. So it was all an act from Jackie. Talk about two-faced! And to think for a moment, I'd thought she might be OK.

'No one will be her friend,' said Kaylie. 'Like it's *so* obvious that Cat and Becca only hang out with her because they wanted to get in with a famous family. If she wasn't Zac Axford's daughter, I bet they'd have nothing to do with her.

'Yeah,' said Fran, 'everyone knows that Cat only spends time with her because she wants to get off with her brother, Ollie.'

'And Mac and Squidge,' said Susie, 'they're such hangers-on. Wanting to be part of a glam lifestyle.'

'I bet she left her old school because she had no friends there either,' said Jackie.

'Yeah.'

'Yeah.'

'Poor little rich girl,' said Fran. 'I wonder if she knows she's a has-been.'

'We're the Teen Queens and she's the has-been,' said Kaylie, and they all started laughing.

Then I heard the door open and close again. I felt like I'd been stabbed in the stomach and the tears I'd been holding back started to fall. There was no way I could go into class after what I'd heard, especially with red, swollen eyes. I waited five minutes, until I heard the first bell go when I knew that they'd all be in assembly, then I ran for the door and out the school gates.

I went straight down to the Cremyl ferry, then caught the bus into Plymouth. I knew what I had to do next. They'd left me no option.

11

Becoming Invisible

'WHAT DO you mean, you don't want Meena to drive you to school any more?' asked Mum on Saturday morning as we had breakfast.

'There's a bus,' I said.

'But you'd have to walk about half a mile to get it. Don't be ridiculous, Lia. Meena's always taken you to school. What's this really about?'

I took a deep sigh and got ready to explain. My new tactic: I was going to do everything I could to fit in and *not* stand out, and that meant some things had to go. First, the chauffeur-driven lift to school. Second, my watch. I'd bought a new one at the market in Plymouth yesterday — cheap, pink strap, plastic. Third, my clothes. I'd got some new outfits from a discount warehouse — all for under a tenner. From now on, I'd wear my hair scraped back and no make-up. No one would be able to accuse me of showing off. I'd be grey, blend with the crowd. I was going to fit in if it killed me. In fact, more than that; I was going to be invisible so that no one would notice me at all.

'It's really important that I don't stand out in any way, Mum. Being the only one at school who is chauffeur-driven in a Mercedes makes me stand *way* out.'

'But loads of the kids get dropped off or picked up.'

'Yeah, but not in this year's Mercedes. And the others get picked up by their mums and dads – not by the housekeeper.'

'Are you saying you want me to drive you in?'

'Yes. *No*.' Mum drives a silver Porsche. Imagine what they'd make of that! 'No. But how about Meena drives me in in her car? Her old Ford wouldn't stand out so much.'

'Has that girl been getting at you again?'

'No,' I lied. 'I just want to fit in, and it's so different to my old school, that's all.'

Mum didn't look like she believed me. 'Well, you're going to have to wear a paper bag over your head, Lia. You're a stunning girl, and I'm not just saying that because I'm your mum. You'll always stand out in a crowd.'

'Not if I dress down and don't wear any make-up.'

'Lia, have you looked in the mirror lately? You look just as good without make-up as you do with it on.'

'I have to blend in, Mum. It's really important. Please support me on this.'

Mum sighed. 'I'm not happy about this, Lia. Something's

not right and I get the feeling that you're not telling me the whole story, but . . . if that's what you want, then fine. I do understand how important it is at your age not to feel like the odd one out. So Meena will take you in her car from now on. And you're going to wear drab clothes . . . I don't get it, but fine.'

It seemed to work to a degree. Nothing major happened. The Clones just ignored me or sniggered if I ever said anything within their earshot. I could deal with that. I no longer wore anything to school that would draw attention to me. I stopped putting my hand up in class when a teacher asked a question. Meena picked me up in her old banger. I made sure I saw Jonno out of school and kept out of his way in school. If I saw Kaylie or one of the Clones coming, I'd turn and walk the other way. They'd won, they knew it, and they seemed to lose interest.

As the weeks went on and life settled down, I carried on seeing Jonno. However as I began to feel slightly better, I also began to feel that Jonno and I didn't have much in common. I found I was making excuses so that I could hang out with the old crowd – Mac, Becca, Squidge and Cat. Jonno preferred coming up to the house to going out, so he could watch the footie with Dad, and it just wasn't fun like it was with my mates.

We did spend a little time on our own, though – going for a pizza, to a movie, round the Old Town in Plymouth. Those were the times when I began to realise that it wasn't really happening for me with him. We didn't talk in the way that I've been able to talk with boyfriends in the past and, some of the time, I felt like Jonno was just agreeing with me and not really listening when I tried to share some of my ideas or views about things. There were only two topics of conversation that Jonno was interested in: sport and music. And it was getting boring. That and his new joke collection, which had made me laugh in the beginning, but was starting to wear a bit thin. Every time I saw him, he had a new one for me.

'How do you make Kaylie's eyes light up? Shine a torch in her ear.'

'Why does Kaylie hate Smarties? Because they're hard to peel.'

'What's the difference between a Kaylie Clone and a supermarket trolley? A supermarket trolley has a mind of its own.'

'What does a Kaylie Clone do when someone shouts, "There's a mouse in the room!"? Checks her highlights.'

'What's the similarity between a Brazilian rainforest and Kaylie O'Hara? They're both dense.'

And on and on they went. I think he got the jokes from the Internet, then adapted them. I think the jokes were his way of being supportive, but as the weeks went on, I was beginning to wish he'd just shut up about Kaylie. I didn't even want to hear her name.

Thank God for Squidge. He phoned one Saturday afternoon when Dad and Jonno were ensconced in their usual positions on the sofa and asked if I'd go up to Rame Head with him.

I leaped at the chance. We took the dogs with us and had one of the best afternoons I've had in ages. Cat told me that Squidge plans to do a film about the tiny church up there. It's right on the peninsula, on top of a small hill that looks out over the sea. There's something about the place. It's magical. I always feel so peaceful there, like nothing in the world matters.

'So how's it going with lover boy?' he asked as we made our way up the steps to the church.

'Och, he's football crazy,' I sang in a Scottish accent. 'Football mad.'

Squidge laughed. 'Not your scene, huh?'

'No thanks. I think he should be dating my dad – they're clearly madly in love.'

'It must be hard for you sometimes . . .'

'What do you mean?'

'All the trappings that come with you. Fab house. Your dad. You must get hangers-on.'

'Yeah. In fact, I overheard Kaylie and the Clones saying

that you and Mac were only interested in me because of the glam lifestyle.'

I expected him to laugh it off, but Squidge looked serious. 'Just be careful, Lia,' he said. 'Sometimes you don't know who your real friends are.'

I wasn't sure who he was talking about, but I didn't want to pursue it and ruin our afternoon. It did make me wonder, though. Cat? Becca? Mac? Who was he referring to?

Gutted

12

THE FOLLOWING Tuesday morning, I was going into school as normal and spotted Cat and Becca just inside the gates. They were deeply engrossed in conversation about something and didn't see me until I'd almost got up to them.

Becca jumped as soon as she saw me and nudged Cat to shut her up.

'Oh,' said Cat, looking awkward. 'Lia.'

'What were you talking about?' I asked. 'You looked totally absorbed.'

Becca glanced guiltily at Cat. 'Oh, nothing,' she said.

'Um, we were talking about the show,' said Cat.

Yeah right, I thought. My heart sank. I knew they were lying.

As we walked into school together, I felt gutted, even more so when I saw Cat look at Becca and make a face, as if to say, Oh dear, she almost caught us. I felt like turning around and running. It was the last betrayal. Cat and Becca, my two best friends. And now even they were talking about me in secret.

It was too much. I no longer knew who to trust. I was beginning to think that maybe changing schools had been the worst idea of my whole life. I resolved that when I got home, I'd speak to Mum about going back to my old school. I had my friends up there and even though it would mean being away from home again and I'd miss Mum and Dad, at least Star and Ollie were in London and I'd be away from this nightmare.

In the break, I went off to find Squidge. At first, I thought that I wouldn't say anything to him as I know that Cat and Becca are his friends too, but somehow I felt I could trust him. He had tried to warn me about who my real friends were.

'I just don't understand it,' I said after I explained what I'd seen. 'I really thought that there were no secrets between Cat, Bec and me, and now . . . I don't know what to think. They were clearly talking about me.'

Squidge shook his head. 'No. You've got it wrong. They *are* your mates. Honest. Look, they were probably trying to protect you.'

'Against what?'

'Same ole, same ole. Kaylie.'

'No,' I said. 'She's been OK lately. Lost interest.'

'I don't think so . . .'

'Why?'

Squidge bit his lip.

'Oh, please Squidge. If they're doing something I don't know about, please tell me. Please.'

'Look, promise you won't say that I told you . . .'

'Promise.'

'Apparently Kaylie's still trying to stir it about you. She told Cat and Becca that you'd been slagging them off to her.'

'*What?* I never even speak to Kaylie. That's mad!'

Squidge shrugged. 'Well, she is, isn't she?'

'How do you know this? When did it happen?'

'Last night at rehearsal. I saw her talking to Cat and Becca, then Becca told me what she'd said.'

My stomach tightened into the familiar knot. 'And what did she say?'

'Something about you saying that you only hung out with Cat and Becca because they were nice to you when you first arrived and now you can't shake them off. Then she told them that really you wanted to be in with Kaylie and her lot and that's why you've been so upset about them not accepting you.'

'But surely they wouldn't believe her? I'd never slag them off. Why didn't they phone and ask me? Why didn't they tell me about it this morning?'

Squidge faced me squarely and put his hands on my

shoulders. 'Because they didn't believe a word of it and didn't want to upset you. Look, Lia. They're your best mates. They know what Kaylie's like.'

'Do they? *Do* they? But they were whispering about me this morning. I just don't know who to trust any more. And . . . and on Saturday, you said to be careful about who my real friends were.'

'I didn't mean *them*, you doofus,' said Squidge.

'Then who?'

This time it was Squidge's turn to look uncomfortable.

'Who?' I insisted.

Squidge hesitated for what seemed like ages. 'OK. Jonno,' he said finally.

'Why? He's not in with Kaylie,' I said. 'He doesn't even like her.'

'I know,' said Squidge. 'Look, forget I even said anything. It's probably just me coming over all big brothery about you.'

'Oh, tell me, Squidge. Do you know something about Jonno that I don't?'

Squidge glanced around the playground to make sure no one was listening. 'Not exactly. Just . . . you know what we were talking about on Saturday. About hangers-on. Well, sorry, but I think that's what Jonno might be doing. When you talk about him, it sounds like he used you to get in with your dad. You know he's desperate to get into the music business when he leaves here. He must know that your dad could help him and it sounds like he spends more time with him than you.'

I couldn't deny it. It had begun to really annoy me lately, and privately, I had been thinking of calling it a day with him. Not so much because I thought he was a hanger-on, but because I didn't think I really fancied him any more. There was no chemistry – not on my side anyway. Even though he was good looking and nice, I wanted more than that. I preferred to be with someone I could really talk to and have a laugh with, and if I had a boyfriend, I wanted one who made me feel tingly when he kissed me. Snogging Jonno was like eating porridge. A bit dull.

'I hope I haven't spoken out of turn,' said Squidge anxiously. 'In fact, take no notice of me. Deep down, I'm probably jealous.'

'Jealous?'

Now Squidge looked *really* awkward. 'Look, got to go. Class starts in a minute.' And with that, he turned and fled.

Squidge jealous? That stopped me in my tracks for a minute. Could he possibly fancy me? I felt my brain do a gear shift, as I'd never let myself imagine being with him. But we do get on well. He's so funny and full of life and new ideas, and he has the most amazing brown eyes, with thick black lashes and a lovely wide mouth . . . Hmm. Jealous? Maybe he felt the same about me. Yes, interesting. Very interesting.

13 Vicars and Tarts

'SO PLEASE, no secrets,' I said to Cat and Becca when I caught up with them at lunch-time. 'I know that Kaylie was stirring it again, but please, tell me when she tries a stunt like that.'

'We didn't want you getting upset,' said Becca. 'And it wasn't as if we took any notice. In fact, Cat asked how many times she'd have to flush before Kaylie would go away.'

I laughed. 'I'd be more upset if I thought you weren't my mates any more. I knew something was going on when I saw you this morning. I felt awful. I thought I'd lost you. I'm sorry, I guess I'm getting paranoid with everything that's been going on, so please, no secrets from each other.'

Cat looked at Becca questioningly and Becca gave her a nod.

'We were talking about you, Lia,' she said. 'It's true. But not what you think. We weren't talking about Kaylie – I wouldn't waste my breath. No. We were trying to think of a surprise for you. We know you've had a rough time lately, and we wanted to do something to cheer you up.'

'Just be my friends and always tell me what's going on. That's the best thing you could ever do.'

'Yeah, but we wanted to do *something* . . . I don't know,' sighed Becca. 'It's like you haven't been yourself lately. You've been sort of defeated, like a shadow of yourself. You're so quiet. You can even see it in your posture. You've stooped in on yourself – it's as though you're trying to disappear.'

'I am,' I said. 'I don't want anyone to notice me.'

'But that's not you,' said Cat. 'It's like Kaylie's rubbing you out somehow. We wanted to do something to bring the old Lia back. Make you laugh again.'

'Like what?'

Well, that's what we were trying to decide. A movie, a sleepover . . . dunno. We didn't know if you'd like to do something on your own or whether you'd want Jonno along.'

'OK, seeing as we're being totally honest, I don't think I want to go out with Jonno any more.'

'Why?' asked Becca.

I shrugged. 'Don't know. I mean, he's a really nice guy and cute and everything, but I don't think we've got a lot in common.'

'This isn't part of your campaign to be invisible, is it?' asked Becca. 'You've ditched the watch, the nice clothes, the Mercedes and now you're going to ditch the cutest boy in school, all so that Kaylie O'Horrible won't give you a hard time . . .'

Speak of the devil. At that very moment, Kaylie came out of the loos and made a beeline for us. In her hand, she had a pile of envelopes. Oh, here we go, I thought. Invites to one of her do's.

'Hi.' She smiled at us all, then turned to me and handed me an invite. 'Look, Lia, I just wanted to say, let's bury the hatchet and start again. I've been thinking about that e-mail you sent and you're right, we should try to get on. So, bygones be bygones, etc., and please come to my party on Saturday.'

I think my mouth fell open. 'Oh . . . right. Thanks,' I said as I took the envelope from her.

She gave invites to Cat and Becca as well. 'I thought I'd have a theme party this time,' she said, 'so it's fancy dress. Vicars and Tarts. All the boys are coming as vicars, so all the girls are coming as tarts. Should be a right laugh.'

Becca pulled a face at her as she went off. 'What a cheek! I don't believe it. At rehearsal, she fed us a pack of lies about you and now she swans in and gives us invites as though nothing was said. Huh! Bury the hatchet? Her? More like she wants to bury it in our backs. So no. No way

I'm going to one of her stupid parties. Not if you paid me.'

'Me neither,' said Cat. 'She might think she can just wave and we'll all come running. No way. No, let's put these invites in the bin.'

'No, wait,' I said. 'I think we should go. She's put out the hand of friendship and I bet that wasn't easy for someone like her. Please. I don't want to go on my own, so please come with me. I . . . I want to give it a try.'

Becca looked at Cat.

'Why is getting on with Kaylie so important to you, Lia?' asked Becca. 'She's a Class A bitch. You don't need people like that in your life.'

I felt a moment's panic. I didn't want them to think that there was any truth in what Kaylie had said to them about me wanting to get in with her and shake them off.

'I don't want to be a close friend of hers, I don't. I just want it to be all right between us. Like, no stuff . . . no bad vibes. If she is on the level and I don't go to her do, she might think I'm being snooty or something. I'd like to go and show that I simply want to get on with everyone. Then maybe we can put this whole mad thing behind us all and get on with our lives.'

'All right,' sighed Becca. 'But only for you.'

On the night of the party, we had a great laugh getting dressed. Being Queen Party Planner, Mum's got a dressing-up chest full of weird and wonderful costumes from Venetian wigs to Japanese kimonos to Roman togas. At the bottom of the chest, we found some wonderful tarty gear. Rubber skirts, feather boas, blonde wigs, high strappy shoes . . . Becca put on a tiny black leather skirt and black lace bra with a see-through black blouse over it. Cat chose a white see-through top with a black bra underneath – very trashy. And I went for a short, low cut, pink strappy dress, fishnet tights and a magenta pink feather boa. We plastered our faces with make-up and back-combed our hair as high as we could. By the time we'd finished we looked like a right bunch of slappers.

Dad's eyes almost came out on stalks when he saw us totter down the stairs in our high heels. 'And just where on earth do you think you're going, dressed like that?' he asked.

'Party,' said Cat.

'I don't think so . . .' Dad began.

'Fancy dress,' I said. 'Vicars and Tarts, and I think you can tell that we're not the vicars.'

He still didn't seem too happy about it. 'Put your coats on until you get there and I'll drive you.' He glanced anxiously at the three of us again. '*And* pick you up!'

I asked Dad to drop us on the corner of Kaylie's road, as I didn't want to draw attention to his Ferrari. As soon as he drove off, we whipped off our coats, applied a bit more rouge and red lipstick, then tottered up to Kaylie's front door. Becca rang the bell.

A few moments later, a middle-aged lady with frizzy blond hair answered the door. She was wearing a tracksuit and smoking a cigarette. She looked horrified to see us standing there, giggling, on her doorstep.

She took a drag of her cigarette. 'Yeah?'

Suddenly I had a sense of foreboding. There was no sound of music coming from inside or people's voices. The house was quiet and I could see a flicker of light from a TV through the window at the front.

Becca and Cat began suspect something was up at the same time. 'I . . . er, we thought there was a party here,' said Becca.

'Well, you thought wrong,' said Mrs O'Hara, looking us up and down with disapproval. 'And do your parents know that you're out dressed like this?'

'Um, we thought it was fancy dress,' muttered Cat. 'Sorry. Wrong house. Sorry to have bothered you.'

Mrs O'Hara shut the door without another word. She doesn't look like a very friendly person, I thought, walking down the path towards the gate. Suddenly, I was blinded by a flash of light as someone leaped out of nowhere.

'Smile for the camera,' called Kaylie. As my eyes adjusted back to the dark, I could see that behind her were the

Clones – Jackie, Fran and Susie. They were all laughing their heads off. Becca put her hand up to her face so that they couldn't get another picture, but it was too late, Kaylie was clicking away as fast as she could.

Suddenly Becca made a bolt for her, but she wasn't quick enough to get the camera. Kaylie ran for her front door and in a second, disappeared inside. The Clones raced down the road to the left and were out of sight in a minute.

'Come on,' cried Becca, setting off after them, 'let's get them.'

Cat and I tried to follow them, but in three-inch high heels, running was an impossibility. Cat collapsed into a privet hedge in someone's front garden and starting laughing.

'I can't even walk in these things, never mind run,' she moaned.

Becca came back to check that Cat was OK, then looked in the direction that the Clones had gone. 'Oh, stuff them,' said Becca. 'They're not worth it.'

'Yeah,' I said. 'Stuff them.' She put her arm around me. 'It doesn't matter, Lia. Who needs Kaylie or her stupid friends anyway?'

'Yeah,' said Cat. 'So she got us to dress up – like, very funny, ha ha.'

'Yeah, pathetic,' I agreed.

'Let's go back to yours, Lia, and have our own party,' said Cat.

We all sat on the wall and, as I got out my mobile to call Dad, a green Fiesta drove past. It slowed down when the driver saw us.

'Whey *hey*,' called a boy in the passenger seat as he wound down his window. 'Want to spend the rest of your lives with me, darlin's?'

'You couldn't afford my dry cleaning, *darling*,' Cat called back in a very posh voice.

When they realised that we weren't interested, they drove off, thankfully. Cat and Becca began to laugh and I tried to join in, but my earlier sense of foreboding had deepened. Somehow I felt that this wasn't the end of it.

14   The Last Straw

THE FOLLOWING Monday, when I got into school, there was a crowd of people around the notice board in the corridor outside the assembly hall. There seemed to be a lot of giggling going on, so I went to see what the joke was. People often posted jokes that they'd found on the internet, although they didn't last long up there, as usually one of the teachers saw them and took them down. As I approached, one of the boys in the crowd spotted me and nudged the person next to him. Suddenly, everyone went quiet. Kaylie, I thought immediately. Oh no, what has she done now? The crowd parted like a wave and I peered at the board to see what they'd all been looking at. Up on the board was a blown-up Polaroid of Cat, Becca and me, dressed in our tarts' outfits. Underneath it, was written: *The real Lia Axford and her mates. How the little Miss Perfects are out of school. We vote for Ophelia Axford as Slag of the Week. Sign here if you agree.'* There was a whole list of names and a few messages with boys' phone numbers with invitations to call them.

Jerry Robinson from Year Eight whistled and winked. 'Hey, Ophelia, I'll have afeelofya. Get it?' he started laughing. 'Ophelia, a feel of ya. And you look so quiet in school. Call me.' Then he laughed. 'No, on second thoughts, I'll call you. Maybe.'

I tried to smile and make light of it, but inside I felt frozen. I couldn't even cry. This was the last straw. I felt numb except for the knot in my stomach that felt tighter than ever. Suddenly, I couldn't breathe. As the crowd dispersed, I reached up to take down the photo. Just as I reached out, someone put a hand on my shoulder. It was Miss Segal.

'I'll take that,' she said with a grim expression. She took the photo from the board and walked off without a second glance at me.

That's it, I thought as I watched her walk away. My favourite teacher and now even *she* is going to think badly of me. I ran for the girls' cloakrooms and luckily they were empty. The bell went for assembly and I could hear everyone outside heading for the hall. I went into the last cubicle and locked the door. I'd reached the end. I didn't know how to be any more.

First, the boys here thought I was aloof, and now they

thought that I was a slag. I'd tried standing up for myself. I'd tried being invisible. None of it had worked and now Kaylie had even got it in for Cat and Becca and it was all because of me. If I hadn't come to this school, I thought, their photo wouldn't be up on the notice board for the whole world to see. I felt a total failure. I'd let everyone down. I didn't fit in here. And it was probably my fault. So that was it. I would definitely, *definitely* talk to Mum about leaving this horrible school and going back to my old one in London.

I decided to hide in the cubicle until assembly got going, then I would go home and beg Mum to let me leave here and never come back.

It was only a minute later that I heard the cloakroom door open then close. Like before, when Kaylie and her mates came in, I lifted my feet up so that no one would know I was in there. This is insane, I thought, I can't stay at this school any longer. I can't spend the rest of my school years hiding in the loos.

Whoever it was that had come in was looking in each cubicle. Oh, *please* don't be Kaylie, I prayed. I didn't think I could take any more of her abuse.

'Lia, I know you're in here.'

It was Squidge's voice! What should I do, I asked myself . . . ? Maybe if I'm really quiet, he'll go away. He reached the cubicle I was in and tried the door.

'Lia?'

I tried not to breathe.

'Lia. I know you're in there. Look. No one takes Kaylie and her mob seriously. You mustn't take it to heart. Honestly, no one gives a toss. Please come out.'

A moment later, the cloakroom doors opened again and I heard more footsteps.

'Is she in here?' asked Mac.

'Lia?' called Becca.

'I think she's in there,' said Squidge.

It wasn't that I didn't want to speak to them – I just couldn't. I felt numb.

'Hey, Lia,' said Cat softly. 'We know you've seen the photo. So they think they've made fools of us. It's no biggie. We're in this together. Please come out.'

'Yeah, in fact,' said Becca, 'most people think she's a sad loser, stooping to this last stunt. Come on, come out.'

I didn't reply.

'We're not going to go away,' said Squidge.

I heard footsteps go into the cubicle next door and it sounded like someone was hoisting themself up. Suddenly there was Becca's face peering over the partition. She smiled. 'Hey, we've got to stop meeting like this.'

'Is she in there?' asked Cat.

'Yeah,' said Becca. 'Come on, Lia, come out. We can deal with this. Together. Come on.'

I felt so ashamed. So stupid and weak that I couldn't be like them and just laugh it off.

'Come on,' said Becca. 'You can't sit in here all day. Assembly will be over in a minute and people will start coming in before class.'

'I'm so sorry,' I whispered. I got up and unlocked the door. I still didn't feel like going out, but on hearing the lock open, Cat pushed the door and came in and put her arm around me.

'You're bigger than this,' she said. 'Come on. We have to show them that it hasn't got to us. We can't let her win.'

'I'm so sorry,' I said again. 'I wish I could be like you, but . . . I'm sorry. It's like I've just, I dunno . . . I'm going to go back to my old school. I can't take it here any more . . .'

Suddenly Mac stiffened and jerked his thumb towards the door. We all held our breath for a moment as we listened to the footsteps outside in the corridor. Click clack on the floor. Quick footsteps. Alert. Efficient. Not the footsteps of a schoolgirl or boy sauntering to or from assembly. The door opened. It was the headmistress.

'Becca Howard. Why aren't you in assembly? Jack Squires and Tom Macey! *What* are you doing in the girls' cloakrooms? And who's in that cubicle?' She marched forward. 'Cat Kennedy. Lia Axford.' She sniffed the air. 'You've not been smoking, have you?'

'No, Miss,' said Becca.

Mrs Harvey looked us all up and down. 'I don't expect this sort of behaviour from any of you lot. Don't let me see it again!'

Then she turned on her spiky heels and left.

I was still ready to make a bolt for home, but Squidge wouldn't let me leave.

'You know that saying. Take a twig on its own and it's easy to snap. Bind a few twigs together, not so easy to break. Five twigs, even more difficult. There's you, me, Mac, Cat and Becca. They won't break us if we stick together. You're not alone in this. OK?'

'OK . . .' I said, with an attempt at a smile. Dear Squidge, I thought. He's trying his best, and maybe even thought he fancied me, but he doesn't know what I'm like. Pathetic. A loser. Can't fight my own battles. Whingey, wet and full of self-pity. It's best I'm out of here and out of all their lives.

Cat and Becca wouldn't let me go. They marched me, one on either side, to the first class. Although Kaylie and the Clones sniggered when we walked in, it didn't matter any more. I'd decided. Her, her clones and this horrible episode were soon going to be nothing more than a bad memory. Three classes to sit through: double English, then drama with Miss Segal. Then at lunch, I'd slip away. I'd go back to my old school and, at last, the nightmare would be over for good.

15 Role-play Nightmare

'OK, CLASS,' said Miss Segal, looking around the room. I tried not to meet her eyes as I felt embarrassed about the photo she'd taken from the board. 'Today I want to do something a bit different. I know we've done scripts in the past, we've looked at other people's words, other people's ideas. Today, we going to free things up a bit.'

I was hardly listening. In my head, I was calling my old mates in London – Tara, Athina, Gabby, Sienna, Olivia, Isobel and Natalie. I hoped they would still be my friends when I went back to my old school, and that they'd still like me and accept me and not pick up on the fact that, somehow, I'd become a loser.

'Lia?' asked Miss Segal. 'Are you with us today?'

I nodded. 'Sorry. Yes. Just thinking.'

Kaylie sniggered. It didn't bother me. You're history, I thought. I only have to get through this last class, then

I'll never ever have to see you or your stupid friends ever again.

'Right,' continued Miss Segal. 'We're going to do some role-play situations. I'll need a couple of volunteers, then I'll set the scene and we'll see where it takes us. The idea is to improvise. I'm not going to tell you what to say or do, just see what comes into your head.'

Count me out, I thought. One thing I will not be doing today is volunteering for anything like that. Sounds like my worst nightmare.

'OK. First scenario,' said Miss Segal. 'Two people who have some kind of a relationship. What it is, our volunteers have to decide. It can be sisters, family, business partners, whatever. It can be at home, in an office, school . . . you choose, and the rest of us will try and work out what the relationship is. OK. Who's up?'

Mary Andrews and Mark Keegan put their hands up. I watched as though from a distance as they enacted a scene in a bank. It was quite clear. Mark was the manager and Mary was a customer. I wasn't really interested. I looked at my watch. Thirty-five minutes to go until lunch-time. Then I was out of here.

After Mark and Mary had done their role-play, Miss Segal stood up again. 'Good,' she said. 'Now let's make it more interesting. The essence of all good drama is conflict. And how do you create that?'

'Fight, Miss,' said Joanne Nesbitt.

'Arguments,' said Bill Malloy.

'Yes, but what causes those arguments in the first place?' asked Miss Segal.

No one answered.

'Conflict of some sort,' said Miss Segal. 'By putting opposites together we can create that. For example, put two non-smokers on a train. What do we have?'

'People with something in common,' said David Alexander.

'OK. Two smokers together?' asked Miss Segal.

'A smoky compartment,' said Mark Keegan.

Miss Segal laughed. 'Yes, but again, we have two people who get on. Now. Put a smoker and a non-smoker in a room together and what do we have?'

Becca gave Kaylie a dirty look. 'Conflict,' she said.

'That's right. Can anyone think of any other opposites?'

'Vegetarian and meat-eater,' said Sunita Ahmed.

'Good. Any others?'

'Different religions, different politics . . .' said Laura Johnson.

'That's it. Now you're getting it.'

'Rich and poor,' said Cat.

'Popular and not popular,' sneered Kaylie, with a side glance at me.

'Winner and loser,' said Susie.

'Excellent. So, for our next scenario,' continued Miss Segal, 'I want two boys.'

Peter Hounslow and Scott Parker got up and went to the front.

'OK, boys, this time I want you to play opposites. You choose who and where. Let it evolve and let's see what happens.'

Despite myself, I couldn't help but be interested. In front of me, Pete and Scott began to size each other up, then call each other names. Pete started mocking Scott's voice and laughing at him. It wasn't long before the boys were fighting. I knew it wasn't serious as they're best friends out of school, but it reminded me that when a boy is a bully, then it's obvious. Pete was playing the bully and Scott was his victim.

When they'd finished, Miss Segal clapped. 'Excellent, and did you see, as they got into their roles, Pete became stronger and Scott became weaker? Great body language, boys. Scott, you really looked weary and defeated by the end. OK. I think that was pretty clear – the bully and his victim.'

She looked around class and fixed her gaze on me. 'OK. Now let's see how two girls might play out that situation.'

I felt myself stiffen. This was getting a bit close to home and I felt like I wanted to disappear. No way. Look somewhere else, I thought as I stared at the floor, avoiding

Miss Segal's eyes. I felt myself getting hot. I looked at my watch. Only twenty more minutes to go.

Miss Segal's gaze moved on. 'Any volunteers?'

To my amazement, Cat nodded at Becca, then the two of them were up like a shot.

'OK, girls,' said Miss Segal. 'Off you go.'

Cat started to say something and Becca started rolling her eyes and looking away as if she was really bored. She flicked her hair and sniggered to an invisible person. Cat shut up. Then Becca started acting really friendly to a group of invisible people and pretended to hand out cards. She stopped at Cat. 'Oh sorry, not you,' she said, with a toss of her hair. 'You're not pretty enough.'

Someone at the back laughed. I was stunned. She was doing the most perfect imitation of Kaylie. Then Becca walked into Cat. 'Oh *sorry*, wasn't looking where I was going,' she said, with a really false smile. Cat started looking miserable. 'Oh, lighten up, Cat,' teased Becca. 'You're too serious.'

I glanced over at Kaylie. She was looking daggers at Becca. I wanted to die. Becca was on a roll. She spoke to her invisible friends, sniggered, whispered, gave Cat filthy looks.

Finally, she stood in front of Cat with her hand on her hip. 'Whatever kind of style you were going for,' she said, 'you missed.' Then she started laughing again.

When they'd finished, Miss Segal clapped. 'Well done,'

she said. 'And very interesting. I'll tell you why. Because with the first scenario, the boys, it was clear. Pete was the bully, Scott was the victim. But with Cat and Becca, it felt different. Can anyone tell me why?'

A hush had fallen over the class. A few girls glanced nervously at Kaylie.

Miss Segal looked around. I think she felt the tension in the air. 'It's suddenly gone very quiet in here. Come on, class. Why did it feel different?'

Sunita put up her hand. 'With the boys, the bullying was physical. With the girls, it was more subtle. Like, Scott would have had a bruise or a broken arm to show for it. All Cat had was a broken ego. The aggression towards her was almost unseen, as Becca made it all look so casual. Like walking into her accidentally on purpose. Cat might think that she was imagining it.'

'So, what's the solution?' asked Miss Segal.

'There isn't one,' said Sunita. 'You can't tell your parents, as it's not like you've got a black eye or anything, and if you make a fuss, they might make things worse by causing a scene at school and *no one* wants that.'

'So why not go to a teacher?' asked Miss Segal.

'No way,' said Laura Johnson. 'What are you going to say? They might think, What's the big deal? So someone walked into you or didn't invite you to their party. So what. Deal with it. Then you'd feel like a fool. Or maybe the teacher would talk to the bully girl and then the girl might act all sugary-nice to you for a while, but you'd know it was totally false. No, best leave teachers out of it.'

I had the feeling that Sunita and Laura were talking from experience and wondered whether they had once been subject to Kaylie's methods as well.

'So what *do* you do?' asked Miss Segal.

No one spoke for a few moments, then a voice from the back of the classroom started up. It was Tina Woods, a really quiet girl who hardly ever said anything. 'You, er . . .' She nervously adjusted her glasses. 'You cry at home on your own. You hide your feelings and try and get through each day without anyone noticing you . . . You try to be invisible.'

At that moment, the bell went for lunch and people began to shuffle at their desks, anxious to get out, but I was riveted to my seat. Tina had described my experience exactly, as had Laura and Sunita.

'Just before you go,' said Miss Segal, 'I'd like to say that there *are* things that you can do. Most bullies are cowards at heart and must be stood up to, one way or another. Expose them. Because if they're doing it to one person, they're probably doing it to someone else as well. And if not now, they will in another year. I should know. I was bullied at school and it took me a long time to realise that I had to be myself and not to let others define who I was.

OK, you can go now, but I'm here if anyone wants to talk about this further.'

As the class made a dash for the door, I noticed that Tina Woods was hovering in the background. I got up and followed Cat and Becca out the door. I felt stunned.

16 Real Friends

'YOU WERE totally brilliant, Becca,' said Laura as we sat eating our sandwiches in the hall at lunch-time. 'You had you-know-who down to a T.'

Everyone was talking about Miss Segal's class. It seemed that loads of people had stories about being bullied. Tina, Sunita, Laura – even some of the boys had been subject to forms of exclusion, name calling and general nastiness.

'Well, I'm not afraid to say her name,' said Cat. 'You mean Kaylie. And it's the first time I've ever seen her look so uncomfortable in class. And I noticed she scarpered pretty fast when the bell went. Doesn't want a taste of her own medicine.'

'She and her mates made my life miserable last term, just because I wore the wrong kind of trainers,' said Sunita. 'But my parents couldn't afford to buy me the trendy ones.'

'So what did you do?' asked Cat.

'I begged my mum and she saved up and got me some new ones for Christmas,' said Sunita, 'but that didn't work either. Kaylie accused me of being a copycat and dressing like her.'

'You can't win with people like her,' said Becca. 'Best just leave them to rot in their own poison.'

'It's amazing,' I said, 'because there were times when I thought it was just me. That it was my fault.'

'No way,' said Becca. 'There are just some girls who are really mean. Who knows the reason. Like Jade Macey. We could have been real mates. But no, she didn't want anyone else from our school going for that Pop Princess competition. And she was just plain horrible to anyone she saw as a threat.'

'I hate all that,' I said. 'Why can't people just see each other as equals, not as rivals.'

'Way too liberal for someone like Kaylie,' said Cat. 'She sees you as a threat, especially as you took Jonno from under her nose . . .'

'Well, she can have him back.' I laughed. 'Actually, no. Even though I don't want to go out with him, he's still too nice for Kaylie.'

'Still want to leave, Lia?' asked Cat.

I looked at my watch and shook my head. It was ten to one. My plan to run as soon as morning classes ended had been forgotten. Miss Segal's class had changed everything. I realised that I wasn't alone.

'So, what are we going to do to stop her antics from now on?' asked Becca. 'She's made the best part of this term a misery for Lia, and for Tina, Laura, Sunita and probably a load of others too.'

'Confront her, Lia,' said Cat. 'I bet there's enough people to back you up. She'd run a mile. She's OK if she can get you on your own or if she's got her little gang with her, but I bet she wouldn't be so sure of herself if she realised that she's outnumbered.'

I shook my head. 'After this morning, I honestly don't think it's going to be necessary. There's no doubt that everyone in our class knew what was going on. Her behaviour has been exposed all right, and I doubt if she'll be able to get away with it in future.'

'I guess,' said Cat. 'In fact, I think everyone can see what a spiteful cow she is and always has been. I think you'll be surprised at how much anti-Kaylie feeling there is.'

'Count me in,' said Laura.

'And me,' said Sunita, taking a seat next to me and offering me a piece of her Kit Kat.

I felt hugely relieved, as until today I'd thought that Sunita and Laura didn't like me either. I thought no one did. And now I saw that it wasn't that they didn't like me. Kaylie had a hold over a good number of people and they were afraid to go against her. What a waste. All that time worrying what these girls thought about me and we might have been friends all along.

I took a deep breath. 'And do you know, the fact that I let it all get to me so much suddenly seems mad. I don't even like Kaylie . . .'

'Neither do we,' said Laura and Sunita in unison.

'So why have I been so bothered about whether I fit in with her crowd or not?' I said. 'I don't want her as a friend. It's weird – it seemed so important to win her over, but I see now I'll never win her over. And you know what? I *don't* care.'

'That's exactly what I realised with Jade,' said Becca. 'I have some really good mates – you and Cat and the boys – and there I was, getting all strung out about some stupid girl who was just mean. Not someone I wanted to hang out with anyway. It *is* weird, you're right. It can get all out of proportion. We spend so much time wanting to be liked by people who we don't even like ourselves.'

Laura started laughing.

'It's true,' said Laura. 'It's because they're popular . . .'

'Not so popular after today, I don't think,' said Cat. 'And who said they were popular anyway? I think it's a myth they started themselves.'

'It worked,' said Laura. 'Because they didn't like me, I thought no one did. Just because I don't dress and behave like them, they made me feel like I was a weirdo. I wish they could accept that everyone is different and just let people be.'

'Yeah, there's room for all of us,' said Sunita, then she laughed. 'Not everyone wants to be a Barbie and it's not a look I could ever really do – not unless I bleached my skin and dyed my hair.'

'Yeah,' said Laura. 'We don't all have to be like her to have friends. There are plenty of people in our year, and only four of them.'

'Exactly,' said Becca. 'I think it's important to invest in the people you do like – your real friends. It's what they think that counts.'

I nodded. 'That's what my dad said, but I didn't really appreciate it at the time. He was right. There will always be people for and against you and it's pointless wasting time trying to win over some of the people who are against. Spend time with the people who are *for* you. Those relationships are worth it.'

'And that means being totally honest so that we always know that we can trust each other,' said Cat. 'Even if what we say upsets the other. I think trust is the most important thing there is.'

'No hiding anything,' said Becca.

'And no unspoken grievances, as that's how it all starts,' I added. 'So no secrets.'

I felt happier than I had in weeks, like a huge weight had been lifted. At that moment, Squidge appeared at the end of the table and I suddenly found myself blushing. Ohmigod, I thought. Here's me going on about trust and honesty and I have the biggest secret of all. Squidge. I've fancied Squidge for ages and never told anyone.

'To real friends,' Cat said, putting her hand on the table.

Becca put hers over Cat's. 'To real friends,' she said.

I put my hand over theirs. 'To real friends.'

'So things are better since before assembly?' asked Squidge, sitting down at our table and smiling at me. I felt myself blush even more. Totally honest, I thought . . . That means I have to tell Cat that I fancy her ex-boyfriend. Arghh.

A wave of anxiety flooded through me. How would she react? Maybe best if I keep it quiet and not get into it. I glanced over at her and she gave me a big smile back. What am I thinking? I asked myself. She's not Kaylie. She hasn't got a nasty streak. I can trust her, I know I can. And I have to let her know, by being totally honest with her, that she can trust me.

'So what's all this hand stuff about?' asked Squidge.

'A pledge,' Cat replied. 'To friendship, trust, honesty, no secrets and saying what you really feel to the people you care about.'

Squidge looked deeply into my eyes. I knew he was thinking what I was thinking, and once again, I blushed furiously.

***

In the afternoon break, I saw Cat go into the girls'
cloakrooms. It's now or never, I told myself and dived in
after her.

She was washing her hands at the sink and looked up
when I burst in. 'Hey,' she said. 'It's been a good day, hasn't
it?'

'Yeah. But . . . Cat, I have something to tell you,' I
blustered.

She dried her hands and leaned back against the sink,
ready to listen.

'Er, um . . . I know we said we've got to be honest and
stuff, so I'm just going to come out and say it, and if there's
even the slightest objection, you have to say. Promise?'

'Yeah. Promise. What is it?'

I took a deep breath. 'Well, it's like . . . there was
probably something there the first time. No, um . . . how
can I put this? Would you mind if . . . ? No. Er . . .'

Cat laughed. 'Lia, what are trying to say?'

'Um, Squidge.'

Cat looked at me, waiting for me to continue. 'Yeah,
Squidge?'

'I like him,' I said.

'Yeah. Everyone likes Squidge.'

'No. I mean, I *like* like him.'

'You like like him? Oh! You *like* like him? As in, fancy?'

'Yeah.'

Cat grinned. 'But that's brilliant. I always knew he liked you. I mean, *like* liked you.'

'Really? And you don't mind?'

'Me? No, course not! No. Me and Squidge, we're long over. It's funny. Even at the beginning, I had a sneaky feeling that he fancied you. Ages ago, he said he thought you were stunning. So, has anything happened?'

I shook my head.

'Has he said anything?'

'Not exactly.'

Suddenly Cat slapped her forehead. 'D'oh. Stupid me. I bet it was Squidge who sent you that Valentine card! Have you got it with you?'

I shook my head.

'Bring it into school tomorrow and I'll tell you. I know his handwriting, even when he tries to disguise it.'

'But really, really, really, you wouldn't mind if I got off with him?'

'Really, really, really,' said Cat. 'In fact, it would make things a lot easier for me, as although he's cool and stuff, I've always been worried about hurting his feelings. I didn't want him to be on his own. I'd love it if he found someone, and even better if it was you. If he was seeing you, I could date other boys without feeling guilty.'

'Date other boys? But what about Ollie?'

'Yeah, Ollie . . .' said Cat. 'I'll see him when he's down

here, but I think we both know that he's not one for the big serious relationship. I'm sure he sees other girls when he's up in London, and I'm not going to get all possessive. I'm not going to let myself go there. I don't want to get burned.'

'He really does like you,' I said, then grinned. 'He always asks after you whenever he phones.'

'Yeah, but does he *like* like me?' teased Cat.

'Yeah, I think he's got a bad case of *like* liking you.'

Cat grinned. 'Good. Let's keep it that way. I know if I got all heavy with him and started demanding that he tells me what's going on with other girls and stuff, he'd be off. No, I want to keep it casual.'

'Treat 'em mean to keep 'em keen?' I asked.

'Sort of. Though I could never be mean to Ollie.'

'I know what you mean,' I said.

Then we both started laughing. 'What do you mean, you know what I mean? That I'm mean, or are you suggesting some other meaning?'

'You're mad, Cat.'

'Mean, mad . . . is there no end to your insults?' She put her fists up in mock fight just as Kaylie came in. 'Hey, Kaylie, do you mean to be mean, or . . . ?'

Kaylie took one look at us, turned on her heel and fled. Cat and I burst out laughing.

Cat shrugged her shoulders. 'I didn't *mean* anything . . .'

'Don't start that again,' I said.

As we made our way back to class, I realised that I hadn't looned about like that for ages. I'd been so careful about everything I said and how I came across, analysing every look and gesture from everyone and wondering if there was anything behind it. It felt so good to feel carefree again. Plus, now I knew that Cat wouldn't mind about Squidge. The future was beginning to look very promising.

17 White Flag

AFTER SCHOOL, we all piled back to Cat's house.

'I think we should celebrate,' said Cat, going into their kitchen and straight to the fridge. 'Who wants a scone, and oh . . . there's a tub of Cornish cream. Who wants a cream tea?'

'Well, we do live in Cornwall,' said Becca. 'When in Cornwall, do as the Cornish do.'

'Do you have strawberrry jam?' I asked.

Cat rummaged in the fridge and produced a pot of jam, which she put on the table. 'We do.'

Becca read the label. 'Straight from Widdecombe's Farm and on to our hips. Oh, what the hell? It's a celebration.'

Cat rolled her eyes. 'I don't know why you worry about your weight so much. You're just right.'

'Just right for the Teletubbies, you mean.'

I laughed. Becca looks great, but thinks that she's big. She's mad. She's got a great figure.

Five minutes later, just as we were tucking into freshly baked scones oozing with jam and cream, my mobile bleeped that there was a text message. I wiped the crumbs off my hands and checked the message.

'It's from Kaylie. It says, if I dare go to any of the teachers about her, my life won't be worth living.' I laughed. 'How pathetic is that?'

'Oooh scary,' said Cat, putting her hand on her heart and feigning a faint. 'Bite me.'

'Hmm,' said Becca. 'Warning you off going to the teachers. She was obviously rattled by Miss Segal's class. What should we do?'

'Nothing,' I said. 'I honestly don't think it's worth it. She knows what she's done and so does most of our class now. In fact, I wouldn't be surprised if the table turns and she finds people ganging up against her now that they realise that they're not alone.'

'Serve her right if they do,' said Becca.

'Yeah. But you know what, life's too short. I should have listened to Dad. He told me that at one point in his life, the press gave him a hard time. He said it took him years to learn just to leave it. Not retaliate, not to try and put the story straight, just leave it. That's what I'd like to do. She probably only wants a reaction – you know, to see that she's upset me or scared me. That's what gives her the power. But if she doesn't get the reaction she expects, no power. Anyway, I've really had enough of it all . . .'

'Oh, you mustn't leave, Lia,' said Cat. 'Please don't talk about going back to your old school again.'

'Don't worry, I won't. No. Enough of all the bad feelings. I don't want revenge or to get back at her, or to give her a taste of her own medicine, or anything. I just want it all to stop. She leaves me alone, I leave her alone.'

'So, what do we do, then? Wave a white flag to say we don't want to do battle?'

I thought for a moment. 'Actually, that's not a bad idea. Let's send her one more e-mail,' I said.

'What?! After what happened last time?' asked Becca. 'You're mad.'

'What kind of e-mail?' asked Cat.

'Sort of last chance kind of thing . . .'

Becca sighed. 'You're far too forgiving, Lia.'

'No, I'm not. Not forgiving. I'll never forget what she's done, but I do want this to be the end of it now. *Finito. Kaput.*'

'Suit yourself,' said Becca. 'But I think you're mad. You just said what your dad said. Don't engage. Don't have anything to do with bullies.'

'I won't after today, but I just want it to end on a positive note – not with her having the last word with that stupid threat of hers. I want to let her know that I'm not scared and that I'm not in to waging some stupid battle either. We've got years left at school. I want her to be clear about the way it's going to be with me.'

Cat looked at Becca. 'Makes sense.'

After we'd finished tea, we went into Cat's dad's study and turned on the computer.

'Sign it from all of us so that she knows that we're here with you,' said Cat. 'But what shall we say?'

'Dear Kaylie, get lost, you stupid loser,' said Becca.

'Tempting,' I said, 'but . . . can I write it, then if you agree, we'll send it?'

'Course,' said Cat then made way for me to sit down.

Dear Kaylie,
First, your threats don't scare me. In fact, I think they're pretty pathetic. Second, I'm well aware that you might send this round our class again, but who cares? Do what you like. I never wanted any trouble between us and I'm prepared to put it all behind me. I know that after today, a lot of girls are ready to gang up against you, but I think this whole thing should stop here, for good. I propose that tomorrow morning, we meet before assembly and we go in together and show our year that we are all OK and have resolved our differences. I'm not

suggesting that we become friends, as that will
never happen, but I don't want any more crap at
school.

   I'll be outside the school gate at 8.55. The
choice is yours.
Li@ @xford.

Cat leaned over my shoulder and typed in: And C@t and
Becc@.

'You sure you want to send it?' asked Becca when she'd
finished reading it.

I nodded.

Cat leaned over and pressed the 'Send' button.

Kiss

THE NEXT morning, I got up early and put on my favourite track. It's called 'Don't Panic' by Coldplay and it always makes me feel really up and in a good mood. I haven't played it for weeks, but as the words to the song echoed around my bedroom, I found myself singing along. 'We live in a beautiful world . . .'

Mum knocked on my door, then came in and sat on the end of the bed. 'You're feeling happy today. What's happening?'

'I have decided to be myself,' I said.

'Ah,' said Mum. 'Good. At least, I think it is. And what exactly does this entail?'

I sat next to her. 'It means that I'm no longer going to hide who I am or who my family are. In fact, I wondered if you could give me a lift to school today?'

'In Meena's car?'

461

'Nope. In your gorgeous Porsche.'

Mum laughed. 'So what happened to low-key?'

'Not me,' I said. 'That was last month. I've realised we are what we are. I am who I am. I can't spend my whole life pretending to be something I'm not. I'm Lia Axford, my dad's a rock star and I'm proud of it. I've spent so much time apologising for the fact that we live well and I have nice things. Well, I'm going to enjoy it from now on. Why not?'

'Why not, indeed,' said Mum. 'So what's brought on this change?'

'Long story. Just . . . I've realised that I might be quiet, but I'm not invisible. Nope. I'm going to be who I am and happy about it.'

Mum smiled. 'Excellent. Now get a move on or we're going to be late.'

When she'd gone, I got my Cartier watch out of its box and put it back on my wrist. Then I found my Valentine's card and put it in my rucksack ready to show Cat. I picked my best pair of jeans and DKNY T-shirt and put them on. Then I applied a little mascara, a little lip-gloss, a squirt of Cristalle and I was ready.

Cat and Becca were waiting for me at the school gates when Mum and I drew up. Cat whistled when I got out the car.

'Hubba hubba,' she said as Mum hooted, then drove off.
'You look great. You haven't worn your hair loose like that
for ages.

'Thanks . . .' I said as I looked around. 'Any sign of
Kaylie?'

'Not yet,' said Becca.

I pulled out the Valentine's card and showed it to Cat.
She took one look and grinned. 'Definitely,' she said.
'Squidge always was rubbish at trying to disguise his
handwriting.'

I smiled back at her. I was really chuffed that it was from
Squidge. All that time he'd liked me and had never said a
word.

'Hmmm, you and Squidge, huh?' said Becca. 'Cat told
me all about it. I think it's brilliant.'

I grinned. 'So do I.'

After that, we stood and waited. And waited. Finally the
school bell went for assembly.

'She's not going to show, is she?' I said.

Becca shook her head. 'Didn't think she would.'

'Do you mind?' asked Cat

'Not at all,' I said, and I meant it. 'Her loss. Now we'd
better run.'

We made it into the hall just in time and lined up with
the others in our class. There was no sign of Kaylie. It was
only when we were going into our first lesson that Cat

spotted her. With the Clones as usual, and they were going into class. It didn't bother me one bit that she hadn't shown up at the gates. I'd waved the white flag and she'd chosen to ignore it. Fine by me. While we waited for Mr Riley, our maths teacher, to arrive, Cat, Becca and I went over to chat to Laura, Sunita and Tina on the opposite side of the room from the Clones.

'Cat told us about the e-mail, Lia,' said Sunita. 'Good for you. But no show, huh?'

'No show. But no worries either,' I said. 'I couldn't give a toss.'

'I think she could,' said Laura, glancing over at Kaylie. 'She looks dreadful, like she hasn't slept for a week.'

'Good,' said Tina. 'Now she knows how it feels.'

'I think you're right, though,' said Laura. 'It's not that I'm scared of her or anything any more, but I don't want to get into a revenge thing. Like you, I want to leave it and get on with life. Stick with the friends I've got and not think about her. I hate all that bad vibe stuff.'

Excellent, I thought as I looked around. There are some really nice girls in our year and I resolved to invite them over and get to know them better.

'OK, take your places,' said Mr Riley as he came in through the door.

As the morning classes went on, I glanced over at Kaylie a few times, but she kept her head down through the whole lesson, like she didn't want to look at anyone. She did look terrible, but it was her choice not to have turned up at the gates and go into assembly with us. I felt totally indifferent about it. No loss. She didn't want to change, but I did. I felt like the whole ordeal had made me stronger, firmer in my resolve to be true to myself and to my friends, and to spend time getting to know people I actually liked. For the time being, Kaylie's campaign was over and if she ever started up again, she couldn't touch me.

When school ended that day, I went out to wait for my lift home as usual. As I was standing at the pick-up point, my mobile bleeped. Oh, here we go, I thought as I checked the text message. Maybe Kaylie wants to have one last go at me . . . But it wasn't from her. It was from Squidge.

'Do u want to meet 18r?' it said.

I texted back. 'Yes.'

'Meet me at the bttm of ur drive at 7.'

'OK.'

An amazing feeling of anticipation fluttered in my stomach as I tried to envisage what he might want.

He arrived to pick me up on his battered old moped.

'So, where are we going?' I asked as I climbed on the back.

'Rame Head,' he answered.

'But it's dark.'

'I know.'

We rode up the lanes in silence and I wondered why he'd want to go up there at this time. We wouldn't be able to see the amazing view. Not that I really minded. I was alone with Squidge and that was enough for me.

Ten minutes later, Squidge parked his moped in the field near the peninsula, then he unhooked his rucksack from the back.

'What's in there?' I asked. 'It looks really heavy.'

'You'll see,' he said, pulling out a parka jacket. 'Here, put this on. It might be cold up there.'

I put on the coat over my jacket and Squidge led the way with his torch. We trudged across the field that led to the small hill where the church was, then began the ascent up the wooden steps to the church at the top.

'Careful,' said Squidge, shining his torch so that I could see. 'Hold on to the banister.'

'Don't worry, I am,' I said. Apart from the torch light, it was very black out there, as there are no electric lights or lampposts, but strangely, I didn't feel frightened – only intrigued. I looked up at the sky. It was a clear night and I could see a million stars.

When we got to the top, Squidge led me to the side of the church. 'OK, stay here and close your eyes, and I'll tell you when to open them.'

I did as I was told. 'Good job I trust you,' I said.

Squidge did a maniacal laugh, then I heard him walk into the church. What on earth could he be doing? I wondered.

A short time later, he came back out and took my hand. 'OK, you can come now, but don't open your eyes yet.'

He led me around the side of the church, then inside. 'OK,' he said, 'you can open your eyes now.'

I opened my eyes and gasped. 'Wow! It's beautiful.'

The church is tiny – only three metres by four, with three gaps in the walls where once there were probably windows. Inside, it is all grey stone – even the floor. If there was ever any tiling on the floor, it's long gone. Usually, it's cold and damp in there, but this night, it looked like the most magical place on earth. What Squidge had been carrying in his bag were candles and nightlights. Loads of them. He'd placed them all around the floor and on the window ledges and they glowed a soft, golden light.

'This is what it must have been like in ancient times,' said Squidge. 'Imagine coming up to a service here from the village before there was any electric lighting.'

'Amazing,' I said. 'An amazing atmosphere. Like Christmas.'

Squidge produced a flask from his bag. 'And supplies,' he

said. 'I thought we might want something warm, so, cup of tea, vicar?'

I laughed and took the cup he was offering me.

'Actually, it's hot chocolate,' he said. 'Much nicer than tea.'

'So what made you do this, Squidge?'

He shrugged. 'Every time I come here, it feels special. Energising. The locals say that a lot of very powerful ley lines converge here . . .'

'What are ley lines?'

'They're supposed to be prehistoric tracks, joining prominent points on the landscape – likes churches and burial grounds. Stonehenge is on a ley line so are the Stone Circles and the Standing Stones. I suppose you could say that in the same way that rivers carry water, these ley lines carry good energy, which is probably why people used to come to them to worship in ancient times. You know, to soak up the good vibes. Anyway, I always wanted to come up here at night. I've often tried to imagine how it must have been in the old days, so I thought I'd recreate it.'

I looked around at the tiny church bathed in the soft glow of the candles and nightlights. 'Totally magical,' I said. 'Very good energy. I've always felt that too whenever I've come up here. It's like my battery gets charged, if you know what I mean.'

He nodded. 'I plan to film something up here one day. Maybe some scene from the past. You can have a lead role if you like.'

'God. I can't act for toffee. In fact, the only time I got a lead part was when I was five. I was in the Nativity play as Mary and totally forgot my lines. Since then I've been out of the way in the chorus.'

'Well, you *were* only five,' said Squidge. 'And I bet you were very cute. I was in a Nativity play as well when I was little. I played a donkey.'

I laughed. 'Have you always been so sure of what you want to do? You know, to direct films?'

Squidge nodded again. 'Sort of. I mean, I started out taking photos, then Dad got me a video camera and it evolved from there.'

'You've never wanted to act, then – always direct?'

'Oh yes, that way I get to cast the movie and pick the locations and so on. Location is so important, it has to be the right place for the right moment in a film.'

'And what is this kind of location right for?' I asked. In my mind, it was perfect for a romantic scene. I wondered if he thought the same.

Squidge smiled a half-smile, looked full into my eyes and leaned closer to me. I felt my chest tighten and for a moment I thought he was going to kiss me. But he leaned away and the moment was over. 'Something and someone very special,' he said. 'But it's not just for films that you choose locations.'

'What do you mean?'

'I guess having got interested in making films has made me think about a lot of things. The parallels in life. Life is what you make it, just as a film is what the director makes it.'

'Explain.'

'I see my life like I'm making a film. It's like, the camera starts rolling the moment you're born and it films your perspective on life – a view that's totally unique in the universe. Your view. But that's not all. In a film there's a leading lady, a leading man, sometimes a baddie, parts for extras and so on. In your life, you're making *your* film. You've got the lead part, like I've got the lead part in mine. You had a baddie in yours, Kaylie O'Horrible. Thing is, we can choose how the script goes. I'm realising it more and more. Whether we're going to play a hero, a heroine or someone who loses it all. It's choice, just as it is in a script. You make up your own dialogue, your own responses and so on. In your own film, you are the writer, the . . .'

I laughed. 'I get it – the writer, director and producer. At the end, the credits will come up: *My life, starring Lia Axford, Cat Kennedy, Becca Howard . . .*'

'Yeah, exactly. You chose to cast them as friends,' said

Squidge. 'You choose the locations as well, the plot lines, the love interests, the lot.'

'I like that. Creator of my own movie.'

'And the cameras are rolling now,' continued Squidge, 'behind your eyes, seeing it all from your point of view, so you get to be cameraman as well. You choose what to focus on, what details to zoom in and out on, et cetera.'

Well, I'm zooming in on your mouth at the moment, I thought. Everyone at school thinks that Jonno is the best-looking boy in school – well, I prefer Squidge. His face is far more interesting. But it's not just his face, I thought, watching him. It's the way his face lights up when he talks. And he has great style. I love the long black leather coat he wears. It makes him look so cool. Choice, he said. Was it my choice that Kaylie was so horrible to me? Maybe it was, partly, because I fell into playing a part in *her* film and she had chosen me to play the part of a victim. Not any more, pal. I'm taking back control of *my* movie and I want a better role.

'You're staring at me,' said Squidge, smiling.

'Oh, sorry, I was just thinking . . .'

'About what?'

'About choice. I've had such a weird time lately. I was thinking that I didn't feel I had much choice in it. But you're right, I did. I chose how I responded to things. Like that saying – you can either sink or swim. I was sinking for a while back there and now I've chosen to swim. I was letting Kaylie have a major part in my movie, and now,' I laughed, 'she's sacked. I don't want her in the film at all. She can be an extra in the background school scenes. And definitely *no* dialogue.'

'Good,' said Squidge.

'It's funny, because the whole thing with her started after that game of Truth, Dare, Kiss or Promise,' I said. 'Remember on Valentine's Day, when Becca told us all we had to kiss someone and she told me I had to kiss Jonno?'

Squidge's face clouded for a moment. 'Oh yeah, your leading man. How's that going?'

'Ah. I think I'm going to do a recast. I'm the director of my movie. I can do that, can't I?'

Squidge smiled again. 'Sure. Does Jonno know that he's been made redundant yet?'

I shook my head. 'Haven't written the dialogue for that scene yet, but I'm going to work on it over the next few days and tell him next time I see him.'

After this evening, I was more sure than ever that I had to end it with Jonno. I'd only been with Squidge a short while, but he was so interesting. He really thought about things. And not *one* mention of football.

'But forget Jonno for a moment. Thinking back to Valentine's night, you never fulfilled the kiss dare. You said you were going to do it in your own time.'

Squidge was quiet for a moment. 'I will when the time is right.'

I *really* wanted him to kiss me, like I've never felt before. 'And when do you think that will be?'

Squidge did this amazing thing. He smiled with his eyes, then he looked at the floor. 'Right girl, right time,' he said, then looked up into my eyes. 'You can't hurry it. It's like an avocado pear – if you bite into it too soon, it doesn't taste as good as when it's ripened.'

I felt my stomach flip over. If he'd been waiting for me, then I was ready. No doubt about it – I'd never felt this way about a boy, *ever* – not even Ollie's friend, Michael. This felt different. Special. I felt so alive. Hyper, like I'd drunk ten cups of coffee, yet strangely calm at the same time. Life is what you make it, Squidge had said. You make the choices about how you want your movie to turn out. Well, I choose not to be so timid any more, I thought. I want a more fun role in my own film. But is *he* ready to play the next scene? As Squidge continued to look into my eyes, I wondered how to speed up the process.

'Well, winter's over,' I said. 'Spring is on its way, then summer. Good times for things to ripen, I'd say.'

I took a deep breath, took a step towards him and gently put my arms around his neck. He slid his hands around my waist and pulled me close, then . . .

Cue slushy soundtrack as the camera pulls away to fade out.

The End.

Well, it's my film. I can do that. And I think most people can guess what happened next. . .

Cathy Hopkins

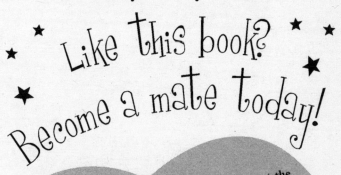

Like this book? Become a mate today!

Join CATHY'S CLUB and be the first to get the lowdown on the LATEST NEWS, BOOKS and FAB COMPETITIONS straight to your mobile and e-mail.

PLUS there's a FREE MOBILE WALLPAPER when you sign up! What are you waiting for?

Simply text MATE plus your date of birth (ddmmyyyy) to 60022 now! Or go to www.cathyhopkins.com and sign up online.

Once you've signed up keep your eyes peeled for exclusive chapter previews, cool downloads, freebies and heaps more fun stuff all coming your way.

☆

www.piccadillypress.co.uk

☆ The latest news on forthcoming books

☆ Chapter previews

☆ Author biographies

☆ Fun quizzes

☆ Reader reviews

☆ Competitions and fab prizes

☆ Book features and cool downloads

☆ And much, much more . . .

Log on and check it out!

Piccadilly Press

☆